CRuK £1-2s

From beach to boardroom, these couples' lives
are about to be turned upside down,
as they discover that secrets and surprises
pave the way to happiness!

Enjoy our new 2-in-1 editions of stories
by your favourite authors—

for double the romance!

with

GREEK BOSS, DREAM PROPOSAL
by Barbara McMahon

BOARDROOM BABY SURPRISE
by Jackie Braun

D0784326

Dear Reader

We hope you like our new look and format!

We want to give you more value for your money—and the same great stories from your favourite authors! Now, each month, we're offering you two Mills & Boon® Romance volumes. Each volume will include two stories. This month:

Hot bosses are on the agenda in…

GREEK BOSS, DREAM PROPOSAL
by Barbara McMahon
&
BOARDROOM BABY SURPRISE
by Jackie Braun

* * *

Sizzling Australian heroes will melt your heart…

CATTLE BARON: NANNY NEEDED
by Margaret Way
&
BACHELOR DAD ON HER DOORSTEP
by Michelle Douglas

For more information on our makeover, and to buy other Romance stories that are exclusive to the website and the Mills & Boon Bookclub, please visit: www.millsandboon.co.uk.

The other titles available this month are: **HIRED: CINDERELLA CHEF** by Myrna Mackenzie and **MISS MAPLE AND THE PLAYBOY** by Cara Colter.

Best wishes

Kimberley Young

Senior Editor, Mills & Boon® Romance

GREEK BOSS, DREAM PROPOSAL

BY
BARBARA McMAHON

MILLS & BOON

To Ruth Johnson, with love and friendship.
You make being in the NSDAR even more special!

First published in Great Britain 2009
Harlequin Mills & Boon Limited,
Eton House, 18-24 Paradise Road, Richmond, Surrey TW9 1SR

© Barbara McMahon 2009

ISBN: 978 0 263 86959 0

Set in Times Roman 13 on 15½ pt
02-0809-50739

Printed and bound in Spain
by Litografia Rosés, S.A., Barcelona

Dear Reader

Come with me to an adventure in the beautiful land of Greece. It's long been a place of fascination for me, and I dream about going there one day to soak up the sunshine and beauty of the landscape. To lie on pristine beaches and tour historic sites. Until that time, I use the places I've visited around the Med to picture how sailing the Aegean would be, how the breezes would feel and how the dynamic and gorgeous Greek men would look. What would be more fun than to travel the Aegean in a luxury yacht, visit quaint isles for their history, or colourful markets with fabulous bargains? All on the arm of a sexy Greek man, of course. As a vacation locale, could we find a better spot? So, come visit Greece with Sara and Nikos, and be swept away on a mini-holiday that will give you the feel of an exotic land we may all one day see.

Love

Barbara

Barbara McMahon was born and raised in the South USA, but settled in California after spending a year flying around the world for an international airline. After settling down to raise a family and work for a computer firm, she began writing when her children started school. Now, feeling fortunate in being able to realise a long-held dream of quitting her 'day job' and writing full time, she and her husband have moved to the Sierra Nevada mountains of California, where she finds her desire to write is stronger than ever. With the beauty of the mountains visible from her windows, and the pace of life slower than the hectic San Francisco Bay Area where they previously resided, she finds more time than ever to think up stories and characters and share them with others through writing. Barbara loves to hear from readers. You can reach her at PO Box 977, Pioneer, CA 95666-0977, USA. Readers can also contact Barbara at her website: www.barbaramcmahon.com

CHAPTER ONE

SARA ANDROPOLOUS leaned over to view the pastry from all angles. It looked perfect. Satisfied, she slid it onto one of the delicate china plates and drizzled a bit of honey on top. Two mint leaves completed the presentation and she smiled. One down, five more to do in less than five minutes.

Working swiftly, she finished the last in less than the allotted time. Perfection.

She'd been on her feet for five hours, yet she felt as fresh as if she'd just started. She loved creating works of art for consumption. Time flew, and she was absorbed in her work to the exclusion of all else.

"See how this pleases your guests," she murmured in a one-sided imaginary conversation with Nikos Konstantinos.

When Sara had first arrived in Greece four months ago, her temporary assignment at the τραγο´υϖδι αο´ερα, Windsong Hotel, several miles from Thessalonika had seemed like an answer to prayer. She'd been trying to find a way to get a toehold in Greece for so long, it was amazing to her how swiftly things had fallen into place. No one suspected her real intent. The sudden opportunity to move to Greece had been impossible to refuse. She'd left her friends, sublet her flat, and headed for the Aegean with one thought in mind—find a way to make contact with her grandmother, Eleani Konstantinos.

As the yacht gently bobbed on the sea, Sara wondered for the nth time if she were really any closer to her goal. It had seemed meant to be when her friend Stacy had discovered that Sara's grandmother had remarried and found where she had been living all these years. When Stacy had then told her five months ago about an opening at the exclusive Greek resort owned by the grandson of the man her grandmother had married, Sara had applied instantly for the job. Amazingly, she'd been hired within two weeks of her first interview. Being Greek herself and knowing the language had been a big plus. But she also liked to think her accomplishments had commanded the attention of the interviewer. The lavish salary she was getting indicated they expected no less than outstanding work.

So far things had progressed better than she'd expected. After only four months in Greece, it was nothing short of miraculous that she'd been promoted to temporary chef on Nikos Konstantinos's luxury yacht. With any luck, at some point, they would put in at the island his family owned—the key to getting to her grandmother. How she was to accomplish the next step was beyond her at the moment. Still, she was closer than ever. Time would present the opportunity she needed.

Stretching her muscles, she placed the desserts on the elegant silver tray and put it on the open area of the counter where the steward would pick it up to deliver to the guests in the main dining salon. It was after nine and she was just about finished for the day. She felt revved up, wide-awake and not at all ready to go to bed, though she'd been up before six every morning to prepare breakfast.

The chef on the yacht *Cassandra* had become suddenly ill with appendicitis, and she'd been selected to fill the role until he recovered. As the chief chef at the resort had explained when selecting her for the assignment, their boss, resort owner Nikos Konstantinos, had guests expected for a week's cruise around the Aegean and needed someone versatile enough for all meals and desserts. The chief chef had recommended her even though she was the newest member of the kitchen staff. She still couldn't believe her luck. At this rate she'd finally meet her grandmother before the month was out!

Her intelligence unit, as she called her friends in London who had rallied round to help her get to Greece once they'd learned of her goal, were certain her mother's mother was living on the Konstantinos family island in the Aegean. Strategically isolated for privacy, the island offered no way to gain access unless a family member brought guests. Since her letter had been returned unopened, her phone call refused and no e-mail address available, she knew no one would vouch for her. To the contrary, she suspected if she petitioned Nikos Konstantinos directly, he'd have her fired on the spot and erect even stronger barriers between her and her grandmother. She was not going to put that to the test. She'd find a way onto the island on her own.

If she could just meet the woman, maybe she could ignore some of that stiff Greek pride that apparently ran rampant in her mother's family and tell Eleani Konstantinos about her daughter's death, and the last words her mother had said—how she wished she could have re-conciled with her parents. It had been too late by the time Damaris Andropolous had uttered those words. She had died two days later.

Sara wanted to carry them back, heal a breach that had split the family for almost thirty years. She had been working more than a year to achieve that aim to fulfill the promise she had made to her mother just before she died.

Was the end really in sight?

Looking back, the best thing her mother had ever done was insist Sara learn Greek. Most of their family friends in London had been of Greek descent, a close-knit community of Greek expats who had loved to celebrate special occasions together. Her friend Stacy swore she loved the English lifestyle more than anything, yet she, too, had studied their ancestors' language. Sara knew her fluency in Greek had landed her this job, she was sure of it. She had had no difficulty in adapting to life at the resort. It was a delightful change from the rainy weather she'd left in London and she'd thrown herself into her job with determination that had obviously paid off.

As she put the pots and bowls she'd used to prepare the evening meal in the sink to soak, Sara thought about how she'd approach her grandmother—if she got the chance. Stacy had been a font of information, relying on the gossip of her own cousins who still lived in Greece. Sara's grandfather had died several years ago, and Eleani had remarried Spiros Konstantinos, head of the legendary Konstantinos Shipping empire. Sara had scrambled to find out as much information as she could about the family, only to come up with very little.

They obviously used a good deal of the money they made ensuring privacy.

"I'm late. Sorry. Won't happen again,"

Stefano said as he swooped up the tray of desserts. The steward was late at least once a day—and always claiming it wouldn't happen again. She had gotten used to it and if Nikos Konstantinos didn't care, she certainly didn't.

"Looks delicious, as usual. I'll get it up to the guests." He talked so fast Sara sometimes had trouble understanding him. She made sure he had all he needed for the guests, then began preparing a tray for the crew.

When Stefano returned, he leaned against the door and let out a long breath. "So the daughter is turning up her charm. I suspect this is a cruise to ensure the lovely Gina Fregulia and Nikos have a chance to get to know each other better. Her father is hinting for marriage, you know. And it doesn't seem as if Nikos is resisting at all."

"Now how would you know that?" Sara asked as she worked. She silently urged him to continue. The more she knew about the Konstantinos family, the better able she'd be to deal with them, she thought.

"It's no secret. The man's thirty-four years old. Past time to marry and start a family, else who will inherit all the money?"

Sara looked up at that. "You're thirty-five. Are you married?"

Stefano laughed. "It's different for me. I get to see beautiful women every day. Sail the Aegean on every cruise. Maybe I will settle down one day. But I don't have two fortunes to leave when I die."

"Two?"

"Nikos didn't follow his father and grandfather into shipping. But he's still the sole heir after his father. He's making a small fortune in his own right with the resort and all the collateral businesses. Wish I had some of that money."

"I'm sure we all do. Actually, we get some by doing our work properly," Sara said mischievously, smiling at the steward.

"I meant, have it to spend without working. It'll be interesting to see how the relationship between Miss Fregulia and the boss pans out."

"Do you think it won't?" Sara asked, curious. She longed to ask a dozen questions, but didn't want to give rise to suspicion.

Stefano gave a shrug. "The way I hear it, Nikos loved his first fiancée. I never knew the full story of the breakup, but for a long time, he had the temper of a bear. Arranged marriages are a bit passé for those of us in the regular world, but in the world of huge fortunes, not so uncommon. I think Nikos Konstantinos will marry for the good of the resort, and to provide heirs for the fortunes. The Fregulias are big in wine in Italy. Their fortunes surely match those of Nikos. At least he doesn't worry about being married for his money. I predict a match made in business."

"An oracle," Sara said, finishing the last touch on the desserts for the crew. "I wish them happy." A happy Nikos meant a more amiable man if she ever had to call on him for access to her grandmother.

"I expect Gina Fregulia will be happy if she gets her hands on Nikos's millions."

"Thought you said she was wealthy."

"Her father is, subtle difference. Nikos will be the prize," Stefano said.

Sara shook her head. Stefano called their boss by his first name around the staff, but she knew he'd have infinitely more respect when in the presence of Nikos Konstantinos. At least she thought he would. She had yet to meet the man. Didn't care much one way or another if she ever met him, as long as his yacht docked on the family island at some time while she was still aboard.

"The captain won't be having dessert. He's returned to the helm to relieve the mate. This looks nice for the crew," Stefano said as he lifted the second, less elaborate, tray full of delicious pastries.

"We should have our food as nicely presented as the guests," Sara said, putting the finishing garnishment on the last plate.

Sara followed Stefano to the aft deck where a table had been set up for the crew to use. Those already seated had left her a place at the end since she didn't normally join them until dessert. Except for Stefano, the rest of the men were around her mother's age. They had probably sailed on the Konstantinos yacht for years.

Sara relaxed slightly. Her duties for the day were completed. The gentle breeze that swept by as the yacht plowed through the sea made it most pleasant to be outside. It was a cool relief from the hot kitchen. The stars were growing brilliant against the darkening sky. Only the running lights from the yacht and the illumination spilling from the salon disturbed the velvet darkness.

Once she'd finished eating, she considered relaxing on one of the loungers and just studying the sky. With little ambient light, the stars seemed to multiply. She saw more each night than she'd ever seen in London.

They'd be stopping at anchor soon. The Aegean rocked the boat gently each night. She loved it. Maybe she should consider looking for a permanent berth on some ship once her task had been completed.

"Thank you," one of the crew said as he rose. "It's good."

One by one the others rose and thanked her. Sara was beaming when Stefano left to clean the kitchen. He'd removed all the dishes and utensils, leaving the table bare, except for her glass of water.

One of the men went to sit near the aft rail, gazing out across the sea. The others left, presumably to other tasks or for an early bedtime.

Sara enjoyed the night air for a short time, then went back to the galley to check on preparations for breakfast. Once she had that done, she'd call it a night.

She had been longer on the aft deck than she thought. The galley was gleaming. Stefano had finished and vanished. She would have enjoyed some company in the quiet space while she mentally reviewed the checklist for the ingredients she would need to bake individual quiches for breakfast. She'd make a pan of sweet rolls and cut up fresh fruit. The larder of the galley was bigger than the pantry she had in her flat. The yacht was spacious and outfitted to suit the most discriminating tastes.

Humming as she double-checked everything, Sara was startled when she heard the door open behind her. Turning, she stopped in surprise. No doubt about it, Nikos Konstantinos had come to the galley.

In a land where all men seemed to be handsome, she was momentarily taken aback. Feeling tongue-tied like an idiot schoolgirl, she could only stare for a long moment, feeling every sense come to attention as she gazed at him. He had wavy black hair and a tan that spoke of hours in the Aegean sun. Dark eyes gravely regarded her. He seemed to fill the doorway, his head barely clearing the lintel. He was over six feet, with broad shoulders and a trim physique. The white dinner jacket he wore seemed out of place on a ship, yet suited him to perfection. Bemused, Sara wished her friend Stacy could see how the rich dressed for dinner—even on a private yacht. This man would take the crown for good looks. She felt a frisson of attraction, and the surprise shocked her out of her stupor. He'd think she was an idiot if she didn't say something.

"Can I help you?" she asked. For a moment she felt a pull like a magnet's force field, drawing her closer. Looking away for a scant second, she was vaguely pleased to note her feet were still where they had been. She hadn't made a fool of herself by closing the gap between them.

"You are the chef replacing Paul?" he asked in disbelief.

Sara almost groaned in delight at the husky, sexy tone of his deep voice. She wanted to close her eyes and ask him to recite some lengthy passage just to hear him speak. But Sara Andropolous was made of sterner stuff. Tilting her head slightly, she gave a polite smile, ignoring her racing heart and replied, "I am."

Be very wary, she warned herself. This man held the key to the Konstantinos family island. She dared not do anything to jeopardize that. But for an instant she forgot all of that as she took in his stunning good looks. The tingling awareness seemed to grow with each tick of the clock.

He narrowed his eyes slightly. "I had not expected a woman so young," he said softly.

"Age has little to do with accomplishments," Sara replied, her back up now. What, a woman still in her twenties, though barely, couldn't be as great a chef as one in her fifties? So much for instant attraction. Reality slapped her in the face. He came from the same world that had ended so cruelly for her mother thirty years ago. What did he know of deprivation, hardship, heartache? Or working one's butt off to get ahead? She'd fought long and hard to achieve the level she had attained. Age had nothing to do with it. Sheer dog-headed determination and drive had.

While not precisely the enemy, Nikos Konstantinos was, nevertheless, not a friend either.

"My apologies, I didn't mean to imply it

was. You caught me by surprise, that's all. I came to compliment you on tonight's meal. My guests were most pleased. The lamb almost melted in our mouths."

Sara was pleased with the compliment and equally surprised her new boss had taken time to come to tell the chef in person.

"I am Nikos Konstantinos," he said. As if she wouldn't know.

"I am Sara Andropolous," she replied. Would he recognize the name from the one letter she'd sent months and months ago? Or had he not been the one to refuse it and have it returned to sender?

"You are finding everything you need?" he asked.

"Yes. The galley is perfect."

"As are the meals you are preparing. I am pleased."

She felt a warm glow. She had worked hard to achieve her goals. She would fight tooth and nail to keep her position. But not, it seemed, today. The man she now worked for was satisfied.

"I believe in passing along compliments so people know their work is appreciated," he commented.

She studied him a moment longer not knowing what to say. He nodded his head once and left.

Nikos Konstantinos had not followed in his father's and grandfather's footsteps, but had made his mark in the hotel industry. Since building the Windsong, his impact on Greek tourism had been assured, Sara had been told more than once. The employees of the hotel bragged about its success, and with good reason. The excellent staff had had a lot to do with it, after all. The resort was rumored to have a waiting list of more than a year for a reservation. Guests not staying in the hotel could sail into the wide harbor, rent a slip at the lavish marina and use all amenities of the resort—including dining in one of the six fine restaurants. Those staying at the resort could choose which restaurant in which to dine each evening or arrange for room service to deliver and serve a meal as elegantly on a private terrace or balcony as in any of the five-star restaurants.

She was surprised he was as young as he was to have accomplished all he had. Maybe she should have returned the compliment. But then, he had started with a wealthy family backing him; he had probably leapfrogged over growth pains others had to endure.

She returned to her task. Their backgrounds couldn't be more different. Sara had been raised without a twopence to spare. Fighting her way above the poverty level, she'd put herself through culinary school by working endless hours in kitchen sculleries to afford the training needed to rise above the level of short-order cook. Perseverance, determination—and yes, even some of that stiff-necked pride from her mother—had pushed her through and to success.

Whereas Nikos had probably merely spent one month's allowance and had the Windsong built with a snap of his fingers. Nikos, she thought, like they were friends or something. Mr. Konstantinos, she corrected herself silently. If his guests continued to be pleased, he would be, as well. Which meant he'd keep her on board longer. Fingers crossed it was long enough to visit the family island.

Heading for her tiny cabin a short time later, Sara grew optimistic. She'd met the owner and he was satisfied with her work. Surely that meant things were still looking up for her plan.

Sara knew she'd been unbelievably fortunate that the chief chef had recommended her for this cushy spot. There were five other crew members in addition to herself. With the guests and Nikos, that made twelve. Nothing like the number of dishes she had to prepare in one of the resort kitchens each evening.

Her first sight of the yacht had inspired a touch of awe. It was beautiful—sleek, gleaming white and riding with a high bow off the water. The main body looked to be longer than her apartment in London and the aft deck could have easily hosted a party for fifty. That's where she and the other crew could spend off hours. At least the owner was generous with his staff.

Sara frowned. She wasn't sure she wanted to list admirable attributes. Nikos Konstantinos might be one of the sexiest men she'd ever met, but he was no more than a means to an end for her. She had better not forget that. Besides, Stefano had said this was almost an engagement cruise—a chance for Nikos to decide whether to marry the daughter of a business associate. Sounded cold to her. It also mirrored the same circumstances her mother had been in years ago—an arranged marriage. At least this time it sounded as if the prospective participants were not averse to the plan.

She was astonished to find herself attracted to the man. For a second she had almost forgotten what she was doing and been tempted to flirt. A handsome man, a lonely woman, the perfect romantic setting.

How dumb would that have been?

CHAPTER TWO

NIKOS left the galley to return to the suite that served as both office and bedroom when on board. His chef had been a surprise. Her dark wavy hair had been tied back, with tendrils escaping to frame her face. Her large brown eyes had revealed a wariness that had surprised him. He was used to the awe in which some held him. This was somehow different. Yet her manner had been professional. He'd detected a note of annoyance with the comment about her age. Nikos almost smiled. Touchy—weren't all great chefs? Though the only ones he'd ever met before had been male. A female chef was a novelty. At least she had not instantly tried to flirt and garner more interest.

He had grown weary of the flirtatious ways of the women he met. If he thought a single one would be interested in him if he had not a dime to spare, he might feel differently. But he'd learned early on that most women wanted one thing—to live a life of luxury—preferably off the proceeds of a susceptible male. His own aborted engagement proved that.

It was as if life were a lottery and he one of the prizes. Nikos did not like to consider himself conceited, but maybe he had grown so with the attention of so many lovely women over the past ten years.

He found Sara's totally professional attitude refreshing. What would it be like to have people judge him on his own merits? To have a friend who wanted nothing but him as he was?

George Wilson and Marc Swindard were the only two friends to come to mind. Perhaps because they'd shared so many holidays at school when it was too inconvenient for each of them to be flown home. He would send them both e-mails and catch up. Maybe they could get together soon. The demands of business could be consuming. He was guilty of not making more of an effort to get away. But a short trip to New York or London in the near future could be arranged.

Of course, if the idea of marrying Gina Fregulia grew, maybe he'd be contacting his friends to announce his engagement. This time the engagement would be more likely to endure—no lies of love and passion to cloud the issue. He found Gina attractive. She certainly knew how to entertain and moved in the same social circles he did. She'd be a definite asset to the restaurant side of the resort with her knowledge of excellent wines and the contacts her family had.

Nikos pushed open the door to the suite and loosened his tie. He had a little time to catch up on business before he retired for the night.

When Stefano brought his breakfast promptly at seven the next morning, Nikos had been working for almost an hour. The yacht rode at anchor during the night and Nikos had taken advantage of that to have a quick swim in the sea at dawn before showering and dressing for the day. Satellite connections kept him in constant touch with the resort and anyone else who wished to contact him—such as his father, who called just as Stefano put the tray on the desk.

"Have you checked on your grandfather lately?" Andrus asked when Nikos answered the phone.

"Is there a problem?" Nikos asked. It was rare his father spoke of family matters. The shipping business was even more consuming than hotels, especially to Andrus. He had lived for the family shipping company as long as Nikos could remember—to the exclusion of everything else.

"He has some idea about buying another boat to use to get from the island to the mainland. He says the old one is too decrepit."

"It's in perfect running order," Nikos said. He made sure maintenance was always current on all the family's watercrafts.

"I think he wants a new one, smaller, that he can drive himself. But he's eighty-two years old. Too old to be jaunting all over the Aegean by himself," Andrus said in disgust.

"Did you tell him that?" Nikos asked, already knowing the answer.

"Do you think I'm crazy? I thought you could visit, convince him to keep the ship's crew and make sure he doesn't do something foolish."

"My grandfather is not a foolish man," Nikos said mildly. His father asked him to act as intermediary between them from time to time. It was the closest to familial affection his father got.

"When were you there last?"

"A month ago," Nikos replied.

"Can you get away soon?" his father asked.

Nikos gazed out of the wide window at the sparkling sea. "I could when my guests leave. I'm entertaining the Fregulias and Onetas right now."

"Next week, then. Let me know." His father hung up.

"Want to know how my own business is going?" Nikos said as he hung up the phone. To his father, if one wasn't in shipping, it was of no account. "Or how about my plans to ask Gina to marry me?" He knew the answer to that one, as well: do as you please. Nikos didn't mind anymore. His father wasn't going to change—any more than his grandfather would. If the old man wanted a powerboat so he could operate it himself, he'd get one. Nikos wasn't going to try to talk him out of it. More power to him. He hoped *he* was as active when he was eighty-two.

Nikos poured a cup of coffee, surveying the meal. An individual portioned quiche lorraine centered the plate. A fresh fruit compote accompanied it, as well as two slices of a rich walnut bread. How early had Sara risen to have this prepared by seven, he wondered?

He knew so little about his temporary chef. He admitted to being a bit intrigued by a woman who had risen so fast in a field dominated by men. Yet the chief chef had recommended her. That spoke volumes. The fact that she was pretty didn't hurt, either.

He shook his head and picked up the reservation schedule for the next month. He had other things to do besides think about his temporary chef.

At noon Nikos consulted with the captain and arranged for the ship to stop on one of the smaller islands not too far distant. It would offer his guests a chance to visit the local market and see some of what the Aegean islands had to offer.

Nikos instructed the captain to give the crew the afternoon off and then set sail again at seven. That would allow for dinner on board and some after-dinner conversation before going to his suite for the night.

Shortly after the island came into view, Nikos received a communiqué from the resort. He went to take the call, only to be told his assistant was busy trying to deal with a power outage at the sprawling resort—no power to rooms, pools, common areas or kitchens. When they docked at the island, Nikos sent word to Gina he would be tied up for a little while but urged the Fregulias to go on ahead and he'd catch up, if the situation could be resolved soon. Tapping his fingertips on the desk, he chafed at the distance between him and the resort. He wanted to be right there finding out what had gone wrong, handling the emergency. With the portable phone held to his ear, he went to the cabin's wide windows.

It was market day on the island. Colorful canopies lined the streets, fluttering in the breeze, shading the wares and goods for sale. The small population seemed to turn out in force to see what bargains they could get, and he watched as Gina happily went down the gangway with her parents and the Onetas, the other couple cruising with them. Soon they were lost from sight as they began exploring the market.

Fifteen minutes later he'd been briefed on the cause of the outage—a power cable severed by road construction near the outer perimeter of the resort. Nothing to be done except wait. The generators had been started and for the most part the resort was operating as usual. Nikos instructed his assistant to keep him informed and hung up. Nothing he could do from the ship.

He started to leave to find his guests when he realized he hadn't seen any of the crew disembark when he'd been at the window. He'd given instructions they were to have the afternoon off. Glancing at the bridge, he saw it was empty. He went to the kitchen to see if any were there. Pausing at the doorway, Nikos's gaze went straight to Sara. She was even prettier in daylight. He frowned. He had no business thinking about her at all.

She was wrapping a platter while Stefano lounged against one of the counters chatting. When he saw Nikos, he straightened up, almost coming to attention.

"Did you need something, Mr. Konstantinos?" he asked.

Sara looked at him. "Did you want lunch? I

had it nearly prepared when I heard the change in plans. Are you hungry?"

He looked at the sandwich wraps artistically arranged on a platter. Stepping closer, he reached beneath the plastic wrap and took one. Biting into it, he recognized good Greek cheese and olives. And a hint of some spice he wasn't familiar with. It was delicious.

"As it happens, I have not eaten. There was a minor crisis at the resort, so I sent my guests ahead. Perhaps you could prepare me a plate and bring it up." He'd eat lunch before leaving the ship. No sense in wasting food, or her efforts.

"Yes, sir, right away, sir," Stefano said.

Nikos's eyes met Sara's. "Actually, I thought Miss Andropolous could bring it up. It would give her a chance to see more of the yacht. The captain has also gone ashore, so I could show you the bridge, as well."

She glanced at Stefano and shared his look of surprise.

"Thank you, I would love to see the rest of the ship. I can bring you a plate in ten minutes," she replied. "The crew decided to eat on board and then we're all going exploring."

Nikos nodded once and then left. He wasn't sure why he'd made the offer. He'd never done so before. But then, he'd never had a woman chef before, either. For a moment Nikos wondered if he'd lost his mind. He was considering marriage to Gina Fregulia. He's spent less than a total of ten minutes with Sara Andropolous. Yet he could postpone finding Gina to show a stranger his ship? Maybe the sun was getting to him. To single out a crew member went against everything he normally did. Yet there was something fascinating about the woman. And she was only bringing his lunch.

Sara knocked on the door in exactly ten minutes. He heard her say something and wondered if she'd needed Stefano to guide her to the suite.

He opened the door and caught a glimpse of Stefano disappearing around the bend.

"Come in." He stood aside as she entered, carrying a tray with his lunch—a plate piled high with delicacies and an iced beverage.

She looked around and headed for the low table in front of the sofa. Placing the tray carefully, she straightened and smiled in delight as she walked straight to the windows. "Wow, this is fabulous. You are so much higher than our quarters. What a great view of the harbor. What island is this?"

"Theotasaia, a small island whose inhabitants depend upon fishing for a living. Today is market day. The perfect entertainment for my guests."

"They like to shop?" she asked, still looking from the window.

Nikos crossed to stand beside her. The colorful market was spread out before them, the canopies still fluttering in the breeze.

"I do not know them well," he said. "They seemed content enough with the suggestion."

Sara looked at him. "You did not go with them."

"I was needed here. There was a power outage at the resort." He briefly told her the situation. He turned back to the plate she'd prepared. There was plenty of food.

"Did you eat?" he asked.

"I nibbled as I was preparing lunch. May I go out to the upper deck? I'll wait there until you eat—for the tour."

"I'll be along in a few minutes."

Sara let herself out of the stateroom and hurried to the upper forward deck. Being around Nikos Konstantinos was unnerving. She couldn't forget she was hoping he'd get her access to her grandmother. But he disturbed her equilibrium. She vacillated between wanting to stay away, lest she let something slip, and getting to know him better. On the surface he was just the kind of man her mother had run away from—wealthy, self-assured and maybe a touch arrogant. And in the midst of arranging a marriage to a woman who matched his fortune. Did Gina Fregulia really want a marriage like that?

Stepping out onto the deck, Sara immediately felt the warm breeze blowing from the sea. The sun was almost directly overhead, the sky a cloudless blue. She went to the railing and looked down. It was quite a distance to the sea's surface. Gazing around, she looked behind her at the wide windows of the bridge.

If her mother had married the man her father had picked out for her, would she have enjoyed luxurious yachts and visits to Aegean Islands? The reality had turned out far differently from what her mother had once envisioned when she'd run away with Sara's father. But her pride had kept her from admitting a mistake and returning home to seek forgiveness.

Sara still hadn't come to any conclusion when Nikos joined her a short time later.

"Come, the captain is not on the bridge. We can see everything and he'll never know," he said with a hint of amusement in his voice.

She laughed, intrigued by the hint of mischief in her boss. "You're not afraid of your captain, are you?" she asked as she followed him to the side door and stepped inside.

"He does not consider the bridge a sightseeing stop for guests. I do what I can to keep him happy," Nikos replied.

She couldn't imagine the man afraid of anything. He carried himself with such an air of competence and assurance, she knew he could do anything he wanted. Interesting that he humored the captain.

The bridge had a 360-degree view. The wide windows had been tinted slightly to keep off the glare from the sea. The wheel was more like an automobile's than the wooden spoke-handled ones of old. With all the gadgets, dials and computer equipment, she marveled at how the captain managed all with only one mate to back him up. Or maybe that was why—everything that could be automated had been.

"Wow, this is fantastic," she said, enjoying the view. "Surely the captain wouldn't mind showing this to guests."

"He is an excellent man and I don't want to jeopardize his staying."

"Like he's about to quit," she murmured. From what she'd learned from the rest of the crew at meals, this was a cushy assignment, and every one of them was grateful for their position.

"If he does, it won't be because I ruffled any feathers," Nikos said, coming to stand closer to Sara and pointing to the west.

"Thessalonika is that way." He swung his arm a bit more. "Thessaly is almost due west of us." Another swing. "And Athens is that way."

"But not close," she said, feeling the heat from his body as he stood so casually near. She could smell his aftershave, a woodsy scent that had her senses fluttering. She wanted to step closer. See if there was some special chemistry between them.

Appalled at her thoughts, she moved away. She would be the most foolish woman on the planet if she thought anything would ever come between her and the fabulously wealthy heir to the Konstantinos shipping fortune. Not to mention Nikos's own fortune from the resort.

"Tell me more about this little island," she said, looking over the rugged terrain. The only flat ground seemed to be where the town had been built. White homes with red tiled roofs filled the small valley. A few had been built at the lower levels of the hills. Several weathered fishing boats bobbed nearby. Probably the majority were out working.

"It only recently became a place for ships to stop. Ten years ago their docks couldn't service a ship with a deep draft. It was suitable only for the smaller fishing boats, but nothing like the *Cassandra*. Now I bring friends here from time to time. I thought my guests would enjoy it."

"Did you get the crisis resolved?" she asked.

"For the time being. We await repair of the main cable, but the generators will suffice until then."

"So now you can join your guests onshore. I shouldn't hold you up," she said, turning a little. He'd stepped closer, and she almost bumped into him. Her senses went on high alert. Her awareness gauge shot up. He was too close; she felt as if he were taking the air and leaving her breathless again.

"Come and I'll also show you the main square of the town. Time enough to find my guests. We're not leaving until seven this evening."

Sara blinked at that. Was he serious? The host of the yacht going off for an afternoon with the hired help? What was wrong with this picture?

"Do you think that wise?" she asked in a husky voice. Her heart was tripping so fast she thought he must hear it, or at least see it pounding in her chest.

"Why wouldn't it be?"

"Maybe because I'm your chef?" she asked. Hadn't Stefano said he expected to hear of an engagement between Nikos and Gina? What kind of man would spend the afternoon with another woman if his almost-fiancée was nearby? Her instincts rose. He was the kind of man she wanted to stay away from.

"It is only an afternoon in a market square. Come if you like. Or say no."

She nodded, looking away. She was not responsible for how Nikos Konstantinos behaved. She needed more information if she wanted to get on the family island. Maybe this was the chance to find out more about his family—and satisfy some of the curiosity she had about him.

"I'd love to see the square. I'll need to be back around five to have dinner ready by eight. But until then I'm game."

If the crew on the yacht thought it odd the owner was escorting the new chef when he had guests visiting from Italy, no one said a word. Ari had drawn guard duty, and he was at the gangway to make sure no unauthorized person came aboard. He gave a two-finger salute to Nikos and grinned at Sara.

In only moments they were in the midst of the crowd that clogged the streets where the market was set up. Old women all in black carried string sacks in which they put the produce they bought. A small boy walked beside his mother carefully carrying a fresh loaf of bread wrapped in paper. Children's laughter rang out, mingled with the rise and fall of bargaining debates and the spiel of those with less popular items trying to entice buyers.

It was more fun than she'd had in a while, Sara thought. Her mother would have loved it. She felt a pang when she remembered how her mother had spoken so fondly of her childhood memories. Sara nodded to the vendors, sampled one of the sweets—walnuts and honey—and danced out of the way of several children running through the marketplace.

Nikos caught her arm to steady her. She felt the touch all the way to her toes. Catching her breath, she looked at him. "Thanks."

Oh, goodness, those dark eyes looked fathomless. His face was angular and masculine. His hair was tousled just a bit from the breeze. She wished they could have met under other circumstances.

But what other circumstances? If not for her needing access to his family island, they would never have met in a thousand years. Their lifestyles were too distant.

"Why, Nikos, you took care of the emergency already?" A tall dark-haired woman seem to spring up from the ground beside Sara.

As she looked at the woman, Nikos released his hold.

"Gina." For a moment he said nothing. Sara wondered if that was resignation in his eyes, but it couldn't be. Wasn't this the next Mrs. Nikos Konstantinos? Or was she a friend from Thessalonika?

The woman slipped her arm between his and his chest and leaned against him slightly. "I lost Mama and Papa. I knew the yacht was the best place to go if I got lost. But now I have you to show me the sights. I saw the cutest church on the town square. I would love to see inside."

Sara watched her for a moment, wishing Stacy could be here. She'd make some snide comment, which would have both of them laughing at the obvious ploys of this Gina. Yet the woman had to know she was special to Nikos. Sara mentally sighed. She had known spending the afternoon with a fabulously wealthy man was beyond her reality.

"Sara, may I introduce Gina Fregulia, one of my guests for the cruise. Sara is responsible for the wonderful meals we are enjoying."

"Oh, the quiche this morning was just delicious. I couldn't eat it all, of course, I do have to watch my figure. But what I sampled was simply divine. You're so clever. I can't cook." She glanced up at Nikos with a simpering smile. "But I don't need to. We have a cook for that. I do have other talents."

"I'm sure you do," Sara said softly in English, just imagining what talents the voluptuous Italian woman had.

Nikos caught her eye, amusement evident in his. She must have misread the earlier emotion.

"Well, I'm looking for fresh produce to enhance tonight's meal. Enjoy visiting the church," she said briskly and turned.

"Sara," Nikos called.

She turned.

He hesitated a moment as Gina clung. "Tell them to charge it to the yacht, they will know how to collect."

For a split second she had hoped he was calling to reissue his invitation to see the town square together. To dump his guest and spend the afternoon with his chef. Ha. Gina was much more his type. He had been kind to offer to show her around. She relieved him of his impetuous offer.

Waving gaily, she turned and plunged into the crowd, hoping to lose herself quickly before the false smile plastered on her face dissolved and her disappointment showed. She would have liked to explore the island with someone who knew it. That was all.

Sara ended her afternoon at a small taverna near the docks. Fishing boats arrived every few minutes and she watched as the catch of the day was handed from the smaller crafts to a large ship that had tied up only moments before the fishermen returned. Most of the fish went into cold storage in the ship that probably took it straight to the mainland. Some fishermen carried their catch straight to a series of tables with running water to clean the fish and pass it along to one of the booths at the market.

Giving in to impulse, she went to buy some fresh catch to serve for dinner. She could rearrange her menu and knew the fresh fish would be excellent.

When she returned to the ship, she saw Nikos standing near the rails, talking with his guests. They were seated on the cushioned chairs dotting the upper forward deck.

Just before she looked away, he glanced

around, his gaze catching hers. For a long moment he merely stared at her. Then slowly he raised his glass in silent toast.

Someone—probably Gina—said something and he looked back. Sara hurried on board, her nerves tingling. Would he seek her out again before the trip was over?

Why would he? she silently asked.

CHAPTER THREE

ONCE the yacht stopped for its nightly anchorage, Sara felt an unexpected rise in anticipation. She and several of the other crew members were lounging on the aft deck, enjoying the evening. It was much cooler tonight. She'd brought a sweatshirt. The breeze that blew constantly was refreshing but chilly. She listened to the conversation more than contributed. Now that the ship had dropped anchor, she wondered if Nikos would come again to thank her for the meal. She'd taken extra pains with tonight's dish, broiling the succulent fish to perfection.

Probably not. He'd merely been kind to a new employee last night. He expected good work; she delivered. And he'd also been hospitable when he'd offered to show her around the upper deck of the yacht. She didn't think he was the type to mingle with his employees on a routine basis. With the rest of the crew lingering on the aft deck, even if he wanted to speak to her again, she doubted he'd do so in such a public place.

And why would he want to? She wasn't a regular member of the crew. Once the chef with the ruptured appendix recovered, he'd be back in his galley and she'd be back at the resort looking for another way to contact her grandmother.

Unless she could somehow get to the family island before that.

One by one the crew members rose to depart to their quarters. When only Sara and the captain remained, she changed seats to be closer so she could ask him some questions. She wanted to be able to turn the conversation to access to the island.

"Have you been in charge of this ship long?" she began.

"Since it was commissioned. Before that, I was captain of a ship for Mr. Andrus Konstantinos, Mr. Nikos's father. I have served the family for almost twenty years."

"An ideal job, I'd say, sailing around the Aegean all the time."

"Ah, but sometimes we go further—into the Med and to ports west of Greece. One summer I took the patriarch and his new bride to Spain and Morocco. It was a beautiful summer sail."

That had to be her grandmother he was talking about. The senior Konstantinos was now married to Eleani. "How long ago was that?" she asked.

"Many years now. More recently we have sailed to Egypt and to Italy."

"Do you have any family?" she asked, wondering how they managed his being from home for long voyages.

"Only a brother and his children. His wife died two years ago. They are mostly grown, but I see them at holidays if not required on board. Have you sailed a lot?"

"No, this is my first trip."

"Lucky for you seasickness is not a problem."

"If she'd gotten sick, she'd have been in a real pickle," Nikos said from the shadows.

The captain turned his head and nodded a greeting. "Mr. Nikos. Did you require something?"

"Just a brief break from the work that never ends. I came to check up on my chef and compliment her on the excellent dinner tonight. The presentation added to the delicious taste of the fresh fish."

Sara surreptitiously wiped her damp palms on her slacks and tried to keep her breathing under control. "I'm pleased you and your guests enjoyed the meal."

"As did we all," the captain added. "Aeneas did well in recommending Sara. We all enjoy Paul's food, but Sara has brought new dishes to the table that the entire crew appreciates."

Nikos walked to a side railing. The ship bobbed gently on the sea, the breeze blowing from the bow. "Tomorrow I think we should find another island for our guests to visit. They seem to grow bored easily," Nikos said.

"I can't understand it myself," the captain said. He rose. "If we are to depart early, I will retire now."

"After seven. I want a swim first," Nikos said.

"Absolutely." He bade them both goodnight.

Sara was the only one left on the aft deck

with him. She should say something. Or maybe he wanted to be alone and knew his guests wouldn't intrude in this area.

"So you swim each morning before we weigh anchor?" she asked, gazing over the starlit surface of the Aegean. The water was dark and smooth, almost like a mirror to the stars.

"If time and weather permit."

She smiled. She couldn't picture herself swimming each day before starting work.

"Would you care to join me?" He half turned to look at her.

Sara was startled at the invitation. She thought about it for a moment. It was hard to be swimming when she should be preparing a meal. "I'd better not. I have omelets planned for tomorrow and fresh walnut bread again. I'll need time to have it all ready for your guests."

"Come for fifteen minutes. You can work around that," Nikos urged. "Besides, I'm the one who eats early, and the crew. My guests haven't had breakfast before nine since they've been on board."

"Okay. No, wait. I did not expect to swim. I didn't bring a suit." She would love a chance to swim in the sea to start the day. It had never crossed her mind that she'd actually have an opportunity to do so or she would have packed a swimsuit.

"We have extra suits on board. Sometimes guests don't plan to swim, either, and then change their minds. I'll have Stefano bring you one."

"Thank you," she said. She hoped Stefano would not suspect there was more to the invitation than there really was—merely a time to go swimming before beginning the day's work. She didn't want to give rise to gossip that could harm her chances of staying on board.

"I usually start around six, swim a half hour, shower and dress to be ready to work at seven," he said.

"Early," she murmured. It was already close to midnight.

"It's a routine that suits me well."

"So you swim mornings at the resort, as well?" she asked.

"Weather permitting. Sometimes in the sea, sometimes in one of the pools."

She tucked that piece of information away. Maybe she'd get up early once in a while for a swim herself, instead of swimming in the pool at midnight after her work was finished each day.

He studied her in the faint illumination of the anchor light. "How are you adjusting to being on the sea? You did say you weren't seasick."

"It's challenging to cook in such a small space, but the captain keeps the boat on an even plane so I don't have spills or liquids sloshing over. Stefano keeps it clean once I'm finished preparing the meal. Actually, I'm enjoying myself." She was surprised to say it, but it was true. She'd been so focused on trying to find her grandmother, she had overlooked how much she was enjoying the experience of working in this situation.

"I'm glad," he said.

She glanced away, feeling the attraction that flared whenever he was near. She knew it was only a part of her visit to Greece in which she didn't have to calculate ways to get to the island. Sooner or later Nikos would return to his family home. With any luck, she'd still be aboard when he did. She should make the most of this opportunity, but couldn't think of a thing to say to ingratiate herself with him. She so wanted to get to the island—just for an after-noon. That's all she'd need.

"It's late. I'll see you at six," Nikos said.

"Good night," Sara replied. She'd see him again in a few hours. They'd swim together and then she'd be back in the galley. Wait until Stacy heard.

Sara had spent her time while preparing this evening's meal imaging Nikos enjoying every bite. She'd also thought about when he'd offered to play guide and the anticipation she had felt. She hoped his guests enjoyed the food, as well. But the reality was she was cooking for him. Wasn't the old adage something about the way to a man's heart was through his stomach? She didn't want to get to his heart—just his island.

Sleep proved difficult. She knew she had to trust in luck to get her what she wanted. And so far her luck had been spotty. None in trying to contact Eleani Konstantinos, good luck in landing a job at the resort. No luck in finding a way to the Konstantinos's island on her own. Amazing luck in getting a berth on the ship. Now could she hope that luck held? Or was there something she could do to press it?

By six-fifteen the next morning Sara still

didn't have a swimsuit. She debated forgetting the entire idea and dressing in her regular resort uniform of khaki slacks and navy shirt with the resort's logo on the left side then heading for the galley. In the light of dawn, maybe Nikos had a change of heart.

The soft knock went almost unheard. She crossed to the door. Stefano grinned at her when she opened it, holding out a small box. "Compliments of Mr. Konstantinos. He said to meet him at the aft deck when you're ready."

She took the box, thanked him and shut the door. The swimsuit was a brand-new one-piece in a lovely teal color. She pulled it on. It fit perfectly. Tying her hair back, she slipped on her robe, not having any other swimsuit cover-up, and headed for the aft deck, her heart pounding. Would the other crew members resent her swimming with the boss? Or was this a common practice that she was making more of than it warranted?

Nikos stood by the back railing. He turned when he heard her and watched as she crossed the space in her bare feet. Without her working shoes, which gave some elevation, she was more conscious than ever of his height.

Sara tried not to be intrigued by the broad shoulders and well-developed muscular chest. It was hard not to imagine herself drawn against him, feeling those muscles hold her close. She longed to trail her fingertips across his tanned skin, to feel the texture, the warmth and strength.

Then the reality slapped her. He was someone she needed in order to accomplish her goal. That was it. Otherwise he lived the kind of lifestyle she was wary of. She should never forget that.

"Ready?" he asked.

"Yes." The air was cool. Would the water also be? She slipped off her robe and walked to the railing, peering over. "Do we just jump in?" she asked. They were still eight feet or more above the water.

"No." He flipped open a section of railing, indicating ladder steps built into the boat. "We climb down to that swim board. It's a platform to get on and off the ship."

It was not wide, maybe eighteen inches out, running the width of the ship. Nikos showed her how to use the ladder and in only a couple of moments they stood side by side on the platform.

"Now," he said, diving into the blue water.

Sara took a breath and followed.

It was heavenly. The water was cool but not cold. The faint pink still showing in the wispy clouds in the sky was the first thing she saw when she surfaced. Turning, she saw the boat not far away. Looking around, she saw nothing but sky and sea and ship.

Nikos broke the surface a dozen yards ahead of her and began swimming away. Sara smiled at the pure sensual enjoyment of the moment and began to swim after him. She loved the water, and one of the perks of working at the resort was the swimming she could enjoy during her time off. Very different from her life in London.

She was beginning to wonder if she should turn back when she saw Nikos had stopped and was treading water. Catching up with him, she grinned in delight.

"This is fabulous. What are your guests doing still asleep? They should be out enjoying a swim."

Nikos stared at her for a moment, then glanced back at the yacht. "I think Senora Fregulia is not so fond of a swimsuit. Senor Fregulia is too focused on business, and getting her hair mussed is not Gina's thing. The Onetas take their lead from the Fregulias. It is of no matter. I hope my guests are enjoying themselves, even if we do not share liking of the same activities."

"What about the crew? Surely some of them would like to swim."

"Occasionally when we are at anchor they do. Mostly not." Nikos shrugged. He didn't much care about the other crew members at this particular moment. He was enjoying the obvious pleasure Sara derived from the early-morning swim. She was open in sharing in her emotions. No guile. No flirtation. Was it the novelty that intrigued him? Or the mysterious chef herself who had come to work for him?

She obviously liked her position and had given no hints she wanted more. She didn't pester him with dozens of questions about his life, about his likes and dislikes. Sara took each moment as it came. She was enjoying the water and it showed. Definitely a novelty after the jaded women he usually met at receptions and parties.

She wore her femininity unselfconsciously,

moving with grace whether walking across the deck or touring the bridge. She was comfortable with who she was. Witness the wet stringy hair that had escaped her tieback. She merely swept it away from her face and gazed around in delight.

Nikos didn't mix business with pleasure. No matter how much he enjoyed being with her, he would never overstep the bounds of employer-employee. He still didn't understand the impulse that had caused him to issue the invitation. He was glad he had, however. If only to enjoy her pleasure in the simple exercise.

"I'd say I'd race you back to the boat, but you're a stronger swimmer than I am," she said. "This is so lovely. Can I swim every morning?"

"If you wish," he said, beginning to lazily swim back. "Not when we are in port, however. The water near marinas is not so fresh."

She wrinkled her nose, keeping up with his slower pace. "Too many oil spots. I've seen the rainbow colors floating on the surface."

"We'll be stopping at another island today. The ladies loved shopping yesterday. Today's island won't have a market, but there are shops and cafés. There is even an old fort sitting on a bluff with a terrific view. Maybe you can tour that."

"We'll stop before lunch?"

"You get another free pass. I'll take my guests to lunch at one of the waterfront cafés. No lunch preparations needed."

For a moment Sara looked wistful. Was she wishing she could join him? Suddenly Nikos wondered what it would be like to take a few days off. Get away from work, from duty, and just enjoy Sara's company. Maybe when this cruise was finished he'd find out. Unless he became engaged to Gina by then. The thought surprised him. He'd started the cruise with that intent. Was he having second thoughts? The alliance would work to the benefit of both. Yet momentarily he'd forgotten his intent, his interest in Sara overriding his common sense.

"We're going to have a lot of food left over if you keep changing the meals," she commented.

The ship was getting closer every moment. When they reached it, she'd disappear to change and get to work. Nikos knew he'd not see her again today—unless she lingered on the aft deck after dinner. He could tell her again how much his guests enjoyed her cooking.

When Nikos was dressed for the day, he went to his desk and powered up his laptop. First order of business, catch up on e-mail and check in with his assistant at the resort. By now the power should have been fully restored. But there would be other minor crises to deal with. While he worked, Stefano brought his breakfast. An omelet as light as air, loaded with mushrooms, onions, spinach and green peppers was the first thing he saw. The walnut bread on a separate plate was still warm. The coffee was strong and hot. As he ate, he tried to visualize Sara preparing the meal. He frowned. He had no idea how cooks worked. His education was sadly lacking. One day he should check out the galley and see her in action.

When his cell phone rang, he answered.

"Nikos, it is your grandfather," the familiar voice said.

"I know. I recognize your voice." Nikos smiled. He had spent many summers on the island while his parents traveled. It still remained his favorite place.

"Your assistant tells me you are on another cruise. Where this time?"

Nikos filled him in and waited. There was usually a reason his grandfather called at this early hour. Informal family chats were unheard of.

"I'm thinking about buying another boat," he finally said.

"Oh?" Nikos suspected his grandfather knew his son had called Nikos.

"I wanted you to vet it for me. And don't be telling me I'm too old to buy a new boat. This one is for Eleani and me to go out together. No privacy otherwise."

Nikos shook his head. The *Cassandra* offered plenty of privacy and was available whenever his grandfather wished. But he understood the older man's reasoning. Last night he'd been very aware that he and Sara hadn't been alone.

"I am committed for another three days, then must return my guests to the resort and await their departure before I can come home," Nikos said, glancing at his calendar. He had no important meetings or commitments the following week. "I'll come after that."

Nikos always found it easy to relax on the family island. It had been a while since he'd visited. He could enjoy his grandparents' company and really take a few days away from work.

"Good, plan to stay awhile. We have not seen you in a long time."

"I will stay a few days. Give my regards to Eleani."

He hung up, his mind already returning to the situation at hand. Why shouldn't his grandfather and his wife enjoy a small boat? They might be older, but they were both perfectly capable of running their own lives. His own grandmother had died when Nikos had been a boy. When Spiros had remarried, to a widow, Eleani, Nikos and his family had accepted her as Spiros's wife. She'd had no one. That had been almost ten years ago. She had easily become a vital part of their family and had been the best thing for his grandfather. Nikos liked her warmth and devotion to Spiros. And she'd shared that warmth with the rest of the family when they'd let her.

Nikos hoped he was as active when he was in his eighties. Hard to imagine now reaching that age. He could not picture himself married, much less very much in love with a wife in fifty years.

It was stupid to cast all women in the same light as Ariana, but he had a tendency to do just that. She'd professed undying love when they'd been engaged. But once he'd caught her with another man in bed, he'd had trouble believing it. The truth had been that she'd wanted the lifestyle Nikos could offer. She didn't love him; she loved being with men—rich, poor, young, old. Ariana hadn't been too particular.

To a young man who had been in love, it had been a double blow. First, that she hadn't loved him and second, that he hadn't been wise enough to realize that before finding proof. He'd learned the lesson well, however. Unless a woman had a fortune to match his, he would never consider her in the matrimony stakes.

Gina would make a perfect businessman's wife. She was polished, aware of the demands of work and brought a wealth of contacts with the wine industry in Italy.

Yet still he hesitated. If left to him, he probably would not marry. Families were overrated. He knew from his own experiences and shattered expectations that it was an institution best handled carefully. Currently he set his own goals and had no one to blame except himself if things didn't go as he wanted. A wife would be an additional responsibility. Still, he did want children, some boy or girl to leave the resort to. To teach the ways his fore-fathers had lived for generations. Would Gina be that wife?

He didn't have to decide on this cruise, but he wasn't getting any younger.

He quickly scanned his messages, replying to two that were urgent. Shutting off his laptop, he rose, ready to face his guests and offer some of the hospitality of the small island they were heading for.

The ruins were spectacular. He'd taken other guests on a tour of them in the past and everyone had raved about the antiquity of the stones and the view of the sea that seemed endless.

He hoped the Fregulias and Onetas would like it, as well.

Four hours later Nikos knew this particular outing hadn't met with the same success as the visit to the market had the day before. The three couples had walked around the cobblestone streets of the old town, stopping in several shops but purchasing nothing. The morning was winding down. There was time for a quick visit to the ruins before a late lunch, but his guests seemed disinclined to continue.

Senor Fregulia wanted to visit a taverna. His wife wanted out of the sun. Nikos knew what Gina wanted but the more she seemed interested in him, the less he felt interested in her. Was it just the normal reluctance of a man to commit to one woman?

"It is so hot," she complained for the tenth time.

"Perhaps we should return to the boat and continue the sail," he suggested.

"No, I wish to visit the taverna. A drink of fine wine while sitting in the shade and watching people would suit me better than the boat. I seem to be prone to a touch of seasickness," Senor Fregulia said, heading in the direction of an outdoor café.

"I wish to see into some more of the shops," Senora Fregulia said, looking at her friend. An instant later Senora Oneta agreed.

Gina was pouting. Nikos wanted to shake the lot of them, but his duties as host prevented that. How had the outing turned out to be so annoying?

"Gina?" A young man dashed over and began talking with her in rapid Italian. His speech was too fast for Nikos to follow with the limited Italian he spoke, but the gist seemed to be they had been friends who hadn't seen each other in a long time.

"Excuse my manners," Gina said at one point, linking arms with the young man. "Pietro, this is our host, Nikos Konstantinos. Nikos, my friend Pietro from Rome."

Once introductions had been completed, Gina flirted with Pietro, keeping a careful eye on her father and on Nikos.

"Come, we will all enjoy some wine and watch the boats in the harbor," she suggested, drawing Pietro toward the taverna. "Nikos can tell us all about this quaint little island and the people who live here."

It was obvious to him what she was doing and he had no intention of playing her game of pitting one man against another. If she thought that would spark his interest, she would be very surprised to know his thoughts, which of course he would never voice.

Senor Fregulia waved Nikos over.

"I know you are a busy man. We can entertain ourselves this afternoon. Go, do what you need to do. What time shall we return to the yacht?"

"By six." Would it be this easy? To have the rest of the day to himself?

"We will return by then." The older man turned to his wife and urged her down the sidewalk with an admonition that she could shop after they'd had some refreshments.

For a moment Nikos watched the group walk away. Duty required he be a good host; good business sense dictated he not alienate a man whose business he wanted. Prudent planning for the future indicated he should get to know Gina better. The truth was he wanted to be on his own—just for the rest of the day.

Turning, he walked back to the harbor. He could call his assistant, get up to speed on the various projects in the works and maybe even respond to some mail if anything crucial was pending.

Just as he reached the wide dock, Nikos saw

Sara walking toward him. She was wearing a floppy hat to keep the sun from her face. Her arms were bare and lightly tanned. She was looking around as she walked. He noted the instant she recognized him. For a moment her smile lit up the harbor, then was replaced with a frown and a wary look.

"Hi. Did you forget something?" she asked as she walked closer.

"No. Where are you going?"

"Sightseeing. The captain said we were all free until six. Was that right?"

"Yes. We will not sail until after that. Dinner at eight."

"Then I'll be back by six, no problem."

She stepped by him.

Before she'd gone three feet, he said impulsively, "Would you like to see the ruins on the mountaintop?"

Nikos wasn't sure who was more surprised—Sara or himself. Vanished was the idea of working. Gone was the concern for his guests. He had enjoyed swimming with her; now he wanted to show her some of the island. See how she related to the history that was so much a part of their culture. Spend some time with someone who didn't expect him to propose in the next minute.

"I would love to see the ruins. Can you spare the time?" she asked. The wariness had not left her eyes.

"The afternoon is free, it turns out. I would like to see them again myself." With a sweep of his hand indicating she should precede him, they walked down the dock to the street. Two cabs were parked nearby, their drivers leaning against the side of one, talking.

Nikos summoned one and in seconds he and Sara were on their way through the town and beyond. The mountain was not very high, sloping gently up from the sea. The lush vegetation that grew along the side of the road served as a green backdrop to the incredible blues of the sea and sky.

Nikos watched Sara as she gazed out of the side window.

"This is beautiful. At times like this I wish I was a photographer or painter and could capture the scene forever."

"You'll have to remember it."

She nodded. "I shall! Thank you for bringing me along. It's fantastic."

Sara felt her heart turn over when Nikos smiled at her comment. She quickly looked back out the window. With butterflies dancing inside, it was safer to feast her gaze on the view of the sea rather than drown herself in Nikos's eyes. She felt that growing sense of awareness sweep through, though she kept her gaze firmly on the distant horizon. She felt tongue-tied. What could she say? Nikos was the type of man her mother had fled Greece to avoid. Surely her daughter wouldn't be so foolish as to fall for him? He was so out of her league.

Yet the trip to the ruins was an unexpected treat. Why had he invited her along?

"Your guests didn't wish to come?" she asked.

"No. They were content to sit in town and watch the inhabitants."

"That sounds nice," she replied politely. In some circumstances maybe. For her the chance to see more of the island beat sitting in one spot all day.

The road wound up the hillside until the vegetation grew thin. Rocky expanses dotted the land, giving way to a deteriorating wall that outlined where the ancient Roman garrison had once stood. When the cab stopped at the graveled parking lot, Sara was delighted with the setting. There were few other cars. With several acres of ruins to view, there weren't enough people to make it crowded.

Nikos held out his hand to assist her from the cab. His fingers were warm and strong as they wrapped around hers. She shivered slightly in response, though the day was quite warm. Pulling away quickly, she walked toward the ruins feeling fluttery and excited and foolish all at once.

He spoke to the taxi driver as he paid him off. The cab turned toward the town.

"So tell me about this place. It certainly has a commanding view of the sea," she said when he joined her, walking toward the walled expanse.

"It was a Roman outpost before the time of Christ. Not a strategic one. Archaeologists have suggested it might have been an outpost for rest and relaxation. The stones that comprised the fort remain, if in some disrepair."

They were a warm pinkish color, huge in size and placed without mortar. The sheer size ensured they did not topple over. Sara regarded them with awe, wondering how men two thousand years ago could have moved them to the summit.

They walked to the parapet, and Sara caught her breath at the beauty of the island and sea.

"If I'd been a Roman soldier stationed far from home, I'd love to have come here for R & R," she said. "Do you ever wonder what it would have been like?"

"More often when I was a child than now," Nikos said. "All of Greece is steeped in ancient history. I wanted to be a Spartan when I was younger."

She glanced at him. "You'd have made a good one, I'm sure."

"Based on?" he asked, amusement evident in his eyes.

"Just a hunch. Of course, I guess I'd really need to see your skill with a spear before passing judgment."

Nikos laughed. "A skill not fully developed, I fear."

Sara smiled and returned her gaze to the sea, feeling the pull of attraction stren; then toward the man standing beside her. He re; ed a foot on the low wall and gazed out, as well. She could feel the warmth of his body near hers and was torn between moving away or moving closer. She did neither, just savored the day and the company and tried to keep a perspective on things.

A group of young children ran across the ruins, yelling and laughing. Sara turned to watch. They were having the time of their lives. Behind them a couple stood side by side and watched indulgently. Sara felt a tug of nostalgia. Her mother used to take her places, usually with one of her friends, and would watch as Sara and her friend ran and jumped and laughed. The excursions had been limited to the parks and gardens they'd been able to afford on her mother's meager salary. But they'd been outings of fun and joy.

She missed her mother. For a moment sadness threatened to overrule her pleasure in the day. Her mother had turned her back on all this at eighteen. Even years later when Sara knew she'd yearned to return home, Damaris had refused. Her pride had not let her return home in disgrace, as she so often said. Her pride had kept her from the one thing she'd longed for. Sara knew about pride, but she was a touch more practical than her mother. If she wanted something, she'd go after it.

"Noisy," Nikos said, stepping away from the low wall and watching the children.

"They're having fun!" she said. "It's what makes wonderful memories of family outings. Would you not have them here?"

Nikos watched silently for a moment, then turned away. "It's hard to take in the grandeur of the place with children running around."

"One day you'll bring your own children to run around here. Don't you have happy memories of similar expeditions?" she asked, walking along the wall, heading for the other side. The fort had been situated on the highest point in the island, commanding a 360-degree view. Perfect for watching from all aspects. And the view of the green of the island, the white strip of beach and the azure of the Aegean had to have made it an ideal family spot.

"No," he murmured.

Sara looked at him in surprise. "Why not?"

"Not everyone associates families with happy children and holidays together," he said.

Sara blinked. "What does that mean?"

"Nothing. Have you seen enough?"

"Not nearly. After we walk the perimeter, I want to explore that curious building in the center."

"Probably where the troops slept. The view is the same from all sides."

"No, it's not. If you are tired of showing me around, feel free to leave. I'm sure I can get a cab back to town." Sara was surprised with Nikos's attitude change. He suddenly seemed to close off and distance himself. Had she said something to offend him? Trying to remember every word she'd just said, she couldn't find anything wrong.

"No, I brought you, I'll stay."

"Gee, what enthusiasm. Go. I'll be fine." Now she felt like an unwelcome burden.

She walked to the far parapet and looked at the view, not seeing a thing. A flare of anger burst forth. She'd been having fun. Maybe she wasn't supposed to have fun with the keeper of the key, as she thought of Nikos Konstantinos. He was the only way to get in to see her grandmother. She needed to remember that.

"Rome lies in that direction," his deep voice

said in her left ear. She turned and almost bumped noses with Nikos.

"I used to wonder if soldiers longed for home or were satisfied serving the emperor wherever he sent them. Even in antiquity, this was a small island, isolated from all the grandeur of Rome, from the excitement the big city held. Were they lonely?" he continued.

"Probably—and missing families and all."

She felt him move away. Aha, *families* was definitely the key.

Sara turned. Nikos hadn't moved that far. Her shoulder brushed his chest. "Don't you like families?" she asked bluntly.

"I have nothing against families," he said evenly.

"You're lucky, you still have your parents and grandparents. I have no one. That's why when I marry, I will fall madly in love with the man. I want us to have lots of children. I want to marry into a large family so my children will have huge celebrations at holidays and birthdays. Lots of cousins, aunts and uncles and loads of love."

"Not everyone is cut out to marry and start a family. Though most do it from duty."

"I agree not everyone is cut out to be a parent, but I think life is enriched by children. For most people anyway," she said, thinking of her own father. He'd abandoned her mother when Sara had been two months old. He couldn't take the interrupted nights of a newborn baby. He resented not having his friends over whenever he wanted. He hadn't liked being a father. And the consequences were ones Sara and her mother had lived with for the rest of her mother's life. Had he ever regretted leaving? She'd never know. She didn't even know if he was still living.

"Families aren't always like you imagine. I often wonder why my parents had a child," Nikos said.

"So, no brothers or sisters?"

He shook his head. "Probably a good thing in the face of things. There were no other children to be ignored and brought out only on occasion to show off." He shook off the memories from his youth. He'd made his way in the business he wanted. As an adult, he could far better understand his parents.

"You're young to be alone in the world. No other relatives?" he asked.

She shrugged. "No one I know. So it's just me, until I find that special man to fall in love with and marry."

"I wonder if marriage is for me," he said.

Nikos took a breath. He usually had more finesse when warning a woman off who might have any matrimonial intentions. Not that he thought Sara was contemplating such a move. She had shown none of the flirting that he was used to. He was thinking of Gina. The trip was proving more important than he'd anticipated. The more he was around Gina, the more doubts crept in.

He knew his duty to his family was to provide heirs. He would need to hand down his grandfather and father's shipping business. Maybe he'd have several children and they could each decide what to do with their lives. He would not force any along career paths they disliked. But was Gina the right woman?

"Everyone has to decide that for himself. If you fall in love one day, you might change your mind," she said.

If she only knew.

"On the other hand, I suspect love is overrated. Good for some, disastrous for others," she added, nodding.

Nikos suddenly wanted to know why she said that. Had she fallen in love and been hurt as he had? If so, she had rebounded with optimism.

"It does work for some," he admitted reluctantly. "My grandfather and Eleani are a perfect example."

"Oh?" she said.

"They married about ten years ago and are blissfully happy together. In fact, my father wishes me to check up on them soon." He frowned, studying the horizon, and wondered why he'd thought to bring that up. He hadn't even told Gina.

"Is there a problem?"

"No. But my grandfather has a crazy idea that my father wants me to talk him out of. If you ever saw my father and grandfather together, you'd understand why I act as a buffer between them. But it gets tiresome." He stopped talking. It was not like him to share any family business with a stranger. Much less an employee. He didn't know what kind of gossip Sara might be.

Sara looked at him oddly, then turned away.

"I know a path that leads to one of the beach villages if you're up for such an adventure," he said. She had no interest in his family situation. The sun was high overhead, and despite the breeze, the air was growing uncomfortably warm with the heat reflected from the stones. They could enjoy the walk and then find a taxi to return to the dock.

"It's mostly shady," he added. "Or I can arrange for the taxi to return here to pick us up."

"Sounds more like an adventure to walk back down. Do you want some water before we start? I brought a couple of bottles," she said, rummaging in the small tote she'd slung over her shoulder. She handed him a bottle and opened the second one, taking a long drink.

"Warm but wet," she said with a grin.

Nikos drank the entire bottle, wondering what Gina would have made of the situation. She would have complained the ground wasn't suitable for her shoes. The water was warm and not cool. The sun was too glaring.

But he was not interested in taking her to ruins. Yet, as he watched the children running and shouting and obviously having the time of their lives, he knew he'd want to bring his own children if he ever had any. He'd want them to know and love their country's history as he did.

Try as he might, he couldn't picture Gina with them.

Sara, yes.

The thought startled him. Sara still had that starry-eyed wonder as she took in everything. She'd urge the children on and demand to know every aspect of the history of a place to share with them. And probably make up stories about where the men had been from, or what they had left behind.

The trail to the village was well marked and wide enough to walk two abreast. Just a few yards from the ruins, trees began. The leafy canopy soon dappled the path in shade, lowering the temperature significantly.

"Lovely," she said as they walked in the quiet. The noise from other visitors at the ruins faded completely when they made a sharp turn. The trail made a series of switchbacks to enable the path to be easily navigated while ascending or descending the steep hill. "I imagine this dates from the Roman times. Soldiers probably used this very path to go to the village for supplies," Sara said, envisioning men traveling up and down the trail.

"Maybe. Would you have liked cooking for the garrison?"

"Most men seem to appreciate good cooking. I'd make the best dishes in the Empire, and soldiers would long for this duty station," she said, falling into the fantasy.

"I'd improve my spear prowess to get the duty assignment."

Sara laughed. "No need. I'm happy to cook for you aboard the *Cassandra*."

"And I'm happy to eat your meals."

"Ah, how gallant. If I served oatmeal for breakfast, would you say the same?"

"Depends. I suspect your oatmeal would far surpass that which I ate at school in America."

"Ah, so that's the trace of accent I hear when you speak English," Sara said. They'd spoken Greek most of the time, but she'd heard him once or twice speak in English and been intrigued by the faint accentuation on some words.

"I went to university there for two years for

postgraduate work. Stayed in a variety of hotels to get an idea of what I liked and wanted for my resort."

"I've never been. Maybe one day," Sara said.

It was after two by the time they arrived at the fishing village. Sara was ravenous and uncertain how to respond when Nikos suggested they stop for lunch at one of the tavernas lining the small fishing harbor. She agreed and then had second thoughts.

Colorful umbrellas shaded the tables. The food was plain but delicious—fresh fish, grapes and some local wine. Conversation was awkward.

"Is your Italian supplier's wine better than this?" Sara asked as she sipped the delicate white wine, casting about in her mind for other topics. The one in the forefront was too dangerous.

"This is excellent. Perhaps I should explore having more Greek wines," Nikos said, as he sipped from his glass.

"Do you make all those decisions?" Sara asked. "Seems like you would have hired others to do that."

"For the most part I delegate to the different

departments of the resort. But I do like to keep an eye on every section. I shall suggest this to the sommeliers of two of our restaurants. Are you also a wine connoisseur?"

"Nope, not at all. But I know what I like," Sara said. She smiled as she gazed around. Her milieu wasn't small cafés with plain fare. She loved cooking meals with drama and flair. But that didn't mean she couldn't appreciate the appeal of a quiet place, and good basic food.

"Thank you for today. It's been a treat," she said.

"I'm pleased you've enjoyed it."

"In Spain they have siesta after lunch. Eating makes me sleepy," she commented, finishing the last of the food on her plate. Maybe she'd return to the ship and lounge on the aft deck, dozing a bit.

"In half an hour, you could swim again. Care to join me on a short swim? I have some diving equipment on board."

"I thought you said swimming near docks wasn't a good idea."

"The yacht has a small runabout. We'll go out into the sea a distance, away from the shore."

Once again Nikos had surprised her. Warily she examined the pros and cons of another swim. The pros would obviously be the joy of swimming in the sea. And maybe getting more information from the man. Opposed to that was the proximity to Nikos. She was drawn to him each time they were together. The last thing she wanted was some kind of connection that would hinder her goal. She had nothing in common with the man. In fact, she wasn't sure she even liked him. But her body seemed to have other ideas.

"Very well, I'll go swimming. I'm not sure about the diving," she said at last. And hoped she wasn't making a mistake. But she was only in Greece for a short time. Why not make the most of unexpected chances?

Two hours later Sara and Nikos had changed, commandeered the small runabout from the yacht and set out. He'd convinced her to try diving. After donning the cumbersome scuba gear, Nikos and Sara slipped into the sea. The water was like silk against her skin. The sun sparkled on the surface like a million diamonds. Sara was treading water, feeling awkward with the air tanks strapped to her back, while Nikos once again explained the rudimentary aspects of scuba diving. She pulled down the face mask and stuck the mouthpiece in her mouth. Taking a breath, she found the air was cool and a bit dry, but she filled her lungs, excited about this adventure. It struck her as a bit odd that the man she was using to find her grandmother was willing to teach her how to dive. To even spend time with her. She would not look a gift horse in the mouth.

His hand grabbed hers. "Once we're under the water, if you feel any discomfort or become nervous, squeeze my hand and we'll surface immediately. We are not going deep."

She nodded. He put his mouthpiece in and motioned with his free hand to begin.

She took a deep breath and held it as they slipped beneath the water. She'd done a little snorkeling on a vacation in Spain a couple of years ago, so expected the crystal clarity of the sea. A moment later she let her breath escape and breathed again. It was magical, being beneath the water's surface and still breathing. She felt an affinity with the fish.

Nikos began swimming slowly, his hand tugging her along. She kicked her flippers and soon was swimming beside him. His fingers linked with hers and he matched his own pace to hers so they were in sync. Sara kept her eyes forward, resisting the urge to watch Nikos swimming. His body was honed from exercise and swimming. His broad shoulders and tight stomach muscles made her own heart flip over. She'd much rather watch him than look for any fish, but peripheral vision was severely limited with the face mask and it would be too obvious if she turned her head.

Nikos swam in a large circle, not wanting to be beneath the water too long on Sara's first time. She seemed like a natural. Surfacing at one point, he asked her how she was doing.

"This is the greatest thing in the world," she said once she removed her mouthpiece.

"Good." He released her hand. "Try it on your own."

She nodded, her eyes sparkling behind the glass. She repositioned her mouthpiece and dove beneath the water. He remembered that first rush when he'd started many years ago. Lately he'd been too busy to go diving. Maybe he'd take a few days at the island. There were several coves where colorful fish proliferated. Maybe Sara would like to see them.

He trod water for another moment. When he went to the island, he wouldn't need Sara. She could resume her work at the resort restaurant. He'd have only the captain, the mate and Stefano as minimum crew for the short distance between the resort and island.

Unless he decided differently. Replacing his own mouthpiece, he dove after her.

She wasn't where he expected. He swam faster. Had she run into trouble? Then he felt a tug on his ankle. Flipping over, he bumped into Sara. From the laughter in her eyes, he knew she was all right and playing. She kicked away, on her back, watching him as she moved through the water. He surged after her.

Suddenly she was gasping. He caught her under her arms and swam swiftly to the surface. Pulling the mouthpiece from her mouth, he held her above the water while she coughed.

She pushed back the face mask and gasped for air. A moment later she looked at him ruefully.

"First rule of scuba diving—don't laugh," she said. She coughed again and drew in a deep breath.

"Is that what caused this?"

She nodded, her hand resting on his shoulder. "You looked so surprised when you saw me, I couldn't help it. I forgot about being underwater. When I laughed, water came in my mouth. Thanks for the rescue."

"Enough for today."

She looked around. The small boat they'd used to get away from the dock and *Cassandra* bobbed several hundred feet away.

"I can swim back. I'm fine now that I have my breath back." Without volition, her fingers began rubbing small patterns on his smooth skin. She could feel the muscles contract beneath her as he kept them both above water. Did she have her breath back? Being so close to Nikos was robbing her of air again. Her legs tangled with his as they lazily kicked to keep upright. Her left side was pressed against him.

He swept back his own face mask and gazed into her eyes, his gaze then dropping to her lips. Sara licked them. Salty. She wrinkled her nose.

Nikos's eyes took on a distinctive gleam. "You look delectable," he said in that low, sexy voice.

"You've got to be kidding," she said. "My hair is hanging in strings. I have no makeup on and I'm covered in salt water."

He leaned forward the scant inches separating them and kissed her.

CHAPTER FOUR

SARA kissed him back. Her tongue met his. His slow kicking kept them upright while the kiss went on and on. She hugged him, her hand brushing against the top of his tanks, the breathing hose and straps separating her from his skin. She wanted to be closer, impatient to drop the tanks and have nothing between them.

Then reason returned. Slowly she pulled back, her eyes wide as she gazed at him. He looked at her lips again, then into her eyes.

"This is *so* not a good idea," she said. For a gazillion reasons. Yet she couldn't move.

"Why is that?" he asked.

"Relationships between boss and employee always end badly—usually for the employee." It was not her first reason, but one that would suffice.

He released her and swam back a foot or so. "This was merely a kiss. You are correct, relationships between working people don't end well."

Sara sank to her chin, turning to swim toward the runabout. He'd shown pity on a lonesome crew member and with his free afternoon offered to show her how to dive. He'd probably wanted to go alone. She was not reading anything into their afternoon. Not even the kiss. People kissed others for various reasons.

She refused to explore why she'd kissed him back. Enough to have enjoyed the afternoon. She didn't need anything further from Nikos Konstantinos.

The kiss had surprised her. But she'd not been able to help herself and had returned the kiss. Magical—like the entire cruise. The sooner she had her wits about her, the better.

Sara reached the boat first. She tried to pull herself in, but the weight of the tanks offset her balance too much. Rats, now she'd have to rely on his help, and that was the last thing she wanted. If she could levitate herself in, she'd do so.

Nikos pulled himself easily into the small craft, shrugged out of his tanks and went to the side to assist Sara, lifting her without difficulty. Once standing on the rocking boat, she unfastened her own straps. Before the tanks could slide off, he lifted them from her shoulders, carefully placing them in the rack built into the back of the boat.

"Thank you again, I enjoyed the diving," she said politely, refusing to meet his eyes. If the yacht hadn't been so far away, she would have struck out swimming to avoid this awkwardness.

"My pleasure." His deep voice sent shivers down her spine. Could they recapture the ease they'd enjoyed before? Did she want to?

He pulled up the anchor and started the motor. Sara sat in the seat next to his and gazed straight ahead. The day had been magical. She would ignore the change after the kiss and remember the good part. Her friends would want to hear every detail when she returned. And she'd tell all—except about the kiss. Some things were too private to share.

It took less than ten minutes to return to the *Cassandra*. One of the crew heard the motor and was there to take the lines and secure the small boat when Nikos stopped. He turned and offered his hand.

She smiled politely and took it to step to the swim platform and then up the ladder to the aft deck.

"Oh, Nikos, where have you been?" Gina leaned over the side, eyeing Sara as she climbed swiftly up.

"Took advantage of the time for some diving," he said. "What are you doing here?"

"The captain said you'd be returning on the aft of the boat, so I came to wait. You should have told me you wanted to go swimming."

Gina continued to watch Sara ascend. When she reached the deck, Gina walked over. "Aren't you the cook?"

"Chef," Sara corrected, walking back down the deck toward the door to the lower decks.

"We didn't go swimming, Gina," Nikos said as he reached the deck. "We went diving. You said you didn't know how or I would have invited you."

"I could have gone swimming," Gina was saying to Nikos as Sara walked through the door and headed for her cabin. Let him explain to his guests why he'd taken the hired help diving and ignored his invited guests.

As Sara stood beneath the minuscule shower a few moments later, she wondered why herself. He certainly had the choice of a wide variety of women. She knew a half dozen who would love to trade places with her. So why had he spent the day with her? Was it because he recognized a kindred spirit who also loved antiquities? She hardly thought so.

By the time Sara had the evening meal prepared, she had regained her equanimity. The duck *à l'orange* was perfection. The lightly steamed vegetables *al dente* and nutritious. Once the dishes were served, she'd send the crew's meals out and begin to work on the dessert. Not that all the delicacies were consumed each evening. She had her suspicions about which guests did not eat the sweets. Their loss. The triple-chocolate mousse cake tonight would melt in their mouths, the bitter chocolate flakes on the frosting a contrast to the sweetness of the mousse. It was one of her favorite desserts. She'd made a double batch to make sure the crew had enough. And she could indulge, as well. Nothing like chocolate to set things right.

Stefano returned for the desserts a short time later, and Sara took her own dinner to the aft deck. Those crewmen off duty were lounging in contentment.

"The dinner was great," one called when she stepped out.

"I'd have more dessert if there is any," another said, holding up his empty plate.

Sara smiled; she loved it when people appreciated her efforts.

"There's more. Help yourselves, or ask Stefano to get you another piece." She sat at the end of the long table, eating while she listened to their desultory conversation. The gentle rocking of the boat was soothing. The air was cooler than earlier, but quite pleasant enough to sit outside. If she were in London now she'd be slogging away in some hot kitchen, making dishes to order and dashing around to find everything she needed with other chefs working at frantic speed, as well. Maybe after she found her grandmother she'd consider working for a private club or household or yacht. She enjoyed planning the meals and preparing them at a more leisurely pace.

That day was still a long way off.

Sara didn't leave the aft deck when she finished eating. Stefano cleared the dishes. One by one the rest of the crew bade her good-night and left. Soon darkness fell and she felt alone standing by the railing as she gazed over the sea. The surface was calm, almost glassy, reflecting the stars that pierced the night sky. When the moon began to rise, its sliver of light cast a delicate pale yellow trail across the sea. She felt almost as if she could step out and walk along it all the way to the moon.

Nikos watched Sara from the bridge. She stood so still as she gazed across the sea. He wondered what she was thinking about. The captain looked up from the chart he was reviewing by the small lamp.

"Is everything all right?" he asked.

"Yes. The cruise is going well," Nikos replied, still watching Sara. He wanted to go down to the aft deck and steal a few minutes of peace. Today's kiss had shown him how dangerous that would be. It had just been a kiss. And if he had resisted that impulse, their time together could have continued. Now he had to distance himself before she thought there was more to his wanting to spend time with her than an escape from the duties of work.

That thought firmly in mind, he'd refrained from going down to the aft deck tonight. But it didn't stop the desire to do so.

"We head for Mazure tomorrow?" the captain asked.

Nikos swung around. "No, head for home. I'm cutting this cruise short. I'll explain to my guests tomorrow." With a nod he left. The sooner he got his guests on their way, the sooner he could head for the family island. The return was only one day ahead of schedule. He'd treat them to a lavish suite at the resort to make up for it. And he'd head for his grandfather's. He still had not asked Gina to marry him. After today he wasn't sure he wanted marriage. He would bide his time a bit longer, bid the Fregulias farewell and think about the future when he was on the island.

And say goodbye to Sara.

In his office a few moments later, he was churning with frustration. He'd only been with the woman a few times. Once back into the swing of things, he would forget her soon enough. She'd be cooking in the kitchen of the farthest restaurant at the resort; he'd be at the other end in his offices and suite of rooms.

"Blast it!" he rasped out, slamming his palm against his desk. She was pretty, talented and content with her life. She had not made a single overture that could be misconstrued. Unlike him.

He sat in his chair, leaned back and gazed out of the darkened window.

What if he continued to see Sara for a while? The novelty would wear off and he'd be on to the next woman on the horizon. Maybe marriage wasn't for him. At least his father had settled on one woman.

Sara's appeal was her unique spin on things, which made her intriguing. Once back in his normal routine, he'd soon miss the witty repartee of women of his own social set. He'd miss the gala dinners, the receptions. He'd find her enthusiasm and wonder boring after a while and begin to long for the more sophisticated, cynical women he knew.

But until then, could he continue to see Sara?

Why not take her to the island? The thought came unbidden.

Why not, indeed. She seemed content to be on the boat. He knew she liked swimming, standing in the dark watching the stars, diving.

Would she be equally content going to formal receptions, meeting dignitaries and businessmen who played an important role in developing Greece? Wearing designer dresses and expensive jewelry? Any woman he developed a relationship with needed the sophistication to move in his world.

He knew how to play the game. He wanted his resort to become world renowned and knew what it took to get there. But sometimes he longed for quiet, tranquility and genuine people. Like Spiros and Eleani. They were content on the island, or traveling when the mood suited them. They entertained and also spent time alone enjoying their own company.

He could find that tranquillity at the family island. His father wanted him to stop in. His grandfather had invited him. He'd go.

And he'd take Sara with him.

The next morning Nikos rose early. Ignoring his computer and the work that awaited, he donned his swimming trunks and grabbed a towel. In less than ten minutes, he was on the aft deck, contemplating the sea. He'd had all night to think about his plan. If Sara kept her distance as she had yesterday on the runabout, he'd have a harder sell. If she showed some sign of interest, he'd move ahead.

"Good morning," she said from behind him.

Nikos let out a breath he hadn't known he'd been holding as he turned slowly around.

Sara dropped her own towel and cover-up on one of the chairs. Her hair was bound back in a ponytail. She didn't look directly at him, but he didn't care. She'd come to swim. He would take that as the sign he wanted.

"Good morning. I hoped you would come to swim."

She looked at him in surprise. "You did?"

"You seemed to enjoy it. Why not take advantage of the opportunities?" He thought that sounded reasonable. Which was not at all the feeling he had seeing her again this morning. He felt a most unreasonable attraction.

"My thoughts exactly."

He wished she'd smile. Her eyes lit up when she did. But her expression remained solemn.

He opened the railing gate and gestured for

her to go first. She descended the steps quickly and without a word dove into the sea. He followed. She was ahead of him, swimming leisurely. She didn't seem angry or upset. Just distant.

She bobbed up and trod water, looking around. The sun was rising, the air crisp and clear.

"Is it always this beautiful?" she asked when he stopped next to her.

"Always."

She grinned at that and shook her head. "What about the storms? Wasn't one of Shakespeare's plays based on a severe storm in the Med?"

"Ah, but this is the Aegean, always perfect." He relished her grin. What could he do to keep it there?

"And never any storms?" Her doubt was obvious.

He shrugged. "Only if nature's awesome power can be described as beautiful."

She rolled her eyes at his attempt to describe the storms that sometimes erupted without warning and were the bane of sailors. No body of water ever escaped storms.

"Today will be clear, however," he reassured her.

"And duty calls," she said, turning to swim back to the *Cassandra*. "I need to get breakfast ready for your guests."

"And for today's meal?"

"Eggs Benedict."

"A favorite of mine," he said, keeping pace with her.

She frowned. "I didn't know that."

"Now you do." He would not let her retreat.

"So tomorrow will be oatmeal," she retorted. Reaching the swimming board at the back of the yacht, she held on while kicking her legs lazily in the silken water.

"No oatmeal."

She grinned again. "We don't have any on board anyway. But it's good and nourishing."

"Fine for a cold winter's morning."

"So should I wait for such a cold snap?"

He felt foolish talking about oatmeal, but at least Sara hadn't scurried up the ladder and disappeared into the galley. Twice she'd grinned at him. Could he go for three?

"I'll come up with something different tomorrow," she promised.

"Actually, there will be no need."

"What do you mean?"

"We're returning to the resort this afternoon. I'm cutting the cruise short."

"Why?"

Nikos hesitated. "Family business," he said.

"Oh." She grabbed hold of the support and lifted herself onto the swim board and then scrambled up the steps to the deck. "I'll make today's breakfast special, then," she said, leaning over the rail to see him. "And lunch on board?"

He nodded.

She disappeared from view.

Sara's heart pounded. Family business. Did that mean something was wrong? Not with her grandmother, she hoped. While she had no warm feelings for the woman, she desperately wanted her to read her daughter's last letter. It meant so much to Sara that her mother's mother knew how much her daughter had loved her and wanted to return to Greece. How much she regretted her impetuous marriage and asked for forgiveness.

All through breakfast Sara speculated on

what Nikos had meant. Would he be going to the family island? Would he take the *Cassandra* and its crew? Even if he did, she'd learned it was less than a three-hour cruise to the island. There was a chef in residence on the island, so he undoubtedly would feed the smaller crew. A ship's chef would not be needed.

And she had no other incentive to offer. She couldn't hope that the chef fell ill like the ship's chef she was substituting for had.

Could she smuggle herself on board? Hide in the stateroom? Or did the crew sweep through before sailing to verify no stowaways? Just her luck to be found. Then what would she say?

The word about the change in plans swept through the crew quickly. Stefano told Sara and she pretended she didn't know and asked what he'd heard. "Why the change, do you know?"

"He is probably tired of his guests," Stefano said as he waited for the plates for breakfast.

"He would cut the trip short for that? I thought he was interested in Miss Fregulia."

Stefano shook his head. "He never has cut short a cruise before and sometimes he can get some very demanding guests. But it's only a day early. The captain said we were returning, no reason given. I'm not privy to the captain's orders. Nor the path of true love—or at least the proposed walk down the aisle."

"Nor am I. Just curious." Raging with curiosity, was more like it. "What happens with the *Cassandra*? Do we stay aboard?"

Stefano shrugged. "I also work at the resort. If he does not plan another trip soon, I would resume my duties there. As you would, I'm guessing."

"Probably." At least she had the job at the resort. And if Nikos took another cruise, maybe he'd ask for her. Oh, no—wait. The regular cook for the yacht would be ready to sail again in only a few weeks. If the ship didn't go out before that, she would not be included on the next trip.

It had seemed destined when she'd landed this berth. Now without ever getting close to the family island, she was going to miss the opportunity. She would not wish sickness on anyone, so she couldn't keep hoping the regular chef would not be able to go the next time. But one quick trip before he was well would suffice.

"I'll return as soon as they finish lunch to

clear the galley and stow any nonperishables. The rest will be taken to one of the restaurants," Stefano said as he hoisted the tray laden with breakfast plates. "We'll wait until the guests take off before leaving—just in case they want any last-minute assistance."

"I'll make sure my cabin is clean," she said, wiping off one of the counters.

Sara packed quickly. It didn't take long. She'd only been aboard a few days and her clothing was almost entirely resort uniforms. Suitcase by the door, she went to the porthole in her wall and gazed out. She could see land in the distance. They'd be back at the resort soon. And she'd accomplished nothing.

Sara went up on the aft deck as the resort came closer and closer. The wind blew her hair back when she leaned over to look toward the direction they were heading. Shading her eyes with her hand, she looked up to the bridge. Nikos stared down at her. She caught her breath and looked away. For his sake she hoped the family situation was not an emergency.

Leaning over the railing, she watched as the yacht was tied to the dock, the gangplank lowered and the passengers disembarked. Gina held on to Nikos's arm as if she'd fall without his support. Senor and Senora Fregulia followed with their friends behind. No one seemed particularly upset, Sara thought. Maybe the family situation was a happy event—like a new baby born or someone got engaged.

"We're leaving," Stefano said from the doorway. "The *Cassandra* sails again this afternoon. Captain wants to talk to you on the bridge."

"I'll go straightaway, then pick up my bag." She walked over and offered her hand. "It's been a pleasure, Stefano."

"It was mine," he said as he shook her hand. "I hope we sail again together," he said formally. "I'm sure to see you around the resort." With a slight nod of his head he turned and walked back down the short corridor.

Sara climbed up to the bridge, loving the view of the resort from this height.

"You wanted to see me?" she asked the captain when she entered the pilot house.

He looked up from some papers he was reading. "Ah, Sara Andropolous. Mr. Konstantinos would like you to remain on board. We sail again in a few hours and he has requested you sail with us."

"I'm happy to stay," she said, thinking what an understatement that was. "To where do we sail next?" she asked, almost crossing her fingers and toes.

"To the Konstantinos family island."

Sara almost jumped with joy at the news. But conscious that all things could change, she merely nodded and smiled. "I like sailing on the *Cassandra*. I look forward to extending my time on board."

"Your meals are excellent. It's no wonder Nikos wishes you to remain. I've enjoyed each one you've made."

She smiled in delight. "Always words to warm a cook's heart. Thank you."

She did a little skip as she headed out. Walking down carefully to the main deck, she went to the railing and looked around. There were several luxury yachts moored in the resort's marina. Three smaller boats were also tied up. The activity on the docks seemed lively and she enjoyed people watching.

There was one person she was especially watching for.

CHAPTER FIVE

SARA sat in the shade of the aft deck writing to her friend Stacy when Nikos appeared. She had not left the ship, not knowing when it might sail and not wanting to miss her only chance.

"I brought your mail," Nikos said, handing her a slim stack of envelopes.

"Thank you." She glanced at them—all from friends at home. She smiled, looking forward to catching up on all the news. She had pretty much brought Stacy up to date in her letter and asked her to tell all their friends the situation.

He sat on the side of the chaise next to hers. "The captain spoke to you?"

"About staying aboard? He said we would be going to your family's island. I've never known anyone to own an island."

"It's small, been in my grandfather's family for generations."

"Descendant from the Roman times?" she asked, thinking of their trip to the ruins.

"Hardly. It's not strategic at all. In fact, the only way in and out is by sea or helicopter. No roads. And only one stretch of really usable beach. The rest is rocky."

"Sounds private."

"For various reasons it suits the family."

"So this is your vacation after your cruise?"

"No, family business. We'll only be gone a few days, once we leave port. However, bad weather threatens for the next couple of days. Just as well we brought the Fregulias and Onetas back when we did."

"What—storms in your perfect Aegean Sea?" she asked with a smile.

He nodded, amusement in his eyes. "So we'll make a run for the island when the captain thinks there's a window of opportunity. In the meantime, since we'll be leaving on short notice, I appreciate your staying close."

She lifted her tablet. "I have letters to write. More, I'm sure, once I read those from my friends."

He glanced at them, then at her.

"One from a special friend?"

She fanned them out and nodded. "Stacy and I have been friends since starting school. From the thickness of the envelope she's written a lot."

"I was wondering about a particular male friend."

She looked again, then caught his meaning. Meeting his eyes she narrowed hers.

"That's really none of your business, is it?" He may hold the key to getting to her grandmother, but he didn't run her life.

He looked away, studying the masts of a large sailboat tied up nearby. "I was taking a friendly interest in an employee."

"I prefer to keep my private life just that—private." Plus she hated to admit to this dynamic man that there was no one special in her life.

He nodded and rose. "As do I as a general rule. Someone will let you know when we get under way. If you'll excuse me, I have work to do. We will run with a minimum crew."

Sara stared after him when he left, wondering what kind of complex she'd developed because of her background. The man had been cordial to her and she'd just about bit his head off. She didn't want to give herself any ideas, so had nipped any personal talk. She couldn't get past the man's background, so different from her own. Yet had her mother not stood up to her own father and refused to marry the man he had chosen for her, Sara would have had a very similar background to Nikos's.

Instead, her childhood had been a struggle. With no father in the picture, and a mother scarcely trained for work, money had always been tight. But her mother had made the best of things. Sara remembered happy evenings with only grilled cheese sandwiches for dinner. It hadn't mattered, her mother had made it fun.

She leaned back, lost in thought. She missed her mother so much. Damaris Andropolous had had a hard life, nothing like what she had once expected. Sara wished she'd lived to enjoy some of the fruits of Sara's work. By the time Sara was earning enough money for a lovely flat, nice secondhand furniture and friendly neighbors, her mother had been too ill to enjoy it.

Life wasn't always the way one wanted, she

knew. Sara was alone in the world—save the grandmother she'd never met. She had no illusions the woman would embrace her with delight. She'd hand her the letter and that would be that. Sara had a full life in London. Her visit to Greece made for a nice change, but it was not permanent. She longed for the familiarity of home.

Stefano arrived with another crew member in tow, each carrying bags of groceries. Sara went to put things away, chatting amicably with Stefano as he helped.

"We will likely eat breakfast on board and the rest of our meals with the staff at the island," he said. "That's the way it's been in the past."

"Tell me what you know about this family island," she said, hoping to glean some more information about the Konstantinos family.

"It's pretty. The house is huge. The servant quarters are quite spacious, and we can use the beach unless there's a house party, when it's reserved for guests. I like making the trip. For the duration of Nikos's visits, we're on call, but never needed. Lots of downtime—and we get paid."

"Sounds good. Will they need my help in the kitchen?" she asked, wondering how to ask the questions she really wanted to know— when and where might she see Eleani Konstantinos.

"No need," Nikos said from the doorway.

She spun around, surprised to find him at the galley entrance.

"We have a fine chef who cooks to suit my grandfather. As Stefano says, you have the days to yourself. Will you get bored?"

"I doubt it. If there's a beach, I'll go swimming."

"There are some coves around from the main dock that offer a variety of colorful fish if you care to go diving."

Stefano kept stowing the groceries, but Sara knew he was listening avidly. Had he known Nikos had taken her diving? She felt her face grow warm remembering that dive—and the kiss that followed. Surely they'd been too far from the boat for anyone to see.

"Sounds like something to think about," she said, conscious of Stefano's presence. Did Nikos mean to go with her? Or after only one short lesson, would he trust her on her own?

Did others of the crew dive? She didn't want to go with anyone else.

Nikos didn't seem in a hurry to leave. He leaned against the doorjamb and watched as she checked off the ingredients and Stefano stowed them. What was he doing?

"Did you need something?" she asked.

"No. Just wondered what was for dinner. It's supposed to storm through the evening so we will stay put for the night. The aft deck isn't protected. No need to cook if you don't wish to. We can take our meals at the resort."

"Or we take our meals in our rooms in inclement weather," Stefano said.

"Then if you wouldn't mind cooking, it would save the crew going out into the bad weather," Nikos said.

"So individual trays," Sara murmured, wondering if Nikos sat in solitary splendor in the dining salon or invited the captain to join him.

"Perhaps you'd care to join me this evening once the meal is prepared."

Sara stopped and stared at Nikos.

Stefano stopped and stared at both of them, his head turning like a spectator's at a tennis match.

Sara's heart rate doubled. She studied him for a moment. "Why not? Thank you for asking. When I have everything ready, I'll ask Stefano to bring up the tray."

Nikos glanced at Stefano. The steward stared back, obviously at a loss for words. "If that suits you, Stefano."

"Of course."

Nikos nodded and turned to leave.

Sara looked at the steward. "Something tells me he doesn't often ask the chef I'm replacing to eat with him."

"Never. But then, Paul is not a beautiful woman."

Sara laughed nervously. What had she just agreed to? "Neither am I, but thank you. I think I'll prepare lamb with mint jelly. He liked it last time I made that."

"As far as I know he has never been a picky eater," Stefano said, busying himself with the last of the grocery placement.

"How long have you known him?" she asked.

"I've worked for the resort for six years. And been steward on the *Cassandra* for almost five. I wouldn't say I know him, precisely."

And never been asked to eat with him, Sara guessed. She didn't know whether to be wary he had asked for her company or annoyed at the barrier it might raise with other crew members. She had to work with these people. She didn't want any resentment.

Nikos wondered if he was making a mistake. He stood near the tall windows of the dining salon awaiting dinner. Stefano would bring it up in only moments. And Sara would come up, as well. It was unheard of for him to invite a crew member to dine with him. Though he and the captain had shared many meals on the bridge, he'd never shared one in the main salon unless guests were present and they wished the captain to share in the festivities. As to the rest of the crew, Nikos occasionally ate on the aft deck with them, but none had ever eaten in the salon when he was aboard.

The trip to the island would of necessity be brief. He had already been several days from the resort. But he hadn't seen his grandfather in several weeks and wanted to spend a few days with him. He and his wife always made Nikos feel at home and urged him to stay as long as he could. The island held the best memories of Nikos's childhood. He remembered exploring, learning to dive, learning to pilot the yacht. And his grandmother's loving smile. Spiros's second wife, Eleani, was as loving as his first. What was his secret to finding women to love him and for him to love?

He'd thought Ariana would be someone to grow old with. That relationship had proved false and left him wary of women and their motives. While he'd dated over the years, it wasn't until he began to consider Gina as wife material that he'd grown serious. Until he met Sara.

She was nothing like the woman he wanted for a wife. She lacked…what? The cosmopolitan veneer he was used to? That made him feel cynical. Yet he was just as skeptical of her own delight in all things. How long would it take to find the key to Sara? Did she long for fame as a chef? For a high-prestige job? Or just pots of money and the lifestyle that went with it?

"Dinner, sir," Stefano said, arriving with the tray. The table had been set a half hour ago. The steward placed the tray on the stand and began serving.

Sara entered, her cheeks rosy from heat in the kitchen. She'd obviously changed for the meal, wearing a simple dress instead of the resort uniform.

When they'd been seated, served and Stefano had left, Nikos poured a bit of wine in her glass. "A bottle from our own islands."

She took a sip. "Lovely. So have you re-thought Greek wines?"

"The resort has always served local wines, but perhaps we'll expand the offerings. In addition, I have a new agreement for the next three years with Senor Fregulia. After that time I'll review the consumption rate of both and make a decision."

Sara longed to ask about Gina. But since Nikos had never brought up the subject, she couldn't. But it seemed odd that he would dine with her if he were on the brink of asking another woman to marry him.

"Maybe the head chef at the resort will think up a special dish to go with the island wine and when ordered the sommelier can suggest this variety," she said, nervous. Now that it was the two of them, it felt like a date. What would they talk about? Diving? The resort? Or could she steer the conversation to families and Eleani Konstantinos in particular?

She glanced at the windows on which rivulets of water ran down. The rain had started shortly after the groceries had arrived and not let up since. The ship bobbed by the dock, obviously impacted by the winds accompanying the storm. It had grown dark early with the storm.

"So it's a good thing we didn't head out," she said, tasting the lamb. It was delicious. If nothing else, she'd fall back on describing how she had prepared the meal.

"We would have had a rough ride, but the *Cassandra* is very seaworthy, and this storm would have been a mere inconvenience, not a threat."

"I wonder if I would have been seasick," she said, watching him take a bite of the lamb.

"Delicious," he said as he savored the flavors.

Sara smiled, relaxing a tiny bit. "Thank you."

Talk revolved around the ship as they ate the meal. Sara asked how often he sailed, where he had been, what his favorite places were. By the time they finished, Sara was feeling much more at ease. And knew more about her boss. His experiences far surpassed hers in travel. This was her first extended stay anywhere outside of England. She loved listening to him talk about America and even his few months in the UK.

When they were finished Stefano quickly dispatched the dinner dishes and brought the trifle Sara had prepared. He also brought a bottle of brandy from the sideboard and two snifters. Pouring hot coffee from a silver pot, he stepped back and eyed the table, then looked at Nikos.

"Thank you, Stefano. You can clear the rest in the morning."

Stefano bowed slightly, set the coffeepot on the table and left.

As soon as Sara finished her trifle, she folded her napkin and looked at Nikos.

"Thank you for inviting me to eat with you. I think I'll return to my cabin now."

"So soon?" Nikos asked. "It is still early. What would you do in your cabin?"

"Read, make plans for the next few days' breakfasts." She felt her nerves stretched taut.

She resisted drawing closer to the man, yet every minute she spent with him was making it harder to resist. She tried to remember all her mother had said about the strong Greek men who rode right over women and their interests. So far she had seen no evidence of that, but she scarcely knew the man.

"Stay. The night is young. If you like, we can take our brandy up on the bridge. It's dry under the shelter, yet we'll be able to see the resort lights through the rain."

She placed her glass carefully on the table. "What do you expect from me? If I didn't know better, I'd think you're flirting. I'm confused. I thought rumors said you were on the verge of marriage with Gina Fregulia."

Her question caught him off guard. What did he expect? She worked for him, which precluded any close tie. Was he just fighting against tying himself down with one woman when he married? Or did he really want to know more about this particular woman?

"I want nothing except a pleasant evening. And perhaps a diving partner when we reach the island. The only family members there right now are my grandparents, who are not quite up to the activities I enjoy. Consider this a perk of the job. Beyond that, I expect nothing. And for the record, I did not ask Gina to marry me."

"A diving partner," she clarified, confused.

He shrugged. He was surprised that she knew of his earlier plan. Yet it was no secret. Gina had not given any evidence of being upset when she had left, but he knew she too had expected a proposal on the cruise.

She dropped her gaze to her brandy.

"Still, if you are close to becoming engaged, it wouldn't do to spend much time with another woman. It might give rise to the wrong impression." She looked up at him thoughtfully and added, "Even if it might be more of a business arrangement than a love match."

He laughed softly, amazed at her daring.

"Don't you believe in love?" she asked.

He took a breath. Talking about his family didn't come easily. His roommates at school had heard the complaints, the frustration and then the resignation. Usually he maintained a careful facade that revealed nothing of his true feelings. Sara wanted to know more. Did he wish to tell her? Where to start and where to stop? Should he share the history of him and Ariana as well?

"Never mind," she said. "I changed my mind. You keep your secrets and we'll see how it works to be diving partners." She poured cream into her coffee and sipped, her brandy only half-gone.

Her disinterest acted as a goad. "It's no great secret. I don't want a marriage that would end up like my parents'. They had one child—me, but I didn't fit into their plans or lifestyle. Nannies, tutors and boarding school made up my childhood. The few times I returned home for summer holidays or Christmas, I was lucky to find them at home one night to catch up on my life before they were off to another function or short trip abroad. If it hadn't been for the island and the time my grandparents took to be with me, I might as well have lived my entire childhood in a boarding school."

She stared at him. "Not much of a family life for a child," she said slowly. "So different from mine. It was just my mother and me. My father vanished shortly after I was born. She gave me the best home in the world, despite our financial difficulties. I always thought if we'd just had a bit more money, things would have been perfect. Maybe I was viewing things wrong. Time and love are far more important than all the money in the world." As her mother knew when she'd lost both her parents' love and their money. It had been the loss of family she mourned.

"My parents are too wrapped up in themselves to care for a child. I feel the same way about the resort. It is very demanding. It would be a mistake to marry, father a child and then ignore him or her while putting the resort first."

She tilted her head slightly, thinking. "I don't believe you would do that. Firstly, you know what it's like and would cherish your child too much to put him through what you experienced."

He shook his head. "How can anyone be sure?"

Sara bit back her comment. She thought his view of marriage and families was sad. He'd obviously never experienced the close tie that love brought. Was that the Greek way? Marry for business or convenience, not for love.

Not that she had fallen in love, but she knew what it was like from observing her married friends. And one day she hoped she'd discover it for herself. She wanted an emotional tie as well as the legal one. As had her mother. Only, she hoped her marriage, should she ever have one, would end up much happier than her mother's.

She drank the last of her coffee. She liked being around Nikos too much even when their opinions differed. He kept her guessing where he would lead the conversation next.

Time to leave, however. She dare not risk her emotions on a man who would do perfectly well without her.

She rose. "I really am retiring now," she said.

He rose and bade her good-night.

She turned toward the door feeling just a twinge of disappointment that they hadn't connected on a basic level.

"Sara," he said softly.

When she turned, his eyes were focused on her.

She licked her lips, her heart racing. Butterflies had a field day in her stomach, and Sara felt as if time stood still. She recognized desire. That much was clear. She yearned for another kiss, but hesitated. It would only make her compare him to every man she kissed after Nikos; what if she became spoiled by his kisses and never found another to measure up?

Granted, she'd only been kissed in the sea, hardly the stuff of romance. Yet she had dwelt on that experience more than any other in her life.

"Sara?" he said again, stepping around the table and walking directly to her.

She stepped closer and lifted her face, her gaze fastened on his.

He closed the distance and cupped her face in his hands and kissed her.

CHAPTER SIX

His lips were warm as they pressed against hers. Slowly he swept his tongue against her lips, seeking entrance to her mouth. Sara complied, stepping closer, longing for him to wrap her in his arms and keep the kiss going forever.

He must have read her mind as his hands moved to lift her hair, then slide down her back and pull her into closer contact. The kiss deepened, and Sara felt like she was floating. Desire flared. She actively kissed him back, her tongue dancing with his, her arms holding him as tightly as he held her. Only the lack of breath caused her to pull back eventually, gasping.

He continued to kiss her—first her cheek, then along her jaw, then a long slow slide down her throat to the rapid pulse point at the base. Then back up the other side.

She stood still as if afraid the slightest movement would end the magic. When he covered her lips again she responded. It was glorious. She could fall for this man. If he kissed her once a day, she'd probably be content to stay forever in Greece.

The thought filtered in, then struck with clarity.

She pulled back slightly, feeling dazed and confused. And guilty. She had no business becoming involved with Nikos Konstantinos. He was practically engaged to another woman. And she was trying to use him to gain access to her grandmother. Nothing was working in her favor. She suspected he would be a dangerous enemy. She dared not provoke him or lead him on. He would feel betrayed once he knew the truth. She could not aggravate the situation by sending false messages.

He opened his eyes and looked at her.

"I need to go to my cabin," she said quietly, disentangling herself from his embrace.

He started to say something but Sara held up her hand. "No, don't say a thing. This was not *just a kiss*. I can't do this."

She fled from the salon. Once she reached

her small cabin, she shut the door softly and leaned against it. Blowing out a puff of air, she tried to get her roiling senses under control. She could feel the blood pounding through her. She was still breathing faster than normal. Good grief, she was attracted to Nikos as she'd never been to anyone else. And falling for the man was a guaranteed heartache.

She pushed away and went to the small porthole to gaze out at the rainy night. It was too dark to see much; only the dock lights cast faint illumination on the ship. The resort glowed in the wet evening. Had everyone else aboard gone to bed? She checked her watch. It was after ten. Early yet.

You're stalling, Sara, she admonished herself. She could not get sidetracked by an attraction to Nikos. Granted he was gorgeous and successful. He had been more than kind in showing her around the island, teaching her to dive. But she knew he had no intention of becoming involved with her. Was this just a fling before settling down? The thought made her sick—and did not jibe with what she knew of Nikos. He was too honorable. So…maybe the lovely Gina was out of the running. That still didn't give her a chance.

"Darn it," she said aloud. The first man she'd met she really felt an attraction to, and he was off-limits. She knew he would end up disliking her once he knew she'd used him. Was there any way to keep a relationship?

Friendship—she didn't want that, she wanted more.

She lay back on her bunk and relived the kiss. Magical, no other word. Did he know he could melt her insides with a sexy look? Did he care? He probably had women falling all over themselves to impress him.

To fulfill the promise made to her mother, she had to focus on her goal—give the last letter to her grandmother.

But she wished she could dally a bit with Nikos Konstantinos. It would make her Greek trip the ultimate fantasy.

The next morning Sara rose early. She'd slept fitfully during the night, soothed by the sound of the rain, waking as each dream cast her into Nikos's arms. She was glad for the dreary morning sky. Working would help.

She prepared an omelet again for breakfast, with an assortment of fresh fruits and a delicious coffee blend she hadn't tried before. She nibbled as she worked.

With only a minimum crew and Nikos, the workload was easy. Would she need to prepare any other meals besides breakfast? That would depend on the weather. It took less than a half day to reach the island. Once there another chef would be in charge. Maybe she could offer her assistance.

"I'll take up the captain's plate. He says we're leaving this morning," Stefano said.

"It's still raining," Sara said with another quick glance out the window.

"But not windy, which is the bad part of a storm. Rain can't hurt the boat."

She nodded. "There, take it away. That's for Nikos, that's for the captain," she said pointing out the two plates. "Do we eat in our rooms for breakfast, too?"

"We'll stand around the counter for breakfast. We don't have a lot of rainy days on the ship."

After breakfast Sara stepped out on the aft deck, keeping beneath the small overhang to stay dry. The air was humid, the rain warm to the touch when she extended her hand. If they hadn't been in the marina, could she have gone swimming? What a novelty—to swim in the rain. At home it was usually too cold in rainy weather to swim.

She stayed awhile enjoying the change in weather, then turned to return to the galley. Stefano was about through with the dishes. He glanced up.

"The captain asked if you'd like to come to the bridge to watch as the yacht left the marina. I've done it a few times. Gives a different perspective to things," he said.

"I'd love to." She'd relish a chance to see how the yacht was actually operated.

"Take a fresh pot of coffee. It's cool up there and the captain commented he especially liked today's blend," he added.

Fifteen minutes later Sara entered the bridge, two coffee mugs and a coffeepot in hand. She stopped when she saw Nikos standing at the high chart table, reviewing the charts with the captain. Heat washed through her.

He looked up casually and nodded. "Good, you brought more coffee."

The captain smiled. "Come in. We'll be pushing off in a few minutes. I thought you'd like to watch. Without much of a crew to cook for, you will have more free time."

"Thank you. I brewed a fresh pot," she said, walking over and placing the two mugs on the flat surface near the charts. Pouring the coffee carefully, she refused to allow even one drop to spill on a chart. But it took all her concentration. Her instinct was to watch Nikos.

She handed one mug to Nikos and one to the captain.

"You didn't bring a mug for yourself," Nikos commented, taking a sip and watching her over the rim of the cup.

"I didn't know you were here or I would have brought another."

He offered her his.

Sara drew in a sharp breath, hesitated, then slowly reached out and took it. The coffee was hot and fragrant. She took a couple of swallows then returned the mug, feeling an intimacy at the gesture. Moving to the wide windows, she looked at the activity on the dock. Despite the rain, men were working, wearing bright yellow slickers.

"So the storm won't affect our trip," she said.

"Not unless the wind kicks up again," Nikos replied. "And we're hoping it won't."

"The last weather report indicated the worst had passed," the captain murmured, checking a list as he flipped switches and checked gauges.

She watched another minute, then made up her mind. She could act like an idiot and avoid the man as much as possible or take advantage of the invitation to the bridge and learn all she could.

She spun around and almost marched to the high table with the charts. "So what are we looking at?" she asked, peering at the yellow page with blue lines swirling around.

"A depth chart of the sea between here and the island. We are looking for deeper water, which will minimize some of the wave action. We want as smooth a journey as possible," Nikos said, moving slightly so she could see better.

He put his arm over her shoulder and pointed to a series of irregular circles. "This shows the topography of the sea floor. Here are depth indicators." She watched as he pointed out aspects of the chart and the route they were planning.

"How will you know where these are from up here?" she asked.

Nikos removed his arm and looked at the captain. The older man gave a concise explanation of the depth sounder and GPS positioning to which Sara was able to listen and understand without Nikos's touch rocketing her senses.

"I thought you just hopped aboard and took off," she said at the end of the explanation.

"More or less if we use the heliport. My father usually uses that as it's faster than ship, but I prefer the *Cassandra*. Since the weather has kicked up a bit, we're looking for a smoother passage than the usual route we take. We'll be there by lunchtime."

"So if it takes you hours to get there, I bet shopping is a two-day affair."

"There are islands nearby which offer shopping and other amenities. My grandfather wants a new runabout to get to the nearest one. Takes about forty minutes in a smaller boat."

"Your grandparents are there now?" she asked. She couldn't be this close and bear to learn her grandmother was elsewhere.

"Of course, they're who I'm going to see."

She nodded and looked back out of the window.

Sara enjoyed watching the men on the dock cast off the lines. She marveled at how the captain could maneuver such a large ship away without a scrape anywhere. The rain had not abated. The large wipers on the front windows kept the glass clear. She smiled as she felt the power of the engine when they went to cruising speed sometime later.

Turning, she met Nikos's eyes. He was standing on the far side of the bridge, leaning against the glass watching her. He raised an eyebrow in silent question.

"This is fantastic. Do you ever drive the yacht?" she asked.

"Sometimes."

"He is as proficient as I am," the captain commented. "Perhaps with not as much practice, though."

"Who has time to command a yacht when a resort needs a firm hand?" Nikos asked.

"So who is running the resort while you are away?" Sara asked.

"I am. The marvels of modern electronics. I have a laptop here that connects to the main computer at the resort. My assistant can manage the day-to-day activities. I am always available if he needs me."

"Will I meet your grandparents?" Sara asked. She might as well find out from the get-go.

"Do you wish to?" he asked.

She shrugged, trying to show a casual demeanor. What would another crew member do? She didn't even try to guess—none of them had been invited to the bridge since she'd been on board.

"Just wondered."

"My grandfather knows all the crew—except you. He'll want to meet you. In the meantime, you can swim in the sea, enjoy the island. We have some beautiful flowering gardens. A nice gazebo near the beach. I'll take you to one of the coves to dive—there are some amazing sponges and fish there."

"Sounds like a vacation, not work," she said. He still hadn't answered her question. It looked as if it would be up to her to find a way to meet Eleani Konstantinos.

Once the ship was under way, Sara grew bored with watching the rain on the windows and the gray sea that stretched out to the horizon. It would have been lovely had the weather been good. She gathered up the mugs and the coffeepot and thanked the captain for the time on the bridge.

Nikos opened the door for her and followed her into the narrow passageway.

"Thanks for the chance on the bridge. I'll get these back to the galley and see about what to prepare for lunch."

"We'll be at the island by lunch," he said. "And the crew eats with the island staff. You're done for the day."

"Oh."

"Dump the cups and come to the aft deck. We can sit in the lee of the wind and stay dry."

"I'm not sure that's a good idea," she said slowly. Her first inclination was to say yes. Yet, after his explosive kiss last night, the last thing she should do is place herself in the path of temptation.

He stopped her and swung her partway around. "Come for a little while," he coaxed softly, his eyes warm and dark.

Her heart skipped a beat. This was *so* not a good idea.

"Okay. Unless it gets too wet."

"It won't."

She went first to the galley, then stopped in her cabin for a sweatshirt. It was part of the uniform, with the logo of the resort clearly embroidered over her heart. She stared at herself in the mirror. "Do not forget this is only a means to an end. You are not going to get any more attached to the man!"

Sara had a feeling she was lying to herself. The attraction she felt for Nikos was not something she controlled. Maybe her tactics were wrong. Maybe she should be around him as much as possible—to see if once she saw the flaws he was bound to have, it would lessen the pull.

Nikos was already on the aft deck when she stepped out. The overhang had kept the three feet of deck closest to the main structure dry. The wind hadn't touched it. The air was cooler than she expected. The wake was white against the steely gray of the water.

She shut the door and walked to stand beside him. Nikos had pulled two chairs over and dried them. The towel was on the floor.

Sitting, she looked at him.

"So, what shall we talk about?"

He groaned softly. "If we have to talk about what to talk about, we have nothing to say."

"Do we?"

"You mean after last night?"

"Of course."

"You mean a chance to kiss a beautiful woman after a pleasant evening together?"

"Good line. I think I've heard it before."

He shrugged. "So I need to polish my technique."

"I don't think you need to change a thing. It's clear you like your lifestyle and I live a very different one. I told you."

He tilted his chair back, resting against the wall. "And if I don't see them as that different?"

"Trust me, there's a world of difference between us. You are rich, I'm not. You evidently were neglected as a child. I was not."

"Not neglect. My parents gave me the best that money could buy."

"Neglected by them, however. The greatest gift parents can give their children is their attention. My mother and I did so much together. Even when I was a rebellious teenager. She loved me. There was never any question."

"Some people are not meant for marriage. My parents aren't the only reason."

"So what else? Burned at love?"

"You might say so. Now I wonder if I really loved Ariana at all. It was an advantageous match."

"What are you talking about?"

"My engagement—surely you've heard the tale."

She shook her head. "I thought you didn't ask Gina Fregulia. So there was another engagement that ended. Were you heartbroken?" she asked sympathetically.

He gave a harsh laugh. "Hardly. Mad as hell. Ariana was beautiful and pleasing and professed to love me. Our relationship was meant to be, she said a hundred times."

"Uh-oh, I think I've heard this tale before," she murmured.

"Do you want to hear it or not?" he asked.

"Yes." She closed her mouth tightly and looked at him.

He looked away. "Damn, I don't want to explain. Sufficient to say my loving, meant-to-be fiancée found our own relationship wasn't quite enough, so she found other meaningful relationships with as many men as she could."

"Ouch," Sara said. "Tacky."

He looked at her in surprise. "Tacky? Is that all you have to say?"

"Well, you said your heart wasn't broken. So then it was probably embarrassing to end the engagement if others knew why. But her behavior definitely was tacky. You're well rid of her."

He nodded. "Well rid of any suggestions for future alliances as well—unless the rules are clearly defined. In the meantime I'm content with the way my life is going."

Sara thought about what he said. She felt the tension in his words. Maybe he had been hit harder by the betrayal than he wanted to admit, even to himself. And for a moment her heart softened. No one should be in love and have that love thrown back into their face by such wanton betrayal.

She had a hard time picturing Nikos Konstantinos heartbroken, but he might have been and hidden it from the world. She wanted to reach out and touch him with sympathy but refrained. She didn't know how that would be received.

She began to relax. Hearing he had problems with life like anyone else made him seem more normal or approachable. Not the mighty millionaire resort owner living in an ivy-covered tower. Did she dare spend time with him? They'd never have to be alone—except when diving. He had never made an untoward comment or move on her. And she'd be leaving soon. Putting distance between them would be the best solution in the end. Despite her love of what she'd seen of Greece so far, her home was in London. Her friends were there. Her memories. Her mother was buried there.

She had a few days. She dared not reveal that being with him rocked her emotions. That kissing him was the most glorious feeling ever. That she longed for more when reality kept slapping her back. They had no future. She should adopt that as her mantra.

She dared not give voice even to herself of what she feared might happen—that she'd fall madly in love with him and end up going home with the world's biggest heartbreak. He might like to kiss her, but his barriers were well established. She was not some femme fatale that men fell for. He'd already set his course—

marriage to Gina, business arrangement. She shivered. It sounded so cold and sterile. She wanted love, heat, passion and loyalty that lasted a lifetime.

Take the time on the island as a gift. One day she could look back on her great adventure in Greece. Were all Greek women destined to heartbreak? Her mother had been betrayed yet had loved the man she gave up her family for. She had never found another to love after he had left. And her pride had kept her from admitting she'd made a mistake and returning home. Sara dearly hoped she would not follow in her footsteps. Pride was well and good in its place. But not to the detriment of love and family.

Nikos shifted his focus to the sky. "I think this storm will last all day. Not the best way to see the island when we arrive. It's quite beautiful with all the flowers in the garden."

"So are the gardens at the resort," she said, feeling oddly adrift now that her goal was drawing closer. She had not thought beyond handing her grandmother the letter. What next?

"I took the advice of grandmother Eleani for the gardens. She loves flowers and worked with a landscape architect to design the gardens at the resort."

"That's what you call your grandmother," she asked.

"My real grandmother died when I was a teenager. About ten or eleven years ago my grandfather married a widow—Eleani. She is a delightful person, warm and friendly and openly adores my grandfather. I can't help but love her because of that. As you may have gathered, my family is not very demonstrative. Except for Eleani."

Sara was hungry for any information about Eleani. But would it appear odd if she questioned Nikos? She was wary of getting to know too much about him. Wouldn't that lead to expectations that she couldn't fulfill? Once he knew he'd been the reason for her presence, as a key to the island, he would be furious.

Again she bemoaned that she'd met him only as a means to an end, and then had become attracted to him. Why couldn't life be easy for once?

"So tell me why you know as much about running this boat as the captain," she said, deliberately changing the topic.

"I love the sea. When I was younger I was always after the captain to show me how, so he convinced my grandfather to let him give me a crash course of several weeks. We loaded up on supplies and set off. It was one of the best summers of my life. I learned about charting, learned how to read the weather, how to sound for depth. How to dive. We were gone eight weeks and it flew by like the wind. By the end of the summer, I could pilot the boat as well as the captain. I had grown proficient in diving and received a good overview of the Aegean, to boot."

Nikos told her of the villages and cities they'd visited. How he had crashed into more than one dock and had been the despair of the captain whenever he turned the yacht into a port. Sara laughed more than once, as she knew he wanted. He was a natural storyteller and she listened avidly to every word, relishing the deep tone of his voice and the fluttering inside that occurred whenever she was near him. She was growing used to being in constant turmoil around him.

When he wound down, he asked her about her favorite summer. She told him about the trek through Scotland she and her mother had made—despite the rain and cold weather. How they ate at pubs each night and tried to like haggis, but gave up midway through their trek and switched to porridge.

At Nikos's expression, she laughed, remembering he didn't like oatmeal.

"So how did you end up a chef?" he asked.

"I like to cook. My mother quoted that saying 'Do what you love and you'll never work a day in your life' to me from when I was a little girl. I learned to prepare simple Greek dishes at her side when I was quite small. It seemed like a logical career for me."

"And it's worked out?"

"There's a bit of a bias against female chefs. Especially in some of the more posh restaurants in London—the ones where I could really explore all kinds of exotic dishes. But I'm still young. I'll keep pushing ahead. The fact I've worked for your resort will add a fillip to my résumé. Maybe I'll have better luck when I return to London."

"And must you return?"

"It's my home." Now they were getting close to her secret.

"But not too soon," he said.

Sara shrugged. She knew she would not have a job once Nikos discovered why she'd been working at his resort. Yet he'd been the one to ask her to accompany him to the family island. In a way, he'd facilitated part of her quest. Would he see it that way? Would he understand why she'd had to resort to subterfuge to reach her goal?

She wanted to forget about seeing her grandmother. The thought shocked her. Ever since her mother had gotten sick, Sara had wanted to reach Eleani. Two years and counting. How could she even for a moment consider coming this far and not contacting her?

Yet being with Nikos had made her more interested in this exciting man than in seeking some unknown woman who had let her only child leave and never resumed contact. What good was any of it going to do at this late date? Her mother was dead. She had tried to heal the breach and been rebuffed. Why should Sara try?

Because of a promise.

She had made her mother a promise, and Sara would stand by her word.

No matter who got hurt? a small voice inside whispered. No matter that her mother would never know one way or the other?

A promise was a promise. She had to keep hers to her dying mother.

Nikos looked at a seagull gliding on the wind.

"We're getting close," he said.

Sara looked around. "How can you tell? It all looks the same as it's been since we left the resort."

"Birds live on land. This one is either from our island or Patricia, the nearest island where you can shop." He glanced at his watch. "Besides, we've been traveling long enough."

So their time together was ending. Maybe it was for the best.

"Despite what you say about your family, you're happy to be going home, aren't you?" she asked.

He nodded. "The island is special. The best place for our family—when we all gather together. I won't see my parents this visit, but my grandfather holds a special place in my heart. I owe him more than most grandchildren owe their grandfathers."

"Family ties are the hardest ones to break. They are strong no matter what the circumstances," Sara said slowly.

"True. I'd do anything for him."

She nodded, studying him gravely. "No matter what he asked?"

Nikos shrugged. "I can't imagine him asking anything I would not be willing to do."

"Even if it were hard or seemed pointless at some stage?"

"Even then. If it meant enough for him to ask me, it would mean enough for me to do it."

Sara looked away. Nikos had reaffirmed her own beliefs. At least they had that in common—not that he'd ever know it.

"Did I miss something?" he asked.

"What?"

"The conversation turned very solemn all of a sudden."

"I was just asking about commitment and family ties. Sometimes things happen. Promises are made. Remember that."

"I think I can remember that—things happen, promises are made."

She laughed, forcing away her dismay and focusing on the moment. She'd caught a glimpse of Nikos's attachment to his family's island. She suddenly yearned to see it—through his eyes if possible.

Before long he rose and peered over the railing toward the bow.

"There it is." The excitement in his tone had Sara jumping up and going to stand beside him. He drew her in front of him, holding her steady against the motion of the yacht. She peered around until she could see ahead. Rain hit her in the face, but she could see the silhouette of an island dead ahead.

Sara leaned back against Nikos's chest. She felt the shelter of his arms as he steadied them on the railing of the ship as it rose and fell meeting the waves head-on. She could stay here forever—though they'd be soaking wet in a few minutes

"It doesn't look like much today, but see it in the sunshine," he said by her left ear. "When we get closer, you'll see the house on the highest point, with gardens surrounding it like a beautiful, colorful skirt. The beach is pristine and we work to keep all oil and waste from the yacht away from the sand. The cove I told you about is around the leeward side."

"It's larger than I thought it would be," she said, as the island seemed to gain in size every bit closer they came.

"A few square miles. There is a small compound behind the house where the servants have their homes. Even a guest house, which my parents use when they visit."

Even more important than finding her grandmother, Sara would find out where Nikos called home. See what kind of place he loved. Find out more about boyhood escapades. While he sounded as if he'd led a solitary life, he'd also had this glorious place to explore. Despite what he felt as a lack of parental involvement, they had done a fine job in giving him a safe place to live as a child that he still cherished today.

Sara definitely didn't feel that way about the flat she'd grown up in. The best thing said for it was its proximity to the public gardens.

A deckhand was on the dock waiting to tie up the *Cassandra*. Other than that, no one was in sight.

Sara and Nikos had returned to the bridge to watch the docking procedure. Now the captain turned off the engines and snapped up his chart portfolio. "So we are here. Sailing again when?" he asked Nikos.

"A few days at least. You're free to do whatever you wish here. I'll contact you in plenty of time to prepare for our return trip. It will undoubtedly be after the weekend."

Since it was Tuesday, Sara could look forward to at least five days to see over the island. She hoped the weather would clear so she could go diving again. And see the flowers in the garden. Her heart pounded—and find her grandmother. But she was trying not to think about that step now that it was here.

"You will all take your meals at the main house as usual," he continued. Looking at Sara he said, "A respite from your duties. Feel free to visit the house kitchen if you wish, but Dimitri and his staff will prepare our family meals."

She nodded. They were to stay aboard during the visit. No need to have employee quarters prepared when their cabins suited. She was glad she'd brought along a couple of mystery books. Without reading to look forward to, she'd be bored to tears with the inactivity in the rain.

An older man walked down to the dock, an umbrella carefully sheltering him from the rain. He had a furled umbrella in one hand.

"I see your grandfather," the captain said.

"I'd better go." He hesitated a moment, looking at Sara, then nodded and left the bridge.

Sara moved to the window closest to the pathway and tried to get a good glimpse of her grandmother's second husband. He was as tall as Nikos, she thought. Perhaps Nikos would look like him when he was old.

A feeling of regret swept through. She would not get to see him grow old. Their paths would have diverged long before either of them was old. She wished for him a happy life. Maybe Gina, or someone like her, would change his warped views of family and would love him forever.

She hoped she'd find a man like that, who could make her forget the past and sweep her away into a future of love and happiness. She sighed softly and watched as Nikos met the older man on the dock and they hugged. He took the umbrella his grandfather offered, and in only moments the two of them disappeared from view as they went up to the house.

CHAPTER SEVEN

SARA didn't see Nikos the rest of Tuesday. She took one of her books to the aft deck, pulled over one of the chaises and dried it off to sit in the fresh air and read. When the wind shifted, she felt the drizzle and gave up and went below. She could have joined the men in the salon, free for their use while on the island. But she didn't relish the card game they were playing and couldn't concentrate on her book with the noise of their conversation.

Not that she was exactly engrossed in the story. She kept wondering when Nikos was coming back.

Sara fell asleep in her cabin with the book across her chest. Sometime later she woke when there was a knock on her door.

She jumped up and tried to become fully awake. Opening the door, she saw Stefano.

"We're going up to the house for dinner now. Want to walk up with us?"

"Yes. Just let me run a brush through my hair."

"We'll wait at the gangway," he said, turning away.

The rain had stopped, but every shrub and tree between the dock and the house dripped. The late-afternoon sun shone beneath the lingering clouds, making the drops of water sparkle like jewels.

"Tomorrow should be a good day," the captain said on the walk. "You can go swimming if you like."

"I would like. The cabin is a bit small for being stuck inside all day," she said.

He laughed. "You should have come to the salon."

"I had a book to read."

"Stefano said you were napping. The book not compelling enough?"

"Guess not," she replied, smiling up at the older man. "But if I am ever troubled with insomnia, I'll know what to read."

Dinner was quite festive with the boat crew greeting staff members of the house like old friends. Sara was the odd person out but was quickly introduced to the others.

When the captain complimented her to the chef on her desserts, the chef's eyes took on a speculative gleam.

"Perhaps you could spare some time to work with me while you are here."

"I'd be very delighted," she said. It would fill the days, which now seemed to stretch out endlessly. Nikos would make a difference—if he had time for her. In the meantime, she'd never been so conscious of their situation as now, when he was upstairs with the person she had come to Greece to see, and she was so close but still a floor away with no clear-cut way to meet Eleani.

Soon after the meal ended, Sara returned to the yacht. She watched the house for a while, the lights shining like a beacon on the hilltop. She couldn't hear any sounds, but could imagine the talk and laughter. For the first time, she felt like an outsider. Eleani was her grandmother just like Spiros was Nikos's grandfather. She had as much right to be there as he did. Yet no one knew that, and she doubted she'd be welcomed once the facts were revealed.

Waking early the next morning, Sara debated going swimming. With only one ship tied up, surely the water would be clean enough near the dock. Going around to the beach might be risky. She dressed in her swimsuit, pulled on shorts and a shirt and went topside to determine if she dare risk it.

"I was hoping you'd get up early," Nikos said when she stepped out on the aft deck.

He sat in a chair near the rail, relaxed and wearing swim togs and a shirt.

"Want to go for a swim before breakfast?"

"Is the water clean enough here?" she asked. Had he been waiting for her?

"Sure, but I was thinking of a cove around the lee side of the island. It's sheltered and has very colorful fish. We could snorkel until hunger drives us back."

"Sounds great."

He motioned her to the side and pointed down at a small runabout tied to the dock. "I had one of the men pull it out of the boathouse. Perfect for putting around the island."

Sara was soon riding in the small boat, watching Nikos as he skillfully maneuvered it around the yacht and, keeping close to shore, began to go around the island. The sun was just above the horizon, not yet as burning hot as it would become later. The air was soft against her skin as they skimmed across the water.

When he turned into a small cove, Sara looked around with interest. Foliage grew to the water's edge on most of the horseshoe-shaped cove, flowers blossomed in profusion. The tiny sandy beach, almost in the center of the cove, was pristine.

The water was crystal clear. She could see every aspect of the sandy bottom and the colorful fish that swam lazily around when the boat stopped and was carried forward by momentum. He lowered an anchor and soon they were stopped.

Nikos pulled snorkeling gear from the small locker. Sara took off her shirt and shorts and accepted the mask and breathing tube. Donning the mask and flippers, she stepped off the boat into the silken water. It was cooler than a bath, but not cold like the water off the English shore.

They swam for more than an hour, Nikos leading the way and pointing out things as they went. When they kept still, fish would swim within touching distance. A kick of a flipper would send them darting away.

Breaking the surface at last, Sara pushed her mask up on top of her head and shook off some of the water. Nikos surfaced beside her.

"This is a wonderful spot," she said, treading water.

"My favorite on the island."

"Can you get to it over land?" she asked, studying the unending greenery that lined the shore.

"There's a path, if it hasn't gotten overgrown. But it's easier and cooler to come by boat."

"Time for me to head back for breakfast?"

He glanced at his waterproof watch. "The kitchen staff will have it set out by now. We can eat on the terrace. I told the captain you were not going to cook this morning and that they should avail themselves of the house's breakfast buffet."

She nodded, suddenly aware that she and Nikos were in a similar situation to one before—when he'd kissed her in the sea. She felt anticipation rise with nerves and tension. Would he kiss her again?

Not wanting to tempt fate, she turned and began to swim to the boat. Nikos passed her and reached the craft first. He drew himself up and over the side with his strong arms, then turned to offer a hand to Sara, easily pulling her from the water in one swoop.

She stumbled a bit on the rocking boat and fell against Nikos. His skin was cool from the water, but warmed instantly where she pushed against him. Sara felt the water dripping down her back from her wet hair, felt the heat rise between them and wondered whimsically if there was steam evident from the heat she generated. But she would not be accused of flirting.

Had the trip been her subconscious at work? She loved the feel of the man, the energy and desire he evoked while kissing her. Just being near him was extraordinary. But she never wanted him to suspect. How horrible if he thought she came swimming just so they would end up kissing.

So much for her resistance. He followed her

and drew her into his arms. Despite her own thoughts only seconds ago, she didn't resist. When his mouth covered hers, she put her arms around him. Dimly aware she was being reckless, she didn't let that stop her. She'd tried; her resistance wasn't strong enough. There would be little likelihood of Nikos giving her the time of day after she revealed who she was and that she'd deliberately sought out a position at his resort in hopes of gaining access to the island. But until then, she wished every moment to be as special as this one.

He broke away a few moments later, resting his forehead against hers and staring into her eyes. "Hungry?"

For you, was the unbidden thought that popped into her mind. But she knew he meant food. "Yes. A bit."

"Time for a quick shower before breakfast," he said, stowing their gear and pulling in the small anchor. Once under way, Sara felt cool as the water evaporated from her skin. And itchy from the salt. She glanced at Nikos as he handled the boat with assurance. She didn't get it. The more she was around him, the more he puzzled her. The scuttlebutt from the ship was that he was on the verge of getting engaged. He so did not act like a man almost committed to one special woman. He said he wasn't engaged, but he'd never said he wouldn't be one day.

From what her mother had told her about the wealthy families of Greece, Nikos didn't fit the mould. Granted, if he proceeded with a business marriage, it would be similar to her mother's situation. Yet the antagonism she expected against such a man and arrangement vanished. For a few moments she wished she had the chance of an arranged marriage—if the groom was Nikos.

"So we all eat up at the house this morning?" she asked.

He nodded. "It's buffet style, to allow for different times people wish to eat. Lunch will be at one and dinner at seven. But breakfast is from eight until ten."

"Sounds like a hotel," she commented, wondering how many people were around to need such a big window of time for the first meal.

He shrugged.

"Your grandparents are well?" she asked a few minutes later. So far she wasn't sure how to proceed. She couldn't just march in and demand her grandmother's presence.

"In top form. Today I'm going with my grandfather to see the new boat he's buying. To appease my father."

"Why can't your father check it out?" Sara asked. If Nikos's father was so concerned, shouldn't he be the one here?

"Business before family," Nikos said. He chuckled mirthlessly. "Speaking of which, much as I have deplored my father's focus on business, I find I follow in his path. With my absence from the resort last week for the cruise and now being here for a few days, I'm going to have to work when I return from the boat shopping expedition."

"On the *Cassandra*?" she asked.

"I have an office in the main house that ties directly into the one at the resort."

Sara thought he worked hard enough, but didn't feel she could offer that observation. She wondered if she dared explore the grounds while he was tied up. And if her grandmother just happened to be in the garden, wouldn't a meeting be completely acceptable?

Sara showered quickly, towel dried her hair

and pulled it back. Before she left her cabin, she pulled the letter from her bag and folded it over, tucking it in one of the pockets of her shorts. Just in case.

Breakfast was on the terrace that overlooked the sea. Sara suspected every terrace around the mansion overlooked some portion of the sea, since the island wasn't that large. Two of the crew were talking as they drank coffee. Their empty plates showed they'd already enjoyed a large breakfast.

The buffet would do the resort proud. Silver chafing dishes gleamed in the sunshine. Eggs, bacon, sausage, breads, sweet rolls and fresh fruit lined up ready to tempt everyone who walked by. Fragrant coffee brewed at the edge of the buffet table. Sara piled her plate high. Swimming before breakfast gave her a big appetite.

"Do enjoy the chef's offerings. He gets very annoyed with guests who nibble at a token amount and then leave most of it on their plates," Nikos said as he stepped behind her and began placing food on his own plate.

Sara glanced at him in surprise. Looking around the terrace, she saw only members of the crew and the members of the household staff she'd met. Should he be eating with them?

"I can sympathize. Don't worry, I like food. The eggs look light and fluffy even after steaming in the chafing dish for a while. And the fruit is icy cold. You're fortunate in your chef."

"I know that and he knows that. Luckily he and my grandfather came to an agreement that makes them both happy, so there is no fear he'd leave for a better post."

"Wise man, your grandfather. A truly gifted chef is in high demand."

"And you, are you in high demand?" he asked as they moved along the buffet.

"I'm getting there. Every job I've had is moving me along. One day I'd like to be able to set my own salary. And pick exactly where I'd like to work."

"And that would be?" he asked, gesturing to an empty table near the edge of the terrace, an umbrella tilted to shade it from the early sun.

"I used to think London. Now, maybe the Greek Isles," she said with a smil . "Or a ship that sails the world."

"It's nice to see the world. I enjoyed my two

years in the United States and the various hotels and resorts I visited on my summer school holidays."

Nikos watched as Sara began to eat. Her comment about settling in the Greek islands had surprised him. And instantly had him raising barriers. She'd never tried to coax him into giving her something she wanted. Even a job recommendation. Nor had she ever flirted. She was totally unlike the other women he knew. Yet once she'd made that comment, he felt as if the balance between them had shifted. She worked for him. He was merely enjoying swimming and snorkeling with someone with similar interests.

If she thought staying would allow for more involvement, she was mistaken.

Yet the thought of her leaving also filled him with disquiet. Sara was refreshing to be around. She was totally content with her own accomplishments and goals. She didn't try to pretend she was anyone else.

He'd surprised his grandparents last night when he'd mentioned one of his crew was interested in diving and he planned to spend some time enjoying that activity.

They didn't say anything, but Eleani had smiled and suggested he have her come to meet them. His grandfather had echoed that, saying he wanted to meet the newest member of the *Cassandra*'s crew. He already knew all the others.

It was one thing to enjoy diving with Sara and another to give rise to any speculation on her part that he was looking for more. He'd made it as clear as possible he was not in the marriage field. He knew she'd heard about Gina and his tentative plans. As long as she knew the rules, she'd have no reason to expect more from him than he could deliver.

That wasn't why he'd brought her to the island.

He didn't wish to examine too closely exactly why he had. He only knew the more he grew to know her, the more she intrigued him.

He stood when she rose and watched as she left the terrace and headed back to the ship. For the first time ever, Nikos regretted having the strong sense of duty he'd had ground into him. He'd much rather go after Sara, pack a picnic lunch and return to the cove—just the two of them.

Duty called, however.

Once he'd finished his coffee, he went to his office, called his assistant and became engrossed in the daily challenge of running a world-class resort. When his grandfather was ready, they'd go check out the boat he was interested in buying.

Sara watched the clock. She'd been told lunch would be at one and hoped Nikos would take a break to eat when she did. The yacht's galley had been designed by a professional. She had no trouble inventorying supplies, especially the spices and herbs. They were an important part of any dish, so it was crucial these were kept fresh and fragrant. She made a list of ones that needed to be replaced. The rest of the staples were sufficient for the next few meals she'd planned. Had they been departing on a cruise, she would have shopping to do. By the time that happened again, Nikos's regular chef would be recovered and ready to return to work.

She sat on the high stool at the counter and gazed out the porthole. Would she like being a chef for one family? She thought of the captain and his years of service for the Konstantinos family. She enjoyed working in different environments, but the benefits and security of a long-term assignment like he had did hold a certain appeal.

Especially if she ever married.

She began to think again of home. Once back, she'd try to find a position that would offer career potential. She'd have the lovely memories of her Aegean adventure to remember—especially how a dynamic Greek millionaire had kissed her in the warm waters of the sea.

Stefano stepped inside. "We're going up to the house for luncheon."

Sara smiled and hopped off the stool. "I'm more than ready. I can't believe after the humongous breakfast I ate that I'm hungry again, but I am. And I want to see what Dimitri has done this time."

"One chef taking ideas from another?" he joked.

"Only with permission. I am learning more and more about Greek food. My mother was not much of a cook, so we were limited in what we ate. Now I'm having such fun discovering new recipes and taste sensations."

As Sara approached the big house, her anticipation grew. Would Nikos share his meal with her again? Or was breakfast the only meal he'd have until dinner? She knew he had enjoyed all the meals she'd prepared for him and his guests on the cruise, but did he keep different hours when he wasn't entertaining guests?

The lower terrace was again set with two large tables and a long buffet table near the house. The grapevines winding around the arbor provided shade from the noontime sun. The table where she'd shared breakfast with Nikos looked forlorn when the other tables were obviously set for the meal.

The higher terrace was set with one small table. A silver-haired man sat watching the group as Sara and the others approached the lower terrace. The captain waved in greeting and the man nodded in reply.

Sara knew that was Spiros Konstantinos, Nikos's grandfather. She wished they were closer so she could get a better look. Then she was distracted by the greetings of the household staff.

Sara sat between Stefano and Ari. The captain

sat at the head of their table. A silver-haired butler sat at the head of the table where the household staff sat. He could also see the family's terrace and how the waiter was doing there.

From her vantage point, Sara could barely see the table on the other terrace. There were flowers growing in large containers, softening the angles of the house, almost enclosing the terrace. A large trellis shaded that terrace, as well, thick with grapevines offering a green canopy overhead.

She could smell the delicious aromas from the buffet table and glanced around. No one was serving themselves yet.

"We wait for Mr. Konstantinos to be first," Stefano said, leaning close. "Once the family has been served, we are free to enjoy ourselves."

Nikos came out onto the terrace then, escorting an older woman. Sara felt her breath catch as she knew she was looking at her grandmother for the first time.

The woman was as tall as Sara, slender and walked with a regal bearing. Her hair was dark, threaded through with silver. She smiled and waved at the crew and staff, then greeted her husband. Nikos pulled back the chair to seat her, then took a seat to his grandfather's right.

Nikos glanced around and looked at Sara. She felt the connection almost like a touch. A second later he turned slightly toward her grandmother, obviously in response to a question the woman posed.

The Konstantinoses were soon served their meal, and the staff then was free to partake of the lavish buffet the chef had created. She loved the spinach, feta cheese and walnut salad that she'd had before. In one of the hot chafing dishes was fresh lamb, grilled to perfection. In another a chicken dish. Another held fish. Sara sampled everything. She had to ask if the chef would share some of his recipes. The food was delicious.

As before, she ate quietly, listening to the conversation flow around her. She knew most of the staff had worked together for years, and she was definitely the newest member.

Lunch was followed by freshly brewed coffee and tea. Sara sipped some of the sweet tea that smelled so much like passion flower. She missed being on the aft deck of the boat, bobbing gently in the water. But this was the next best thing. She'd have to remember every detail to share with Stacy and her other friends.

Nikos approached their table when the meal was over. Several people looked up in surprise. Stefano jumped to his feet.

"Do you need something, sir?" he asked.

"No. Finish your coffee. My grandfather wishes to meet the newest member of the crew," he said.

Sara nodded slowly and rose. She felt odd ever since seeing her grandmother for the first time. Now Nikos was inviting her to meet her—unbelievable. Should she take advantage of this opportunity and give Eleani the letter? Or wait and hope for a more private moment? The envelope suddenly felt as if it was bulging out her pocket.

"Should I be meeting them at the luncheon table? Not the office? Is that proper?" she asked softly.

Nikos laughed. "Entirely proper. We'll talk diving and boats and maybe you can offer some insights to my grandfather about my resort, which he and my father think is a waste of time when I could be working in shipping."

"You love the resort," she said without thinking.

"I do. And I find the stringent regulations and many requirements necessary in shipping to be very dull. But my grandfather and father are convinced one day I'll get my priorities straight and quit the resort."

"I can't ever see that happening." How could they be talking about such mundane topics when she was about to meet her grandmother for the first time?

As they approached the table on the upper terrace, Sara had eyes only for the woman seated there. As they drew closer, she searched for any resemblance to her mother, but found little. Maybe in the way she held her head. In her eyes? Her mother should have been the one walking across the terrace. How could this gentle-looking woman have been so hard-hearted as to reject her only child?

"Grandfather, this is Sara. Temporary chef aboard the *Cassandra*. Sara, Spiros Konstantinos, my grandfather, and Eleani, my grandmother."

"How do you do?" Sara said, remembering to smile at the older man. Her muscles felt strained. Now that she was face-to-face with her grandmother, she wanted to dash away.

"Do sit with us. It's lovely for Nikos to find someone to join him on his diving forays. It's too dangerous to dive alone. I'm afraid my diving days are behind me. Though I do love a nice paddle in the sea," Eleani said, smiling.

Nikos held the chair for Sara, who was glad to sit down. Her knees felt definitely wobbly.

"Who doesn't like swimming in the sea?" Spiros Konstantinos asked. "Where are you from, Sara?"

"I've been working at the resort in Thessalonika. When the chef on the *Cassandra* got sick, I was tapped as his replacement."

Spiros looked at Nikos. "Interesting. How did you know she liked to dive? Was it something you asked the chief chef to check into?"

Nikos leaned back in his chair, completely at ease. Sara thought she'd shatter if anyone touched her, every nerve in her body was so keyed up. She looked at her grandmother again. So close. Should she hand her the letter?

"She likes the sea. We went swimming and I asked if she'd like to try diving. She takes to it like a natural. And no, I had no inkling of that before we sailed."

"Nothing very deep yet, though," she said,

wanting to make a contribution to the conversation and not sit like a star-struck groupie doing nothing but stare at Eleani. "I love it. Seeing the colorful fish, the contour of the bottom of the sea—it's all so different from swimming on the surface."

"Has Nikos taken you around to the cove?" Eleani asked.

"We went snorkeling for a while this morning. Maybe tomorrow we'll dive," he said.

Sara wondered when she and Eleani would ever have a moment alone. That's all she would need.

"Sounds like a good plan. Have you and Spiros settled on the boat?" Eleani asked Nikos.

"Nikos thinks it's fine," Spiros answered testily.

"And is not putting up roadblocks like Andrus?" she asked with a fond smile at her husband.

"He has more sense than that." Spiros glared at his grandson as if challenging him to deny the statement.

Nikos laughed softly. "You say that because I'm agreeing with you."

Spiros nodded, his eyes suddenly twinkling as he studied Sara. "I think you and your diving friend should spend the afternoon exploring the coves. Maybe tonight you can take her to Patricia."

"Spiros," Eleani said. "Nikos has made plans." She gave him a very meaningful look.

"Actually, I've put some plans on hold," Nikos said. He looked at Sara. "Would you like to go to dinner at a favorite spot of mine on the nearby island?" he asked her.

"I never turn down a chance to try new places," she said. If his grandparents didn't find it odd he'd invite her out, she wouldn't refuse. "Good Greek food?"

"The best," he replied.

There was a small sound from Eleani. Everyone looked at her. She stared at Sara.

"For a moment you reminded me of someone," she said slowly.

Sara wondered if it was her mother Eleani had seen. She glanced at Spiros and Nikos. They didn't seem to find anything suspicious.

"I understand you're buying a new boat. To get to Patricia," Sara said to Spiros, hoping to distract Eleani from further speculation.

"I'll finalize the deal soon. Nikos tested it, checked the specs and said it looked fine to him. The captain of the *Cassandra* has vetted it as well. I take delivery soon. Are you a boating enthusiast?"

"Actually my first time on a large boat was when I started working on the *Cassandra*. I enjoyed the cruise very much. It was a bit tricky at first, learning how to prepare meals when the floor beneath my feet didn't remain level and still."

"Try preparing food in a gale," Eleani said with a smile. "Remember that trip to Sardinia, Spiros, when it was so stormy, and then Paul got seasick and I tried to prepare a simple meal? We ended up eating cheese and bread and drinking wine from a coffee cup with a lid so it wouldn't splash everywhere."

"We made it through and with perhaps a better understanding of the travails of our cook," he said with a fond look at his wife.

The conversation stayed on extraordinary experiences on boats over the years. Sara laughed at some of the stories, and her eyes widened a time or two when the outcome could have been drastically different. She was charmed by Spiros Konstantinos. And she was puzzled by her grandmother. She didn't seem the kind of woman her mother had made her out to be. Eleani came across as a warm and loving woman. She obviously adored her husband and was fond of Nikos. This played so differently from Sara's expectation. Where was the hard-hearted woman she'd thought to find?

The letter burned against Sara's leg. For a moment she considered standing, handing it to Eleani and returning to the yacht. Something held her back. It would be better to be alone with the woman, not have her surrounded by the men of her family.

Nikos glanced at his watch. "I hate to break this up, but I have an important call coming in about five minutes."

Sara stood up. "It was nice meeting you both," she said. If they only knew.

"I'll be down at the ship by six," Nikos said, also standing.

She nodded and walked away, longing to turn and question her grandmother without delay.

But, selfishly, she wanted an evening with

Nikos. That would really be a date. She might as well make her last day at the island memorable.

It was shortly before six when Nikos boarded the *Cassandra*. He'd worked straight through after leaving the lunch table.

He looked forward to showing Sara the neighboring island of Patricia. While not large, it was considerably larger than the family one. The main center had many shops and cafés. The seaside town still had a definite charm that appealed to visitors. And the food was excellent. They'd take the runabout. No need to take the yacht.

He checked the galley on the way to the aft deck. It was pristine but empty. Stepping out on the deck, Nikos hoped she was there. He didn't want to have to figure out which cabin was hers.

Sara sat in the shade, reading. Two of the crew were also on the deck, one sleeping in a chaise, the other with a fishing line tossed over the side of the yacht. For a second Nikos wondered what he'd do if he caught a fish. Who was going to prepare it if the chef was dining on Patricia that evening?

Sara looked up. "Hi." She wore the same dress she'd worn when they'd dined in the salon. He hadn't thought about it, but she'd hardly had time to pack another since she didn't leave the ship during the few hours they had at the resort.

The fishing crewman turned to see who she was talking to. Seeing Nikos, he started to get up, but Nikos shook his head.

"Ready?" he asked Sara.

"Yes," she said, rising swiftly.

In less than ten minutes they were in the runabout heading around a point of the island. When they reached the open water, the wind kicked up. Nikos looked at her.

"Not too much?"

"It's wonderful," she said, raising her face to the setting sun. "Business satisfactorily completed for the day?" she asked. Nikos loved the way the wind blew her hair back. He remembered the silky feel and couldn't wait to touch it again. Concentrating on driving the boat, he tried to ignore the rising desire for Sara.

"Yes. The evening is mine."

"Your family island is lovely. You're lucky to have such a place to visit. Will it be yours one day?"

He glanced at her and nodded. "But not for a long time, I hope."

"So you need to get married and have children to leave it to," she commented, her eyes shut.

Who would he pass it on to? The thought surprised him. For the first time he thought about the future in terms of family. His grandfather was growing old. Already in his eighties, he wouldn't be around forever. There were few bonds as strong as those between Spiros and Nikos. He had never felt the same love from his own father. When Spiros died, it would leave a huge gap in Nikos's life.

And what would fill that gap? Work at the resort? To what end?

After the cruise, he wasn't sure he was ready to ask Gina to be his wife. He wasn't looking for the love his grandfather had found twice. Some men were luckier than others.

But he realized he had no one to teach to dive, to share the beauties beneath the sea with—except friends. No child to instill with family history and to leave his life's work to. What happened when he grew older?

His grandfather was proud of Nikos's accomplishments. He knew his father respected what he'd accomplished, even if it wasn't in shipping. But he wanted more than respect. Nikos realized he wanted love. He'd thought he'd found it with Ariana, only to be shown how false that had been.

Could he find it elsewhere? Did it even exist?

"Thank you for bringing me today. It's another memory to add to my Aegean summer memories," she said.

Summer memories. Nikos had a few special ones himself. Was that what Sara thought of this, a memory of a summer spent in Greece? Would she really return to London after a while? He expected her to resume her job at the resort when Paul was well enough to rejoin the *Cassandra*. Would she stay a year, maybe two or three and then return home?

He wasn't sure he wanted Sara to leave.

CHAPTER EIGHT

SARA loved Patricia. From the first moment she stepped from the dock area onto the old cobblestone streets she was enchanted. White buildings almost touching, red tiled roofs peaked, flowers everywhere, it was a dazzling town. The sidewalks were narrow, scarcely giving room for them to walk side by side. Twice when they met others, Nikos pulled her close with an arm around her shoulders, to allow the others to pass.

"I want to see everything," she exclaimed.

"Fortunately, that won't take long. It's a small town," Nikos replied.

He steered her to the town square where the old church dominated one side. The other sides were crowded with shops and small cafés. Sara was tempted to stop at one of the tavernas for a drink but didn't want to spend the time sitting when there was more to see before it got dark.

"Come, I think you'll like this one," he said as they rambled around the old square. Entering one of the specialty shops, Sara stood transfixed for a moment. It appeared the shop had all the spices in the world. She drew a deep breath, savoring all the different aromas she could detect.

"Wow, I could spend an entire day here!" She began walking up one aisle and down another, stopping from time to time to sniff a special spice or herb. Gathering small bottles of different spices as she walked, she glanced at Nikos from time to time, worried he'd be bored and anxious to leave.

He patiently walked beside her, looking around with interest.

"This will have to do," she said, her hands full of small bottles. "I can't wait to use them in special dishes. Fresh spices and herbs make all the difference."

Nikos insisted on carrying the shopping bag when they left.

"I called for reservations at seven," he said. "We don't want to be too late returning to the island. Another shop or two, then we must head for the restaurant."

"I'm ready now if you want to head that way," she said. "Tomorrow maybe I can try a dish or two with the spices. Do you think Dimitri would let me use his kitchen?"

"Yes. As long as you let him assist. He's always looking for new food to please my grandfather."

"Then I'll ask him. I can't wait."

They walked along the sidewalk, gazing into the windows, stopping once or twice to discuss something they saw.

As they approached the restaurant, Sara was struck with how ordinary it looked. She'd expected a man like Nikos to go for an upscale place like the restaurants at his resort. This looked homey and friendly—almost like a family place.

Which it proved to be when they entered.

Instead of some elegant, quiet, dignified restaurant, this one was huge, boisterous and loud. Families and couples vied for room at the many trestle-style tables. The food was served family style—huge bowls and platters set in the midst of every table from which customers helped themselves.

They squeezed into a spot near the door and introductions were hastily made, first names only. Two of the men at the table knew Nikos and asked after Spiros. The conversation was lively, the food plain but marvelous. Sara ate her fill in record time. The lamb was tender and flavorful. The vegetables were prepared exactly as she enjoyed. And the crusty Greek bread was delicious. The wine was plentiful, as well, poured from a pitcher.

"Nothing pretentious here," she murmured at one point.

"No. Do you mind?" Nikos asked, leaning closer to better hear her.

"I'm having the time of my life. This is great." She almost had to shout to be heard, but she didn't mind. The lively atmosphere was infectious. She wasn't sure why his grandfather had urged him to bring her to Patricia, but she was glad they'd come. This was the kind of gathering she and her mother had attended in London whenever there was a celebration. She almost expected to look around and see her mother or one of her friends.

At nine, several musicians filed onto the small raised platform at the back of the large room and began to play. Immediately couples left the tables for the dance floor to join in the traditional Greek dances. Sara was enchanted. "I didn't expect this," she said.

"It's a local place, not for tourists. Do you dance?"

"Some. We had lots of Greek friends in London. Our parents made very sure none of us forgot our heritage. This is a kind of line dance, right?"

"Right. After this comes a *ballos*, a couples' dance."

"Ah." She looked at him with a challenge. "So you do that one?"

"We do," he said, holding her gaze.

Sara could feel the anticipation rise as she stared back. The *ballos* was a romantic dance—definitely for couples. Had he danced it with Gina? Being Italian, she probably did not know the traditional Greek dances. Whereas Sara, on the other hand, had been schooled well.

She tore her gaze away and looked at the dancers on the floor. The music made her blood pound—or was it the proximity of Nikos Konstantinos?

When the next dance began, the crowd greeted the music with a roar of approval. Sara clapped her hands and rose when Nikos did, pleased to show him she knew as much about their heritage as someone raised in Greece.

The dance was fast and fun. It followed the age-old romance tradition—flirtatious and sassy. Definitely masculine versus feminine role playing. As they whirled and stamped and came together, then parted, Sara laughed in sheer joy. She had loved going to celebrations in the neighborhood. The expatriate Greek community in London had been closely knit. Engagements, weddings, christenings and funerals had brought the entire community together. Of course, there was no dancing at funerals, but other causes to celebrate were embraced with enthusiasm and traditional music and dance.

When the dance ended, the musicians moved on to another, this one a traditional line dance, with one of the older men from town leading. She and Nikos laughed, danced and shared in the delight of the night.

It was late when Nikos said it was time to leave. Sara was tired but buoyed up by the exuberant dancing and the friendly locals who had included her as if she'd been born there. Being with Nikos had a lot to do with it, she was sure. They still had the boat ride back to the island.

The moon had risen, a silvery crescent high in the sky. Once on the boat and heading away from Patricia into the night, Sara glanced around, not seeing anything but stars, moon and sea. She hoped Nikos knew where they were going. He piloted the craft with confidence. She was content to sit back and remember the evening's frivolity. She glanced at Nikos. This was a side of him she'd never expected— steeped in tradition, reveling in neighbors and casual dining. And dancing with the best of them.

"I could tell you enjoyed yourself," he said, once they were on the open sea.

"It was great fun. I hadn't expected dancing."

"And I didn't expect you knew our dances."

"Why not? I'm as Greek as you. Of course I know them. And more."

"Usually we learn them as children."

"As did I," she said, remembering some of

the events she and her mother had attended. Then an old memory flashed into her mind. They'd been at a wedding of a friend of her mother's. When almost the entire group of guests rose to dance, her mother had looked sad, commenting that no one had danced at her wedding.

Sara gazed across the sea. How much had her mother missed by her impetuous marriage? If her parents had helped her instead of repudiating her, would she have found happiness with another man and married him? She could have had more children, followed a traditional Greek woman's life. Maybe not lived any longer, but she would have been happier.

"I've dated Greek women who don't know the dances," Nikos said.

She shrugged. Her happiness had faded as she thought about Nikos seeing other women. Yet what would she expect, that he was celibate? He was too dynamic and involved with life not to date and enjoy the companionship of others. It wasn't as if she had any special claim.

Nikos guided the boat by rote. He'd traveled from Patricia to the island many times and could probably find his way home blindfolded. He felt wide-awake after the dancing. Sara's expertise had surprised him. Ariana had not enjoyed dancing—at least not their traditional Greek dances, which were fast and strenuous. She had preferred going to modern nightclubs.

He no longer cared about Ariana. She'd made sure of that when he'd discovered her lies. Any feelings he'd felt for her had shattered. Trust was too fragile to repair once it had been broken. So why did he use her to compare other women to? As a reminder of treachery and betrayal? Or as a barrier against falling for someone else? Love made a man foolish. He was beyond that time of his youth, though seeing his grandparents again had him wishing for more in life than the suitable marriage to someone like Gina Fregulia. Was he in danger of changing his views on marriage?

He glanced at Sara. She seemed pensive.

"What are you thinking?" he asked. He expected tiredness, but at least a happier face as she remembered the evening.

"Sad thoughts," she said, turning toward him. The faint light from the control panel didn't illuminate her face at this angle. She was in shadow, with only the light of the moon showing her silhouette.

"After the dancing we did? Impossible." Unless she regretted the evening coming to an end. He did. He could dance with Sara all night.

"I was thinking of one of the wedding festivities we attended when I was younger. My mother had almost cried when she spoke of no one dancing at her wedding."

"Didn't she have a traditional Greek wedding?"

Sara shook her head. Nikos wondered why she hadn't. Sara didn't speak much about her family. Only to say that her father had left them when she was very young and her mother had died last year. What had it been like growing up in London? She spoke perfect Greek, knew their dances, the food. Obviously, her mother had wanted to maintain the connection. Yet she had no other relatives. Why had her parents moved to England? Why not stay in Greece and forge ties with neighbors to aid the small family?

Sara had started out intriguing him. The more time they spent together, the more she fascinated him. It wasn't only the physical attraction, though he enjoyed kissing her, touching her, feeling her warmth against him. He wouldn't mind a closer connection, but she'd never given any sign she'd be interested.

Except for her kisses. Maybe he should push the issue and see where they went.

She was unlike most of the women he associated with. She reminded him a little of Eleani—Sara was warm and friendly and kind. Maybe that was what set her apart. She was kinder than Ariana had been, that was certain. Gina last week had been catty in some of her remarks. He never remembered Sara saying anything unkind.

They arrived at the dock with no problem. He tied the lines to the cleats and helped Sara from the boat. They walked silently to the gangway for the yacht. He escorted her up and stopped on the forward deck.

"I'll say good-night."

"Thank you for dinner and the evening. I had a wonderful time," she said politely.

"Everyone is probably asleep, but I feel as if we are on display. Who knows who can be watching," he said, leaning over and brushing his lips against hers.

He turned her around and gave her a gentle push. "Go to bed, Sara. I'll see you tomorrow."

He turned and left the yacht, wishing the evening could have ended with Sara in his bed. The thought surprised him. He wasn't thinking just tonight, either. What would it be like to wake up with her each morning? Spend time together when he wasn't working? She liked to dive, to swim. She was a terrific dancer. And she cooked like a dream. What was not to like about Sara Andropolous?

As he walked up to the house, he idly considered a life with a woman like Sara. He knew love existed. Spiros had loved his first wife and was devoted to his second. A man could learn a lot about marriage studying his grandfather.

Intellectually Nikos understood people could fall in love and share their lives happily and with true contentment. He'd asked Ariana to marry him thinking they'd have the perfect modern marriage—similar interests and friends that would enable them to have the kind of life both enjoyed. He had loved her only to be disillusioned with her betrayal.

She had wanted more than his love—more

men and more money. Would things have been different had he already achieved the success he now enjoyed? No—love would overlook finances. She had not loved him, not the way he wanted.

Reaching the house, Nikos turned and looked at the yacht, almost invisible against the dark sea. For a moment he debated returning, going to her cabin, asking her to stay a while longer. Common sense took over. If she was amenable, she would be as keen tomorrow as tonight. And if she shot down the idea, he'd rather it be later.

The next morning Nikos rose early and went for a morning swim at the beach. The sand was being raked by one of the groundskeepers. The yacht showed no activity. He dropped his towel, pulled off his shirt and plunged into the sea. The water felt cool and invigorating.

He swam some distance out and then floated for a little while. Hearing splashing, he looked at the shore. Sara was swimming out toward him, still some distance away.

Treading water as she approached, he ignored the feeling of satisfaction that blossomed. Her coming out this morning had to mean she enjoyed the early-morning swims as much as he did.

"Hi," she said a moment later. She shook her head and water drops splayed all around.

"I thought you'd sleep in," he commented. She was beautiful in the soft morning light, even with her hair wet and hanging around her face. Her eyes sparkled with enjoyment.

"Couldn't sleep in. Not in the habit. With no meals to plan or prepare, I have a lot of time on my hands. Maybe I should return to the resort. I'm sure not earning my salary here."

"Aren't you enjoying being here?"

"Too much. I'll get spoiled," she said with a grin.

He wanted to spoil her, give her jewels and dresses and make sure she never lacked for anything.

"Except before I do return, I want a couple of recipes from Dimitri. That salad the other day was delicious. I figured out all the ingredients except one. Which is the one that makes it so special. Do you think he'll share?"

"I expect so. If not, tell him I said he should."

She laughed. "If he does not wish to share, I certainly wouldn't threaten him with you."

"Why not?" The more he knew her, the more she puzzled him. Wasn't that the way of the world? Get what you want no matter how it's accomplished?

Ariana would have used every bit of power she had to obtain her own ends. He looked away. He must stop comparing Ariana to every other woman he met. Sara was nothing like her. End of comparison.

"You're up as early as I," she said, lazily dog-paddling around. "Why not take advantage of this brief holiday and sleep in?"

"Feels too much like I'm sleeping the day away."

"What do you have to do today?" she asked.

"Work, what else."

She splashed water on him. "Play is what else," she said before diving beneath the water before he could retaliate by splashing her.

The chase was on. Nikos knew he was the stronger swimmer, but he let her get ahead before giving chase. When he tagged her, she came to the surface and laughed.

"You need to watch that laughter," he warned, coming closer. "You're going to drown one day if you're not careful."

She laughed again and nodded. "I'll try not to laugh underwater. Now I'm it." And she surged toward him. He'd been expecting it and swam to one side, diving deep and moving parallel to the shore.

They played until both were breathless. Then Nikos took her hand and drew her closer.

"I didn't get a proper good-night kiss last night."

"No one was awake on the yacht," she said, entwining her legs with his, encircling his neck with her arms, pressing against the length of him.

"It felt like prying eyes were watching from every porthole."

He felt her laughter as she kissed his jaw. "So?"

"So I don't want to put a burden on you by being seen with me."

"Everyone on board knows your grandparents asked to meet me. What's to know? It's not as if we have a torrid affair going."

"It's not as if I don't want one," he said.

Her start of surprise showed him she'd never considered it. Damn. Surely she didn't think he kissed every woman he knew like he kissed her.

Maybe he should show her what they could have together.

He pulled her close and kissed her with all the pent-up desire that consumed him. She kissed him back, her mouth sweet and hot, her arms holding him closer as the kiss went on until he forgot where they were. The water closing over their heads was unexpected. Breaking the kiss, he kicked up and when they bobbed to the surface, he released her.

"You're too dangerous in the water," he said. He released her and began swimming toward the shore.

Sara swam beside him.

"So?" he asked when their feet touched bottom and they walked the short distance to shore. He saw her towel beside his on the pristine beach. The groundskeeper had left. They were alone.

"So what? Breakfast? I'm starving, how about you? I'll whip something up in the galley just for you," she said.

He ignored her attempt to change the subject. When she picked up her towel, he followed suit, drying his chest as he watched her watch him. "I meant an affair and you know it."

She shook her head sadly. "Sorry, Nikos, I'm not into affairs. Tempting though this would be, I want something special when I marry."

"What if you don't marry?" he asked, annoyed at her statement.

"Don't say that. I want to marry for love and be loved forever. I want kids and ties and a feeling of belonging. If I don't get them, I'll feel life has cheated me. I'm holding out for what I want."

"Until then, we could have fun."

"Sure. What happens if I fall in love with you?"

He stepped back involuntarily. "I told you I'm not looking for love."

"Just a suitable marriage, allying two business families."

"There is something wrong with that?" he asked stiffly.

"Not if that's what you want. But what about love? Don't you think that would make a marriage so much better? Look at your grand-parents—they obviously adore each other."

"My parents made a suitable marriage."

"Oh, and from what you've said, that's been

a success for the two of them—but not the kind of family I want."

"It works."

"Don't you want more for yourself and your children if you have any?"

He hesitated a moment.

Her comment bothered him—especially in light of his thoughts from yesterday about who he had to leave his life's work to, who was there to share the cove with. Who could he teach to dance the traditional dances?

What would it be like to have children with Sara? She'd spoil them to death. But she'd love them to pieces. And her husband—would she also love him to pieces?

"You have to be the world's biggest idiot," Sara told her reflection after her shower ten minutes later. She still had wet hair, was wrapped in a clean towel and had wiped off the small mirror in the minuscule bathroom adjacent to her cabin. "Looking the way you do, he asked you to have an affair, and you go all high-and-mighty and say no."

She sighed and turned. She could never have taken Nikos up on his suggestion knowing he would find out soon enough who she really was and her reasons for wanting to visit his island. She couldn't add further betrayal to that by becoming intimate with him if she wasn't being totally honest.

She knew he wasn't in love with her, but obviously the attraction she felt was met by his own desire. How fabulous it would be to make love with Nikos. They could find seclusion at the cove, enjoy each other's bodies, then go swimming. She loved to swim, and her newly acquired basic skill in diving. Would she ever get another chance?

Taking a determined breath, she donned her clothes. Not likely after today. She was going to find Eleani and give her the letter. After that, the entire Konstantinos family would likely expect her to swim to the next island to get off this one as soon as possible.

It couldn't be helped. Long before she met Nikos she'd made her mother a promise. She was honor-bound to keep it, no matter what it did to her tentative relationship with Nikos Konstantinos.

Sara prepared a light breakfast. Her nerves were growing taut with the concern about meeting Eleani. Sipping hot tea, she remembered all her mother had told her about her life before running away to marry Sara's father. Nothing could hurt her mother now. Sara could fulfill her last wish and move on.

At ten o'clock, Sara left the yacht and walked up to the gardens surrounding the house. She felt much the way she thought a condemned prisoner must feel. It was fate, nothing more, but she wished she could predict the outcome.

Stepping onto one of the flagstone pathways, she wandered around the gardens. Normally their beauty and tranquillity would prove soothing. Today she only saw opulent luxury that had been denied her mother. The pots of flowers they had sometimes been able to afford for their windowsill had been all her mother had. She'd talked often of the lovely gardens at her childhood home. She would have loved the gardens here on the island.

Turning a corner, she stopped. Eleani Konstantinos sat on a wooden bench in a clearing, gazing at a basket of cut flowers. She looked up and smiled.

"Sara. What a pleasant surprise. Come sit by me. Where is Nikos?"

"Working." She stepped closer, her eyes never leaving Eleani's.

"He works too hard. He gets that from his grandfather and father, I expect. Will you two be going diving later?" She patted the bench beside her in invitation. Slowly Sara walked over and sat on the edge.

"No, I don't believe we'll go diving again," she said slowly. Reaching into her pocket, she pulled out the letter and handed it to the older woman.

"What's this?" Eleani asked, reading her name on the envelope.

"A letter I was asked to deliver," Sara said, watching, noting the faint lines around her grandmother's eyes, the soft tones of her skin, the silver in her hair.

Eleani studied the handwriting for a long moment, then slid her finger beneath the flap and tore open the envelope. She withdrew the two pages. Catching her breath, she began to read.

Sara watched her. She felt the hot sun beating down on her head, but didn't seek shade. The play of emotions across Eleani's face had her wondering exactly what her mother had written.

All she'd told Sara was that she had a letter for her mother, for Sara to promise she'd get it to her.

She'd fulfilled her mother's last wish. Sara rose and turned away. She could go home now.

"Wait!" Eleani said. "Sit back down."

Sara turned and looked at her. "I've done what I came to do."

Tears spilled from Eleani's eyes. "My daughter is dead," she said brokenly.

Sara nodded. "She died more than a year ago."

Eleani shook her head, crushing the letter against her breasts. "My baby, my poor, poor baby. How could she die? She was too young to die. Ah, my beautiful Damaris. My precious baby girl," she said, leaning over and sobbing.

Sara was totally taken aback. This was not the reaction she had expected.

Sara looked away. "I'm sorry this is unexpected news."

"Unexpected? I never thought to hear from her again. But at least I had the consolation of knowing she was happy in England. I have missed her every day since she left."

Sara whipped around and stared at her. "She was not happy. My father deserted us weeks after I was born. Mum had no skills for work, she'd been raised as a pampered daughter of a wealthy family. Do you know she scrubbed floors because that was a skill she could quickly acquire? We had the help of friends, handouts, Mum used to call them. They seared her soul. She hated that." But not as much as she hated the thought of returning to her parents' home and admitting she'd been wrong.

"I didn't know," Eleani whispered, "The one time we tried to contact her, she refused. Her father said to leave her to her life. We did the best we could. Now she's gone. I'll never see her again."

Eleani covered her face and cried.

Sara frowned. This was not going the way she thought it would. It distressed her to see anyone so distraught. Awkwardly she patted her shoulder, wishing now that she'd just left the letter on a table to be discovered.

She didn't know how long she sat there, staring across the garden toward the sea, seeing in her mind the small, old apartment she and her mother had shared until Sara had begun earning enough money to help pay for a better place. She saw her mother's looks fade as poor nutrition and the stress of her life wore away her youth and health.

She glanced around the beautifully land-scaped setting. The money used for just one season of gardening would have changed her mother's life drastically. She felt numb. She missed her mother. She wasn't sure bringing the letter had been wise, now that the deed was done.

What had her mother written? To take care of Sara? She had said she wanted to make sure her daughter was taken care of.

Sara was a grown woman with an excellent career ahead of her. She didn't need someone to take her in at this stage of her life.

She heard the steps and turned to watch as Nikos stormed toward her.

"What the hell have you done to my grand-mother?" he asked in a low growl.

CHAPTER NINE

SARA watched him approach. She could almost feel the waves of suspicion pouring off him.

She rose and faced him. "I was asked to deliver a letter and I did."

"Eleani, what is it?" Nikos asked, sitting beside the woman and drawing her into his arms. He rubbed her back, glaring at Sara.

"What was in the letter?"

"I don't know. It was sealed."

"Who is it from?"

"My mother."

Nikos frowned, saying soothing words to Eleani.

"I'm Sara Andropolous, Eleani's grand-child."

The statement stopped Nikos cold. He stared for a long moment. Giving way to anger, he bit out an epithet. His gentle hands soothed his grandmother.

"I didn't know she had a child, much less a grandchild," he said a minute later.

"My mother ran off to get married when she was eighteen. Her parents cut her off because she chose to find her own husband. I find the entire situation sordid and inexcusable."

He swung back at that. "You find it inexcusable. What about lying and cheating to gain access to my grandparents' home? Wreaking who knows what havoc? I find that inexcusable!"

"I never lied to you nor cheated. I was hired to work in the kitchen at the resort. I used my skill and experience, which would be hard to cheat with. You're the one who allowed me to work on the *Cassandra*. You're the one who insisted I stay on board when you came to your family's island. You are the one who introduced me to them the other day."

"Stop it, both of you. I can hear your voices from the house." Spiros rounded the corner and took in the scene. "Eleani, my love, what is wrong?" He immediately went to his wife. In the confusion of Eleani telling her side and

Nikos telling what he knew, Sara spun around to leave.

Guessing her intent, Nikos moved swiftly to her side.

"You can't waltz in here and cause this uproar and think you get to leave without further explanation."

"What further explanation do you need? I gave her the letter. There's nothing more," Sara said, starting to feel again. She wanted to weep, knowing she'd damaged whatever had been building between Nikos and herself. Still, honor had demanded she carry out her mother's last wish. Which she had—at a personal loss. Now she just wanted to leave. She felt nothing but resignation and regret.

Spiros sat beside his wife. Eleani had stopped crying and leaned against him tiredly. His face was set in anger. His eyes flashed when he looked at Sara. Saying nothing, he reached for a handkerchief to dry Eleani's eyes.

"I would like an explanation, young lady," he said sternly.

At that, Eleani looked up and saw Sara and Nikos.

Sara felt a spurt of anger. "Didn't your wife tell you she had a daughter in England? She was my mother. Before she died Mum asked me to deliver a letter to her mother. I've done just that."

"I know about Damaris," Spiros said slowly. "It saddens me to learn she is dead. We had hoped at some time she'd return to Greece to see Eleani."

Sara frowned. This didn't make sense.

"She couldn't come home. Her parents had told her if she left she would not be welcome to return," she said. "How could you? She was a teenager, sheltered and protected. Her one fling ended disastrously, but did her parents come to her aid? Did they forgive a youthful indiscretion and take her back home to help? No! Her father said he would disown her. How true that was."

"It wasn't like that," Eleani said sadly. She struggled to sit up.

"Now you wait until your mother is dead and come to disturb my wife?" Spiros asked.

"My mother asked only that I deliver a letter she wrote to her mother. I never knew the details of the letter. I do know she refused to return home until she was too sick to make the trip. As soon as I can get off this island, I plan to get as far away from here as I can. I'm sorry to have been the cause of such upset."

Eleani began crying again. "Don't go," she said forlornly.

"Where would you go?" Spiros asked.

"London, where I belong. Away from people like all of you."

Nikos made a sound of surprise. "People like us?"

"Uncaring, unfeeling, sanctimonious rich people who only want things to go their own way and never mind family members who don't fit in with the path you decide they should take. Like my mother. Like you yourself, Nikos."

Spiros turned in surprised to look at his grandson. "What has Nikos to do with this?"

"You and his father pressured him to join the family shipping firm. Pressured him for marriage with a 'suitable' woman—translated to mean 'equally wealthy'. What about what he wants?"

Nikos shrugged when his grandfather looked at him.

Sara wasn't finished. "Instead of following your dictates he made his own way. Do you ever really see what he's done? Ever give him praise for fighting against the current and still coming out with something marvelous?" she continued, impassioned.

Spiros looked back and forth between Sara and Nikos. "It is true I wished for Nikos to join our shipping firm. But I see now it would have been a mistake. It was hard enough to let go the reins when Andrus took over. Two strong personalities are more than the company can bear. Nikos added to the mixture would have been a mistake. He was wise to go into a field he chose."

"And to have done so well," she added.

Spiros's features softened a fraction. "So you stand up for Nikos?"

"I'm not standing up for anyone but me. I'm stating facts."

"Then listen to this fact," Eleani said. "Damaris ran out on her wedding. We were the ones who had to tell Alexis she wasn't coming. We had to face our friends, business acquaintances, family and say our daughter had shamed us in front of everyone. She ignored all we had done for her and ran off with an irresponsible man who wanted access to our money. Your grandfather was heartsick. It pained him greatly, and he refused to have any more to do with her while she was with your father. But had she left him, we would have welcomed her home—despite the shame she brought to our family. Even now, when I see Alexis, I am embarrassed. He is such a nice young man. She would have done so well to marry him. He says he has no hard feelings, but she had to have hurt his pride if nothing else. He loved her, you know."

Sara stared first at Eleani then at Spiros. She was taken aback by the revelation. Had her mother lied all these years? Or merely glossed over the details of the truth? Either way, she had painted an entirely different picture in Sara's mind.

"Come, sit down and tell us about Eleani's only child," Spiros said gently.

Sara was very aware that Nikos was standing at her side. She went to a chair and sat gingerly on the edge. He moved to stand farther away, gazing out to the sea.

"You need to stop crying now, Eleani. Listen to what Sara tells us," he said gently.

Eleani nodded, blotted her eyes again and leaned against Spiros as if for strength.

Sara didn't know where to begin. She ached for the difficulty of her mother's life. And from Eleani's reaction, she had believed her daughter had led an entirely different life.

"I only know the past from what I was told. My mother had hardly been in England six weeks before she knew her parents had been correct about the man she'd run off with. It had been romance, pure and simple, that had persuaded her to leave her family home. She had believed herself to be in love. She railed against the intractable demands her father had made—marrying to ensure the family coffers. She had believed my father to be different from who he truly was. She did not have the wisdom to see reality. She was eighteen for heaven's sake."

"She wasn't forced to wed Alexis. We thought she was captivated by him. He was only six years older, and very much in love with Damaris," Eleani said. "We were pleased. His family is very respected."

"So why did your mother not return home once she realized her mistake?" Nikos asked.

"No money. No welcome." Sara hesitated a moment. "Pride. And she was pregnant with me. She said she wrote to her father asking for help. He refused. She swore over and over she would never ask again."

Eleani gave a small sound. "Ah, that stubborn pride of the Marcopusoses. Always I had to fight against it. For years I asked him to find our daughter. He finally gave in and said he'd have a private detective locate her. Weeks later he said Damaris was happy with her life and that was the end of it. He must have approached her and been rebuffed and rather than tell me, he concocted such a story."

Sara shook her head, frowning. "When my father vanished, she was not yet twenty, a single parent with no skills. One of her friends helped by watching me nights after her own day of work so Mum could go and clean offices. That was the best job she could get for a long time."

Eleani groaned softly. "My precious baby girl," she whispered.

"Go on," Nikos said.

Sara turned to look at him. "I'm telling this."

"Not fast enough."

"Let her proceed at her own pace," Spiros said.

"We lived in a section of London with a large group of Greek expats. It was the best thing on one hand—everyone knew everybody else. We shared the language, the food. But it constantly reminded my mother of all she'd lost."

Slowly, as if viewing the scene for the first time, Sara continued. "It was only after she was diagnosed with cancer that she began to talk about contacting you. We learned from mutual friends of her father's death and your re-marriage. My mother wrote a letter and mailed it. It was returned. By then she was really ill. She wrote the one I brought today. After her death, I tried contacting you. I ended up here."

"I thought she was happy," Eleani repeated. "Stanos told me that."

Had her mother's stiff-necked pride kept her from her home? Sara remembered some of the pretending they had done when she was younger—to preserve her mother's standing with her friends. Excess pride. None of it mattered anymore. She'd fulfilled her promise. "That's it. May I go now?"

"No. Stay. I want to hear all about Damaris and you," Eleani said. She lifted the letter. "Damaris asked me to watch out for you."

"I don't need watching out for." She had her own share of the family pride.

"Bad choice of words. How about having close contact with your grandmother," Nikos said.

Sara flashed him a look and then returned her gaze to Eleani. "What do you want to know about Mum?"

"Nikos has raved about your cooking. How did you choose that profession? Did Damaris ever learn to cook? We had a chef at home so she never learned as a child," Eleani said.

Sara smiled in memory. "Mum was okay as a cook, at least by the time I noticed such things. But nothing special. She loved the big gatherings best when everyone brought something. Authentic Greek food was what she craved, but we also ate English. I think some of my reasons for going into food preparation was to explore new dishes in self-defense against Mum's limited choices."

Talking helped show Sara she no longer felt the burning ache of loss after all the months.

She could remember her mother with pride and happiness, not overwhelming grief.

"I'll have Marsa bring you some refreshments. Talk as long as you wish," Spiros said gently, standing and motioning to Nikos.

Nikos watched for a moment. Sara was like a stranger to him. For days he'd been intrigued by her—now he knew the reason she behaved so differently from others. She genuinely did not want anything from him but transportation to the island. Now that she'd achieved that, what?

Would she try to worm her way into her grandmother's affections—become her only heir? Eleani was wealthy enough Sara could quit her job and live the life her mother should have enjoyed.

"Do you know more?" he asked his grandfather when they left the women behind and were alone.

"No. Eleani told me long ago that she had a daughter she hadn't seen in years. I only knew Stanos by reputation. He was a hardliner—had his own rules and stiff-necked pride. I think I can see him in a temper, cutting off his only child."

"He had a private detective look into her life. He would have reported that Damaris was a single parent, that there was a little girl."

Spiros nodded, studying his grandson. "What of you, Nikos?"

"What about me?"

"Sara isn't the person we thought her to be. She's more than a crew member of the *Cassandra*. I will welcome her into our family as I would any relative of Eleani's."

"It's your home, do as you wish. I'm returning to the resort as soon as the captain can get the *Cassandra* under way," Nikos said. He'd return to work and forget about the pretty chef. There'd no longer be a need for Sara to continue to work. He'd instruct his human resources office to begin a search to fill her position.

The sooner he was consumed with business, the better.

"Don't leave before Monday. That's when you originally planned, right? Stay and visit with your grandfather a little longer. Give her a few days to visit with Eleani."

Nikos hesitated, then nodded once. He'd stay for his grandfather's sake.

"Sara's right, you know. I never told you how proud of your accomplishments I am. You have made a major contribution with the resort. I am proud of you and so is your father."

Nikos smiled slightly. "That's stretching it, don't you think?"

Spiros shrugged. "I'm sure if he thought about it, he'd be proud of you."

"You seem to be taking Sara's revelation in your stride," Nikos said.

"I was shocked when Eleani first told me she had a daughter. Hard as it is to hear the truth, it is best to find out. Too many lies have gone by in that family. Maybe Eleani will gain some peace knowing Sara. And I hope neither makes the same mistake Damaris and her father made."

"Not likely," Nikos said, looking back out the window. "Sara is no naive eighteen-year-old. She's almost thirty, has worked her way up in a grueling profession. Been on her own for a while. And definitely wasn't born with a silver spoon in her mouth."

"You're angry with her. I know. It's understandable."

"She used me to get to Eleani. I don't like being used."

"That's not all," his grandfather said.

"That's all I'm focused on now," Nikos said. "I'll tell the captain we leave at first light on Monday." He left before his grandfather could say any more.

Nikos went to the room he used as an office. He sat and turned on his computer. But when the screen came on, he didn't see it. He heard Sara telling him she had no family. She'd lied.

Or did she truly believe that? Eleani seemed more than willing to accept Sara.

She'd used him. Had all their time together been with the sole aim of getting to the island? The mutual interests? The kisses? What was truth, what false?

Thank God he'd never pushed for more.

So he'd wait for Monday. Escort Sara back to the mainland and wash his hands of her. Blast it!

By lunchtime, Sara's nerves were stretched tight. She'd spent the morning talking with her grandmother. She'd finally come to believe the woman had had no inkling of the dire straits they had sometimes lived through. She began to soften the stories, glossing over the hardships Damaris had faced, trying to put a happier note on everything. She didn't want to cause Eleani any more distress than she already felt. Again and again she looked at the letter and then at Sara.

By the time Marsa announced lunch, all Sara wanted to do was flee to the yacht and see if the captain would take her to the next island.

But she rose when Eleani did, used the proffered powder room to freshen up and went bravely to the terrace where lunch was being served.

Today she was escorted to the family table. She saw the crew's table on the lower terrace and wished she was going there instead.

Spiros joined them a moment later.

"Nikos has work to do. He's eating inside," he explained to Eleani.

Sara knew the truth. He couldn't even stand to be around her for the length of a meal. She was surprised at how much that hurt. For a few magical days she'd enjoyed herself. It was time to pay the piper. She was not some glamorous socialite like the ones Nikos was used to. She'd used him to get to Eleani. But she'd lost a lot along the way.

After an awkward lunch, Sara excused herself and headed for the boat. The first person she saw was Stefano who asked her if the rumors were true—was she Eleani Konstantinos's granddaughter?

"Stefano, do not listen to rumors," she said, brushing past him and going to her cabin. She pulled on her swimsuit, covered it with shorts and a top and grabbed a towel. She wanted to be alone, to think and to swim and to find some peace.

She approached the captain about taking the runabout.

"Where are you going?" he asked, not saying no. He'd also probably heard the rumor.

"Around to the cove Nikos took me to. I'll stick close to the island and anchor on the beach."

"Do you know how to run the boat?"

She nodded. She'd watched Nikos. It didn't look hard.

The captain inclined his head. "Take drinking water and don't swim deeper than where you can stand."

Sara smiled, warmed he was concerned enough to lecture her on swimming safety. And smart enough to know she needed to be alone.

"I'll be careful," she promised.

She banged the dock twice trying to get the runabout away, but once she had it pointed in the direction she wished to go, she was set. In only moments Sara felt as alone as anyone could. There was only sky and sea and a bit of an island. And heartache.

When she reached the cove, she nosed the boat to the beach. Holding the anchor and line, she jumped out and dragged it up on the shore. Satisfied the boat wasn't going anywhere, she waded back for her towel. She swam first, staying close to the shore, back and forth as if swimming laps. When she was almost too tired to lift her arms again, she waded ashore and moved her towel to a spot of shade where she lay down and tried to keep her mind empty.

But scenes from the day replayed. Nikos's anger. His aloof stance by the window. His hard eyes. She couldn't get any of them to vanish and wondered if she'd be doomed to repeat those scenes over and over all her life.

Finally the soothing warmth of the breeze and the gentle lap of the sea lulled her into the welcomed oblivion of sleep.

When Sara awoke, she was not alone. Nikos sat not five feet away. She sat up slowly, glancing around. There was no other boat.

"You came by the path?" she asked.

"You took the boat."

"I thought you had work to do."

"I finished and thought I'd take a swim."

She gestured to the water. "Have at it."

"You should not have gone swimming alone. It can be dangerous."

"As if you care," she replied petulantly. She wished she could recapture the feelings she'd had when they'd been here before. Blinking her eyes to keep tears at bay, she stared across the sea. Why had doing the right thing for her mother ended so badly for her?

"I do not wish an accident to befall anyone," Nikos said. After a moment he spoke again, "Why didn't you tell me? We talked about family. Why not say you were estranged from your grandmother?"

"I was afraid you'd know instantly I was trying to reach Eleani and stop me."

"Things might have been better if left as they were."

"I promised my mother I would do my best

to see her letter reached her mother. Would you have me renege?"

"Your mother is dead. She would not have known."

"But I would have known I hadn't kept a promise. Would you have broken a promise, Nikos?"

He was silent for a moment. Then reluctantly he said, "No, I would have honored my promise as you did. I think there might have been a better way to handle things."

"I tried the normal means. I could not make contact. It seemed like an act of fate when I got the job at the resort. I was so close. And when I was chosen to work on the *Cassandra*, I knew it was right. I'm sorry you feel I used you. In a way I guess I did, but I never lied to you about anything."

He didn't say anything, just stood and walked to the water. Sara watched as he dove in and swam away. He turned when he was some yards off shore and began to swim parallel to the beach. The cove was not wide. He swam laps. Sara watched every stroke, wishing he'd asked her to join him.

She rose and picked up her towel, shaking

off the sand. She waded to the boat and tossed in her towel, then plunged into the silken water. Keeping out of Nikos's way, she swam hard, trying to tire herself out so she could sleep tonight. If he didn't arrange transportation for her soon, she'd have to stay through the weekend. How awkward that would be. She'd have to explain things to the crew—not that it was any of their business, but they had befriended her when she joined on and it was the right thing to do. If it fed gossip, so be it. Better than rampant speculation.

Sara lost track of time. She plowed through the water, growing tired but pushing on. Zoning out while swimming helped her forget everything. There was only the water and the sky. Finally almost too tired to move, she stopped to tread water for a moment. Looking around, she spotted Nikos in the boat. For a second her heart skipped a beat. Would he leave her here? She'd never find the pathway back.

Unlikely. He sat in the boat, watching her. She began to swim slowly back. Her arms and legs felt like limp spaghetti. Her breathing was still hard. But she also felt at peace for the first time since she walked up to the house that morning.

"Need a hand?" he asked when she reached the boat.

She shook her head, standing in the shallow water.

"Then push the boat off and get in. It's time to go back."

She went to get the anchor. Nikos coiled the line as she brought the anchor to the boat. She pushed the bow away from the beach, facing it seaward. Then she scrambled aboard. Taking her towel, she dried her face and arms. Tying it around her, sarong fashion, she sat in the copilot's chair. Nikos had started the engine as soon as she boarded, and once she was seated he opened the throttle until Sara felt as if they were flying.

Before long they were tied up behind the looming back of the *Cassandra*.

He turned off the engine and looked at her.

"Now what?" she asked.

"My grandfather would like you to join us for dinner," he said evenly.

She thought about it for a moment. "Okay, I guess."

"I thought you'd say that," he replied.

She looked at him. "What do you mean by that?"

"It seems likely that having made your presence known to Eleani, you'd expect to enjoy the benefits of being her granddaughter."

"You think that's why I told her? I don't know her at all. I don't consider I'm due any benefits of being her granddaughter. She owes me nothing. I owe her nothing."

"You're wrong. If what she says is true, and I believe it is, she didn't know about you."

"She should have taken the time to find out," Sara grumbled.

"Women of her generation usually bend to their husband's dictates. Her husband told her Damaris was fine. What was Eleani to think— that he lied?"

"He did lie."

"But she would not have thought that. If anyone is at fault or to blame about anything, it's Stanos. He's dead, so can't be held accountable. She should have known, and maybe she should have tried herself to find Damaris—especially after he died. But she didn't. She thought everything was the way it was to be. Now she knows the truth. Give her a chance."

"So which side are you on? You practically accuse me of kissing up to her for the so-called benefits—which you don't think I'm entitled to. Then you defend her actions and suggest I get to know her better."

"The relationship between you and your grandmother is not my business. You two have to find your own way."

"And the relationship between us?" she asked challengingly.

"There is no relationship between us." Nikos stood and stepped to the open part of the boat.

"There is. Or was. Even though you don't want to call it that, we had the beginning of a relationship," she said, standing and balancing herself against the rocking.

"You may think so."

"Come off it, Nikos. I know you don't want to be burned again like with Ariana. But every woman on the planet isn't after your money. I liked being with *you*. Except for dinner last night, I haven't cost you anything but your time. Admit it, we were becoming friends. And

it sure seemed like you were pushing for more
with those hot kisses."

"Hot kisses," he repeated.

She felt herself grow warm as she glared at
him. He knew they were hot. And as much as
he denied it now, she knew there had been a
spark of something between them.

She also knew that spark would never have
a chance to become a full-blown conflagration.
She had put paid to that notion with her actions.

"What time is dinner?" she asked.

"Seven."

"I only brought my uniforms and the one
dress I wore last night."

"I'll take care of that."

By the time Sara reached her cabin a few
moments later she longed for a hot shower.
She'd really love to soak in a tub, but that kind
of luxury wasn't available aboard the
Cassandra—at least not in the crew quarters.

The shower did a lot to refresh. Drained after
this morning's confrontation and the swimming she'd done, Sara lay down for a nap.

At six-thirty there was a knock on her door.
Opening it, Sara was surprised to find one of

the maids from the house. She held a box out for Sara.

"For you. A dress for tonight," she said. Smiling briefly, she turned and fled as soon as Sara took the box.

Sara closed the door and placed the box on the narrow bunk. Opening it, she stared for a long moment. The dark burgundy color was rich and perfect for her coloring. Lifting it, she stared. It was formal enough for dinner and beautiful enough to make anyone wearing it feel like a princess. Slipping it on a few moments later, Sara wished she had a full-length mirror. She studied as much of herself as she could. The dress fit like a dream. She liked the way it brought out her coloring. Her dark hair gleamed. Her cheeks were pink with anticipation. She felt very special. How nice of her grandmother to send her the dress to wear with dinner.

Or had it been Nikos? His words echoed. Heat washed through her. Had he bought the dress? Where? Unless he'd gone to Patricia. Not a short hop in a car, but at least two hours of his time.

Not likely. But what was the likelihood of

such a beautiful dress just lying around the house waiting for someone her size and coloring to show up to wear it?

At five minutes to seven Sara walked up to the house. She could see the lower terrace was already set for the staff's dinner. The table on the upper terrace was bare. Going to the front of the house, she knocked on the door. A moment later Nikos opened it. He was wearing a dark suit, white shirt and maroon tie—almost the color of her dress.

"You are family, Sara, no need to knock. Come in. My grandfather thought it best if we eat inside tonight. Not so many distractions."

Like the crew watching their every move, Sara thought. "Fine." She stepped inside, looking around with interest. The high ceiling and white walls gave the illusion of coolness even in the warmth of the evening. Wide windows in the salon were open to catch the breeze. The furnishings were a bit heavy for her tastes, but obviously old and much loved if the patina was any indication.

"You look lovely," he said.

She looked at him. "Did you buy this dress?"

He looked thoughtful for a long moment,

then inclined his head. "I thought it was the perfect dress for you."

"It is. Thank you." She didn't want to tell him how special it made her feel. Now, knowing he'd bought it for her alone made it even more special.

"Sara, you are here. Welcome," Eleani said. "We are ready to go in to dinner." She seemed nervous. Nikos offered an arm to each and escorted them into the lavishly appointed dining room. Eleani smiled when she saw Spiros. The connection was obvious—she relied on him.

Sara felt a touch of envy. With her mother dead, she had no one to rely on. She so longed for a close connection with someone—a person she could trust with anything and know he would always be there for her.

Involuntarily her gaze flicked to Nikos. He had seated her and was talking with his grandfather. His manners had been exquisite. His demeanor all that anyone could expect. But the ease between them was gone.

"Welcome, Sara," Spiros said.

Nikos's dark eyes were unreadable.

Dinner was awkward. Eleani tried to carry

on a normal conversation, but kept looking nervously at Sara. Nikos said little, eating and watching Sara. She felt as nervous as Eleani obviously was, with his gaze constantly on her. At one point she almost told him to look away.

As soon as dinner was finished, Sara hoped she could escape. Despite the lovely dress and all the discussion she and Eleani had shared that morning, she was out of place. She did not belong.

"Shall we move to the salon? It's more comfortable there," Eleani said.

"Perhaps I'm needed on the ship." She looked at Nikos. "Will I be taken back to the resort in the morning?"

"No, we sail as scheduled on Monday."

"Very well." So he didn't wish to get rid of her instantly. She wanted to bring up the situation about her job. So far at least he hadn't told her there was no job waiting at the resort. Yet, it would be too awkward for her to stay. She wanted the comfort of familiar things and friends. She'd return to London as soon as she could.

"I'll escort you back to the ship, if you wish to leave now," he said, rising.

"I can manage."

He didn't reply, just came around to pull her chair back and gently take her arm.

"Dinner was delicious, Eleani," he said.

"I'll tell Dimitri you said so." Her smile was wobbly. "Good night, Sara. Perhaps you'd like to have breakfast with me in the morning—just the two of us on my balcony."

Sara was surprised at the invitation. "Thank you. What time should I be here?"

"Around eight," Eleani said, her smile growing warmer.

Once Sara and Nikos left the house, she said, "I'm surprised you didn't have me shipped off already. Why wait until Monday?"

"It's only a couple of days. Time for you to get to know Eleani."

"Your idea or your grandfather's?"

"It was his idea but I agree with him. You may think I'm without feelings, but Eleani has always been very kind toward me. I think she deserves a chance."

Sara mulled that over.

"And I think you do, too," he said after a moment.

"A chance for what?"

"To build family ties."

"Oh." Sara tried to see his expression, but it was too dark.

"So we call a temporary truce?" she asked.

"We are not at war," he replied.

"You're angry."

He walked along for a few seconds, then said slowly, "Would you expect me not to be?"

CHAPTER TEN

OVER the next two days Sara spent more time with Eleani than alone. She saw Nikos only at dinner. Breakfasts were spent with her grandmother on her private balcony. Lunches were often shared with Spiros and Eleani. She answered endless questions and asked many herself about her mother as a young child and then as a teenager. It was a bittersweet time. The easy acceptance that Eleani showed should have been for her mother. And the awkwardness she felt now around Nikos tore at her heart. They'd meshed so well once upon a time.

She knew she never should have had secret thoughts about them developing some kind of relationship, but she had. Stupidly, she'd fallen in love with the man. Now he ignored her. He used work as an excuse, but she knew he had time enough to spend hours with his grandfather. Doing right should bring a reward, not sever something special. Though she was fooling herself if she thought Nikos would ever consider her as more than an employee who liked learning to dive. Still, her heart ached when she saw him.

On Sunday afternoon she sat with her grandmother on the large upper terrace, enjoying the serenity of the gardens and the view of the Aegean. Clouds built on the horizon, but seemed too distant to take seriously. The breeze from the sea was pleasant and fragrant after skimming across the blossoms.

"Sara," Eleani said after a quiet lull in conversation. "Spiros and I want you to move here with us."

Sara turned to look at her in surprise. "I can't do that," she said.

"Please. Think about it at least. I missed so much of Damaris's life. I can never make up for that. But you can have a different life than you've known. Stanos left a small fortune. I have more money than I can ever spend, so you would never be a burden. Please. It would mean so much to me to have you here."

Sara shook her head slowly. "Thank you. I appreciate the gesture. But my home is in London. My friends are there." Her mother was there as well. Somehow Sara had never thought of leaving London permanently.

"Don't say no right away. Think about it," Eleani urged.

"I'll think about it but don't believe I'll change my mind. Perhaps I could come to visit from time to time. We hardly have had time to catch up on everything." Maybe a holiday, a few months away would give time for Nikos to get over his initial anger. Maybe they'd be able to be friends of a kind again.

She pushed away the thought that by the next time she came to visit, he might be married to Gina. How would she deal with that?

"Of course you must spend holidays here. But think about living here—if only for a year or so. We know lots of people, have visitors frequently. You can go to Thessalonika, Athens, I could show you where Damaris grew up. There is so much to see in Greece. It's your heritage, after all."

"I know. I'll think about it." Sara was

starting to feel pressured. This was not something she wanted. Especially with Nikos already angry at her. He would think she'd planned it all along. Ariana had wanted money; he'd think she did as well.

It was *family* Sara wanted. Could she turn down Eleani's offer? She was growing fond of the older woman. Instant love had not sprung forth. But the more she knew about her, the more Sara could see her as a victim of circumstances and her upbringing. Maybe she could not have done things differently regarding her daughter. Sara would never know.

And as Nikos had suggested, she was giving Eleani a chance.

After lunch, at which Spiros also had extended an invitation for Sara to stay, she decided she needed some time to herself. She said she wanted to swim before the clouds developed into rain, and went back to the yacht.

She donned her swimsuit and gathered her things and a book to read on the beach, then went to find the captain to see if she could use the runabout again. He was on the bridge reviewing charts.

Nikos was with him, dressed in shorts and a

T-shirt. She stopped short at the doorway, thrilled as always to see him. The T-shirt hugged his muscles lovingly. She swallowed, wishing things were the way they once had been.

"Do you want something?" he asked, catching sight of her.

"I wanted to use the runabout if that's okay. I wanted to go swimming once more before leaving tomorrow."

He raised an eyebrow. "I thought you'd be staying."

She frowned and slowly shook her head. "I'm not staying."

Nikos glanced at the captain and then moved around the high table. "I'll take you to the cove. You shouldn't swim alone."

"I was planning to stay close to the shore."

"I'll take you," he repeated.

The ride in the runabout was in silence. Sara didn't have anything to say and Nikos was obviously still angry.

Anchoring on the beach, Nikos shut down the engine and looked at her.

"My grandfather said you were invited to remain here with them."

She pulled her top over her head and shimmied out of her shorts. "Eleani invited me. I said no."

That surprised Nikos, she could see.

"Why? Isn't that the entire goal? Get to know your grandmother, spin her a sad tale and end up living the life of luxury? The island has to be several steps up from the flat you shared with your mother in London."

She wanted to knock him overboard. "That's your style of thinking, not mine. My goal as you call it was to deliver the letter my mother wrote just before she died. I thought you'd kick me off the island that same day. I have no plans to stay here."

He looked skeptical. She gave a sound of disgust and stepped over the side of the boat. How dare he think she was looking for an easy berth. She realized then and there he had not really learned anything about her in the days they'd spent together. How could she even think herself in love with such a man? Unfortunately, the heart had its own reasons.

Nikos watched Sara swim away from the boat as if being pursued. Was she spinning another tale, or had she really refused to stay? Was it temporary until she could make arrangements at home or was she seriously not planning to move to the island?

It made sense that his grandfather's wife would want Sara living with her—Sara was her only grandchild. Eleani was a woman full of love and devotion to her family. She would love to have Sara to spoil and be with. Especially after having missed her entire life up to this point.

Nikos tried to think of other women he knew who would refuse such an offer. Carte blanche on anything. Never having to work again. Shopping, luncheons, parties—who would prefer to work in a hot kitchen?

No, Sara had to be holding out for higher stakes. Maybe she wanted a share from Stanos's estate that should have gone to her mother.

He frowned, watching her as she swam. That didn't fit with what he knew about Sara.

They had talked. In-depth discussions of things like families—and promises. He remembered her comment about doing the right thing no matter what. She evidenced a strong sense of honor.

If that carried through, she would not stay. Her quest had been completed.

Did that mean she'd return to London?

Nikos refused to examine why that thought rankled. He had already decided to dismiss her from the job at the restaurant. Now he wondered if that would be wise.

No sense alienating his grandparents. She'd either give it up herself and return to London or change her mind and accept Eleani's offer.

He stepped off the boat and began swimming after her.

As Sara drew near the curve of the cove, she turned and began swimming back toward him.

When they met, they both stopped swimming.

"Want to go diving?" he asked. Seeing her so close, hair wet around her face, eyes sparkling with the delight she found swimming, he had the urge to kiss her again. How dumb was that?

"I'd love to." She looked at the sky. "Will the storm hit soon?"

He glanced around, studying the growing gray clouds, still far enough away to be safe. "I think we'll have an hour or so and still have a margin of safety to get back to the dock."

"Then I'd love to."

They donned the scuba gear from the runabout and were back in the water in less than ten minutes, exploring beneath the surface.

Nikos swam a bit behind Sara, to better keep an eye on her. He could tell she continued to find delight in the beauty beneath the sea. She chased fish, explored encrusted rocks on the sea bed and swam near one arm of the cove then pointed up. Surfacing, he followed her up.

She raised her face plate and took out her mouthpiece.

"Can we go a little around the side, to see the rocks?"

"The current's a bit tricky there. You have to watch for surges. Are you sure you're up to that?"

She thought about it for a moment. "Have you done it?"

"Many times. Some of the rock formations are amazing. It's not very dangerous, just be cautious."

"You lead, I'll follow you."

"I'd rather be able to see you."

"Then side by side?"

"You stay on the sea side, let me be closer to the rocks." If a surge came, he would be able to manage things better than she would.

"Thanks." Pulling down the face mask and popping the mouthpiece back in, she dove beneath the surface.

The exploration was fascinating. It had been a while since Nikos had been over this section and seeing it anew as if through Sara's eyes had him appreciating the beauty even more. He should take time to enjoy pursuits he enjoyed—like diving. He may not like what Sara had done, but he was suddenly grateful to her for rejuvenating his love for diving.

They turned just as a wave surge hit. For a moment Nikos was slammed against a rock, Sara bumping into him. He caught her before she could be swept to the rocks and held her close. The pressure abated and he kicked away, giving a wider berth to the rocky shore than before.

She pointed upward, but he shook his head and pointed back toward the cove and the boat.

In only a few moments they reached the boat.

When they surfaced and Sara took off her face mask and mouthpiece, she looked at him. "That was wild. Are you okay?"

"Fine." His left shoulder and part of his back burned like fire. He knew he'd scraped the skin, and probably bruised some muscles with the impact. At least it had been him and not Sara.

"You must have hurt something. My bumping into you wasn't a light tap."

"I've had worse." He looked at the clouds, now moving swiftly across the sky, some early fingers already overhead. "I say we get aboard and back to the dock."

She looked up and quickly nodded. "It looks like it's getting darker by the minute."

Nikos levered himself out of the water and into the boat, pulling Sara in a moment later. Divesting himself of the air tanks, he winced when the strap rubbed against his shoulder.

"Let me see," she said, half turning him. "Oh, oh, it's bleeding. Do you have a first-aid kit aboard? You don't want that blood getting all over you and everything else."

"No first-aid kit. It'll be okay." It was starting to burn. The sooner they got back, the sooner he could take care of it.

"Wait." She picked up her shirt, and before Nikos guessed what she was doing, she tore off a strip from the hem. Folding the rest into a large pad, she formed a makeshift bandage and covered the bleeding skin. "I'm not sure this will hold," she said, trying to tie it on with the strip. "Put your shirt on over it, it'll help hold it in place," she said.

Helping him pull on the shirt, her hands brushed against his chest, against his back. Nikos drew in a sharp breath, her touch doing nothing to alleviate the pain of the scrape but raising his blood heat by several degrees. Finally she was satisfied.

"That'll hold until we get back," she said. "I think you need to see a doctor."

"I'll be fine. Let's go." He began to pull the anchor in. It dragged across the sandy beach but came readily. In less than five minutes he had the motor going and was backing away from the beach. The sea was running higher than when they started. Once out of the shelter of the cove, they felt the force of the wind. The water was choppy with large swells breaking every few moments.

He kept the boat on course and they made

the dock safely. Two crewmen were there to help tie up. Bumpers had been placed between the *Cassandra* and the dock as the force of the wind bumped it into the floating dock.

"Brewing up quite a storm," one of the men said.

"You're bleeding through the shirt," Sara said.

"I'll be okay once I get into the house." His shoulder was stinging. Still, once he washed off the salt water, he'd have a better idea of how bad it was.

"Go in and get changed," he said as they walked along the dock.

"Are you going to be all right?" she asked.

He didn't want her worried, but it was nice to have her so concerned. "I'll be fine."

He waited until she hurried up the dock and then headed for the house.

Once under the shower, Nikos knew the injuries were more than superficial scrapes. He'd need help with taking care of them. He dried off, donned a pair of khaki pants and then tried to see what he could do. He saw the blood oozing from a couple of deep cuts. The rocks had been irregular and sharp. If he'd been at the resort, he could have called upon the nurse he'd hired in case guests needed anything.

Sara was wet by the time she reached the house before dinner. The rain had started shortly after she and Nikos returned. She'd showered, dressed and then watched the rain the rest of the afternoon as it poured down. She hoped Nikos wasn't as injured as he looked. With all the blood smeared around, it was hard to tell.

She'd donned a windbreaker and scarf to try to protect herself from the weather, but it proved futile as the rain was relentless. An umbrella would have been useless with the gusting wind. Finally she reached the front door and was sheltered by the portico. Knocking, she waited impatiently for it to open.

"Miss." One of the maids opened the door wide and urged her in. "Let me take your wet things. I will bring you a hair dryer," she said, as Sara took off the windbreaker. Her shoulders were damp, but would soon dry. Her hair was dripping, however.

"I'd appreciate it," she said.

The maid hurried away just as Eleani came down the stairs.

"Goodness, Sara, you are soaked."

"The maid is getting me a hair dryer. The rest of me isn't as wet and will dry soon. It's really raining hard. How is Nikos?"

"Men! They think they're above being injured just by thinking that. Two of the cuts are deep. But there was nothing to be done but use adhesive to tape them together. I have some antibiotic ointment so I used that and bandaged the area. He should know better."

"We didn't expect the surge in the water."

"A storm was brewing, anyone could see that," Eleani said with exasperation.

Sara nodded, feeling guilty that her desire for swimming had cause havoc.

The maid returned holding a hair dryer. "If you wish, you can use this powder room," she said.

"I can get you some dry clothes," Eleani said.

"I'm fine. If I can dry my hair, the rest will dry soon. It's not that cold."

Shortly, Sara joined Eleani and Spiros in the main salon. He expressed concern about their diving and Sara explained how they'd left the cove. It was at her request, yet Nikos was the one who had suffered.

"Dinner," one of the servants announced.

"Shall we?" Spiros offered his arm to Eleani.

Sara rose. When she entered the dining room, she did not see Nikos.

"Is Nikos joining us for dinner?" she asked.

"He should be here by now. Probably got tied up on some call." Spiros turned to the man waiting to serve them. "Check on Nikos for me, would you?"

"At once."

Taking their seats, they talked desultorily for a few moments until the man returned.

"He's asleep on his bed. Should I waken him?" he asked.

"No, let him sleep, Spiros," Eleani said, placing her hand on her husband's. "It will help the healing. We can send up a tray after we eat."

"Fine."

Sara missed Nikos being there, even though the last couple of meals had been uncomfortable with him glaring at her. At least she knew him, they'd shared parts of their lives with each other. It was not the same with the two older people she scarcely knew, and one of whom she still had mixed feelings about. Sara still couldn't reconcile her grandmother's actions or lack thereof. Yet the more they talked, the more she grew to know the woman. Eleani had loved Damaris. That much was clear.

After dinner Sara offered to take up a tray for Nikos. Spiros agreed and soon one was brought from the kitchen. She followed the older man's directions and turned left at the top of the stairs. The house was large, with seven bedrooms, she'd been told. The flat she and her mother had shared would fit in the main salon and leave room to spare.

The door was slightly ajar when she approached. Balancing the tray, she knocked. There was no answer. Pushing the door, she saw Nikos was sprawled across his bed, on his stomach, asleep. She opened the door enough to enter. Setting the tray down on a small table near one of the tall windows, she crossed to the edge of the bed.

"Nikos?" she said softly.

He looked just as formidable asleep as he did when awake. His hair was tousled. He was bare from the waist up and the white bandage was a stark contrast to his tanned skin.

She felt odd watching him as he slept—as if she were intruding. She was also fascinated. Glancing around, she saw a straight chair, which she brought over so she could wait for him to waken. The dishes were covered; they'd keep the food warm for a little while. She wanted to reach out and touch him, feel the warmth of his skin, maybe even lean over and kiss him as if she had the right.

She sat and waited, watching him sleep and thinking of how she might have done things differently. Perhaps it would have resulted in a different outcome. Maybe she could have salvaged their growing friendship, if nothing more.

Sara lost track of time. She was about to leave when he stirred.

"Nikos?" she said softly.

He opened his eyes and looked at her. For a moment she felt cherished. Then his awareness kicked in and his gaze grew hard. "What are you doing here?" He rolled over, groaned softly and sat up. Reaching out, he switched on a bedside lamp.

"Damn, this shoulder hurts more than I expected," he said, rotating it a bit.

"Don't start it bleeding again. Eleani said two of the cuts were deep." She jumped to her feet and reached out as if to stop him. She pulled back her hands when she realized what she was doing.

"I brought you some dinner, but didn't waken you as I thought you'd need the sleep. It's probably cold by now," she said, going to the table and lifting one of the plate covers. Steam rose. "Maybe not."

He rose and crossed the room. He reminded her of a panther on the prowl. Barefoot and bare-chested, he moved with elegant grace. The play of light and shadows on his skin had her fascinated.

When he reached the table, he took a fork, cut a small portion and popped it into his mouth. Shrugging, he pulled a chair closer. "It's warm enough and I'm hungry enough to eat anything."

"I'm sure Dimitri would be happy to warm it up or prepare you something else," she said.

"Don't hover. Sit." He pointed to a chair and took another bite. "It's fine. I've had worse." He looked at her. "And better."

"Will we still leave in the morning?" she

asked, pulling the straight chair closer to him and sitting.

He nodded. "This storm will blow out by then."

It was already dark outside. Rain coated the windows.

Sara was content to watch him eat, as she had been to watch him sleep. She was storing memories to last a lifetime. She'd already decided that once she returned to the resort, she'd turn in her resignation and return to England. Her task was done. She wanted familiar people, places. She wanted the love of her friends and the trust she couldn't have with people who suspected her motives for everything.

So this might be the last time she'd be with Nikos. She treasured every moment.

"Did you eat?" he asked.

"With your grandfather and Eleani," she said.

"She's your grandmother, you can call her that," he said slowly.

She shrugged.

"You know." He took another bite, ate it slowly then looked at her. "Your mother could have come back and confronted her parents. She didn't need to try to reconcile by mail. Did you ever think of that?"

"Of course I did. I even asked her several times why she didn't. It was the family pride. She had as much as her father, I think. And I truly thought she was content enough with life in England. Her getting sick showed me how much she had missed Greece all her life. Even if she hadn't reconciled with her parents, she could have made a good life for us among her friends and in familiar settings of her former home in Greece. But she refused to even visit."

"Don't tell me you never had a vacation or went on a trip," he said.

"We took lots of trips, to the north of England, to Scotland, Wales."

"That money could have been spent on airfare to Greece. So since she didn't, how important was it to her to return to her parents? Maybe her death was just the excuse you needed to come here and meet Eleani and worm your way in."

Sara took a breath with the shock. She thought they'd gotten past this with the dive and all. Nikos still thought she was after money and nothing else.

Slowly she rose, replaced the chair where she'd found it.

"Good night," she said with dignity and left the room.

"Sara, wait," he called, coming after her.

He caught up with her at the top of the stairs, reached out to take her arm to stop her from descending.

"Let me go. You've made your position clear over and over. I don't know why I ever thought you were someone special. You are cynical and jaded and haven't a trusting bone in your body. You should spend your life alone so you never have to wonder if anyone loves you or only your money. At least your parents have a life that they want—even if it didn't include you. At least they reached out and tried. You do nothing but hide away in your resort and spurn anyone who tries to get close to you." She yanked free and almost ran down the stairs.

"Sara, wait," he called.

She threw open the front door and dashed out, but pulled it shut carefully behind her so no one else in the house would know how angry she was. It was hard to see the wide path in the dark, rainy night, but she could see lights on board the *Cassandra* and took off almost at a run.

Tomorrow they'd return to Thessalonika and the next day she'd be back home in London. She could hang on that long. She had to. What choice did she have?

CHAPTER ELEVEN

"Nikos?" Spiros said behind him.

Nikos slowly closed the front door he'd wrenched open after Sara had fled. Turning, he looked at his grandfather.

"Is something wrong?"

"No. Sara and I argued. She left for the boat. She'll get soaked."

"She can dry off there. Eleani had hoped she'd stay the night. I'll have to tell her Sara has already left. What I won't tell her is that she left so precipitously."

Nikos headed back to the stairs.

"Are you all right?" his grandfather asked.

"I'm always all right."

But it was a lie. Nikos realized that when he stepped back into his bedroom. His lonely bedroom. When he'd been younger, he'd been so full of hopes and dreams. He would not have a marriage like his parents'. He would find a beautiful woman who would love him. Who would want to have all the closeness of family he saw with his grandparents and that his own parents had spurned.

Ariana was that woman, he'd once believed. She had proved false and it had changed him. Now for the first time in years, he thought about his old dreams. A home, family, children. The insight that had shocked him before returned. Who would he teach about the island's history and special places? Who would he regale with family stories, from the war to the rebuilding, to the exploits of his grandfather and father? If he did not marry, did not have children, the family ended with him.

But he needed more than children. He wanted someone who came to a marriage with dreams similar to his own. Was someone out there—waiting for him?

What if Sara's dreams matched his? He could get past the way she'd used him if they did. Had the way she'd been with him only been talk? What if she'd been that way to gain his sympathy in case things didn't work out as she'd planned, and she needed to enlist his help?

He looked at the bed, remembering that first moment when he'd awoken and had seen Sara. For a split second it had felt absolutely right. As if he expected her there, and there she was.

She'd never once asked for anything—unlike other women who wanted trinkets or wanted to be seen in nightclubs, not spend quiet evenings on the aft deck of a yacht.

Damn, if he could just trust his own feelings.

He had once before and had been proved wrong. Dare he risk it again?

The sun rose the next morning in a cloudless sky. Sara had her things packed before the *Cassandra* began its engines. She had sent a message to the house thanking them for their kindness and saying goodbye. She knew they might be up already, but she had no desire to speak to anyone.

Stefano brought her some breakfast, croissants and rolls, freshly baked by Dimitri. She hadn't got the recipes she'd wanted. So be it.

She knelt on her bunk and looked out of the small porthole as they pulled away, watching as the house on the hill grew smaller until the *Cassandra* swung round and the house was lost from view.

She felt numb again. They would reach the resort before lunch. She'd contact the travel desk and see what the earliest flight to London was. She didn't need to worry about leaving anyone in the lurch by her departure. The kitchen at the resort had made arrangements when she'd been chosen to serve on the *Cassandra*. The yacht wasn't scheduled for another cruise that she knew of. By the time it was, its regular chef would be ready to come back.

It wouldn't take her long to clear out her room at the resort. Maybe there'd even be a flight out today.

As far as her relationship with Eleani was concerned, she'd write. They could gradually build up a connection. Or maybe not. Sara had done as her mother had asked. Her life was not her mother's. Eleani was a relative, but there was only a tiny bond between them. It might grow or not. Sara didn't care at the moment.

She refused to think about Nikos. He'd made his position clear numerous times. She had been dumb in the extreme to even hope for a difference in him. She refused to admit she loved him. He would never love her in return, and she did not want to end up like her mother, always pining for a man who had left and would never be back.

The knock on her door later had Sara's heart leaping in expectation. She opened it, disappointed to see Stefano there.

"The captain asks if you'd like to watch our arrival from the bridge."

She considered it. But shook her head. "Please tell him thank you, but I'll stay here. I'll be ready to leave when we dock."

She closed the door, knowing she was closing off her last chance to spend some time with Nikos. It was not worth the pain of saying goodbye again for a few moments in his company. She preferred to make the break clean and final.

When they docked at the resort she was ready. She watched from her porthole until she saw Nikos striding away from the ship. Then she went to find out how soon she could be on her way to England.

Luck was with her. She booked a seat on a

7:00 p.m. flight to London. Packing the things in her room swiftly, she arranged to have her bags picked up and delivered to the taxi she'd take to the airport.

She went to the kitchen to tell the chief chef she would not be coming back to work. It was hard. She'd enjoyed the weeks she'd spent in the kitchen and all she'd learned about genuine Greek cuisine. She vowed she'd keep it up when she returned home.

It was time to leave.

She looked neither left nor right but went straight to where the taxis picked up and delivered guests. Pointing out her bags, Sara was on her way. She gazed unseeingly out the windows as they sped through the traffic and on to the airport. Despite her best efforts, her heart was aching. Tears flooded her eyes and she brushed them impatiently away. She'd learned about doing without her heart's desire from her mother. Maybe the Andropolous women were destined not to find happiness with the first man they fell in love with. It didn't mean she had to settle for anything but the best. Someone who was above all the other someones in the world. Would she ever find it again?

She loved Nikos Konstantinos. The admission hurt. She rubbed her chest and tried to shake off the ache. She hardly knew him. She'd forget about him within weeks of getting back home.

Liar, an inner voice said.

Sara knew she'd never forget Nikos.

She paid for her ticket, checked her luggage and made her way to the concourse to await the flight. She couldn't wait to see Stacy and tell her everything. Or almost everything. Sara wondered how long it would be before she could talk about Nikos without revealing how she felt.

The preliminary boarding began. She'd be home in a few hours.

"Sara," Nikos said.

She looked up. "What are you doing here?" she asked, astonished to see him.

"I want to talk."

"You can't be here. Only people with tickets can be here. Besides, they've called my flight."

"I bought a ticket. It was the only way. But I don't want to use it. I don't want you to use yours. I want to talk."

"We have nothing to say. You've made that perfectly clear—especially the part where you think I'm angling for money, no matter who gets in my way."

"I think I was wrong about that."

"What? You *think* you were wrong about that. You were totally wrong!"

People began to watch them. Sara glanced around, seeing the curiosity on their faces.

"Go away," she said, looking anywhere but at Nikos.

"If I go anywhere, it'll be to London. If we have to sit side by side on the plane and hash this all out, I'm good to go."

"We are not sitting together on the plane."

He held out his boarding pass. The seat number was adjacent to hers.

"How did you manage that?" she asked suspiciously.

"Money has its uses. I bribed the ticket agent."

"That's just wrong."

"Not as wrong as your leaving before we have a chance to talk—really talk. Sara, don't go. Stay here in Greece. Get to know Eleani. Get to know me."

"You? What do you have to do with my re-lationship with my grandmother?"

"Nothing. Do what you want with her. Stay for me."

She didn't understand. "I'm going home."

"Make Greece your home. You speak the language, know the food, the traditions—the dances. Stay, make your life here—with me."

Now Sara knew she was confused. Nikos wanted an arranged business marriage. He couldn't be proposing.

"Exactly what are you talking about?" she asked.

It was his turn to look around at the avid audience they had. Frowning, he held out his hand for hers. "Come with me. I'd prefer some privacy."

"Nothing you have to say requires privacy, unless you plan to blast me for using you to reach my grandmother."

"Dammit, I want to ask you to marry me, but not in front of a hundred strangers," he snapped.

Sara blinked. "Marry?" she squeaked. Had she heard him correctly? The man who thought all women were after his money and couldn't love him. The man who wanted a business marriage with a woman of equal fortune was proposing to her? Poor, working woman Sara Andropolous?

No, she had not heard him correctly.

Someone in the group of passengers clapped. Soon dozens took up the applause.

Sara felt the heat rise in her cheeks. "Did you just propose?" she asked. How dare he propose in front of a hundred strangers.

"I did. You have enough witnesses."

"You don't want to marry me."

"If you would come with me as I asked, I would explain."

She rose and picked up her tote. Turning to face the majority of the passengers, she shrugged. "Looks like I'm not going to London after all." With a smile she turned back to Nikos. "This had better be good. If you have me miss my flight for anything less than per-fection, I'm not going to be happy."

He reached out and took her hand, lacing his fingers with hers, raising them to his lips for a brief kiss.

"If you would just say yes, it would make ev-erything easier."

"And why do I want to make things easier for you?" she asked, feeling daring. Her heart sang. He had proposed and she had no intention of refusing. But if he didn't know that yet, it wouldn't hurt to draw this out a bit.

He began striding down the concourse. Sara had to run a couple of steps to catch up.

"How did you find me?" she asked.

"I called your room and you didn't answer. It didn't take long to discover you had booked a flight out tonight. My fear was the traffic, that I wouldn't make it before you left. Which means I would have had to follow you to England."

"You could have said something before," she grumbled. "We were on the boat for three hours."

"I wanted more privacy than can be found on *Cassandra*," he said, heading back to the terminal. In less than five minutes they were in the back of his limousine. He flipped a switch, closing the window to the driver's section. He pulled Sara into his arms and kissed her. Thoroughly.

Breathlessly she pulled back a few moments later and gazed up into his warm brown eyes.

"Is that a yes?" he asked.

"I thought you were going to explain things," she countered, stalling. She still wasn't sure he knew what he was doing. He really wanted to marry her?

"Time enough for all the explanations in the world once you tell me you'll marry me. I love you, Sara. I never thought I'd say those words again. I never thought I'd truly feel the emotion again. But I do—when I'm with you. When I think about you. When I dream about you.

"I want to spend my life with you, and have you with me every day. Maybe we'll have some babies together—children we can love together, raise together, and who will give us grandchildren that will delight our souls. Or if we don't, you will always be enough for me. Say you love me. Tell me you didn't just use me to get to Eleani. That our time meant something special to you—as it did to me."

"It did. *Of course it did!* I fell in love with you, too. I was thrilled when you visited me on the aft deck. But your story about Ariana scared me. I knew you were planning to ask Gina to marry you—rumors like that don't stay quiet long. I didn't want to repeat the mistake my mother made. I didn't want to hold on to hope that you would learn to love me. She never stopped hoping my father would return."

"She loved him that much?"

Sara shook her head slowly. "I'm not sure. Sometimes, and especially after talking with Eleani, I wondered if it was just her pride. She'd given up so much for him, she wanted it to come right. Only, for her it never did."

"We won't be like your parents. Nor mine, come to that. I don't mind entertaining or going to parties, but it's you I want to be with. Sailing in the *Cassandra*, swimming in the sea."

"Working at the resort. I can still cook there, right?"

"If you want. Or not, if you don't."

"I do. I love my job. And there's so much more I can learn about Greek foods. If you adjust your hours, we'll be together when we're not working."

"So you have it figured out?"

She smiled and touched his cheek. "It just came to me. It would be the perfect life."

She couldn't believe Nikos Konstantinos was proposing to her. Afraid to pinch herself lest she wake up, she continued to gaze into his warm eyes, brimming with love—for her.

"If we have any children, I want us to raise them, not a series of nannies and tutors. No boarding school."

"But we will show them the island."

"Of course. We can teach them to dive in the cove, swim in the sea," he affirmed. "And explore historic places. Together."

"You're serious about this, aren't you?" she asked with wonder. Who would have expected Nikos to marry a Greek woman who had no money and a job as a chef?

"You still haven't said you will," he reminded her.

"Yes! Of course I'll marry you. I love you, Nikos. Please love me forever."

"I know how you view promises made. I share the solemnity of a vow. I promise I will always love you," he said with a kiss that had Sara convinced of his love.

She had the happy ending her mother had missed. She would embrace it with both hands and never take it for granted. Their love would last forever, of that she was sure. Nikos had promised.

BOARDROOM BABY SURPRISE

BY
JACKIE BRAUN

MILLS & BOON

For my boys, Daniel and Will

DID YOU PURCHASE THIS BOOK WITHOUT A COVER?

If you did, you should be aware it is **stolen property** as it was reported
unsold and destroyed by a retailer. Neither the author nor the publisher
has received any payment for this book.

First published in Great Britain 2009
Harlequin Mills & Boon Limited,
Eton House, 18-24 Paradise Road, Richmond, Surrey TW9 1SR

© Jackie Braun Fridline 2009

ISBN: 978 0 263 86959 0

Set in Times Roman 13 on 15½ pt
02-0809-38966

Printed and bound in Spain
by Litografia Rosés, S.A., Barcelona

Dear Reader

BOARDROOM BABY SURPRISE is my nineteenth book. (Twentieth if you count the first one I ever wrote. It was a train wreck that never got published.) Anyway, each book presents its own set of challenges and rewards. The process is never the same. But it often happens when I sit down to write that the characters come to me first.

That was the case with this book. My heroine, Morgan Stevens, is independent and self-sufficient, but when she finds herself alone and a new mother she is forced to rely on the hero, Bryan Caliborn. As for Bryan, he's used to taking care of situations and looking after people, but in Morgan's case he finds himself drawn in emotionally.

Lots of obstacles stand between them and their happy ending—which made the story tricky for me to write, but hopefully makes it that much more enjoyable for you to read.

As always, I welcome your comments. I can be reached through my website at www.jackiebraun.com

Best wishes

Jackie Braun

Jackie Braun is a three-time RITA® finalist, three-time National Readers' Choice Award finalist and past winner of the Rising Star Award. She worked as a copy-editor and editorial writer for a daily newspaper before quitting her day job in 2004 to write fiction full time. She lives in Michigan with her family. She loves to hear from readers and can be reached through her website at www.jackiebraun.com

'My heroine comments that she usually doesn't fall for the tall, dark and brooding type. Neither do I, but we both made an exception in Bryan Caliborn's case.'
—*Jackie Braun*

CHAPTER ONE

SEATED in the tastefully decorated reception area at Windy City Industries, Morgan Stevens gripped the upholstered arm of the chair and panted as discreetly as she could.

Breathe, she coached herself. In…out…and again.

The jagged edge of the contraction was just beginning to wear off when the secretary returned through one of a trio of doors on the opposite wall.

The name on the woman's desk plate was Britney. It suited her to a T. She was young, attractive, model-slender and crisply fashionable in a fitted black suit, bold-print silk blouse and a pair of killer heels. In comparison, Morgan felt decidedly dowdy in her pastel-colored maternity tent and the comfortable flat sandals that were the only shoes that would accommodate her swollen feet.

"I'm sorry, but Mr. Caliborn is busy and can't see you," Britney said, working up a smile that looked about as sincere as a shark's. "Might I suggest you make an appointment before coming by next time?"

Why? So he could be conveniently gone when she got there? No way. Morgan had been trying to reach Bryan Caliborn for months. She laid a hand on her protruding midsection. Nearly nine of them. The only correspondence she'd had in return, if it could be called such, was a letter from his legal counsel advising her that Mr. Caliborn disputed her allegation of paternity. In fact, he disputed knowing her. He considered her claims nothing less than extortion, and he would sue for damages if she continued to make them.

More than hurt and insulted by his threat, Morgan was outraged. If he didn't want to play a role in their child's life, fine. He should just say so. But to say they'd never met, well, that was beyond defense, legal or otherwise. She never would have taken Bryan Caliborn for such a ruthless, heartless man. Nor had he seemed slow, but he had to be if he wasn't aware that all it would take was a bit of DNA to confirm Morgan was telling the truth. She'd hoped, apparently in vain, to avoid that sort of ugliness.

Rising awkwardly to her feet, she returned the young woman's smile with one that was equally insincere. "Fine. Please pencil me in for his earliest availability."

"Let me just check his calendar and see when that might be," Britney said.

Morgan saw no sense in arguing with the secretary. She would deal with the elusive businessman herself. And she would do so now. While Britney walked behind her desk, Morgan headed to the door through which the woman had appeared a moment earlier. She assumed it was Bryan's office. Opening it, however, she found it was a conference room, a conference room that was filled with suit-clad professionals seated around an oblong cherry table. File folders were open in front of them, not that they were looking at the pie charts and bar graphs. They were gaping at Morgan. But it was the man at the far end of the room who held her attention.

Handsome? No. A better word would be *arresting*. He had dark, almost black hair and eyes of the same fathomless hue. His face was angular with sharp cheekbones and slashing brows that, at the moment, were pulled down in a frown. The nose above his sculpted, flesh-toned lips was thin and just crooked enough to give it character.

Morgan swallowed. Even seated, it was obvious he was tall and powerfully built. Never in her life had she been attracted to the dark and brooding sort, but something about this man was definitely appealing. She told herself it was only because he seemed oddly familiar.

That thought shattered when he spoke. She'd never heard a voice like that before. He didn't break the silence so much as pulverize it. His words boomed through the room like a thunderclap when he demanded, "What is the meaning of this?"

"Sorry," she began, backing up a step only to bump into the secretary, who took Morgan's arm. The gesture seemed more like an effort to detain rather than to steady her, which irritated Morgan enough to prompt her to say, "I need to speak with Bryan Caliborn, and I need to speak to him right now. I thought he might be in here."

"He is." All eyes turned to the big man at the end of the table, who was now rising to his feet. He was every bit of six-four, maybe six-five, and every inch of him radiated power and authority. Again she had the odd feeling that she knew him, but it came as an utter shock when he said, "I'm Bryan Caliborn."

"No." Morgan shook her head, sure that she had heard him wrong. "You're n—"

She didn't finish the sentence. Her water broke, releasing in a gush to form an unbecoming puddle on the polished parquet floor. The secretary let go of Morgan's arm and jumped back, anxious to protect her Marc Jacobs pumps from harm. The people seated around the table gasped in unison, pulling back in their seats, as if Morgan's condition were contagious. Only the man who claimed to be Bryan moved. Swearing richly half under his breath, he stalked around the table toward her.

"Sorry," Morgan whispered, though she felt more mortified than apologetic.

She would have left then, turned and run away—or waddled as the case may be—but as her luck would have it, another contraction began to build. She angled away from him, hoping to make it to the reception area's couch to wait out the worst of it. She made it only one step before grabbing the door frame and sagging against it. Using the other hand to support her abdomen, she fought the urge to whimper. Nothing was going as planned. Nothing *had* gone as planned in a long, long time.

"Britney, call an ambulance," the big man barked. To Morgan he said, "I take it you're in labor."

Labor? She was being wrenched apart from the inside out. None of the books she'd read, none of the classes she'd taken had prepared her for this kind of pain. But she nodded, worried that any attempt at speech would release not only a whimper but a wailing shriek. God, she hurt.

She needed to sit down. She needed some of the drugs she'd learned about in her birthing class. She needed her mother. Only one of those things was an option now, but before Morgan could wilt to the floor, she was scooped up in a pair of powerful arms and carried into the office

that was one door down from the conference room.

He settled her on the leather couch and
returned a moment later with what looked to
be a balled-up trench coat and a glass of water.
He positioned the trench behind her head on
the arm rest and then thrust the glass at her.
Morgan wasn't interested in water. For that
matter, she doubted she could keep it down.
But she dutifully took it and pretended to sip
from the glass. His rigid demeanor told her he
wasn't the sort of man who stood for being
defied. And while she generally wouldn't stand
for being bullied, she was in no shape to put
him in his place.

"The ambulance will be here any moment,"
the secretary said, peeking around the semi-
closed door.

"An ambulance really isn't necessary,"
Morgan began. Not to mention that it would be
expensive for someone who had just lost her
health insurance along with her teaching job
when the school year had ended a week earlier.
The economy being what it was, the district
didn't have the funds for extras like music.

The worst of the contraction had passed, so

she swung her legs over the edge of the couch and planted her feet on the floor. She would go now, exiting as gracefully as her condition allowed. Her car was in the parking ramp adjacent to the building and she could be at Chicago's Northwestern Memorial Hospital in less than twenty minutes, assuming the traffic lights and her finicky compact car cooperated.

What stopped her wasn't the big man, even though he took a lurching step in her direction, but the framed picture on the wall just to the right of the door. In it two men stood arm in arm, one dark and brooding, the other fairer and far less serious. Morgan blinked. She knew those smiling eyes, that windblown brown hair and carefree expression. By turns sweet and silly, this was the man with whom she'd spent seven lovely and, for her, uncharacteristically reckless days in Aruba.

Bryan.

She must have said the name aloud because when she glanced over, the man's gaze also was on the photograph, his mouth compressed into a line so tight that it was hard to tell where his top lip ended and the bottom one began.

"You do know him," she accused, pointing to

the photograph. "You do know Bryan Caliborn."

"*I* am Bryan Caliborn," he proclaimed a second time. "That's Dillon, my younger brother."

Dillon…

Brother…

The words registered slowly, poking through a haze of disbelief. Though a part of her wanted to dispute them, the proof—all six-feet-something of it—was literally standing before her, his arms crossed, his expression ominous and intractable.

Bryan…rather, Dillon—the man who'd fathered Morgan's baby, hadn't given her his real name. This wasn't exactly the kind of revelation a woman needed to hear with motherhood a few centimeters and a couple of hard pushes away. It made Morgan wonder what else he had lied about. What other truths he had obscured with his beguiling kisses and those impeccable manners she'd found every bit as seductive as his smile.

In her best schoolteacher's voice, she demanded, "I want to see him." For good measure, she added, "And don't you dare tell me I need to make an appointment. As you can see, I'm not in any condition to wait an hour let alone a week or two."

"It's not possible," the real Bryan had the audacity to say. She opened her mouth, intending to let loose with a blistering retort. Before she could, though, he said, "Dillon's dead."

Anger abandoned her, evaporating like water on hot asphalt. Bewilderment took its place—bewilderment and a couple dozen other emotions that swirled around in a dizzying mix. Since her legs threatened to give, Morgan backed up to the couch, sinking onto its cushions.

"He's dead?"

Bryan's head jerked down in a nod.

"But how? When?" She asked the questions, needing to know even though the answers really didn't matter. What would they change? Not only was she about to become a single mother, her baby would never know his or her father. She swallowed a fresh wave of nausea. For that matter *she* hadn't known her baby's father.

"Six months ago. A skiing accident in Vail, Colorado." The words came out stilted, made curt by grief. Or was that some other emotion lurking in those onyx eyes?

"I...I didn't know."

"Neither did I." He glanced meaningfully at her stomach. "Where did you and Dillon meet?"

"Aruba. Last August."

She'd gone there alone, using the tickets she'd bought her folks for their thirtieth wedding anniversary. They'd never had a honeymoon. Morgan had wanted to give them one as a surprise. Before she could, though, they'd died in a fluke carbon monoxide accident at their home. Though she wasn't one to make excuses for her behavior, her grief helped explain why someone as levelheaded as she usually was had fallen for the faux Bryan's advances in the first place. She'd been lost, lonely. He'd been charming and a distraction from bitter reality.

"And you...spent time with my brother?" One brow arched in disapproval as Bryan once again glanced at her abdomen.

"Yes."

If she'd felt awkward and conspicuous before, she felt doubly so now. She stood, intent on leaving this time, though where exactly she would go beyond the hospital she hadn't a clue. She was between jobs, between homes and in a strange city without family.

A pair of emergency medical technicians arrived before Morgan could get to the door. They carried black bags and were pushing a gurney.

She held up a hand. "Oh, this really isn't necessary. I can get to the hospital on my own steam. My contractions aren't that close together."

Even as she said this another one began. Just how many minutes had passed since the last? She didn't dare chance a glance at her wrist now.

"It is necessary," Bryan objected. "Assuming what you say is true, that child is a Caliborn."

"Assuming—" She gritted her teeth, and not because of the contraction. She would have stalked out then, but one of the technicians, a kind-faced man with salt-and-pepper hair and a bushy mustache, laid a hand on her arm.

"Let's have a look at you first, okay? We wouldn't want you to have that baby while you're stuck in traffic on Michigan Avenue."

He reminded Morgan of her father, which was the only reason she let him lead her back to the couch.

Once she was seated, the EMT knelt in front of her and pulled a blood-pressure cuff from his bag. As it inflated over her upper arm, she glanced at Bryan, who stared back at her stone-faced. She was coming to know that expression. She could only imagine what he was thinking.

Damn Dillon! Damn him for doing this. And damn him for being dead!

Bryan wanted to throttle his little brother, pin him in a chokehold like he used to do when they were kids and pound some sense into him. Only he couldn't. Knowing that reopened a wound that had just barely begun to heal. Why did Dillon have to go and get himself killed?

Bryan still couldn't quite wrap his mind around the fact that Dill was gone, buried in the family plot at Winchester Memorial Gardens alongside their paternal grandparents and a spinster great-aunt. How was it possible for someone that vibrant and full of life to die? Half the time Bryan wanted to believe that his younger brother was simply off on another one of his irresponsible jaunts, charging his good time to Bryan's accounts.

He'd done that often enough after burning through his own trust fund by his late twenties, Vail being the last wild excursion. Bryan had been furious when his credit card company had called to confirm the charges. Only the best accommodations and restaurants for his little brother. He'd dialed Dill at the luxury hotel where he was staying in a suite that was costing Bryan a few grand a night, and left him a blistering message.

"Grow up, already!" he'd shouted into the receiver. "You're thirty, for God's sake. You have a position at the company if you'd ever deign to work. You need to start earning your own way and stop mooching off me. You do it again and I swear, Dill, I'll call the police."

Of course, he wouldn't have. But he'd been so furious.

Now, sitting in his office looking both terrified and lovely as she answered the EMT's questions and cringed her way through another contraction, was one doozy of an example of his little brother's foolishness. As per usual, it would be up to Bryan to clean up the mess. He'd done that Dill's entire life. Apparently, that applied posthumously, too.

He scrubbed a hand across his eyes. This mess was going to be harder than the others, assuming Morgan wasn't lying about her baby's paternity. That was a possibility given the Caliborn family's net worth. She probably thought she had a big payout coming. Given the state of his brother's finances, she was in for a rude awakening. Unfortunately, determining the truth wasn't as easy as requesting a DNA test. It wasn't because the father in question was deceased. Bryan's DNA could be used to confirm a biological link between the baby and the Caliborns. That was precisely what had him hesitating. He was in no hurry to go through that…again.

He had to say, Morgan Stevens wasn't Dill's usual type. His brother had always gone for flashy women—bombshell blondes, busty brunettes and sassy redheads whose idea of keeping up with current events was to leaf through the tabloids while they had their hair styled. One of the dates Dill had brought to a family dinner last year had actually thought Austria was an abbreviation for Australia.

Morgan appeared to be intelligent and well-spoken, if her phone messages and letters were any indication. She was wearing conservative, if hideous, attire and, despite her advanced pregnancy, didn't appear to be built like a Playboy centerfold.

So, just what had Dill seen in this woman?

Bryan didn't have to wonder what Morgan had seen in Dill. His brother had been good-looking, charming and exceptionally free with his money, which he could afford to be since the money was actually Bryan's.

Gold digger.

It was an old-fashioned term, but Bryan had met enough of those sort of women over the years to know it still applied. Rock stars weren't the only ones who had groupies. Power brokers attracted them, too, though admittedly they were more refined and they tended to be looking for a ring and a Bergdorf charge card.

His ex-wife came to mind. She was remarried to a Texas oil tycoon whose fortune made the Caliborns' look paltry by comparison. And she'd borne the tycoon a son, a son who, for a brief time, she'd allowed Bryan to believe was his.

The scandal had been the talk of Chicago for months after the news broke. The DNA test results had been leaked to the media—even before Bryan had seen them. The gossipmongers had had a field day and they would again if they caught wind of this.

Morgan's moan brought him out of his bitter musings. Her lips parted and she began to pant. Her eyes were pinched closed, her face drawn and dotted with perspiration. She looked incredibly young and scared, especially when she whispered brokenly, "I don't…think I can…do this."

Bryan didn't like weakness. In business, he considered it a character flaw. Oddly, her vulnerability touched him. It made him want to go to her, hold her hand, stroke her cheek and offer reassurance. Absurd reactions, all. He folded his arms across his chest and leaned against the edge of his desk instead.

"Sure you can. You're going to be fine," the EMT told her. "Lie back on the couch now. I'm just going to check to see how far you've dilated."

That brought Bryan upright. He was no expert on labor and delivery, but he'd heard that term before and knew what it meant. On his way to the door, he said, "I'll be outside."

In the reception area, he paced uncharacteristically. He was used to taking charge of any given situation and then taking action. At the moment, he wasn't sure what to do. Should he call his folks, who were currently vacationing abroad, and tell them…what? What exactly could he say? Congratulations, you may soon be grandparents.

Dill's death had been so hard for Julia and Hugh Caliborn to accept. The death of a child, no matter how old, was wrong. It flouted the natural order of things. Parents were not supposed to bury their offspring.

Bryan pictured his mother upon hearing about Morgan's baby. She would be excited and weepy about reclaiming a precious bit of her younger son. No doubt, she would lavish the child with every comfort and amenity. And Morgan, too, by default. She'd done the same with his former wife and the baby she'd been cruelly duped into believing was her first grandchild. Four months before the due date his mother had already made over one of her home's guest rooms into a nursery. Then she'd thrown her daughter-in-law a lavish shower, buying everything left on gift registry afterward. She'd been at the hospital for the birth, crying the happy tears women cry at such occasions. And, eighteen months later, when they'd learned that Caden Alexander Caliborn was not a Caliborn at all, she'd shed more tears, nearly as devastated as Bryan had been.

He clenched his fists. Until he knew for certain this young woman wasn't pulling a very convincing con, he had to protect them. That meant keeping news of Morgan not only from his parents, but from the press.

"Britney," he called as he stalked to her desk. "Not a word of this leaves the building. If anyone in the conference room has questions about who this young woman is or why she came here looking for me today, you direct them to me. Understand?"

"Of course, Mr. Caliborn. You know you can count on me…for anything." Her smile was a just a little too personal for his liking, but he ignored it. In all other aspects, Britney was an efficient and loyal employee. Her apparent crush on him would wane in time, especially if he kept doing nothing to encourage it.

When he turned around, the EMTs were wheeling Morgan out of his office on the gurney. Her head was elevated. Her face was as white as a sheet.

"Will you be coming with us?" the older EMT asked. "We have room in the ambulance if you want to accompany your wife to the hospital."

Wife? He heard Britney gasp and gritted his teeth. Another rumor to dispel.

"She's not my wife," he bit out as the old bitterness returned. He glanced at his ring finger, recalling the gold band he'd once worn. To him, it had been a symbol of his love and fidelity. It wasn't until Camilla had asked for a divorce that he'd learned neither had been returned.

Whatever the EMT thought of Bryan's blunt denial, he masked with his professionalism. "Maybe you could make some calls for her then. It would be nice for her to have some support in labor and delivery, even if it doesn't look like she'll be in there long."

Bryan nodded and glanced at Morgan. In a gentler tone, he asked, "Who should I contact for you?"

Her eyes remained closed and though she was no longer panting; her voice was a breathy whisper when she replied, "No one."

"What about your family, your parents? Give me their number and I'll have Britney call them. They'll want to know."

Moisture had gathered at the corners of her closed eyes. It leaked down her temples now, blending into her perspiration-dampened hair. Weakness, he thought, once again drawn by her vulnerability. Before he realized what he was doing, he reached out and dried her tears.

Morgan's eyes flicked open at the contact. Green, he realized. A rich and vivid green. Like precious twin emeralds. He pulled back his hand and cleared his throat. "Your parents' number?"

"They're gone."

"Where can we reach them?" he asked.

"You can't." Bryan experienced an unfamiliar ache in his chest when Morgan whispered brokenly, "I have no one. No one at all."

CHAPTER TWO

SEVEN hours later, Bryan paced the length of the waiting room, sipping tepid coffee from a disposable cup while his gaze strayed to the large clock on the wall. It was after six, but Morgan remained in labor. So much for the EMT's assertion that the delivery would be accomplished quickly.

What was he doing at the hospital? He didn't have an exact answer, though duty ranked high on his list of choices. Given Morgan's claims, he felt a certain sense of obligation to follow up on the situation. Of course, that didn't explain why the minute the EMTs had wheeled her into the elevator he'd told Britney to clear his schedule for the afternoon, then he'd hopped in his Lexus, arriving at the hospital in record time. The entire way, he'd recalled Morgan's pinched features and heart-tugging vulnerability.

She needed someone. Bryan was the only someone available.

He finished the remainder of the coffee and tossed the cup into the receptacle. If he'd known the birth was going to take this long, he would have lingered at the office or at the very least brought his laptop with him. Duty, he thought again. As Windy City Industries' Vice President of Operations and soon to be CEO, he had plenty of work to keep him busy.

"Mr. Caliborn?"

He turned expectantly at the sound of the nurse's voice. The woman stood in the doorway, a smile lurking around her lips, which he took as a good sign. He hadn't realized he was holding his breath until she said, "The baby is a boy."

Another Caliborn boy. Was this one the real thing? He pushed aside that question and asked, "Is everything…okay?"

"Fine. The baby is perfectly healthy and a respectable seven pounds, eleven ounces."

He cleared his throat. "And Morgan?"

"She's doing well, all things considered. It was a difficult labor, especially toward the end.

For a while the doctor thought he might have to take the baby by caesarean section, but it all worked out."

Because he didn't know what else to say—a rare occurrence for him and not an entirely pleasant one—he offered a curt nod. Then he went to collect his suit coat from the back of one of the chairs. If he hurried, he could catch a couple of members of his management team before they left their offices for the day and maybe go over some of the plans for the company's overseas expansion. But even as he was shoving his arm into a coat sleeve, he was changing his mind. Leaving seemed wrong.

"Excuse me!" he called out to stop the nurse. "I know it's late, but would it be possible for me to see…the baby?"

That's all he wanted, a glimpse at this child who might very well be his brother's legacy and the sole Caliborn heir, as Bryan certainly had no desire to put his heart on the line ever again. For him, marriage and fatherhood were a closed chapter.

"I think that can be arranged." The nurse smiled again before slipping out of the room.

Unfortunately, seeing the baby wasn't as

simple as taking a quick peek in a nursery window so Bryan could assuage his curiosity while maintaining his distance. The newborn was with its mother, the nurse told him when, forty-five minutes later, she led him down the corridor to Morgan's room.

"Don't stay too long," she advised. "Morgan really needs her rest."

He raised his hand to knock. Even as his knuckles grazed the door he wondered what he would say. In a business setting he could hold his own, but he'd never been good at casual conversation with virtual strangers. That had been Dill's specialty.

After his knock, he waited for Morgan to call for him to come in. Instead, the door was flung wide by a bleary-eyed man decked out in wrinkled green scrubs and wearing a sappy grin.

"Have a cigar," the man said, thrusting a cellophane-wrapped stogie into Bryan's hand.

Bryan pegged him to be about thirty, and, given his attire, he'd been at the hospital for some time. So much for Morgan's Oscar-worthy claim that she had "no one." Disgusted with himself for falling once again for a woman's lies, he turned to leave.

"Hey, wait!" The man grabbed his arm. "I take it you're here to see the other new mom."

Other new mom? Bryan shifted back and glanced into the room. A brunette, presumably the man's wife, was holding a blanket-wrapped infant in the first bed. Beyond her, a drawn curtain partitioned the room.

"Maybe I should come back," Bryan said. He already felt awkward and now he was going to have an audience.

"Nah. Come in," the man coaxed, tugging on Bryan's arm. Lowering his voice, he added, "I think she could use some company. The nurses said she went through labor alone and I over-heard them say she doesn't have a husband or anything." His cheeks turned red. "You're not the baby's—"

"No."

Bryan shook off the man's hand and walked to the far end of the room. When he peeked around the curtain, Morgan's eyes were closed. He used the opportunity to study her in a way that would have been rude if she were awake. Matted blond hair and a blotchy complexion offered proof of the hours she'd spent in labor…all alone. It wasn't guilt he felt. He had no reason for that. But something else nudged him. Admiration? She'd certainly shown a lot of grit when she'd burst into the conference room, demanding to see him. As she slept, her brow wrinkled and what he was experiencing shifted, softened. Once again he felt the odd desire to touch her and offer comfort.

From the other side of the curtain, he heard the man talking softly to his wife. Though Bryan couldn't hear the actual words, the tone was intimate. He recalled seeing a bouquet of fragrant flowers and a congratulatory helium balloon bobbing toward the ceiling. When Bryan's wife had given birth, he'd bought out the hospital's floral shop and had lavished her with gifts, including a diamond pendant necklace and matching earrings.

Morgan's side of the room was stark. No flowers, no balloons. No man whispering soft words of love and encouragement. No expensive gifts from a proud father. Bryan swallowed. He tried to picture Dill in the role of new dad. He tried to picture his brother being supportive and taking responsibility. But he couldn't. Even in a situation like this.

What was it Dillon had said upon learning

Bryan was to become a father? After offering his congratulations, he'd added, "Better you than me."

How bitterly ironic.

From the bassinette beside the bed came a faint sound, more like a mewling than a proper cry. Morgan might have been exhausted but her eyes opened immediately at the sound and a smile tugged at her lips.

"I'm here," she crooned softly as she shifted somewhat awkwardly to sit on the edge of the bed. "Mommy's here."

It was then that she noticed Bryan.

He cleared his throat, feeling as if he should apologize for intruding. Instead, he said, "Hello."

"Hi. I didn't realize you were here. I must have dozed off for a minute." She attempted to run her fingers through her hair, only to have them snag in a knotted clump of pale gold. Her cheeks grew pink.

"I won't stay. If I'd known you were asleep…" He shrugged. "I just stopped in to see the baby and… Do you need anything?"

"No." Then she shrugged. "Well, the little suitcase I had packed and ready for the hospital would be nice. I have a hairbrush in it, among other things." Her smile turned wry.

"Where is it? I'll send someone for it."

"At my hotel." When she mentioned the hotel's name Bryan's lips must have twisted in distaste, because she said dryly, "Apparently it's not up to your high standards."

No, it wasn't. The place was little more than a flophouse. He kept that opinion to himself, though the idea of her and the baby—of any young, single woman and helpless infant— staying there bothered him tremendously.

"I'll have Britney bring it by first thing in the morning."

"Thank you." When he backed up a step, she said, "Don't you want a closer look?"

He did. That was why he'd come to her room when good sense had told him to be on his way. Yet he hesitated, oddly more afraid of what he might *not* see than what he might.

The baby was lying on its back. Bryan remembered from Caden's infancy that doctors recommended the position to prevent Sudden Infant Death Syndrome. When Caden had learned to roll over onto his stomach, Bryan had woken up at all hours of the night to check on him, watching his tiny back rise and fall in the low light of the nursery.

"He has hair under the cap," Morgan said.

Bryan spied a few dark brown wisps poking out. Puffy eyes, that deep sea-blue ubiquitous to newborns, were wide open, and though the baby probably was merely trying to focus, he seemed to be regarding Bryan. Finally, one side of his tiny mouth crooked up in a fair imitation of a smile.

Dillon.

Bryan felt as if he'd taken a sledgehammer to the solar plexus. He saw his brother in that little face, not in obvious ways, for the baby's features were too small. But taken in total, they reflected familiarity. Bryan's heart ached again, this pain bittersweet because he couldn't be completely sure he was seeing things as they were or as he wished them to be.

That had been the case once before. And how it had cost him to believe and later find out he'd been deceived.

"What will you name him?" he asked stiffly.

"Brice Dillon Stevens."

He nodded, not surprised that she'd worked his brother's name in somehow. But he

wondered if Morgan had chosen to give the
child her surname because she was unmarried
or because she knew the baby wasn't really a
Caliborn. Of course, that hadn't stopped
Bryan's ex-wife. She'd tossed the child's paternity in his face when their marriage had
splintered apart. She'd stayed with Bryan for
all the months it took her to convince the oil
tycoon he was the biological father.

Bryan's lips twisted at the memory.

"I suppose you listed my brother as the
father on the birth certificate?"

"I did. Is that a problem for you?" Morgan's
voice held an edge that belied her otherwise
fragile appearance. She looked so young and
vulnerable in that hideous hospital-issue gown
that snapped closed at the shoulders. Yet her
direct gaze and even more direct query hinted at
steel.

He ignored her question. "I'll be going. You
need your rest." Before he did, though, he
removed a business card from his wallet and
handed it to her. "If you require anything else,
my private number is on the back."

"Thanks, but I won't be calling. I'm…" She
glanced down at the baby, her expression

softening in a way that tugged at him. "*We're going to be just fine.*"

After Bryan's departure the doubts Morgan had been experiencing for the past several months once again began circling like vultures, picking away at her usual optimism and determination.

We're going to be just fine.

Were they?

What had she been thinking, packing up and crossing state lines without a firm plan in place? That wasn't like her. Of course, nothing about her current situation fell within her personal range of normal. What was she going to do for a job, a place to live?

She hadn't come to Chicago expecting Bryan—er, Dillon—to help out financially, though their child certainly was entitled legally and morally to monetary support. But she had hoped he would offer to pitch in on some expenses, such as the hospital bill. After that, she'd planned to leave up to him how much or how little he wanted to be involved in his son's life both physically and financially. Morgan wasn't a charity case. She had a small settlement from her parents' estate. Unfortunately, the higher cost of living in Chicago was chewing through it more quickly than she'd anticipated.

And now she'd discovered that Dillon not only had lied to her about his identity, but he had been killed in an accident every bit as unforeseeable as the one that had claimed her parents. Gazing at the son they had created together in Aruba, she wasn't quite sure how to feel. Being angry over his betrayal served no purpose. He was gone. She wanted to mourn the man she had known as Bryan, and she did, in the abstract way one mourns any life that is snatched away too soon. And, of course, she mourned him as her baby's father. Morgan had been lucky enough to enjoy a close relationship with both of her parents, but she'd been especially tight with her dad. She'd wanted the same for Brice. God knew her son had precious few relatives as it was, with her parents gone.

As for mourning Dillon as someone significant to her, she didn't. She couldn't. It simply wasn't possible since she hadn't known him well. Indeed, beyond physically, she hadn't known him at all, she realized again, and experienced another wave of shame. She wasn't the sort of woman who engaged in a vacation fling, which perhaps explained why she'd gotten pregnant the one and only time she'd been foolish enough to throw caution to the wind. Or maybe subconsciously she had wanted a child, someone to love and nurture and to help fill up the yawning emptiness she'd felt since her parents' deaths.

Whatever the reason, looking at her newborn son now she had no regrets.

"I love you," she whispered, leaning over to stroke his cheek.

Indeed, Morgan had loved him from the time she'd learned he was growing inside her. But love, even a love this grand and expansive, wasn't capable of obliterating her concerns. And she had plenty of those.

From the other side of the curtain, she could hear the couple discussing who they wanted to act as their newborn's godparents. Judging from the number of names they tossed around, they had a lot of people to choose from. Morgan wasn't completely without relatives, though none lived in the midwest. She did have a small circle of friends back in Wisconsin. A couple of them had urged her to stay in town even after she'd lost her job.

Jen Woolworth, another teacher, one with more seniority who had weathered the latest round of cuts, had been particularly vocal against Morgan leaving the state.

"Hon, you're due soon. You shouldn't be traveling, let alone moving. Stay here with us," she'd urged.

The offer had been tempting. Jen was a dear friend and the two of them often grabbed a cup of coffee after school or hooked up on the weekends for a little shopping and girl talk. But Jen shared a small bungalow-style home with her husband, two rambunctious prepubescent boys and an incontinent miniature poodle they had named Puddles for obvious reasons.

They had enough chaos and no room for another adult, let alone an adult and an infant, even if Jen claimed it would be no big deal to make her boys bunk together in one of the small bedrooms, freeing up the other ten-by-eleven-foot space to serve as Morgan's living quarters and nursery.

The baby fussed. Morgan pulled down her

gown, recalling the instructions she'd received in her prenatal classes. Nursing should have been easy. It was the most natural thing in the world, right? But Brice seemed as baffled by it as she was, and he grew fussier by the minute. Finally, he all-out wailed. It was a pitiful sound, heartbreaking. As tears brimmed in Morgan's eyes, she felt demoralized.

We're going to be fine.

The words mocked her now. Had she really said them to Bryan less than half an hour ago? Had she, even for a moment, really believed it herself?

She wanted to join Brice in crying, but she didn't. She'd never been a quitter and she wasn't about to become one now. Her son needed her. He was depending on her. She couldn't let him down. The luxury of tears would have to wait.

"Let's try this again," she murmured resolutely.

He finally latched on after a couple more false starts.

The flowers—a huge vase full of festive daisies, lilies and delicate irises—arrived as Morgan was putting Brice back in the bassinet.

She couldn't imagine who would have sent her such an expensive bouquet. No one back in Wisconsin knew Morgan had given birth and she didn't know anyone in Chicago. Well, no one except for... No way.

She plucked the little white envelope from its holder among the blooms and tore it open. Sure enough, written in slashing bold cursive under the card's pre-printed congratulatory message was the name *Bryan Caliborn*.

The *real* Bryan Caliborn.

She blinked. Who would have guessed that hard, brooding man could be so thoughtful? An hour later, when a couple of orderlies came to move her and the baby to a private room down the hall, Morgan added the word *accommodating* to his attributes. This room was far more spacious and included amenities such as a plush rocking chair, cable television, a padded window seat and framed reproductions of museum-quality art on the walls.

Just about the time Morgan was beginning to think she'd completely misjudged him, Bryan ruined it with his edict.

That's what the typewritten missive amounted to. It was delivered the morning she was to be released from the hospital by the same snooty receptionist who'd brought Morgan's suitcase by the day before: Britney. The young woman arrived just as Morgan finished dressing in a shapeless, oversize dress. Of course, Britney looked slender and runway chic in a fitted jacket, flirty skirt and peep-toe high heels.

"This is for you." Britney set a large shopping bag on the bed and handed Morgan a note. It was from his highness.

Though Morgan was curious about the contents of the bag, she was even more so about the note.

Morgan,
I have sent a car to deliver you and the baby to new accommodations that you may use for the rest of your stay in Chicago. Your bill at the hotel has been settled in full and I've taken the liberty of having your belongings collected and moved.
    I have asked Britney to accompany you. I will be in contact later this evening to ensure you have everything you need.
                                            Bryan

Relief came first. This was the answer to her prayers. Just the thought of taking Brice to that dingy hotel room that reeked of stale cigarette smoke made her nauseated. And housekeeping and laundry services were included. What new mother wouldn't appreciate help with those time-consuming chores? But Bryan's motive puzzled her. Was he doing this because he believed her or was he merely interested in keeping a closer eye on her? She read the note again, but still was unable to decipher any clues. This time, however, relief wasn't all she felt. It chafed her pride that he'd made the arrangements and moved her things without at least running his plan by her first. She didn't like being told what to do.

Nor what to wear, she added, when Britney scooted the bag closer and said, "Mr. Caliborn told me to pick up an outfit suitable for your trip home from the hospital."

"I have clothes," Morgan objected.

Britney eyed her dubiously before going on. "Yes, well, I brought a couple of selections for you to choose from. I had to guess your size, but I went with loose-fitting styles," she added, her gaze straying to Morgan's midsection.

Morgan knew she still looked pregnant. Not the ready-to-pop balloon she'd appeared to be at her first encounter with the svelte Britney, but a good four or five months gone.

"I have clothes," she said a second time. The words came out forcefully, causing the baby to rouse from his slumber.

"Mr. Caliborn felt you would be more comfortable in fresh things," Britney clarified.

"You can tell Mr. Caliborn—" Morgan began, fully intending to decline the offer, but that was as far as she got before Britney pulled a subtly printed dress from the bag. Then Morgan's only concern was, "God, I hope that fits."

Britney's brows arched. "I can tell Mr. Caliborn what?"

"That I said thank you. And that I will reimburse him."

It did fit. Morgan had to hand it to Britney. The woman not only had a good eye for fashion, she had a good eye for what would look best on Morgan's post-pregnancy body. While nothing could completely camouflage her tummy, the dress Britney had picked certainly minimized it, while accentuating a couple of assets that also had been enhanced by pregnancy. She just hoped Brice wouldn't need to nurse between now and the time they reached wherever it was they were going, because the dress, which zipped in the back, wasn't made for that function.

"Much better," Britney said when she saw Morgan.

Her tone bordered on astonished, but it was hard for Morgan to be offended when she agreed.

"Thank you."

With a curt nod, Britney glanced at her watch. "I've called for an orderly to bring a wheelchair. You've signed your discharge papers, right?"

"I did that before you arrived."

She nodded again and pulled out her cell phone. "Noah, it's Britney. Have the car waiting at the main entrance in fifteen minutes."

Morgan might have felt a bit like Cinderella then, except Britney was hardly fairy-god-mother material and, of course, she had no Prince Charming.

Then Britney said into the phone, "If you see any photographers, call me back immediately and we'll go to plan B."

"Photographers?" Morgan asked as soon as the other woman hung up.

"Paparazzi. Every effort has been made to keep news of you and your son under wraps, but it pays to be cautious."

"I'm afraid I still don't understand."

Britney huffed out a breath. "The Caliborns are a big deal in this city. They're in the headlines regularly for business and philanthropic reasons, but scandals always sell more papers than straight news."

Great. Morgan was a scandal, her son's birth fodder for the tabloids. No wonder Bryan had been eager to find her "alternative accommodations."

CHAPTER THREE

MORGAN stepped into the apartment foyer behind Britney and gasped. She certainly hadn't expected her new place to be a penthouse that offered views of Lake Michigan and the famous Navy Pier from windows that ran the length of the exterior wall.

In the large living room the color scheme was heavy on beige and other neutrals with nary a punch of color. The furniture was tasteful and obviously top quality, and included a baby grand piano that had Morgan's fingertips tingling to play just looking at it, but the place didn't look lived-in. Indeed, every last inch of it seemed as cold as the foyer's Italian marble floor.

"Who owns this place?" Morgan asked. She swore the question echoed.

"Mr. Caliborn. It's his home," Britney replied with a roll of her eyes.

"He lives here?" That came as a surprise. He had such an imposing personality she'd expected to see it stamped on his belongings.

"Since his divorce three years ago." The secretary arched a brow then and asked sarcastically, "What? It's not up to *your* standards?"

"It's not that. It just seems a little…impersonal." Yes, that was the word. It looked more like a showroom in a high-end furniture store than a home. "There aren't even any photographs."

"Mr. Caliborn isn't the sentimental sort."

Morgan wasn't sure she agreed. He kept a picture of Dillon in his office. And she also recalled seeing one of an older couple, most likely his parents. And then there were the flowers he'd sent to her hospital room. She said as much to Britney.

"Don't be so naive, Miss Stevens. Appearances are important to someone in his position. Precautions have been taken just in case the press ever gets wind of you and your…situation. Hence the flowers." Her gaze lowered. "And the new frock he had me select in case some industrious photographer managed to snap a shot of you leaving the hospital. Think of it as damage control."

Damage control? Morgan felt as if she'd been doused in ice water, yet for all that she was steaming mad. Before she could muster a response, though, Britney was moving past her, high heels clicking purposefully on the marble floor before she disappeared through an arched doorway off the living room. Morgan was left with little choice but to trail behind her. After passing through the formal dining room, Morgan caught up with Britney in the kitchen.

"The pantry is fully stocked and so is the refrigerator." The young woman opened the stainless-steel behemoth's double doors, revealing shelves lined with staples including milk, juice, cheese, eggs and butter. The crispers were bursting with a mouth-watering assortment of fresh fruits and vegetables. "Mr. Caliborn said to help yourself and to make a list of anything else you need. He has a housekeeper who comes in twice a week to do the cleaning and laundry. Hilda also takes care of buying his groceries."

So he'd mentioned in his note. But that brought up a most pertinent question. "Where will Mr. Caliborn be staying?"

"His parents are abroad for the summer. He's moved to their residence in Lake Forest for the time being." Britney cast Morgan a quelling look. "It means he'll have a longer commute to work, but apparently he felt you would be more comfortable here than in a hotel."

Some of Morgan's anger dissipated. She *would* be more comfortable here. That went without saying, but Morgan didn't want to displace Bryan from his home and disrupt his routine. She would call him after Britney left. Maybe they could come up with a different solution.

"Besides, the doorman here is vigilant in guarding Mr. Caliborn's privacy, and as such he'll be sure to keep any reporters from slipping up to see you."

Ah, yes. Damage control.

Brice stirred in her arms then. She lifted him to her shoulder and pulled off the little cap he was wearing. Dropping a kiss on his crown, she murmured, "Hey, sleepyhead, are you finally waking up?"

Britney's gaze shifted to the baby. She was a career woman, emphasis on *career*, but surely she wasn't immune to the allure of a newborn. Rather than softening, however, her expression hardened. Apparently, she was.

Still, Morgan asked, "Would you like to have children someday?"

Britney wrinkled her nose. "God, no! Though I suppose *accidentally* getting pregnant can wind up being the ticket to the good life."

Morgan felt sucker punched. "What do you mean by that?"

The other woman snorted. "Take a look around and you'll figure it out."

"You think I'm after money?"

"Yes," Britney said baldly. "And I doubt I'm the only one to reach that conclusion. I suggest you don't get too comfortable with the Caliborn lifestyle. Bryan's noble sense of obligation aside, ultimately, you're not his type."

Two things occurred to Morgan then. First, Britney didn't know that the baby was Dillon's, and second, the young woman had a serious crush on her boss.

Well, Morgan wasn't going to clarify the

situation if Bryan hadn't. Though she longed to assure Britney the brooding businessman wasn't her type either, she kept her mouth closed.

"The bedrooms are this way." Britney click-clacked out of the kitchen, once again leaving Morgan to follow in her wake. "The one at the end of the hall is Mr. Caliborn's. You'll be using the guest suite."

Britney swung open the first door they came to, revealing a large and neatly furnished room. The queen-size bed was outfitted in a taupe duvet. The walls were a couple of shades darker in the same color. A crib, changing table and glider-rocker were set up against the far wall. The pastel-blue bumper pads and comforter provided the only color.

Before Morgan could ask about the nursery furniture, Britney said, "Mr. Caliborn ordered furnishings for the baby. They're top-of-the-line, of course."

"But I have a crib and changing table." They'd belonged to her friend Jen, who had given them to Morgan as a shower gift. For the time being they were in storage with the rest of her belongings.

Britney shrugged. "Now you have two. You'll find diapers, wipes and all that sort of thing in the drawers of the changing table."

"He's thought of everything," Morgan murmured, finding it impossible not to be touched by his efforts, no matter what their motivation.

"Yes. He always does." Britney glanced at her watch, clearly eager to be gone. "My cell phone number is programmed into the telephone. You may call me at any time."

"Oh, that's not necessary."

"Mr. Caliborn thinks it is." With that, Britney left.

Mr. Caliborn thinks…

Mr. Caliborn feels…

Mr. Caliborn has decided…

Under other circumstances, Morgan would have screamed. But as irritatingly high-handed as he could be and as independent as she'd always been, the fact was, she needed someone and he was the only someone available. As she laid Brice down in the brand-new crib in a room that smelled of fresh linens she couldn't help but be grateful they were not back in the claustrophobic hotel room breathing tainted air.

As soon as she could manage it, she would find a job and another place to live. In the meantime, she would suck up her pride and do what was best for her son.

The knock on the door surprised her. It was after eight o'clock that night and Morgan was curled up on the living room couch. The television was on, though she wasn't really watching it. She had too much on her mind to follow the sitcom's quick-paced dialogue.

Britney's confidence in the doorman's abilities aside, Morgan checked the peephole before flipping open the dead bolt. A grim-looking Bryan stood in the hallway, arms folded across his broad chest.

"Hello," she said after opening the door.

Dark eyes surveyed her, no doubt taking in the oversize shirt and unflattering sweatpants. "I hope this isn't a bad time. I forgot my shaving kit when I packed up my things earlier."

"Oh. Sure. Come in." She stepped back to allow him entry.

"The baby sleeping?"

"For the time being," she said wryly. If she

got lucky, she would have another hour before Brice roused and demanded to be fed.

Bryan nodded. "Britney said she showed you around. I take it everything is to your liking."

"Yes." She laced her fingers together. "She mentioned that you're staying at your parents' home in Lake Forest and that they are out of the country."

"They keep a villa in the south of France. Now that my father is getting closer to retirement, they've been spending large blocks of time there," he said matter-of-factly, as if everyone's folks had a second home on the French Riviera.

She pictured the elder Caliborns, pampered, snobbish and every bit as laconic and dictatorial as their eldest son. Heaven help her. Morgan had wanted Brice to have extended family, loving relatives to help fill in the gaps a single mother couldn't. Now she wasn't so sure she would be doing him any favors.

Still, she said, "I had hoped to meet them and to have them get to know Brice. He is their grandson, after all."

"Perhaps on another visit to Chicago," he suggested with a shrug.

She didn't bother to correct his assumption that she was just visiting. It was fast becoming apparent that moving here had been a huge mistake, even if she still felt strongly that she should live in closer proximity to the only family her child had.

"They don't know about me," she guessed.

"No."

"And you're not planning to tell them."

"Not yet."

No need to ask what he was waiting for. Obviously, he required proof of Brice's parentage. She expected him to request a paternity test then. When he didn't, Morgan decided to change the subject.

"I want to reimburse you for the groceries and, of course, for the amount you've had to spend on damage control."

Dark brows tugged together. "Pardon?"

"The bouquet of flowers, the private room and the new dress purchased for me to wear home from the hospital," she clarified. "Britney mentioned that the baby and I would make excellent tabloid fodder and, as such, appearances had to be maintained."

Bryan scowled, but he didn't deny it.

Instead, he said, "No reimbursement is necessary. I wanted you to have those things."

"Well, I insist on paying for my lodgings. When you get right down to it, I'm subletting your apartment." She swallowed, knowing a Chicago penthouse with this incredible view and a rooftop patio far exceeded her limited budget, but she wasn't going to stay here long and pride wouldn't allow her to freeload, especially since Bryan clearly expected her to do just that. "If you'll have a contract drawn up, I'll pay the full rent and utilities for the next month."

"I own it."

Of course he did. "Then, whatever you feel is fair."

"When the month is up, will you be returning to—Cherry Bluff, Wisconsin, isn't it?"

"No, I don't think I'll be going back." Other than her friends, there was nothing for Morgan there. As much as she missed Jen, she could no more freeload off her than she could off Bryan.

"What about your job?"

"I lost it."

"I see." Almost instantly, his dark eyes lit with speculation, suspicion.

Both stung. "I wasn't fired. I was pink-slipped."

"Another word for the same thing, I believe."

"Not from my point of view. I loved my job and I was good at it. The principal hated to see me go, but the school district had to make cuts." She folded her arms. "Perhaps you've noticed that the economy isn't as strong as it once was. Well, in bad times, the arts are the first thing to face the ax."

He appeared surprised. "You're a teacher?"

"A music teacher, yes." She nodded her head in the direction of the baby grand. Her own upright was sitting in storage. "You have a lovely piano. Do you play?"

"Not really."

"Oh." It seemed a waste for an instrument like that to go unused.

He apparently read her mind. "I assume that you do." When she nodded, he said, "Feel free to use it, although it probably needs a good tuning."

"If it does, I'll pay for it."

He sighed, shook his head. Was that amusement she spied in his gaze or exasperation? "Fine, but I'll hear no more talk about contracts and subletting. That subject is closed."

Morgan didn't argue. When she moved out, she would leave a check to cover her expenses. Bryan Caliborn would discover she could be every bit as stubborn as he was. Still, she had to know, "Are you still worried about appearances just in case I'm found out?"

"Among other things," he answered evasively. The enigmatic response as well as the way he was watching her made her wonder what those other things might be.

"Well, for the record, I do appreciate your kindness, even if I feel funny about taking over your home."

"Don't."

One word uttered resolutely. Another edict. It grated against her already raw pride. "You know, you have a very annoying habit of telling me what to do and, now, what to think."

A pair of dark brows shot up, telling her she wasn't the only one who was annoyed. No doubt he wasn't used to being talked to in such a manner. She waited for a blistering retort. Instead, he bowed mockingly.

"My apologies."

Damn him! He was humoring her. "I'd accept them if I thought they were sincere."

"You're questioning my sincerity?"

In her stocking feet Morgan was a full head shorter than Bryan. Even so, she squared her shoulders and raised her chin. "Yes, I am."

"God, you're so damned—" he was frowning when he finished with "—refreshing."

The description threw her, as did the momentary confusion she'd glimpsed in his eyes. "I don't know what to make of that," she replied honestly.

He snorted out a laugh. "Good. We're even then, because I don't know what to make of you."

And he didn't. Bryan usually could read people easily enough. Morgan, however, remained an enigma despite her blunt talk. Interestingly, the more time he spent with her, the more baffled he became. And the more curious. With that in mind, he said, "I'll just get my shaving kit and be on my way."

When Bryan returned to the living room, she was seated at the piano playing softly in deference to the infant sleeping down the hall. In the room's low light, she looked almost ethereal, though the sound emanating from the piano was anything but heavenly. Even to his untrained ears he could tell it was off-key.

"How bad is it?"

She glanced up. "Abysmal. It's a crime what you've allowed to happen to an instrument of this quality."

He nearly smiled at her damning words. She certainly wasn't one to pull punches. "I'd apologize, but I'm pretty sure you'd only accuse me of being insincere again."

"You're mocking me." She plunked out more of the discordant melody.

"Only a little."

She wasn't amused. "I find that almost as intolerable as the fact that you don't trust me and yet feel the need to clothe and shelter me as if I'm some sort of helpless waif."

"Oh, I wouldn't call you helpless. I'd say you've managed quite nicely up till now."

Her eyes widened at the jab.

"Stop it! Just stop it!" she shouted, looking angry and exhausted enough to make him feel petty. "I don't know what your problem is, but it's *your* problem. Not mine. I'm not after the precious Caliborn fortune."

"If I had a dime for every time a woman has said that—"

She slammed the lid down over the piano keys. "And to think I was starting to feel grateful for all of your help. I'd get Brice and leave right now if my car wasn't still parked across town in your company's lot."

He knew he'd regret it later, but he couldn't stop himself from adding, "And if you had someplace to go. But you don't, Morgan. No place to go and no job. Which is why you came to Chicago."

Her eyes turned bright. Her voice became hoarse. "How is it possible that you and Dillon were brothers? I've asked you for nothing. You're the one who insisted on moving me into your apartment, yet you're so suspicious."

I have good reason to be, he thought, calling on bitter memories to make him immune to her tears. He wouldn't be played for a sucker a second time.

"You're right, Morgan. Dill and I are very different men. You'd do well to remember that." He lowered his voice to a more intimate level and added, "Although I can assure you there are certain things I am every bit as skilled at as you found my brother to be."

She shot to her feet, shaking with justified outrage as she poked a finger in the direction of the door. "Out! Get out of here right now!"

Bryan didn't question her right to order him from his own home. He did as she asked, already hating himself for the cheap shot and not at all sure why he'd taken it.

Bryan sat at his desk staring sightlessly out at the Chicago skyline as he levered a gold fountain pen between his fingers. He was too keyed up to concentrate on work, though he had plenty of it to occupy his attention. His agitation had nothing to do with the fact that Windy City's last quarter's earnings were not what he'd hoped they would be. He was thinking about Morgan.

It had been almost a month since he'd last seen or spoken with her. And though part of him knew he owed her an apology for the unforgivable comment he'd made, he couldn't force himself to do so. In fact, just yesterday, after uncharacteristic foot-dragging, he'd hired a private investigator to probe her past. It was

time to find out a little more about Morgan
Stevens than what could be gleaned at face
value. It wasn't just that he couldn't bring
himself to trust her, though that was part of it.
He didn't trust himself and this odd desire he
had to believe she was exactly what she claimed
to be.

Now she'd thrown him for a loop again.
She'd called half an hour ago and left a
message with Britney that she would be
moving out of the penthouse later that day.

That didn't make sense. Nor did the fact that
even though Bryan had a meeting with his
management team in forty-five minutes, he
was pushing himself away from his desk and
preparing to stride out of his office. He needed
to get to the bottom of this.

When he arrived at the apartment door
twenty minutes later, he didn't knock. He let
himself in only to stumble over the luggage
that was stacked in the foyer. She was packed
and ready to go. But she was leaving a bit of
herself behind, he noticed. His beige sofa now
sported a pair of plump red pillows, and a
throw of the same hue was tossed over the
chair. Three weeks in his home and she'd

infused it with more vibrancy and life than he'd managed in three years. But then, this was just a place for him to lay his head at night. He'd stopped wanting a home the day he'd learned he didn't really have a son.

On the coffee table he spied an envelope with his name on it. He opened it to find a check made out to him. The sum had him shaking his head. She was either a clever actress or had too much pride for her own good. Though it wasn't large by his standards, it was probably far more than Morgan could afford. With an oath, he tore it in half before stuffing it into his pocket.

From down the hallway came an infant's shrill cries. He followed the sound, stopping outside the open door to the guest suite. Morgan was at the changing table with her back to him. She'd lost weight. That much was obvious despite the oversize clothing she wore. Her hair was pulled into a ponytail that made her look deceptively young. She was talking in soothing tones as she put a fresh diaper on the screaming baby.

"Hey, hey. Come on now, Brice. It's not as bad as all that," she said. "We're going to be fine, you and me. We're a team, remember?"

The baby quieted, almost as if he understood. More likely, though, the reason was because his bottom was dry and he was being lifted into the security of his mother's arms. The baby eyed Bryan over her shoulder. Brice had more hair now. It stood up on end at the crown. And he'd acquired another chin. He and Morgan made quite a picture, the perfect snapshot of everything Bryan had held dear.

Before learning it was a lie.

He cleared his throat. Upon hearing the sound, she whirled around. The warmth that had been in her tone when she'd spoken to Brice was absent when she told Bryan, "I'll be out in less than an hour."

"It's hardly necessary for you to leave."

"I think it is," she replied.

"Where are you going?"

"Does it matter?"

It did—for reasons he couldn't explain to himself, much less to her. He should be happy she was going. Glad to be rid of her. Except…

"Look, Morgan, I want to apologize. What I said to you the last time I was here, it was… crude."

"Insufferably so," she agreed with a nod.

"But your appalling lack of manners is not the reason I'm leaving. My plan was to stay here until I found employment, and I have."

This came as a surprise. "You've been looking for a job?"

She rolled her eyes. "I know you'll find this hard to believe, but I've always been self-sufficient and I prefer to remain that way."

"What kind of job?"

"I'll be turning tricks in the blue-light district. I hear I can set my own hours," she deadpanned. "A teaching job, of course."

"Were you called back to the school in Wisconsin then?" Oddly, his stomach clenched as he awaited her reply.

"No. I'll be staying in Chicago, at least for the time being."

He ignored the relief that had him wanting to sigh, perhaps because a new worry surfaced.

"Which school will you teach at?" Some of the public ones could be kind of rough. Though he admired Morgan's spunk, it made his blood run cold to think of her going toe-to-toe with some young gang recruit.

"Actually, I won't be in a school." She lifted her chin. "I've been hired by a south-side community center to give lessons as part of an after-school program that's being funded through a Tempest Herriman Foundation grant."

His eyes narrowed. "That doesn't sound long-term or, for that matter, very lucrative. Is it even going to cover your expenses?"

"I don't see how that's your concern," Morgan snapped irritably.

He shrugged. And though it was far from the truth, he reminded her, "Appearances."

"Appearances!" she spat. "If I wasn't holding Brice right now, I'd describe to you, in minute detail, what you can do with your appearances."

"Please, don't hold back. He's too young to grasp words. It's tone that babies this age understand."

"Now you're an expert on children?" She expelled a breath, but then continued in a voice suited to a nursery rhyme, "Maybe it's a good thing you don't believe he's a Caliborn. I don't want my son raised around someone as superficial and self-important as you are."

Bryan ignored the insults. He was a firm believer in quid pro quo, so he figured she was entitled to fling them. Besides, she looked absolutely lovely, with her color high and those emerald eyes flashing in dangerous fashion as she put him in his place.

Stepping fully into the room, he commented conversationally, "I never would have taken you to be the sort to cut off your nose to spite your face."

"That's not what I'm doing."

"No? You're going to move your son, who's barely a month old, out of the safety and comfort of my penthouse and take a job on the city's south side making peanuts. What about health insurance?"

Morgan said nothing, but she swallowed hard and he had his answer.

"No benefits," he scoffed with a shake of his head and then drew closer. "And where are you going to live, Morgan? In some fleabag apartment on a par with that hotel where you were staying before the baby was born? Be reasonable."

"Being reasonable hasn't gotten me very far with you." She abandoned the sweet tone. "You've done your level best to make me feel unwelcome, yet now you have the audacity to act amazed that I'm leaving. What do you want from me? Just what do you want?"

She'd shouted the last question and now the baby began to wail. She looked on the verge of losing it herself. That had him panicked, both because he knew Morgan's tears were the real thing and because the bullying he typically reserved for the boardroom was the primary cause.

"God, don't cry."

"Don't tell me what to do," she countered on a sob. "I've had it up to here with your edicts. I've had it up to here with you. Go away, Bryan. Just go away."

He ignored the directive. In fact, he stepped closer. Close enough that he could smell the scent of baby powder. Close enough that he could have run his knuckles along the underside of her quivering jaw if he'd wanted to. And, God help him, he wanted to.

"Stay, Morgan. Not for the sake of appearances."

"Why then?"

Because I want you to, he thought. I want to get to know you, figure you out. How nonsensical was that? So, he said, "Because it's the right thing to do for Brice."

The fight went out of her. Her shoulders slumped and she lowered her chin. Bryan leaned closer until her forehead was resting on his chest. Brice quieted, too, cocooned between them.

After a moment she sighed. "That's so low."

He laughed without humor. "Yes, but we've already established that I'm a bastard."

She lifted her head and, without heat, admonished, "Don't swear in front of the baby."

"Sorry."

"I'll stay, but only until your parents return. They still don't know about Brice, do they?"

"No."

She shook her head. "Why am I not surprised?"

"They've been through so much pain." The loss of what they believed to be their first grandchild as well as the death of their younger son.

"And you're sure I'll cause them more," she said sadly.

He stepped back, turned away. "I have reasons for being the way that I am," he said slowly. It was as much of an explanation as he could bring himself to give her and more of one than he would have offered anyone else.

"Well, unless you want to live a very lonely life, you're going to have to get over those reasons."

CHAPTER FOUR

BRYAN sat across from his date in the upscale French restaurant, sipping a nice pinot noir and pretending to listen to his date while he replayed the conversation he'd had with Morgan that day three weeks earlier in his apartment.

…unless you want to live a very lonely life, you're going to have to get over those reasons.

She was wrong. He wasn't lonely, he assured himself. Far from it.

"Don't you agree?" Courtney said now.

"Of course," he replied, nodding even though he hadn't a clue as to what had just been said.

All he knew was he had *exactly* what he wanted. Courtney Banks was worldly and wealthy and, okay, every bit as cynical as he was when it came to members of the opposite sex thanks to her own ugly divorce. But that made her perfect. She had absolutely no interest in settling down a second time and absolutely no need for his money. Since not long after his divorce, she and Bryan had gotten together whenever either of them felt the need for a no-strings-attached evening of fun. That's why he'd called her tonight, but now the only woman on his mind was an outspoken blonde about whom he had no business thinking, much less dreaming as he had last night.

"You're not listening," Courtney accused, laughing.

Blinking, he said, "Excuse me?"

"You just agreed with me that the White Sox are a far superior ball club to the Cubs, and we both know what a rabid Cubs fan you are."

He winced. "Sorry. I guess I have a lot on my mind tonight."

"If I didn't know better, Bryan, I might find myself jealous."

He reached across the table and squeezed her hand. "You're not the jealous type." Not to mention the fact that nothing about their relationship warranted the emotion. They weren't exclusive. They weren't committed. Neither one of them had spouted words of love, because, quite frankly, neither one of them wanted to fall in love again.

Courtney's shoulders lifted in a delicate shrug. "I may not be jealous, but I am greedy. When I'm with a man, I want to be the only thing on his mind."

"That's no less than you deserve," he agreed. And more than he was capable of this night. "Would you hate me if we ended the evening early? I'm not fit company."

"*Hate* is the wrong word. I'll be disappointed, though, and so will you. I had plans to model new lingerie." She sent him a smile that in the past had sent blood pumping through his veins. He waited, hoping it would this time, but it had no effect on him.

"It's my loss," he said graciously.

"Yes, it is, and I'm glad you understand that." Her brows rose meaningfully.

He paid the bill and they left the restaurant. After he dropped Courtney off at her Lake Shore Drive address, he should have continued north on 41 to Lake Forest, but Bryan found himself driving south instead. Back into the city. To his penthouse and Morgan.

It was past nine when he arrived at the door. He hesitated before knocking, oddly nervous. Maybe he should have called first. Hell, he shouldn't even be here. What was he thinking? Even as he asked himself this, he raised his fist and rapped three times. If she didn't answer right away, he would go.

The door swung open a moment later. Morgan was dressed in jeans and a T-shirt that she'd left untucked. Her feet were bare, her toenails painted a sheer pink. She'd pulled her hair into a messy ponytail that was a nod to necessity rather than style. Other than a faint sheen of gloss on her lips, her face was free of makeup.

Bryan wasn't sure what to make of the intense awareness that had him sucking in a breath. He only knew it didn't bode well for him.

"This is a surprise," she said.

"It's late and I should have called first," he replied, echoing his earlier thoughts. "Sorry."

"That's okay. I'm up."

"I wanted to pick up a few shirts." Which was a complete lie. "Mind if I come in?"

"It's your home." She shrugged and stepped

back. "Don't tell me you're just getting off work."

"No. I was…out with a friend for dinner."

Her brows rose at the same time her lips twitched. "Is that code for a date?"

He didn't know whether to laugh or sigh. She saved him the trouble of having to decide by asking, "Can I take your coat or won't you be staying that long?"

He shrugged out of his suit jacket by way of an answer and handed it to her. While she hung it in the foyer closet, he reached up to loosen his tie. He was unbuttoning his collar when she turned. She averted her gaze.

"Am I making you uncomfortable?"

"No. Well, not as long as you stop with that button," she said bluntly.

"That was the plan." He laughed self-consciously, and then changed the subject. "How's Brice doing?"

"Oh, he's great." Her expression softened at the mention of her son. "And growing like a weed. He's packed on another two pounds since our last visit to the pediatrician."

"And it looks like you've lost that and then some." His gaze meandered down and when interest sparked he told himself it was a natural reaction that had nothing to do with Morgan personally.

"I've been trying," she admitted. "I have an entire wardrobe I'm eager to fit back into. You may not believe this, but I do own more than baggy shirts." She tugged at the hem of the one she was wearing.

"You look good even in that."

Her cheeks turned pink. "Can I get you a drink or something?"

"I wouldn't mind a Scotch and soda." When her brow wrinkled, he said, "I'll get it myself."

He walked to the wet bar tucked to one side of the room. Though he wasn't much of a drinker, he kept it fully stocked. After filling a glass with ice and soda, he added a shot of Scotch. When he turned, she was seated on the sofa, feet tucked up beneath her, some papers spread out in front of her. Sheet music.

"What are you doing?" he asked, coming around the side of the couch.

"Trying to come up with song selections for a couple of my more advanced students."

That had him puzzled. "You're working?"

She glanced up. "At the south-side community center I told you about."

"But I thought you agreed not to take the job?"

"No. I agreed not to leave your apartment until your parents arrive home from Europe."

"But what about the baby?" he asked.

"Brice comes with me. It's only a few hours in the afternoon." She smiled. "He tends to sleep through most of it, even my beginner students. But when he doesn't there's no shortage of people eager to hold him. The kids adore him and so does the staff."

Her explanation baffled him even more. "I don't understand why you're doing this. You shouldn't be working right now, Morgan."

"I need to. My bank account isn't as flush as yours, which is why I'm still sending out résumés looking for a full-time teaching position."

"But you just had a baby."

"Even women whose jobs afford them a paid maternity leave would be back to work by now," she pointed out. As the soon-to-be head of a Fortune 500 company, he knew this, of course. "If I were still at a school, of course, I would have the rest of the summer off. But working at the community center isn't so bad. Actually, I find it quite satisfying, even if the instruments could all use an overhaul."

"No baby grands?"

"Nope. Not a one. The grant money the center receives only goes so far. I moved my upright piano from storage to the center just so I would have something decent to play."

"Why go to the trouble?"

"The kids." Her eyes lit up. "I've never had such interested students. Some of them come from really disadvantaged backgrounds and dysfunctional homes and yet they are every bit as enthusiastic about music as I am. That makes them a joy to teach."

"You really mean that."

She frowned. "Of course, I do." The baby began to cry then. She rose with a sigh. "Excuse me."

While Bryan waited for her to return, he sipped his drink and paced around the penthouse, noting the new touches she'd added. A floral arrangement sat on a richly patterned runner in the center of his dining-room table. He'd never eaten dinner in that room, he realized. When he ate in the penthouse, he'd either sat on a stool at the kitchen island or taken his meal into the living room to watch television. He missed family meals, the kind where everyone gathered around the table and actually communicated. He hadn't had that with his wife. After Caden was born, Bryan had thought maybe things would change. Of course, they *had* changed, just not how he'd expected or hoped.

Back in the living room he noticed a trio of fat scented candles on the fireplace mantel. They weren't just for show. Their wicks had been burned. He imagined how the room would look, awash in only their light. Cozy. Intimate. Romantic.

He took another sip of his beverage and moved on. A framed picture on one of the side tables caught his eye. In it Morgan was flanked by an older couple. She was wearing a black robe and mortarboard, clutching a diploma and grinning madly. He picked it up to study it. She looked ready to conquer the world.

"That was taken at my college graduation."

He turned to find her standing behind him. He hadn't heard her return. Instead of feeling awkward about snooping—could one snoop in his own home?—he was curious.

"Are these your parents?"

"Yes." She took the photograph from his hands, swallowing hard as she stroked their faces with the pads of her thumbs. In contrast to the radiant woman in the picture, the one standing in front of him was sad. "They were so proud of me."

"You mentioned that they were gone."

"Yes, both of them."

"Sorry," he said as she put the photo back in its place. Then he motioned with his hands. "You've added a few things to the room since you've been here, I see."

"I hope you don't mind."

"No. I like what you've done. It looks nice." In fact, it looked inviting, which was why even though he should be going, he found himself in no hurry to leave.

"Why haven't you?" At his baffled expression, she added, "Made this space more personal."

He shrugged. "I don't know. I guess I just don't see the need."

"But you've lived here for three years. Ever

since your divorce." At his raised eyebrows she said, "Britney told me that."

He walked over to the couch and took a seat. He'd have to have a talk with his secretary. "What else did Britney say?"

"Not nearly enough to satisfy my curiosity," she admitted baldly. "Why don't you tell me the rest?"

"There's really not much to tell. I was married for a few years, but in the end it didn't work out, so we went our separate ways." He shrugged, even though it was hardly that simple.

Morgan settled onto the cushion next to his. "Is she one of those reasons you spoke of before? For being the way you are today?"

He sipped his drink before answering. "Yes." A single word, yet he felt as if he had just bared his soul.

"She hurt you," Morgan said. It wasn't a question, but a statement. "I'm sorry."

Bryan wasn't comfortable with her sympathy, especially because, when one got right down to it, his brother had done quite a number on her as well.

"I've gotten over it."

"Have you?"

Where a moment ago he'd been in no hurry to leave, now he stood. "I should be going. You…you're probably tired."

"Too close for comfort?" she asked. "You only need say as much. You don't need to run off."

"I'm not running." He forced himself to sit again. Then, feeling ridiculous, admitted, "Okay, I'm not comfortable talking about it. It wasn't a pleasant experience."

"I don't imagine the end of a marriage ever is, regardless of the circumstances involved. Are you sure you don't want to talk about it? I've been told I'm a good listener."

God help him, he almost did. He'd kept it bottled up inside for so long. But he shook his head, unnerved by this sudden desire to share. "No. Thanks."

"Okay, but the offer stands."

Out of the blue, he heard himself ask, "Did you love him?"

She glanced away, her cheeks turning pink even before she admitted, "I only knew him for a week."

Seven days and as many nights. Bryan's stomach clenched.

"Some people fall in love at first sight, or so they claim."

Her gaze reeled back to his. "Is that what you want to hear?" she asked. "That I saw Dillon across a crowded room and—*bam!*— lost my heart to him?"

"Yes. No!" His hands were fisted at his sides. He loosened them, shrugged. "It doesn't matter. Your relationship with Dill is no more my business than the relationship I had with him is yours."

That was the end of it, he thought. Discussion over. But Morgan said quietly, "Just for the record, I'm not…promiscuous."

Her face flamed red, giving her words even greater credence. Guilt nipped at Bryan as his thoughts turned to the probe he'd initiated into her background a few weeks back. Call it off, his gut told him. Get the facts, his head insisted. It wasn't like him to be so damned indecisive.

He shoved a hand through his hair. "Dill could be irresistible," he allowed.

"Yes, well, I'm usually pretty good at resisting, but I was at a low point in my life. A really low point. It's not an excuse for my behavior," she said quickly. "But it is a fact."

"Do you regret it?"

"How can I? I have Brice," she reminded him. "If I regret my actions, I'd have to regret him. And I don't. He's the best thing that's ever happened to me."

He swallowed, nodded. "I'll go now."

"Your clothes."

"I'll get them another time." As he started toward the door, he admitted, "I shouldn't have come in the first place."

"Why did you, then?" Morgan asked.

In the foyer, she retrieved his coat from the closet and handed it to him. Their fingers brushed, the contact fleeting. It sent shock waves through him just the same. Need built, both dangerous and exciting. Why had he come? Suddenly, he knew.

"I shouldn't have," he said again.

But she was just as persistent. "Why?"

"You don't want to know, Morgan."

"Yes, I do."

"Because of this."

He dropped the coat to the floor and cupped her face in his hands, drawing her to him even as he leaned down. His mouth was impatient, greedy. Hers was pliant, giving. So much so that even though the kiss began as an almost furious assault, it was an apology, an entreaty by the time it ended.

They stared at one another, their labored breaths seeming to echo off the marble floor. And because all he wanted to do was reach for her again, he scooped up his jacket, yanked open the door and left.

Morgan couldn't believe he'd kissed her. For that matter, she couldn't believe the way she'd responded. How could she expect him to accept her claim that she wasn't promiscuous when she'd welcomed—indeed, reveled in—every second of their intimate contact?

But while she stood in the empty foyer and waited for shame to wash over her, it never came. And when she lay in bed later that night, still too keyed up to sleep, the only regrets she felt were that Bryan still didn't completely trust her and that she hadn't experienced this kind of white-hot attraction for her baby's father.

CHAPTER FIVE

THE following week passed without a word from Bryan, and then a second one did, too. She wasn't sure whether to be grateful or disappointed. She still grew warm every time she recalled that kiss, and, God knew, she thought of it often enough.

Did he?

She managed to push that question to the recesses of her mind only to have it spring front and center again when he called her on Friday evening.

"Morgan, it's Bryan," he said unnecessarily. It wasn't as if she had many callers, let alone a male one with such a deep and sexy voice. "Are you free tonight?"

The question startled her, so it took her a moment to answer. In fact, she didn't answer. She asked a question of her own. "Why?"

"There's something we need to discuss."

That sounded ominous and made her only a little more nervous than the thought that he might be asking her out. Maybe her reaction to his kiss had finally prompted Bryan to seek a paternity test.

"Have you eaten yet?"

She glanced at her watch. It was nearly seven o'clock. "Two hours ago. If a bowl of cereal can be considered dinner."

There was a slight pause. Then he said, "I could pick up Chinese food on my way over. There's a great place just around the corner from the penthouse. Interested?"

Though she wasn't quite sure what to make of his offer, she said, "I like chicken and peapods, skip the egg roll and fortune cookie, and make sure to get white rice instead of fried."

She thought she heard him chuckle. "I'll see you in half an hour."

Unfortunately, he was as good as his word, arriving on her doorstep just as she finished feeding Brice, who'd sent up a squeal almost as soon as she'd hung up the phone. That meant she hadn't had a chance to do anything with her appearance. She was still wearing the loose-fitting tank-style dress she'd put on to go to the center. Her hair was pulled back in a clip at her nape, although several curls had made their escape and whatever makeup she'd put on that morning was long gone.

The baby was in her arms when Morgan opened the penthouse door. Bryan's gaze drifted to the infant, the tight line of his mouth softening. Was it because he saw his brother there? More and more, Morgan thought she caught glimpses of Dillon or some trait that surely was more Caliborn than Stevens.

Or was Bryan recalling that the last time the two of them had stood in the foyer, they'd kissed? His gaze was on her now—specifically, on her mouth. She waited, certain he was going to bring it up. But he didn't and she didn't know whether to be relieved or disappointed. Did that mean she was the only one who'd spent time obsessing over that earth-shattering lip-lock?

He ended the potent silence by holding up a brown paper bag. "Shall we eat in the kitchen?"

She nodded. "No sense breaking out the fine china for takeout."

Morgan retrieved Brice's bouncy seat from the bedroom and joined Bryan as he set the granite-topped island with two plates and cutlery.

Glancing up, he asked, "Can I get you something to drink?"

"That's all right. I'll get it." She set Brice in the seat and poured herself a glass of milk. "Do you want some or would you prefer— what was it?—Scotch and soda?"

"I'll just have water tonight."

She waited till they were seated to say, "So, what did you need to discuss?"

"A couple of things, actually." He selected one of the cartons and forked out some white rice. "First, Windy City Industries would like to make a donation to the community center."

She blinked in surprise. "That's very generous. They'll be thrilled with any amount, I'm sure."

"Not money. Well, not directly anyway. Your supervisor will be notified, but basically you'll need to make up a list of the instruments you require for the after-school program you teach. We'll see to it that whatever is on the list is purchased and gets delivered as soon as possible."

"Bryan, I don't know what to say. Other than thank you, of course." She beamed at him. "You have no idea what a tremendous gift you're giving these children."

He brushed her gratitude aside. "It's not me, Morgan. The donation is coming from Windy City Industries. We believe in being community-minded and supporting worthwhile causes. I thought an after-school music program for at-risk kids was just such a cause and passed the recommendation to the appropriate people at the company to make the final judgment. They notified me today of the gift."

"Well, pass my thanks along to Windy City then." She smiled at him. He might try to distance himself from the donation, but they both knew he was responsible.

"And now to the other matter." He cleared his throat. "Unless their plans change, my parents will be returning from France the Friday after next."

"Oh." She gulped and a peapod nearly stuck in her throat. The hour of reckoning would soon be at hand.

"I'll make the appropriate arrangements once they arrive and settle in," he said.

Then Morgan's eyes widened as another thought crossed her mind. "You'll need your apartment back."

That had been the deal they'd struck when she'd agreed to stay. She'd been paying him for the privilege, not that he'd cashed the checks she'd made out to his name.

"There's no hurry," he said.

Morgan set her fork aside. She'd been looking for a new place, and had a couple of leads on efficiencies that were in her price range. It was time to get off the fence and put down a deposit.

"When do you need me to leave?"

"Whenever," he answered vaguely.

"Don't tell me you're enjoying staying in your boyhood room?" she teased.

He merely shrugged. "Actually, my parents have a guest house at the back of their property. Dill lived there on and off. I've been using it while you've been here. It's quite comfortable, especially since there's a pool and hot tub practically outside my door."

"Well, as long as you're sure I'm not putting you out." She picked up her fork again and pushed a piece of chicken around on her plate.

"Britney mentioned the commute when Brice and I first moved in here."

He frowned. "Britney talks too much."

"I probably shouldn't say this, but she's got a serious case of the hots for you."

It might have been a trick of the lighting, but she thought he blushed. Regardless, he didn't look comfortable. "Beyond the fact that I'm her boss, and not in the market for either a sexual-harassment suit or a serious relationship, she's not my type."

"She said the same thing about me." Morgan wanted to kick herself as soon as the words left her lips; instead she plowed ahead. "What is your type?"

His gaze was steady, piercing, actually. It probably scared most people witless, but Morgan didn't blink. He was good at pushing people away, but she was even better at hauling them close. She came by the talent naturally. Her father had been a pro at getting her to open up and share her feelings.

After a moment, he picked up his napkin. Folding it into smaller squares, he said quietly, "I used to know what I wanted. Now I'm not so sure."

She knew exactly what he meant. Tall, dark and brooding had never been her ideal. Although lately…

He pulled her from her musing by saying, "About the penthouse. Don't worry about packing up for the time being. You're not putting me out. As for my parents, I'll get together with them as soon as they've recovered from jet lag, explain everything and set up a meeting."

"I'd prefer that you set up a visit," she corrected. "A meeting implies business. Business, to me anyway, implies money. I want it to be clear that's not what I'm after. I want a family for my son. Specifically, grandparents, since both of my folks are gone." She tilted her head to one side. "I also wouldn't mind an uncle, since as an only child I can't provide Brice with one of those. Do you understand?"

God help him, he was starting to. More of the old distrust melted away. Morgan was so real and pragmatic. Her feet were planted firmly on the ground. She took on the yoke of responsibility without complaint. He couldn't help wondering, he couldn't help asking, "What in the hell did you see in my brother?"

Her eyes widened. "I…I…"

"Don't answer that question!" Bryan stood so quickly he knocked over his water. The glass cracked and water sloshed across the granite before spilling over the edge and forming a puddle at his feet.

Morgan was up in an instant, grabbing a dish towel to mop up the mess on the island. When she bent down, he knelt beside her, his hand over hers on the towel. "Don't answer the question," he said again, this time more softly. "It came out wrong. For all of my brother's faults, he was a good man."

And Bryan missed him. God, how he missed him.

"I believe that, too." They both stood. "And, since I would love to hear you talk about him more and, you know, share the kinds of things I can pass along to Brice, I'm relieved you feel that way."

He waited until she returned from dumping the soaked towel and broken glass in the sink, to ask, "Why wouldn't I?"

She settled back onto her stool. "Well, the name thing for one. Some people would have been upset about that, especially since I get the feeling it wasn't a one-time occurrence."

"No, it wasn't." He sighed and sat as well. "When he was killed in Vail, the police first notified my parents that I was dead. Since I was having dinner with them at the time, we all realized what must have happened. Still, we held out hope that it was all just a big mistake and that Dill would come waltzing through the door."

"I'm so sorry."

"I flew to Vail to make a positive ID." His chest ached as he recalled the shock of seeing his brother's body on a cold metal slab at the morgue.

"My God! How horrible."

"Yeah, but better me than my mother or father. No parent should have to go through that."

"No parent should have to lose a child, period."

The ache in his chest intensified. There was more than one way to be robbed of that joy. She laid a hand on his arm. How was it possible that such a simple touch could offer so much comfort?

"You're probably wondering why Dillon did what he did." When Morgan nodded slowly, he decided to tell her. She had a right to know. "He was pretty much broke."

If the news disappointed her, it didn't show. Her expression never wavered.

"He had a trust fund, a sizeable one, left to him by our grandparents, same as I did. I invested most of mine. He spent his. Most of it was gone by the time he got out of college."

"Didn't he work?" She did look disappointed now.

"He had a position at the company." Their father would have gladly made Dill a vice president if he'd shown any interest or initiative. "He showed up sometimes, but he didn't put in regular hours. Dill was… He never really grew up."

"And so you let him use your identity and spend your money?" Her tone held an odd mix of disbelief and censure.

"He was my brother. I looked out for him." Guilt nudged Bryan as he recalled that final phone message he'd left. Perhaps that's why his voice was hoarse when he added, "I'd been looking out for him since we were kids."

"Maybe that's why he never grew up," Morgan answered quietly. "He never had to deal with the consequences of his actions."

Anger came fast. Bryan welcomed it since it not only chased away the grief and guilt he felt over his brother, it corralled his wayward interest in this woman who was off-limits to him. She was his late brother's conquest. The mother of Dillon's child.

"I don't recall asking for your analysis," Bryan snapped, even though he knew she'd merely said aloud what he sometimes thought. That between his parents and himself they'd made it too easy for Dill.

"I'm sorry," she said. "You're right. I didn't mean to be judgmental. We all have flaws and, as you said, despite those, Dillon was a good man." Her gaze veered to Brice. "That's what I'll make sure my son understands about his father."

"Thank you."

"You've never held him, you know."

Bryan didn't feign ignorance, rather he ignored the question, forking up a bite of sweet and sour pork instead.

"What is it about him that makes you hold back?" Morgan persisted.

God, the woman was blunt. He knew hardened dealmakers who weren't as adept at going for the jugular. Brice came to Bryan's aid. Without any fussing at all, he spat up all over his pajamas.

Morgan crinkled her nose. "Sorry about that. We're working on his table manners."

"That's all right."

She tipped her head to one side. "You're really not grossed out."

"He's a baby."

"A lot of men would be, unless they're dads themselves." Morgan used her napkin to mop up what she could before scooping the baby out of the seat. It was just as well she wasn't looking at Bryan. Her offhand comment had landed a direct hit.

After she left the kitchen, Bryan picked up his plate and dumped his uneaten dinner down the garbage disposal. His appetite was gone, obliterated by a powerful and confusing mix of emotions. He decided to leave before she started asking more questions that he didn't want to answer. Questions whose answers he was no longer sure he knew.

He was on his way to the bedroom to tell her goodbye when a knock sounded on the door. He could hear Morgan talking to Brice in the nursery. Since she was busy and this was still his penthouse, he decided to answer the door.

Courtney was on the other side, wearing a low-cut black dress and stiletto heels. Just what the doctor had ordered in the past, but seeing her crimson lips bow with promise now did nothing for him.

"The doorman said you were home. Hope you don't mind my popping by. I'm celebrating the fifth anniversary of divorce." She held out a bottle of Dom. "Want to join me? I hate drinking alone."

He glanced over his shoulder, nervous for no reason that made sense. "I'm…I was just on my way out, actually."

"Let's stay in for a little while," she coaxed, walking past him into the foyer.

"I can't stay here." He expelled a breath.

"Okay. We can go to my place," she suggested.

Take her up on the offer, he ordered himself. Go and forget about everything for a few hours. That was what he'd done in the past. But he shook his head. "Not tonight."

"Oh? Not in the mood?" There was nothing Courtney found more exhilarating than a challenge. Her brows rose and she set the bottle of champagne and her handbag on the entry table. "Perhaps I can change your mind."

She reached for him, but before her arms wound around his shoulders Bryan trapped her hands in his. He brought them to his lips for a kiss. The gesture wasn't intended to be seductive. It was a goodbye. He could tell she knew it even before he said, "I'm sorry."

She stiffened for a moment, but then was laughing huskily. "Who is she, Bryan? Please tell me it's not that snooty little secretary that glares daggers at me every time I stop by your office."

He really had to do something about Britney. But back to the matter at hand. "She's no one you know."

Courtney pulled away and turned, regarding him in the foyer mirror. She sounded genuinely interested when she asked, "Is she worth it?"

He glanced toward the bedroom. "It's not like that."

Courtney, of course, didn't see it that way. Turning, she said, "It's exactly like that, Bryan, or you'd still be interested in what I have to offer."

"You do have a lot to offer," he replied in lieu of an answer to her initial question.

Taking Courtney's bejeweled hands in his, he raised them to his lips again. This time the kiss he dropped on her knuckles held an apology.

Morgan, however, was the one who said the words aloud. "I'm sorry."

Both he and Courtney turned. Morgan was holding a freshly changed Brice, her eyes wide and assessing, her expression disappointed. In him?

"Oh, my," Courtney told Bryan. "Now I can see why you said 'not here.'"

"Courtney Banks, this is Morgan Stevens. She's my…she's my late brother's…." He motioned with his hand, not sure what word to use to fill in that last blank.

The baby in Morgan's arms apparently clarified things for Courtney. "Ah. I see."

"I didn't mean to interrupt," Morgan said. She would no longer meet Bryan's eye. "I just wanted to tell you that I'm going to put Brice down."

"I was just going anyway," Bryan said. Why did he feel like such a heel? He had nothing to hide. He'd done nothing wrong. The kiss he and Morgan had shared came to mind. *Liar*.

"Well, thanks for the takeout. It was nice to meet you, Courtney."

"The same here." Courtney gathered up the champagne and her handbag.

He wasn't leaving with her, but Bryan knew that was exactly what it looked like. Maybe that was for the best. "I'll call you when I hear from my parents," he told Morgan.

Her forced smile was the last thing he saw before closing the penthouse door.

"I'll see you to your car," Bryan said to Courtney as they stepped into the elevator.

She was quiet during the ride to the lobby. He appreciated her silence. He didn't want to answer questions right now. He walked her to her car, a sleek red foreign number that was parked in the fire lane.

"You're lucky you haven't been ticketed or towed," he remarked.

"I like to live dangerously," she said with a delicate shrug of her shoulders. Then, more seriously, she added, "Take care, Bryan. Don't let her hurt you."

"She's…we're not in the kind of relationship that allows for one to be hurt."

"But you'd like to be."

He opened the car door for her and ignored the comment. "I can't be hurt, Courtney."

"Sure you can. We both can be. By the right person. And we were in the past, which is why we've sought out one another's company these past few years. It's been safe."

"It's been more than *safe*," he pointed out in an effort to soften their goodbye.

Courtney's laughter was bawdy as she slipped into the driver's seat. "Well, that goes without saying. We've had some good times. I may even miss you." She pointed back toward his building. "If things don't pan out the way you're hoping, be sure to call me. The Dom will be gone by then, but I'll spring for a new bottle."

He smiled, but made her no promises. After his divorce he'd stopped making promises to women. Or maybe he just hadn't met a woman who'd changed his mind. Until now.

CHAPTER SIX

MORGAN grew anxious waiting for Bryan to call. Not, she assured herself, because she felt he owed her an explanation as to how he could kiss her so passionately and fail to mention he had a girlfriend—a gorgeous, perfectly coiffed, perfectly proportioned girlfriend who looked as though she'd just stepped out of the pages of a fashion magazine. No, she wanted to know if he'd spoken to his parents and how they had taken the news about Brice.

Already she'd been apprehensive about meeting the Caliborns. She was doubly so now. She'd conceived a child with one of their sons during a brief fling in Aruba, and now, just months after giving birth, she found herself disturbingly attracted to the other one.

What would they see when they looked at

her? A conniving gold digger? An opportunist? Someone of low moral character?

What would they see when they looked at her son? Would they too question Brice's paternity, perhaps even demand a test? It still surprised her that Bryan hadn't done so yet, because even though his attitude seemed to have softened, he remained detached from the baby.

By the time the following Friday rolled around, she was a bundle of nerves, though it helped to be busy at the community center, so she'd stayed late to help a young girl practice scales. Carla was ten and had just signed up for the program the week before. She was shy and introverted, but, like the other kids, eager to learn.

The girl's fingers stumbled over the keys of Morgan's old upright. Carla missed a couple of notes, went back to find them and winced when the wrong ones came out.

"Sorry."

"Don't apologize. Just do it again. Practice is the only difference between you and me. I've had years of it."

"You think I can be as good as you someday?"

"Maybe even better if you stay with it. Remember to invite me to see you play Carnegie Hall."

"Have you played there?"

"Twice. Now play."

The girl flashed Morgan a grin and started again, this time finishing with only a couple of minor mistakes. In his car seat on the floor next to the piano, Brice let out a delighted squeal when Carla was done.

"See, even the baby thinks you've improved."

"Thanks, Ms. Stevens. I appreciate the extra help."

"Don't mention it. It's been my pleasure. Is someone coming to pick you up?"

"My mom. She told me to wait for her at the front door so she doesn't have to find a parking space."

"Okay. Have a good weekend."

Morgan stood and gathered up some sheet music from a nearby stand. When she turned, Bryan was leaning against the jamb of the door through which Carla had exited. His suit coat was slung over one shoulder and he was watching her with dark, unreadable eyes that left her feeling far too exposed.

"How long have you been standing there?"

"Long enough. Carnegie Hall twice, hmm? You must be very good."

She lifted her shoulders in lieu of an answer. "Are you here for a lesson?"

"That depends."

"On what?" she asked.

"On what you're offering to teach me."

His reply raised gooseflesh on her arms. Morgan cleared her throat and glanced away. "In addition to the piano I play the oboe and clarinet. I'm passable on sex—*sax*."

His brows rose at the Freudian slip, but Morgan noted thankfully that he let it go without comment. He pushed away from the doorjamb and came fully into the room. "My parents are home. I spoke to them last night. They're eager to see Brice and to meet you, too, of course."

Nothing like being tacked on as an afterthought to make one feel welcome, Morgan groused internally.

Brice cooed and Bryan's gaze shifted to the baby, who was batting his chubby fists against a string of colorful rings that Morgan had draped over the carrier's handle. Bryan's expression softened. She saw him swallow hard before glancing away. Did he see his brother in the baby? Was he missing him? Could it be that that was why he sometimes seemed so sad when he looked at Brice? Now wasn't the time to ask such questions, though. Other ones needed to be answered first.

"When do your parents want to meet me? And where?"

He laid his coat on top of the piano and sat down on the bench. "They're leaving that up to you."

That news had Morgan slumping down next to him. The bench was small. Their hips bumped. She could smell his cologne. It was the same scent he'd worn the day he'd kissed her. She was inhaling deeply, even as she tried to focus on the matter at hand.

"The sooner—"

"The better," he finished for her. His gaze was locked on her mouth. She swore he leaned closer for a moment, before he pushed to his feet and took a few steps away. "That's what my parents said, too."

"How about next Saturday?" That would give her a week to rehearse what she was going to say and to find something suitable for her and Brice to wear.

"That leaves where."

"Well, I can't very well invite them to your apartment. Of course, they probably know I'm staying there since you're living in their guesthouse."

"Yes. They think I'm chivalrous."

"I can only imagine what they think of me," she remarked dryly. She turned on the bench and played the opening chords to one of her favorite concertos. "I suppose we could have dinner at a restaurant, although that seems a little impersonal. Not to mention that we wouldn't be able to talk freely without the risk of being overheard." She sent a smile in his direction and added, "My name may not be as well known as your family's, but I'm every bit as eager as you are to keep it out of the tabloids."

"In that case, I suggest that you and Brice come to my parents' estate."

She stopped playing. "You want me to invite myself to their home? Gee, should I tell your mother what to serve for lunch, too?"

He surprised her with a chuckle. "If you'd like."

"I'm serious, Bryan."

"So am I. Outside of my penthouse, the location makes the most sense."

She sighed, because he was right. "Okay."

"I'll set it up." He tucked his hands in his trouser pockets. "Are you heading home now?"

She nodded. "You?"

"I was thinking of stopping off for dinner first. Meal preparation isn't included with my new accommodations."

She smiled. "Mine either. But I've enjoyed having someone to do the grocery shopping for me. Not to mention the laundry and the housework. I'm getting spoiled."

"Somehow, I doubt that," Bryan replied.

He meant it. A woman who would work for peanuts in a community center teaching underprivileged kids the joy of music wasn't spoiled. That conclusion didn't surprise him as much as the fact that he felt Morgan deserved to be pampered and he wanted to be the one doing it.

His gaze dropped to her lips and he recalled that kiss. He didn't like the feelings that had begun to take root. They were the kind that held the potential to grow, spread and blossom into something that terrified him. His dealings with Courtney had been blissfully straightforward. No ties. No lies. No talk of a shared future. Which was why parting the other night had been managed so easily and so affably. There were no messy emotions to get in the way. No explanations required.

But he heard himself offer one to Morgan now.

"Courtney and I...we're not seeing one another any longer."

"Oh?" Her brows notched up. "I'm sorry."

"Do you mean that?" he asked quietly.

She glanced away. "Of course I do. She seemed...nice. And she's very pretty. You made a handsome couple."

"Did we?"

"Yes. You're both very..." She lifted her shoulders. "You turn heads."

He wasn't a vain man. Nor was he one who required his ego to be stroked. But he asked, "Turn heads?"

"You have a commanding presence."

He laughed. "Some people just call me intimidating."

"Do you try to be?"

"Sometimes," he admitted. "It has its uses."

She shook her head. "I think it gets in the way of real relationships. How long were you and Courtney together?"

Bryan thought back. "Since just after my divorce was finalized."

"So a few years. It sounds like it was serious."

"No. It wasn't like that. Actually, it was… pretty casual." He frowned.

"Well, I hope my being in your penthouse had nothing to do with your split."

"No." But it did. It had everything to do with it, Bryan realized, because suddenly *pretty casual* wasn't enough. His frown deepened. "I can't figure out what it is about you that…"

"What?"

He left his previous thought unfinished and said instead, "You don't fit into any mold."

"Then why do you keep trying to force me into one?" she asked.

"Habit."

"It's a bad one. Break it." Her gaze held a challenge.

"I don't know if that would be a good idea." He tilted his head to one side.

"Why?"

A million reasons came to mind. The one he offered rose from his subconscious. "You're dangerous, Morgan."

She blinked in surprise. "Dangerous. Me?"

Yes, he thought. From the moment he'd met her she'd been a blight on his peace of mind. He wanted it back. Even more, though, he wanted…her.

He shot to his feet. He should go. Hell, he shouldn't have come. He could have called Morgan with the information about his parents. He could have had Britney call her, for that matter. But he'd wanted to see her and he'd figured a public place was safer than stopping in at his penthouse.

And so was a restaurant, his libido offered slyly. What could happen in a restaurant with a table between them and waiters and other patrons around?

"Would you and Brice like to have dinner with me?" he asked.

"Now?"

"Now."

"I can't. Sorry. I'm nearly out of diapers and he's going to need to nurse soon."

He nodded. "I understand." Just as well, he decided. Just as well.

"May I have a rain check?"

Bryan shrugged. "Sure."

It was hot when he arrived home an hour later. He'd been hungry when he stopped at the community center. He was starving now and it had nothing to do with the fact that he'd skipped dinner.

He bypassed the main house, even though he knew his parents would welcome a visit from him and would gladly ask their cook to whip up a meal. Instead, he headed to the guesthouse and changed into his swim trunks.

A moment later, he was diving into the deep end of the in-ground swimming pool, powerful strokes taking him to the far side in a matter of seconds. Just before reaching it, he flipped and pushed off the wall with his feet. The water was cool on his heated skin and the exertion took the edge off his frustration. When he hoisted himself out of the water twenty minutes later, his mother was holding a towel, which she handed to him.

Julia waited till he'd dried off and caught his breath before asking, "So, did you talk to her?"

"Yes. I suggested that she come here."

His mother nodded. "Good, good. Well, as long as she won't find that too intimidating."

Rough laughter scraped his throat. "I don't think *anything* intimidates that woman."

"Oh?"

He cleared his throat. "We set it up for next Saturday. I didn't pin down a time. I figured I'd ask you what worked best first."

"See if one o'clock is acceptable and tell her we would like her and the baby to come for lunch." She rubbed her hands together in an uncharacteristic show of nerves. "Do you know what she likes to eat?"

His mother's question had him chuckling since it echoed Morgan's earlier comment. "I can ask her if you'd like."

"Yes. Do that. I want everything to be perfect. Oh, my God." She covered her mouth with her hand for a moment. "I still can't believe it."

"Mom," he began, not sure how to proceed. "There's no concrete proof that she's telling the truth."

"Yes, so you mentioned when we first came home and learned that she'd been here since the end of May." Her tone held censure and more than a little hurt. Julia hadn't been happy that he'd kept Morgan and Brice a secret. His father wasn't pleased either, though Hugh at least understood and accepted Bryan's reasoning.

"Why haven't you sought that proof?" she asked now.

All it would have taken was a swab from the inside of Brice's mouth and one from Bryan's. Since Dillon was dead, short of having his body exhumed, that was the only way to establish a link between the baby and the Caliborns.

"The last thing we need is for the press to get wind of our family requesting *another* paternity test," he said tightly. "The slowing economy is already giving our investors enough reasons to worry."

"Very well, but you've met her, Bryan. You've spent time with her and you've seen the baby. Tell me, do you really think she's lying about Dillon being the father of her child?"

"No. Not lying."

"But you think she could be wrong about… the circumstances," Julia allowed.

I'm not promiscuous.

Morgan's words echoed in his head. Nothing

about her suggested otherwise, so why hadn't he called off the investigation? Why wasn't he just accepting she was exactly what she said she was and Brice was who she claimed him to be?

Perhaps because he was scared to death of the attraction he felt for her.

With a muttered oath, he shoved the wet hair back from his forehead. "I don't know what I think anymore, Mom."

Julia laid her hand against his cheek. It was the same hand that had soothed his hurts when he was a kid. As comforting as he still found it, he knew it wasn't going to set things right this time.

"This must be especially hard for you, Bry."

"It's dredged up a lot of memories," he admitted. "None of them very pleasant to recall. Caden turned five a few weeks ago. I still think about him, you know."

"I know."

"The happiest day of my life was the day he was born." He'd been in the delivery room, gaping like a fool as he'd watched the miracle unfold. "I was the first person to hold him when he came into this world," he whispered hoarsely.

And he'd been among the last to learn of his wife's duplicity thanks to the DNA test results that were leaked to the media.

"We loved him, too," his mother reminded him. Julia's voice was filled with the same tangle of emotions that had Bryan's throat aching and his eyes stinging. "What Camilla did to you—what she did to us all—with her lies, it was wrong. More than wrong. It was cruel. But at some point you have to let go of the past and move on. It pains me to see you so lonely."

"I'm not lonely," he protested.

This was the second time in recent weeks that he'd been labeled as such, the second time he'd been told he needed to move on. He didn't like it.

His mother patted his cheek again, smiling sadly, and even though she didn't say a word, it was clear she didn't believe him.

CHAPTER SEVEN

FOR the next week, Morgan dragged poor Brice into half the stores in Chicago looking for an appropriate outfit to wear when meeting the Caliborns. Nothing in her closet would do. Well, except for the dress that Britney had selected for Morgan to wear home from the hospital in case a picture got snapped. She was averse to it for obvious reasons.

Besides, she'd lost more weight and a few more inches from her waist. She wanted to make the most of it. She owed her improved figure to yoga and running. Not the kind of running that involved lacing up high-performance shoes and heading out into the late August heat. Rather the kind involved in being a single, working mother whose car had decided it needed a rest. The ancient compact had started stalling out regularly a couple weeks earlier.

Usually, after a couple of minutes, it was kind enough to start back up, so she'd put off taking it in. Today, the engine had whined copiously and refused to switch on again. Now it was at a garage being worked on by a mechanic named Vic, whom Morgan hoped wasn't going to try to pad out the price of repairs just because she was female.

She shoved that thought from her mind. She had more important things to worry about, such as what she was going to wear to meet the parents of the now-dead man who had fathered her child. Outfitting Brice had been easy and affordable. As a shower gift one of the other teachers had given her an adorable sailor suit. It was in a bigger size, but he'd grown enough to wear it. Finding something for herself was proving far more frustrating.

All she knew from her brief conversation with Bryan earlier in the week was that his parents were expecting her and Brice at one o'clock on Saturday at their Lake Forest home. Lunch would be served in the garden, weather permitting. Somehow she doubted they were going to gather around a picnic table and eat franks and beans. More likely, the Caliborns would serve fancy little finger sandwiches stuffed with things like cucumbers, alfalfa sprouts and watercress.

"I don't think I like watercress," she muttered as she rummaged through the clearance racks in Danbury's.

It was the third department store she'd been to this day and it would be the last since she had to work later that afternoon. Without her car, she and Brice would be taking the El before transferring to a bus and then hoofing it three blocks to the community center.

From the final rack, Morgan pulled out a yellow sundress. Holding the hanger just below her chin, she asked Brice, "What do you think? The price is right at half off."

He yawned up at her from the stroller before smacking his lips together, clearly unimpressed.

"You're right. The color will make my skin look sallow."

Sighing, she put it back. Another two hours wasted. Or maybe not, she thought, spying the moss-colored suit on a mannequin in the department across the aisle. The jacket was short and fitted with three-quarter-length sleeves and double rows of mother of pearl buttons. The skirt flowed slightly away from the body for a fit that was sure to flatter her post-pregnancy curves without drawing too much attention to the ones she was still working to erase. She steered Brice over to it and then held her breath as she reached for the price tag.

"Oh, my God!" She swallowed. She almost prayed she was right when she said, "They probably don't have my size anyway."

They did.

"It probably won't look good on me," she said.

"Can I put that in a fitting room?"

Morgan turned to find a saleswoman standing behind her. "I—I—" With a sheepish smile, she nodded.

Not only did it fit, it looked fabulous, if she did say so herself. Even Brice gurgled happily as she modeled it in front of the changing room's trifold mirror. Of course, his exuberance may have been the result of gas since he belched loudly afterward.

"How are you doing in there?" the saleswoman asked from outside the door.

"Great. It fits and I love it. But I have one

problem." Other than the price tag. Morgan stared at her reflection. "I need shoes."

She wound up walking out of the store with more than the outfit and a pair of pricy peep-toe heels. She also purchased a new handbag and had made an appointment in the store's salon for the following day. She wasn't even going to think about how much she'd just put on the charge card she kept for emergency purposes.

But late that night, as Brice slept in his crib, Morgan sat at the kitchen table sipping a cup of herbal tea and balancing her checkbook. She'd come home to a message from the mechanic working on her car. The repairs were going to total just a little less than the amount she'd plunked down in Danbury's, meaning she would have to tap the emergency credit card again.

With a sigh, she ran the numbers a second time. In the very near future she was going to have to get a real job, a full-time position that included benefits and a pension. That made her sad. She really enjoyed sharing her love of music with the kids at the center and she felt they got something out of the experience, too.

* * *

Normally, Bryan wouldn't answer his cell phone during dinner, but when he noted the call-back number he excused himself from the table with an apologetic glance toward his mother and walked to his father's study. It was Gil Rogers, the private detective he'd hired to look into Morgan's background. He'd left a message for the man earlier in the day.

"Gil, thanks for returning my call."

"You said it was important."

"Yes. I—I decided I don't need a background check on Ms. Stevens after all. It goes without saying that I'll pay you for your services so far."

"Are you sure?" The detective chuckled then. "Never mind. I guess it makes sense. If it weren't for the baby I'd wonder if the woman wasn't a candidate for a convent. Other than a couple of boyfriends in college and an occasional date, she doesn't appear to have been involved in any serious relationships."

"So she wasn't seeing anyone else around the time the baby was conceived?"

"Not according to the people I spoke with." Gil paused. "I did learn something else, not that it has much bearing on her child's paternity, but I thought you might find it interesting."

"Go on."

"Both of her parents are dead."

"Yes, I know."

"They died together at their home in Brookside. Carbon monoxide poisoning, according to the news clips I was able to dig up. Investigators blamed it on a faulty furnace vent."

"God." The information came as a shock. He sank onto the sofa as he processed it.

"Miss Stevens found them," the detective was saying. "Her folks were still in their bed. Apparently they'd gone to sleep the night before and just never woke up. The story I read included a photograph of her collapsing in the arms of one of the firefighters who'd arrived on the scene. She looked pretty distraught."

Bryan closed his eyes, imagining how it must have been for Morgan and aching on her behalf.

I have no one.

She'd said that all those months ago when she'd gone into labor in his office. How horribly true her statement turned out to be.

"When did this happen?"

"A year ago last spring," Gil replied.

The information jogged Bryan's memory.

More pieces of the puzzle fell into place. She would have been in Aruba just months after burying her parents. Alone, sad…vulnerable.

I was at a low point in my life. A really low point. It's not an excuse for my behavior. But it is a fact.

Bryan recalled her words that day in his penthouse. Unlike Dill, who had made excuses for everything, Morgan wasn't willing to fall back on one, even a very good one. Just as she hadn't claimed to have fallen in love with his brother, nor had she tried to gain Bryan's sympathy. Rather, she'd taken full responsibility for winding up pregnant and alone.

He thought about the check she'd written him for the use of his penthouse. Although he'd destroyed it, she'd sent him two more since then, presumably to cover each month's rent. His brother had used Bryan's name and charged his good time to Bryan's accounts. Morgan wasn't even willing to accept his hospitality.

Perhaps because she sensed his reticence.

"No more," Bryan murmured.

"Excuse me?"

"As I said, I no longer require your services," he told Gil.

"I understand, sir. But I've still got inquiries out with several people. The community where she taught in Wisconsin is pretty close-knit. It's been hard to get many people to talk. Do you want to wait until I've heard back from them?"

"No. As I said, I'll pay you for your time and trouble."

"All right." Gil's tone was reluctant. "I'll mail you a written report along with an invoice."

Bryan flipped his phone closed and tossed it on his father's desk. Then he poured himself a drink from the decanter of Scotch on the adjacent credenza. He drank it in a single gulp, closing his eyes as the liquor burned its way down his throat.

"Bryan?" His mother stood in the doorway, her concern obvious. "What is it? What's wrong?"

He was wrong.

He'd felt that way for a while now, but he had been too stubborn to admit it. He'd allowed the lies of the past to blind him to the truth of the present.

He stared at his empty glass in his hand, an idea germinating. Finally, he said, "Nothing that can't be put right."

Morgan didn't expect Bryan to come into the city to collect her and Brice on Saturday, but when he called Friday evening to tell her when he'd arrive at the penthouse, she didn't argue. Her car supposedly was repaired, but she wasn't willing to press her luck on this day of all days. Besides, she was too nervous to drive.

When the doorbell pealed, her heart was racing. Then she opened the door, saw Bryan and she swore it stopped beating. She'd always found him imposing and dangerously hand-some. Today, in place of the corporate attire she associated with him, he wore tan slacks and a white oxford-cloth shirt open at the throat. He looked younger and far less formidable than he did wearing his usual pinstripes and power tie.

He smiled. She wasn't sure she'd ever really seen him do that. And the word *sexy* got tagged on to her description.

"Wow."

His brows rose in question and she realized she'd uttered the word out loud. As cover for her foolishness, she added, "You're right on time."

"I'm always on time."

"Yes." But she'd been hoping he would be late.

She stepped back to allow him in. When she turned after closing the door, he was watching her. Indeed, he was looking at her as if he'd never seen her before.

"The outfit is new," she said, in case that was the cause for his bafflement. "I felt the occasion called for it. Does it look okay?" Before he could respond, she added, "And just let me say, given what I spent on it, your answer had better be yes."

He didn't smile at her joke. Instead, he said most seriously, "Turn around, Morgan."

Feeling a little ridiculous, she nonetheless managed a slow twirl. "Well?"

"You've done something different with your hair." He made a vague motion with his hand.

"I had it cut. I was due for a new style." The result was a sleeker look that framed her face before flipping up slightly at her shoulders.

"It looks…you look… You're beautiful, Morgan. Stunning, in fact."

He said it the way he said everything: definitively and in a tone that allowed no argument. Not that he was going to get one from her. If the man wanted to call her stunning, who was she to quibble? Unlike Dillon's profuse flattery, Bryan's statement was all the more touching for its rareness. Something stirred in his dark eyes and for a moment she thought— and God help her, hoped—he was going to kiss her again. But then he took a step backward and glanced away.

"We should be going."

The Caliborns' home in Lake Forest boasted more square footage than the elementary school where Morgan had taught in Wisconsin. Given its columned portico and lush landscaping, *grand* was an apt description for it. At the moment, so was *imposing*.

Bryan came around and opened her car door. The gesture wasn't only gentlemanly but practical since she'd made no move to get out. She wasn't a coward, but she briefly considered feigning illness and asking him to take her back to the city. He seemed to understand because he offered his hand to help her out and then gave hers a squeeze of encouragement before releasing it.

"They're good people," he said quietly. "Good people who have suffered some unbearable losses."

Losses. Plural. Before she could ask what he meant, a slender woman of about sixty, wearing work gloves and carrying a trowel, came around the side of the house. She let out a squeal of excitement when she spied them and hurried forward. This was certainly a warm welcome from the gardener, Morgan thought.

"Mom." Bryan's face softened and he leaned down to kiss her when she reached them.

Mom? Morgan had been expecting a Chanel-wearing, diamond-sprinkled matriarch, not this warm and vibrant woman whose lovely face was finely etched from a lifetime of smiles that she apparently had no interest in erasing with Botox. Her hair was solid silver, not white or gray. She wore it short, in a style that flattered her oval face. Eyes every bit as dark as Bryan's dominated that face.

"Here are Morgan and Brice," Bryan was saying. "Morgan, Dillon's and my mother, Julia Caliborn."

"Hello, Mrs. Caliborn." Morgan shifted the baby to the crook of her other arm so she could extend her right hand.

"Call me Julia, please." She extended the trowel before drawing it back with a flustered laugh. "Oh, my. I'm afraid I'm not making a very good first impression. Forgive my appearance," she said to Morgan. To Bryan, she accused, "You're early."

He shook his head, looking mildly amused and all the more attractive for the smile lighting up his eyes. "We're exactly on time, Mom. You just got caught up in your garden again."

"Guilty as charged." She sent Morgan a smile. "I find playing in the dirt a good way to relax. I've been out pulling weeds and pruning plants since breakfast. Being abroad, I missed almost the entire growing season this year. I had someone looking after things here, but my flower beds are in a shambles."

"Unlikely," Bryan said. To Morgan, he added, "My mother is being modest. She's a master gardener and the estate's grounds have been featured in a couple of national publications." His pride was obvious.

Julia waved away his compliments and smiled at Morgan. Then her gaze lowered to the sleeping baby. Her voice was barely above a whisper when she said, "I'd ask to hold him, but I'm a mess at the moment."

She wasn't only referring to her stained clothes, Morgan realized, when Julia's eyes began to fill with tears. One spilled down her cheek and she swiped one away, leaving a smudge of dirt in its place. Morgan's own eyes grew moist. She'd expected this encounter to be emotionally charged for her, but she'd failed to realize how much more so it would be for the Caliborns, given Dillon's death.

"Let's go inside, Mom. Dad can keep us company while you…clean up." He handed her his handkerchief before putting an arm around her shoulders and hugging her to his side as they walked to the front door.

"Your father is probably in his study. Go visit with him while I freshen up. I won't be long."

After Julia excused herself and disappeared up the staircase that curved off from the foyer, Bryan led Morgan through the house, past the living room and formal dining room. Both rooms were every bit as lovely as she'd imagined they would be. They were filled with fine furnishings and stunning artwork, most likely pricy originals rather than reproductions. The rooms didn't appear to be showplaces, but actual living spaces. They exuded comfort and warmth and, Morgan suspected, reflected the home owners' personalities. Very different from Bryan's sterile penthouse.

More of her uneasiness melted away, but it was back in an instant when they entered the study. A man stood at the window with his back to them. He was every bit as tall as Bryan, though not quite as broad through the shoulders. Still, he was physically fit for a man in his sixties. His hair was steel gray and, when he turned, his eyes were the same tawny color Dillon's had been.

"Dad, this is Morgan Stevens. Morgan, my father, Hugh Caliborn."

"It's nice to meet you, sir."

"Morgan." The older man nodded as he stepped forward awkwardly as if not certain whether he should shake her hand or kiss her cheek. Ultimately, he did neither. To Bryan, he said, "Does your mother know you're here?"

"Yes. She came around the side of the house just after we pulled up. She'd been gardening." The two men exchanged knowing looks. "She's upstairs now changing her clothes."

Hugh nodded. Then his gaze dropped to the infant in Morgan's arms. "Bryan tells us that you named the baby Brice Dillon."

"Yes." She held her breath, waited for what, exactly, she wasn't sure.

"It's a nice name." He swallowed.

"I thought so, too."

One side of the older man's mouth crooked up. "He's just a little thing, isn't he?"

"Not so small that he hasn't already managed to take my heart hostage," Morgan mused. She still felt awed by the unprecedented wave of love she'd experienced the first time she'd held him…and every time after that.

"You'll never get it back, you know." Hugh's smile was tinged with the sadness of a father who has outlived a child.

"No," Bryan agreed. The source of his sadness had her puzzled. He cleared his throat then and suggested, "Why don't we all sit down?"

In addition to an expansive desk built of the same wood as the cherry-paneled walls, the room offered seating clustered around a fireplace. Bryan selected one of the oversize armchairs; his father took its twin, leaving Morgan to the sofa. For the next fifteen minutes they talked about inconsequential things such as the weather until Julia, fresh from a shower, joined them.

"Hugh, goodness' sakes, haven't you offered our guest anything to drink?" she chided.

Morgan shook her head. "Oh, no thanks. I'm fine."

"I wouldn't mind a glass of iced tea," Bryan said.

"A fresh pitcher is in the refrigerator. Why don't you bring enough glasses for the rest of us just in case Morgan changes her mind."

Morgan blinked and it took an effort not to allow her mouth to fall open when Bryan rose to do his mother's bidding. Her shock must have been apparent, because after he was gone Julia turned to Morgan and said, "Everything all right, dear?"

"I didn't think anyone told Bryan what to do." She felt her face heat and she cleared her throat. "I mean, it's just that he's so adept at giving orders, I never thought—"

God, she was digging herself a hole. But Bryan's mother was smiling as she sent Hugh a knowing look.

"Bry is much better at giving orders than taking them, which is why I try to give them on a regular basis. Someone has to keep him from becoming too dictatorial." She plucked at the buttons on her blouse as her tone turned nostalgic. "He's always been like that. Not Dillon, though. Instead of making demands, he charmed people to get what he wanted."

Didn't Morgan know it.

"Bryan and Dillon were such different personalities," Hugh agreed. "Sometimes Julia and I wondered if they'd made a pact to be polar opposites just to drive us insane." He chuckled. "Despite their differences, they were thick as thieves. There wasn't anything they wouldn't do for one another."

"It's still so hard to believe Dill's gone." Julia fell silent.

They all fell silent, except for Brice. Before the mood could become too maudlin, he began babbling happily and pumping his fists.

"Looks like you might have a prizefighter on your hands," Hugh said with a chuckle.

"He's an active baby."

"Can I… Would you mind if I held him?" Julia asked.

"Not at all."

Bryan returned to the room just as Morgan was placing Brice in his mother's arms. Morgan wondered what he was thinking as he watched Julia press her cheek to the baby's and close her eyes with a sigh. A moment later, his father was leaving his chair to perch on the arm of the sofa.

"God, it's like looking at Dill all over again, isn't it, Jule?" Hugh's voice was rough with emotion.

"Right down to the little swirling cowlick on his crown." She traced it with a fingertip.

They believed her. Their voices held no doubt, only awe and excitement. Morgan's relief was immense. She'd worried about coming here today and encountering skepticism or at the very least a cool reception. They'd welcomed her and Brice. And now they were accepting them.

From the doorway, the cook announced, "Lunch will be ready in fifteen minutes. Will you still be eating outside?"

"Yes. Thank you, Mae," Julia said. "Bryan,

bring the tray of iced tea. It's too nice outside to stay cooped up in here."

She and Hugh set off with the baby, leaving Morgan and Bryan to follow. On the patio, a scrolled wrought-iron table was already set for lunch with fine china and cloth napkins. Shrubs and plants, many of them past their flowering stage, bounded the sides of the patio and spilled out into the yard. Flagstone paths led from one lush oasis to the next, as well as to a large in-ground pool. Morgan guessed the building beyond it to be the guesthouse where Bryan was staying.

"Your home is beautiful, but this—" She motioned with her arms. "This is breathtaking."

"Thank you," Julia said. "Too bad you missed it when my plants were at their peak." She shot an accusing look in Bryan's direction.

"There's next year," he said quietly.

"Yes. Next year." Julia nodded. "Do you garden, Morgan?"

"No. I lived in an apartment back in Wisconsin. I tried growing geraniums in a pot on my balcony one summer, but they only lasted until the end of June."

"I killed my share of plants, too, before I got

the hang of it," Julia commiserated. She shifted Brice from one arm to the other.

"I can take the baby if you'd like," Morgan offered. "He's small yet, but he gets heavy after a while."

"Oh, no. I'm delighted to hold him." Julia laughed then. "In fact, you might have to pry him out of my arms when you and Bryan leave. You know, if you ever need a night out with friends or a little time to pamper yourself, I'll be happy to watch him for you."

"That's a generous offer."

"There's nothing generous about it. I want to spoil him rotten, as is a grandmother's prerogative." She leaned down to nuzzle Brice's cheek. The baby gurgled in response.

The sweetness of the moment had a sigh catching in Morgan's throat. This is how it would be if her own mother were alive. For the first time since coming to Chicago, she not only felt that she'd made the right choice, but that everything was going to work out. She glanced at Bryan, wondering what he thought of his mother's remark. The pain she saw in his dark eyes came as a surprise.

"Bryan tells us you've been living in his penthouse since the baby was born," Hugh said.

"Yes. I told Bryan it wasn't necessary for him to move out." She colored after saying it, realizing his parents could interpret the statement a couple of ways. "I mean, it's been kind of him to let me stay there, but I could have found another place to live. And I will, of course, now that you're home."

"What does that have to do with anything?" Julia asked. "We've enjoyed seeing so much of Bryan. It's hardly been an imposition for him to stay in the guesthouse."

"I'm relieved to hear you say that, but I think it probably has been an imposition for Bryan, what with the commute and all." Morgan sent him a wry look.

"She's right."

"Bryan!" Julia admonished.

He talked over his mother's objection. "I would prefer to be back in the penthouse, but you needn't look at me as if I'm proposing to throw Morgan and my nephew out on the streets of Chicago to fend for themselves."

Morgan's mouth dropped open. For the first time, he'd called Brice his nephew. For a moment she thought she might have heard him wrong, but when she looked at him there was no mistaking the apology in his gaze. What had prompted his change of heart?

She was so caught up in her thoughts that she missed what else Bryan said, and so it made no sense when Julia clapped her hands together and exclaimed, "That's a great idea! I don't know why I didn't think of it first. What do you say, Morgan?"

"Wh-what?"

"I said, I think you should move in to the guesthouse when I move back to the city," Bryan told her.

"Oh, no. No. I can't do that. You've already been so kind. All of you." She glanced around the table, her gaze lingering on Bryan. "I can't impose on your family's hospitality any longer. It's…it's not right."

"Don't be silly. We'd love to have you and Brice here," Hugh said. "For as long as you want to stay."

"And it will reduce my commute time," Bryan reminded her with a crooked smile.

Julia's argument, however, was the most poignant. "Besides, it's not an imposition. You and Brice are family."

Morgan's mouth fell open as the word

embraced her with all the comfort of a hug. She'd felt so alone, she'd *been* so alone, since losing her parents. Now here were people who had known her for less than an hour offering her not just a place to stay, but a place in their lives.

"Oh, that's…that's so…" Her eyes began to fill, and because she knew it was only a matter of time before she made an absolute fool of herself, Morgan shot to her feet.

She had no idea where she was going, only that she needed a moment of privacy to get hold of her emotions. She followed one of the flagstone paths through a rose-covered arbor, drawn by the soothing sound of rushing water. The pathway opened up to a small waterfall that emptied into a koi pond. Morgan sank down on the nearby stone bench and dropped her head in her hands, giving in to the tears that begged to be shed. When she pulled her hands away, Bryan was standing there.

"I came to see if you were all right."

As he had for his mother earlier, he offered Morgan his handkerchief.

She blotted her eyes—so much for the morning's careful application of mascara and liner—and worked up a smile. "Sorry. I just needed a minute."

"No need to apologize."

"Your mom is very kind and…" She shifted her gaze to the pond. The sight and sound of the water had a soothing effect. Bryan's presence did too. "It's incredibly lonely to be without family. I've got some aunts and uncles and a few cousins I exchange Christmas cards with. But it's not the same."

"No, I don't suppose it is."

Turning toward him, she said, "I never felt cheated to be an only child. My parents were great. Fun, funny. I could tell my mom any-thing, and my dad, he and I…" Her voice trailed off and it was a moment before she could continue. "When my parents were gone it was as if my whole world just stopped having any order. Suddenly, I had no place to be on Sunday afternoons. I had nowhere to go for holidays, no one to call for advice or pep talks."

"That must have been hell."

She swiped away fresh tears. "When I found out I was pregnant with Brice, my first reaction wasn't shock or desperation." She shrugged. "Oh, sure, I wasn't all that excited to become an unwed mother, especially when I found out I was about to lose my job and my health insurance. But part of me was just so relieved that I wasn't going to be alone any more."

"You're not alone, Morgan."

"I know. I have Brice."

"You have more than that." He offered his hand to help her to her feet. Afterward, he didn't let go. His fingers curled through hers. Their palms met. "If you don't want to stay and eat lunch, I'll take you back to the city. My parents will understand."

"No. I'll stay. I finish what I start."

"I've figured that out about you."

The way Bryan was studying her made Morgan feel exposed and self-conscious. Maybe that was why she asked, "What else have you figured out about me?"

"Not nearly enough to satisfy my curiosity," he admitted. "But enough to know I owe you an apology."

"Thanks."

"Shall we?"

He was still holding her hand, the gesture friendly but somehow intimate. Though he merely led her back to the table, Morgan felt a bridge had been crossed.

On the patio, lunch was being delivered. As Mae served grilled salmon sliced over beds of crisp greens and passed out freshly baked hard-crust rolls, a younger, similarly clad woman brought a bassinet out from the house and set it between Morgan's and Julia's seats. It was white and though the wicker appeared somewhat yellowed, the bedding was obviously new.

"Thank you, Carmen." To Morgan, Julia said, "Bryan and Dill slept in this when they were infants. And Caden, too." Julia's face colored and she flashed an apologetic look in Bryan's direction.

Who was Caden?

Morgan didn't ask. Even if she'd wanted to, she didn't get the chance. She and Brice were the topics of interest in this conversation, and so, for the next forty-five minutes she answered Julia and Hugh's questions. It could have had the feel of an interrogation, but it didn't. Indeed, the Caliborns made it easy for Morgan to open up, perhaps because they'd accepted without reservation that her baby was Dillon's son.

The only time she felt awkward was when she talked about what she did for a living. Morgan didn't want her limited financial reserves to color their opinion of her.

"I'm a teacher. Unfortunately, I'm between full-time jobs right now," she admitted.

Bryan had been quiet, though whenever she'd glanced his way, he'd nodded encouragingly. Now he inserted, "Morgan teaches music. She worked in a public school district in Wisconsin, but lost her job due to budget cuts."

"That's a shame, for you as well as for the students. The arts are so underappreciated." Julia's mouth puckered in disdain. "Do you play an instrument then?"

"A few, actually, but mainly the piano."

"And she's passable at the sax." Bryan said it with a straight face, but amusement was evident in his eyes.

God, she hoped she wasn't blushing. Clearing her throat, she said with as much dignity as she could muster, "I was classically trained. My parents had dreams of me becoming a concert pianist, especially after they'd scraped together every penny they had to send me to Juilliard."

"Juilliard?" This from Bryan, who then told his parents, "And she's played Carnegie Hall twice."

"We'd love to hear you play sometime," Julia said.

"I'm afraid I'm pretty rusty at giving concerts. These days, rather than playing Beethoven or Mozart, my time in front of the piano is largely spent helping kids learn notes and scales. I'm working a few hours each weekday afternoon in a community center." She sent a smile in Bryan's direction. "In fact, Windy City Industries recently announced it is making a generous donation of instruments to the center."

Hugh nodded in approval. "Bryan mentioned that at dinner the other evening."

Julia looked puzzled when she added, "He neglected to tell us that you worked there."

"It's a good cause," Bryan said, shrugging.

"A very good cause," Julia agreed. "I'd imagine there are a lot of struggling families for whom private music lessons and quality instruments are beyond reach."

"Exactly. I love it, too. The kids are great, and if it helps keep them off the streets and out of trouble or harm's way, all the better."

"It doesn't pay much, though," Bryan said.

"Bryan, don't be rude," Julia chastised.

Morgan sipped her iced tea. "I'm afraid he's right, which is why I'm still sending out my résumé."

"To schools in the Chicago area?" Julia asked hopefully.

Morgan exhaled slowly. "And elsewhere. The cost of living here is a little more expensive than some of the other communities where I'm applying."

"I have a solution to that," Bryan surprised her by saying. Setting his fork aside, he reached into the back pocket of his pants and pulled out a crinkled envelope. "This is yours."

"What is this?"

"Open it."

Perplexed, Morgan did as he said, and then blinked in shock. Inside the envelope was a check. A check made out to her for the sum of two million dollars.

Bryan watched Morgan's brow wrinkle and confusion infused her expression. Glancing up, she said, "I don't understand."

"It's from Dillon's life insurance policy. He named me his beneficiary."

Shaking her head, Morgan told him, "I can't accept it," and attempted to hand back the check.

He closed his hand around hers. "Yes, you can."

"But it's yours. I don't want money." Her gaze veered to his parents then. "I didn't come here for money. Honestly, that's not…that's not…"

When Bryan squeezed her hand, she stopped talking.

"Morgan, we know that."

"Do you?" The question, dagger-sharp, was directed at him.

"Yes, I do."

Her eyes grew bright and she nodded. "But I still can't take your money."

"It's not my money. By rights, it belongs to Brice. It belongs to my brother's son."

"Bryan's right, Morgan," Julia said.

Hugh was more direct. "Dill was irresponsible when it came to his finances. Money passed through his fingers as quickly as water. Where Bryan invested the trust fund my parents left him, Dillon squandered his. In truth, I'm surprised he thought to take out a life insurance policy. He probably only did it because the father of a girl he dated in college was the principal owner of a large Chicago insurance firm." He coughed, embarrassed. "But whatever the reason, I'm glad he did it. And I agree one hundred percent with Bryan that it should go to Brice."

Morgan turned to Bryan. He was still holding her hand and could feel that she was shaking. "But Dillon named you his beneficiary. He left the money to you."

"He should have left it to Brice. I have to believe if he'd known you were pregnant, he would have. His son is entitled to that money, Morgan."

Put like that, he figured she would agree. Finally, she nodded slowly.

"Okay. For Brice."

"Good. I'll be happy to offer some advice on investments," he told her.

"Investments. Yes. I'd appreciate that." A smile loosened her lips. "I guess I don't have to worry any longer about his college fund."

"It's a wonderful idea to secure his future," Julia said. "But there's nothing wrong with also using some of it in the meantime for day-to-day living expenses, housing, trips and that sort of thing. You won't be spending it on yourself. You'll also be spending it on him."

Bryan could tell she was still struggling with the notion. Most likely because the money in question was to come from his bank account, he decided, when she asked quietly, "Are you sure you're okay with this?"

"Yes." In fact, at that moment, he'd never been more sure of anything.

CHAPTER EIGHT

MORGAN visited with the Caliborns far longer than she'd anticipated. It wasn't obligation that found her there late in the afternoon. It was their warmth and kindness. And, of course, the way they doted on Brice.

"We probably should be going," Bryan said, pushing back from the table.

"I wish this day could last forever." Julia's tone was wistful as she glanced at the baby cooing in the bassinet. "We've enjoyed this visit so much."

"I have, too. We'll get together again soon," Morgan promised.

"We'll look forward to it. It's been a pleasure getting to know you, dear. You're a very nice young woman. Exactly the sort a mother would want for her son."

Morgan smiled, but said nothing. If Dillon were still alive, would they be together now? She doubted it. Before his death, he'd made no effort to contact her. They'd made love, but they'd never spoken of a relationship. Would they have fallen in love, brought together by the shared duties of parenthood? Or, would she have come to Chicago and still wound up damningly attracted to his brother?

"Now that Bryan has given you Dillon's life insurance money, you'll probably want to invest in a home of your own," Hugh said. "But while you're looking, Julia and I still would love for you to stay in our guesthouse."

"Oh, yes. Please say you will," Julia added. "I promise not to be popping in unannounced all the time and disturbing you. Maybe just once a day to play with Brice."

Morgan had to admit, the idea of an extra set of hands held almost as much appeal as the opportunity for Brice to develop a relationship with his grandparents.

"Can that once a day be at two in the morning when he decides he doesn't want to go back to sleep?" she asked with a grin.

"Is that a yes?"

"Yes."

The older woman wrapped Morgan in a hug and rocked back and forth. "I'm so glad."

It was a moment before she stepped back. Then she said to Bryan, "Why don't you show Morgan around the guesthouse before you leave. It's in presentable condition, I hope."

"More or less."

"Good." Julia scooped up the baby. "And take your time."

"We'll be lucky to get out of here before midnight," Bryan groused good-naturedly as they crossed to the guesthouse. His tone was more serious when he added, "I'm glad you agreed to stay here for a while. It means a lot to my parents to be able to get to know Brice and have him so near. They're not very happy with me that I kept him a secret for so long."

"You did what you thought was best," Morgan allowed, though she still felt she was missing some pertinent facts. "And it means a lot to me, too, to have them so close by. Every child deserves at least one set of doting grand-parents."

"They'll spoil him rotten if you're not

careful. Before you know it, toys will start arriving. Big toys like motorized cars and life-size stuffed ponies." He snorted out a laugh. "They're good at that."

Morgan frowned. He sounded as if he spoke from experience, she thought as he opened the door and waited for her to go inside.

The guesthouse was much smaller than Bryan's penthouse, but what it lacked in square footage it made up for in warmth and coziness. The kitchen was outfitted with high-end appliances and warm maple cabinetry. A high counter separated it from the living room. A newspaper was laid out on the counter next to a cup of coffee and a plate dotted with toast crumbs and a small wedge of crust. She pictured him sitting there, combing through the business section as he ate.

"That looks like the breakfast of champions," she teased.

"Making toast is the extent of my culinary abilities." He shrugged. "Don't tell my mother I left dirty dishes out. She'd be appalled."

"Actually, this place is amazingly clean for a bachelor pad," Morgan remarked as he led her down a short hall.

"That's because I'm not here much to mess it up." He opened the first door they came to and switched on the light, revealing a full bath with the kind of tub a woman could do some serious soaking in and a glass-enclosed shower. Pointing to a partly opened door on the other side, he said, "You can access this room from either the hall or the bedroom."

That was their next stop. Once inside, he pulled back the drapes and light flooded in. The room was amply proportioned, although she would have to rearrange the furniture to accommodate Brice's crib and changing table. Bryan read her mind.

"If you take out the desk and move the bed over to that wall, you'll have no problem fitting in Brice's nursery."

The desk in question was piled high with file folders and a laptop computer.

"You're not home enough to mess up this place, but you find time to work here?"

"The company is in the middle of an expansion right now. Since my father is close to retiring, I'm working with the project manager to handle the details and smooth out any wrinkles that develop."

She didn't doubt he was busy, but it still sounded like an excuse to her. "You should be getting out more, spending time with people."

"Who says I don't?"

She folded her arms across her chest. "Does that mean you've found a replacement for Courtney so soon?"

"Would it bother you if I had?"

"Yes." The reply came quickly and left her blinking. It *would* bother her, she realized. A lot. In fact, just thinking about Bryan kissing another woman the way he'd kissed her that one time in his foyer made Morgan want to scream at the top of her lungs. Fortunately, her tone sounded normal when she continued. "You told me that things between the two of you were pretty casual."

"Yes. That's what I want."

Because of his divorce? It had to be. Had he been hurt that badly? "Well, I think you deserve more than that."

He looked mildly amused. "Oh, you do?"

"You're a good man, Bryan."

"Are you sure about that?"

She hadn't been when they first met, but she was now. Oh, he tried to hide it, for reasons that remained a mystery to her. But he was sensitive and fair. The instruments for the community center and the transference of Dillon's life insurance money to Brice were proof of that.

"Yes, I am. And it doesn't hurt that you're also drop-dead gor—"

She ended the description abruptly, but not before he'd figured out where she was heading with it. One side of his mouth crooked up.

"By all means, go on."

When she didn't, Bryan turned the tables on her. "What about you? You're a good person. Drop-dead—et cetera. Don't you deserve more?"

"I stopped thinking about what I deserved the moment I had Brice. I have responsibilities and obligations. I'm a mother now."

"Even mothers can get dressed up and go out on a date now and then, Morgan."

She shook her head. "Not this one."

"Why?"

The way he was watching her made it hard to think, especially since they were standing on opposite sides of an unmade bed whose tangled sheets had her mind straying into decidedly inappropriate territory. "Brice needs me."

Bryan's voice dipped low. It was a seductive whisper when he asked, "Don't you have needs?"

The question was dangerous. The answer that echoed in her head was even more so. Her gaze dropped to his mouth. What she wanted was off-limits and had to remain that way. Morgan couldn't afford to be reckless again. What if things didn't work out? Then what? She would still have to see him. Morgan might not be related to the Caliborns, but her son was. She couldn't afford to jeopardize things.

So she told him, "I have everything I need."

Bryan watched her swallow after making that declaration. She'd sounded resolute, but the way she'd stared at his mouth told him something else.

"Same here," he said.

They were both liars.

It was growing dark when they arrived at the penthouse. Bryan found a spot in front of the building. It didn't surprise her that he came around to open her door. But it shocked her when he lifted Brice out of the car seat.

"I'll carry him," he said when she reached to take him. "That's if you don't mind."

"I don't mind." Quite the opposite. She liked seeing Brice cuddled in Bryan's capable arms as they walked to the building. "You know, I never noticed it before, but you and Brice have the same shaped eyebrows."

His tugged together. "Really?"

"Well, not when you do that."

He stopped walking. "Do what?"

"Frown." Before she could think better of it, Morgan reached up and smoothed out his brow. Afterward, she drew back her hand quickly. To cover her nerves, she quipped, "You do that a lot."

"Do I?"

"I wonder if he's going to be able to intimidate people with a mere glance when he grows up."

"It takes years of practice to perfect. I'll have to get busy teaching him."

Though his comment was offhanded, she hoped Bryan really planned to play a more active role in her son's life. That was what she'd hoped for when she'd stayed in Chicago. That was all she could hope for now.

When the elevator arrived at the top floor, Bryan remarked, "I think someone needs a change of pants."

"Give him to me. I'll take care of him."

"That's all right. I'll do it."

Morgan was aware her mouth had fallen open, but she couldn't seem to close it as she watched Bryan walk down the hall to the bedroom.

Bryan laid Brice on the changing table and rolled up his sleeves. "Try not to move around too much, okay?"

The baby kicked his legs as an answer.

"Never mind."

For the past few months, Bryan had gone out of his way not to hold the baby or touch him, even though at times he'd been tempted. Just being around Brice had brought back too many memories, and even the good ones had made him ache. He'd reached a conclusion, though. He needed to face his demons head-on and step up to the plate as the boy's uncle. This was his brother's son, Dillon's legacy, which was why Bryan wanted Brice to have the life insurance money. But money was a poor substitute for affection. Morgan and the baby needed him. A little scarier was the realization that he needed them, too.

"You'll be happy to know I'm not a novice at this."

The baby merely blinked at him.

"Hey, don't look so unimpressed."

This time Brice yawned and turned his head to one side. Bryan traced the baby's ear from the folded edge at the top down to the tiny lobe.

"It seems we have more in common than our eyebrows. The Caliborn ears. Mine are a little bigger than yours. Your dad had these, too. If you're lucky you'll inherit his ability to make people laugh. He didn't take life too seriously." Bryan shook his head. "He said I did that enough for both of us."

He swallowed then. Missing Dill. Missing Caden. "I wanted you to be his, you know. From the very beginning I wanted you to be his. Just like I wanted Caden to be mine."

"Bryan?" Morgan stood in the doorway. "I just came to see how you were doing."

He cleared his throat. "Fine."

"I can take over if you'd like."

"No. I've changed a diaper or two in my

time." He began unsnapping the blue-striped sleeper, a task made a little more difficult by the baby's flailing limbs. But he finally managed to remove it, along with the soiled diaper. A moment later he was redressing Brice, who was now cooing happily.

"I guess you *have* done that a time or two," Morgan commented.

"You doubted me?"

She nodded. "Sorry. It's just that you don't look like the sort of man who's ever pulled diaper duty."

"It has been a while."

"How long?" she asked softly.

"A few years." Rough laughter scraped his throat. "I guess that diapering a baby is like riding a bike. Once you learn how, you never forget." He lifted Brice to his shoulder. "You don't forget this, either. How they feel in your arms."

"Who is Caden?" she asked quietly.

He closed his eyes. "My...ex-wife's son."

"Oh." Morgan frowned. He could see that his reply had raised more questions than it had answered. "I thought...I guess I thought he was your son."

His laughter was harsh. "I did, too."

The story spilled out, haltingly at first as the words were wrenched from deep inside him. Through it all, Morgan said nothing, listening in that patient way of hers, her expression concerned and sympathetic rather than pitying.

"I'm sorry, Bryan," she murmured. Reaching up, she brushed his cheeks. He'd been crying, he realized. The tears should have embarrassed him. In the past he would have considered them a show of weakness. But they were cleansing and empowering somehow. And he felt stronger.

"I wish you'd told me sooner."

Oddly, so did he. "It's not something I talk about."

"Then I'm glad you shared it with me."

Morgan put one arm around his waist and, pressing her cheek to his shoulder, hugged him. Bryan shifted Brice to his other shoulder so he could hug her back. They stood like that for a long time.

"Can I stay?" he asked quietly. "Just to sleep."

"Yes."

* * *

As Morgan sat in the rocking chair and nursed Brice, she could hear Bryan moving around in the bedroom next door. A moment later the shower switched on. The sounds were routine, domestic and oddly comforting.

After burping Brice, she laid him in his crib. He fussed before settling down, grunting as he wriggled around to find a comfortable spot.

Morgan patted his tummy and recalled what Bryan had revealed. Her heart ached for him. To have been deceived that way by someone he'd loved and trusted had left a lasting scar. No wonder he'd been so cynical and distrustful when she'd first arrived. No wonder he preferred casual relationships with women like Courtney. Would he ever be willing to risk his heart again?

Morgan kissed her fingers and touched Brice's cheek before slipping out of the room. She had no business wanting to know the answer to that question.

It was almost nine o'clock when Bryan joined her in the living room. His hair was still damp from his shower. He wore the tan pants he'd had on earlier and a white cotton

T-shirt he'd culled from his dresser. His feet were bare.

She'd made a bowl of popcorn and was watching an old movie on cable. "Are you hungry?" she asked. "I can make you a sandwich or something."

He settled next to her on the couch. "That's all right. What are you watching?"

"I'm not sure. I tuned in after it started. Want some popcorn?" When he nodded, she shifted the bowl between them.

"You moved the television," he said. "And the couch."

"Yes. It made more sense over there. And, well, once I moved the television, I couldn't leave the couch where it was. I'll move it back when I leave."

"No. That's okay." He glanced around, nodded. "I like it this way. It's more…homey."

Because she didn't know what to say to that, she asked, "Speaking of moving, when are we going to make the swap?"

He rubbed his chin. "Does next weekend work for you?"

"Sure." She wiped her fingers on a napkin. "Brice and I don't have any other plans."

They finished off the popcorn while they watched the rest of the movie. As the credits rolled, Morgan glanced over at Bryan. He'd been quiet for a while and no wonder. His head was resting on the back of the couch and his eyes were closed. She reached for the remote and switched off the TV. It had been a long and emotionally draining day for both of them. If not for nerves, she wouldn't have lasted this long.

I should wake him, she thought. Let him settle into the comfort of his bed. And seek out the refuge of mine.

Morgan reached over and turned off the light. In the darkness she felt his arm come around her, stopping her from rising to her feet. She sank back on the cushion, allowed him to pull her closer to his side. Though she told herself to go, she stayed exactly where she was until Brice's cries woke her five and a half hours later.

CHAPTER NINE

MORGAN was out early Monday morning running errands when the first fat raindrops began to fall. As she hurried to her car with Brice in his stroller the front page of a newspaper caught her eye. The black-and-white photograph of her, Brice and Bryan standing on the street outside the apartment ran four columns wide. She was touching Bryan's face. Smoothing his brow that was so much like her son's, she recalled now, though the photograph made the contact appear far more intimate than that.

It didn't help that the accompanying headline read: Another Questionable Caliborn? This time Windy Cities scion in no hurry to claim child as heir.

Groaning in disbelief, she snatched a copy

from the newsstand. Her dread increased tenfold as she scanned the contents of the article. Not only did it debate Brice's parentage and make insinuations about the character of the single mom who'd moved into Bryan's penthouse, it went on to rehash the horrid details of his divorce and the painful revelation that Caden was not his son. Given how violated she was feeling, Morgan could only imagine Bryan's reaction when he learned that his private life had once again been turned into a public spectacle.

She paid for the paper and tucked it into the diaper bag. She had to reach him, talk to him, offer whatever help or comfort she could. Her hair was damp by the time she reached her car. She quickly buckled Brice into his seat in the back and stowed the stroller. Then she swore under her breath when the engine refused to turn over.

"Not today!" she hollered.

Thumping the steering wheel with the palms of her hands, she debated her options. Bryan would be at the office. She needed to find a phone and call him, warn him. Unfortunately, she didn't own a cell. Yet. She would before the day was out, she decided, making a mental note. She remembered passing an El stop a few blocks from where she was parked. She was a good two miles from Bryan's office. Mind made up, she got out of the car and retrieved the stroller. Covering Brice up with an extra blanket from the diaper bag, she took off at a run.

Bryan was in a foul mood when he stepped off the elevator. He usually arrived at the office no later than seven-thirty, but he'd had a Rotary breakfast across town, followed by a meeting with bank officials. Then he'd run into a snarl of traffic on State Street. It was almost ten o'clock now and in less than fifteen minutes he had a transatlantic conference call scheduled with the site manager and a couple of other managers concerning the London expansion project.

Britney trailed behind him into his office, going over his phone messages as he peeled off his damp coat. It was pouring outside and thunder rumbled in the distance. Everything they said about Mondays was true, he decided, and that was before he saw the tabloid on top of the stack of traditional newspapers he read each day.

At his muttered expletive, Britney said, "I'm sorry, Mr. Caliborn, but I knew you would want to see this."

No. He didn't. But he read the headline anyway and that alone had him shouting, "Get my attorney on the phone."

The young woman nodded, but hesitated in the doorway.

"Is there something else?" He almost hated to ask.

"Yes." Her tone cooled considerably when she said, "Miss Stevens phoned you. Twice in the past hour. I'm guessing she saw the news-paper as well."

Bryan closed his eyes and sighed. To think he'd believed this ugliness was finally over and forgotten. Not only had his past been dredged up, Morgan and Brice had been dragged into it. That just plain ticked him off. Somebody's head was going to roll.

"Get her on the phone first."

"I would, but she didn't leave a call-back number."

He frowned. "She wasn't at home?"

"No. She was calling from a pay phone." Britney tugged at the hem of her jacket. "Not that it's any of my business, Mr. Caliborn, but do you think Miss Stevens could be one of the unnamed sources?"

"What?"

"In the story. It relies heavily on them."

"What on earth would Morgan have to gain by making herself the center of a scandal?" he snapped.

"I don't know. Some people enjoy notoriety and the attention. I mean, she showed up here in labor, burst in on your meeting." She coughed delicately then. "And it can pay well."

"You think Morgan sold this story to *City Talk* for money?" He wasn't angry, but incredulous.

"I hope not. For your sake, Mr. Caliborn. You've been through enough of this kind of thing. If there's anything I can do to help you, anything at all, I'll be glad to do it. But I felt the need to raise the possibility since so much of what is printed here is, well, inside information. Who else would have known that you were so generously allowing her and her baby to live in your penthouse, even though obviously you were suspicious of her claims about the baby being yours?"

"What do you mean by that?"

"You hired a private detective to investigate her sexual history." At his raised eyebrows, she said, "I put through the invoice Gil Rogers sent with his report last week."

She also had to have read the report to know what the man had been investigating.

Bryan held up a hand. "Stop right there. I can think of a few people wise to those details, which, by the way, aren't exactly the facts. That's why I know Morgan didn't plant this story. She wouldn't have gotten things wrong. As for needing money, Morgan is a wealthy woman in her own right these days."

"She…she is?"

"Yes. But I agree this information came from an inside source. When I find out who's responsible for this story, and I will, that person won't be working here. In fact, it would be better for that person altogether if they resigned their position and cleared out their desk before I had to ask them to do it."

Her face paled beneath her blusher. He had a sick feeling he'd just found his Judas.

"If Morgan calls back, put her through immediately."

"But the conference call…" Britney began.

He meant it when he said, "Interrupt me, if need be. She's more important."

When the conference call from London came, he still hadn't heard from Morgan. Bryan didn't like it. Where was she? Had she seen the story? Was she being hounded by reporters? Unfortunately, he had no choice but to wait.

Bryan's mood didn't improve as he listened to the site manager rattle on about cost overruns and a couple of snags the construction crew had encountered with local officials.

Rubbing his forehead, he asked, "How much extra are we talking?"

The sum had him swearing. From the doorway, Britney cleared her throat. "Hold on a minute, John." He covered the mouthpiece with his hand. "Do you have Morgan on the line?"

"Actually, she's here."

Relief flooded through him. "Get her a cup of coffee or tea if she prefers and tell her I'll be with her in a few minutes."

It was nearly half an hour, though, before he was finally able to wrap up the call. He'd found it difficult to concentrate on the site manager's concerns with Morgan just outside his office, especially when he heard Brice start to fuss.

When he finally hung up and stepped out into the waiting area, his mouth fell open at the sight of her.

"My God! Are you okay?"

"I'm fine." She didn't look fine. Her hair was soaked and plastered to her head. Her clothes were equally soggy. Brice had fared better thanks to the stroller's hood and an extra blanket. Now that he was sipping from a small bottle of juice, he was perfectly content.

"What happened?" Bryan asked once they were alone in his office.

"I had to see you."

"Morgan, you're soaked to the bone." And cold, too, he thought as he watched her shiver. He helped her out of her wet coat and put his suit jacket around her shaking shoulders. Together they sat on the leather couch, the same couch where she'd once writhed in labor.

"I got caught in the r-rain. My car broke d-down again."

"That thing is a hazard," he said as he rubbed her back.

"Agreed. It's gone to the scrap heap as of today. But that's not why I'm here, Bryan." She shifted so she was facing him, green eyes filled with concern. "I don't know how to tell you this, but—"

"You've seen the article in *City Talk*."

She winced. "You know."

"Britney brought in a copy." He frowned. "That's why you rushed here in the rain?"

"I tried calling from a coffee shop and again at the El stop, but this seemed the sort of thing you should be told in person anyway. I'm so sorry."

She meant that, he knew. "It's not your fault. Hell, you and Brice are as much victims as I am. More so, when you get right down to it. You only got dragged into this because of the Caliborn name."

She tilted her head to one side. "It's a good name. One worth standing up for. Fight back, Bryan."

"Oh, I plan to. I've already spoken to my attorney about bringing a libel suit against the publisher. He thinks we have a good case, despite my standing as a quasi-public figure. They printed half truths and outright lies without making any effort to verify the facts."

"Tell me about it. They make me out to be some sort of…" She shook her head, left the sentence unfinished.

It was his turn to apologize. He pulled her against him, dropped a kiss on her temple. "I'm sorry you got thrown under the bus with me."

"That's okay. I'm pretty resilient."

"I know." But she didn't deserve this. He stood and helped her to her feet. "Now let's get you and Brice home so you can get out of those wet clothes."

Morgan didn't expect Bryan to stay after he delivered her and the baby to the penthouse. Especially after they spotted a photographer hanging around outside and the doorman told them a couple of reporters had tried to sneak into the elevators. But he didn't leave. Instead, he offered to change and entertain the baby while she took a hot shower and put on fresh clothes.

She did so quickly, pulling her still-damp

hair into a ponytail and not bothering with makeup. She didn't want to keep him waiting too long. Surely he had to get back to the office. But when she joined him in the living room, Brice was asleep in his swing and Bryan was in no hurry to leave.

He was sitting on the couch with one foot propped on the coffee table. He'd removed his suit jacket when they arrived. His tie was loosened now, too, the sleeves of his crisp white shirt rolled halfway up his forearms.

"It's almost lunchtime. Are you hungry?" she asked.

"Not really. You?"

"No." She'd felt queasy since seeing that headline. She plunked down next to him on the couch.

"I called my parents to let them know. A neighbor saw the paper in the grocery store and had already given them the news."

Grimacing, Morgan asked, "What did they say?"

"Well, they weren't happy about it, but they were more worried about me." He sent her a smile. "And you. They're especially glad you're going to be moving into their guesthouse. You and Brice will have more privacy there. They'll see to it."

"But isn't my moving there likely to raise more speculation? The last thing I want to do is cause your parents to be hounded by reporters or have photographers camped outside their front door."

He leaned forward, rested his elbows on his knees. "They have a suggestion for how we can prevent that. They want to call a press conference, Morgan." One side of his mouth rose. "Steal the gossipmongers' thunder, as my dad put it."

"A press conference?"

"They want to make it clear to everyone that Brice is a Caliborn. They don't want it to seem as if we're hiding something or are somehow ashamed of the situation." He turned, touched her face, his fingers lingering on the curve of her cheek. "But it's your decision. They're leaving it up to you."

She glanced away. "The details make it all seem so sordid."

"You don't owe them details. Just the basic facts. Brice is Dillon's son and you came here to connect with your baby's family. There's no shame in that."

"No shame in that," she repeated. Being an unwed mother wasn't as big a deal as it used to be, but that didn't mean Morgan was eager to have all of Chicago discussing her situation over their morning coffee.

"None."

She nodded as she rose and crossed to her sleeping son. Lifting him out of the swing, she dropped a kiss on his forehead. "I'm going to put him in his crib."

Bryan was still on the couch when she returned. "We don't have to say anything," he told her. "You don't owe anyone any explanations. My parents will understand."

"No." She shook her head. "I told you to stand up, fight back. I need to, too. Your parents are right. In the absence of the facts, the lies will just continue being spread."

He stood, crossed to her. Hands on her shoulders, he asked, "Are you sure?"

"Yes. I won't let my son be the subject of rumors."

Bryan pulled her close for a hug. He intended the gesture to offer reassurance, but it morphed into something else as the seconds ticked by. She fitted perfectly in his arms, soft curves molding against him. He turned his head slightly so he could breathe in her scent. It was nothing overpowering, a hint of citrus and soap. His lips brushed her temple as his hands stroked her back, and just that quickly, the need he'd tried to keep banked was stoked to life.

"Morgan." He sighed her name. "God, I wish…" He covered her mouth with his to prevent the words from slipping out. They were too frightening, too damning to utter.

Her arms came up, her hands gripped his shoulders. He felt her fingernails dig into his flesh through the fabric of his shirt, letting him know that this need wasn't one-sided. Bryan took everything she offered and still wanted more. He'd never been this greedy or felt half this desperate. His fingers brushed her cheek, stroked the column of her neck and then found the buttons of her blouse. As he nibbled the sensitive skin just below her ear, he slipped the first one through its hole. When the last one gave way and his fingertips brushed the valley between her breasts, he was rewarded with a moan of pleasure.

"You're in—"

"Insane." Morgan finished as she pushed

away, pulling her blouse together. Her hair was mussed, half of it hanging free from the ponytail.

The breath sawed in and out of Bryan's lungs. Actually, he had been thinking intoxicating, incredible.

"I— We can't do this!"

He almost argued the point. He thought they could do it, very well and to both of their satisfaction. But he knew that wasn't what she meant.

"Can we pretend this never happened?" she asked.

They'd done that after the first time he'd kissed her. It hadn't worked for him then. It wouldn't work now. But Bryan nodded anyway. "If that's what you want."

"I think it's for the best, given everything that's involved here."

Bryan retrieved his coat. Though his body was burning with need from their all-too-brief encounter, he said, "It never happened."

After he left, Morgan flopped down on the couch. She was mortified by her behavior. The way she'd kissed him. The thoughts that had gone through her mind at the time. Just thinking about them now had goose bumps prickling her flesh, heat curling through her… tears blurring her vision.

A year ago, confused and in mourning, she'd allowed Dillon to seduce her. She was every bit as confused now, but no seduction was necessary on Bryan's part. She wasn't sure when or how, but the fact was irrefutable. She'd fallen in love with him.

CHAPTER TEN

THE Caliborns called the press conference for the following afternoon. It made no sense to put it off, Morgan knew, especially now that the mainstream media had started sniffing around, too. But given what had transpired between her and Bryan twenty-four hours earlier, she was a nervous wreck. How was she going to stand in front of a crowd of probing reporters and explain that her relationship with Bryan was strictly platonic?

She wore the outfit she'd purchased to meet the Caliborns just the weekend before. Though she'd deposited the check Bryan had given her, she'd hardly had time to shop for something new. Vaguely, she wondered if someone would notice it was what she'd had on in the photograph that had been snapped. As for Brice, it didn't really matter what he wore. Morgan planned to have him wrapped up tightly in a blanket, allowing only minimal exposure. She wasn't about to let her son's image be exploited so they could sell more papers.

Bryan sent a car for her. The conference was slated to begin at ten o'clock at the Windy City offices. She arrived just after nine and was quickly ushered inside the same conference room where she'd first encountered the real Bryan Caliborn. He was at the end of the same long table, standing rather than sitting, and instead of a file folder, a bank of microphones was in front of him. He looked every bit as handsome and authoritative as he had that day. The only difference was that instead of scowling when he spied her, his eyes lit up and he smiled.

Julia and Hugh were there, too. Julia gave Morgan a hug and took Brice, who had fallen asleep on the car ride over. Hugh hugged her as well.

"Damned vultures," he muttered. "For all the good things Windy City Industries has done in this city, you'd think they'd show some restraint on private matters."

When Hugh released her, Bryan was there, holding out a cup of tea like a peace offering. He didn't hug her, but he did squeeze her arm when he asked, "Nervous?"

"Yes." For reasons that had more to do with the man in front of her than the throng of reporters assembling outside. "I suppose you're better at this sort of thing than I am. This is my first news conference."

"I've done several, but I'm nervous, too. I'd much rather be talking about business than about my private life," he said ruefully. "Did you read over the notes I sent last night?"

She nodded. He had e-mailed Morgan a set of questions he felt they were likely to encounter and suggestions for how they should respond. Basically, all she had to be was honest, but brevity was the key.

"Remember, don't offer them anything they don't ask for, and feel free not to answer any question that makes you uncomfortable. They're not entitled to all of the details," he said.

She hoped it wouldn't come to that, because clamming up would defeat the purpose of such a press conference. They wanted the media to get their fill and then go away, otherwise the story would grow legs and keep running.

A knock sounded at the door a moment before a young woman poked her head inside. "The waiting room is full. Should I start sending them in, Mr. Caliborn?"

"Give us five more minutes," he said.

"Who's that?" Morgan asked.

"My new secretary." His mouth tightened.

This came as a surprise. "What happened to Britney?"

"She wisely decided it was in her best interests to resign."

They stood at the end of the room, Morgan holding Brice and flanked by the elder Caliborns. Bryan was just in front of them at the microphones. The long table kept the reporters and photographers at a distance, though close enough that Morgan saw eagerness and speculation in some of their expressions. When the noise died down and everyone had filed into the room, Bryan cleared his throat and gave his prepared statement.

"Thank you for coming here today. As you know, a story about my family recently ran in *City Talk*. It was poorly researched and full of innuendo and outright lies. My attorney will be filing a libel suit on my behalf. In the meantime, we asked you here today to set the record straight.

"First of all, the baby in question is a Caliborn."

Camera flashes popped and a couple of reporters shouted out questions. Bryan ignored them and kept talking. "His name is Brice Dillon Stevens. He is my late brother's son."

The room erupted into a frenzy then. He gave up continuing with his prepared remarks and pointed to a reporter.

"Leslie Michaelson with *City Talk*," the woman began. "I didn't write the original story that appeared in my newspaper."

"Rag, you mean," Julia inserted. The comment, coming as it did from such a demure and usually pleasant woman, had most of the reporters snickering.

The woman cleared her throat and went on, "We were led to believe, by a source very close to you, that the baby was yours. Do you deny that Miss Stevens had been contacting your office for months, seeking an audience with you regarding her pregnancy?"

"Miss Stevens did contact me looking for her baby's father. Dillon was not here, so I referred the matter to my attorney."

Morgan was impressed. What he'd said was true, he'd just left out enough information to give a different impression—much like the woman's *City Talk* colleague had done in the original story.

"My question is for Miss Stevens," another reporter chimed in. "How did you meet Dillon Caliborn?"

"I met him while vacationing. I found him very charming, and I was very sorry to learn of his death."

The man opened his mouth to follow up on the question, most likely to fill in the gaps left by her response, but Bryan called on another reporter before he could.

"Mr. and Mrs. Caliborn, is there any doubt in your mind that Miss Stevens's child is your grandchild?"

"None whatsoever." Julia beamed.

"He's a Caliborn through and through," Hugh agreed. "If he chooses, he'll be the one standing before you one day, putting you in your place instead of putting up with your nonsense."

That caused a rumble of uncomfortable laughter from their ranks.

The reporter wasn't deterred, though. This time he addressed Bryan. "In the matter of the son your former wife conceived while married to you, a paternity test was performed. Was one done this time?"

Morgan chanced a glance at Bryan. His expression was inscrutable, but she knew the pain the question caused and it was all she could do not to shout for them all to go away and leave him alone.

"No test was necessary. Unlike my former wife, I trust Miss Stevens."

"Is that why you hired an investigator to probe her background and report back on any other men she might have been seeing at the time of the baby's conception?"

Morgan hadn't seen that question coming. It landed like a prizefighter's uppercut. She let out a little gasp, which she camouflaged by clearing her throat. "I'll take this one," she said.

More flashes popped. Holding the baby so his face wasn't visible to the cameras, she stepped to the microphone.

"I requested the investigation." Morgan didn't question why she felt the need to stretch the truth, only that, even though she was hurt by the revelation, it seemed the right thing to do. "The Caliborns accepted my son and me right away. They have shown me nothing but kindness. But given what the family had been through in the past, I wanted them to be assured of my claims. Even though they saw no need for a definitive paternity test, I wanted as many facts as possible on the table."

"Are you still living in Mr. Caliborn's penthouse?" someone shouted.

"I will be moving out today and he will be moving back in. He's been very gracious to let me stay there as long as he has, and I've appreciated his kindness."

"Where will you move to?"

"Do you really think I plan to give the lot of you my new address?" she asked with wry laughter.

The reporters and photographers laughed as well.

More questions were asked, all of them anticipated and as such easily answered. Then Bryan announced, "This will be the final question."

Morgan nearly sagged with relief until she heard what it was. Then she stiffened.

"Mr. Caliborn, what exactly is your relationship to Miss Stevens?"

Had the question been directed toward her, she would be stammering over her words. But not Bryan. Without hesitation and in that tone that brooked no argument, he said, "My relationship to Miss Stevens is obvious. Her son is my nephew and since my brother is no longer alive I feel an obligation to look after both of them."

His words echoed what Britney had told Morgan when she'd moved into the penthouse: *Mr. Caliborn takes his responsibilities very seriously.*

The answer was jotted down in the man's notebook, apparently accepted as the truth, but Morgan didn't want to believe it could be possible that while Bryan was attracted to her and finally trusted her, duty was his main priority.

Bryan was grateful to see the last straggling queue of reporters file out of the conference room and pile into the elevator.

Once they were gone, Julia wilted onto one of the chairs with a sigh. "I think that went well."

"For a feeding frenzy." Hugh grunted. "But at least it's over and done with now."

Morgan was leaning against the far wall, jiggling the baby in her arms and staring intently at a spot on the carpet. She was quiet, far too quiet for Bryan's liking, and he suspected he knew the reason.

"Mom, would you and Dad mind taking Brice into my office? I'd like to talk to Morgan alone for a minute."

When the conference-room door closed behind his parents, he turned to her. "That was pretty brutal. How are you holding up?"

"I'm fine."

Liar, he thought. But he didn't call her on it. He'd lied as well. By omission, when it came to Gil Rogers, but still.

"Look, Morgan, about the private investigator," he began.

She shook her head to stop his words. "Don't, Bryan. There's really no need for you to explain. I didn't know you'd hired one, but I knew that you didn't trust me. You made that pretty plain."

"In the beginning, yes. But that was before—"

Before he'd gotten to know her and realized what a strong, brave and determined woman she was.

Before he'd kissed her and his ordered world had begun spinning into chaos.

Before he'd fallen in love with her.

The last revelation was too new and staggering to ponder let alone share. Love? Good God! He hadn't seen it coming. Of course, he hadn't predicted any of the recent events that had occurred in his life.

Morgan was watching him, waiting for him to continue.

"I let past circumstances color my judgment. I meant it when I told the reporters you're nothing like my ex-wife. I should have seen that right away. I should have believed you."

"I understand, really." But her arms remained wrapped around her waist, her body language stating quite plainly that something was troubling her…something had hurt her.

"Still, I'm sorry. I made things more difficult for you in the beginning than they needed to be, especially given everything you were already going through. I know what happened to your parents."

"The detective?"

He nodded guiltily. "I can't even begin to imagine how horrible that must have been for you. And then, in my stubbornness, I cheated you and my parents out of months of time together."

That wasn't what he was most sorry for, though. Most of all, he was sorry about Dillon. Not only because his brother had lied to Morgan, charmed and seduced her in Aruba, and then walked away without a backward glance only to die in a tragic accident and leave her child fatherless. No. Bryan was sorry that Dillon had been the Caliborn brother to meet her first.

"It's okay. In the end, things have worked out the way they were meant to." Something in her words struck him as ominous, though he couldn't put a finger on what before she motioned toward the door and asked, "Do you think that's the end of it?"

"God, I hope so." Running a hand over the back of his neck, Bryan added, "I don't want to be dodging reporters' questions and photographers' flashbulbs every time I leave the

office or arrive home. That's why I tried to
spell out the facts as clearly as possible so they
won't look for more."

She offered what passed for a smile. "Well
then, I'd say mission accomplished."

Immediately following the news conference,
Morgan moved out of the penthouse as
planned. Bryan moved back in. Her personal
effects were gone, but reminders of her were
everywhere. In the red accent pillows and
throw, the scented candles and the dining-
room-table runner she'd left behind. Even in
the rearranged living-room furniture. She'd
turned his place into a real home during the
short time she'd lived there. But it didn't feel
like a real home now that she and Brice were
no longer in it. When he came home from work
late the first evening she was gone, the penthouse just felt big and empty, and, yes, he
could finally admit it, lonely.

He was lonely.

In the weeks that followed, it became clear
that his relationship with Morgan had changed
along with their addresses. Did she regret the
stolen kisses they'd shared? She'd told him

they should forget they'd ever happened and apparently she had. Bryan, however, hadn't been successful. He lay awake each night, torturing himself with memories of what had been as well as what he wished had transpired… what he still wished would happen. But none of it seemed possible when Morgan smiled at him so politely and kept him at a distance during visits that she made sure were conducted under the watchful eye of his parents.

It was killing him. She seemed not to notice.

CHAPTER ELEVEN

In the middle of November, Morgan found a house. She'd fallen in love with it at first sight. It was a two-story Tudor in a quiet, tree-lined neighborhood of older homes just a few miles from Bryan's parents' place. Compared to that house, it was small, but with four bedrooms and three and half baths spread over two stories, it more than accommodated her and Brice's needs.

It had a big yard with a couple of mature oaks whose fat limbs were perfect for supporting a tree house or a tire swing, and while the landscaping was nice, Morgan was sure Julia could give her plenty of ideas on how to improve it. The owners had already relocated to another state, which meant she could move in as soon as the paperwork was completed. If all went as planned, she and Brice could be in their own home by Thanksgiving or at the very least Christmas. The idea appealed to her. Even though she enjoyed staying in the guesthouse and the Caliborns respected her privacy, she wanted her own home, a place on which she was free to put her own stamp.

Today, Bryan was coming by to see the house. She'd asked him to, wanting his opinion since she would be plunking down a chunk of Brice's inheritance to pay for it. She waited for him in her car in the driveway. The vehicle was new, purchased a couple days after the old one had left her and the baby stranded in the rain. It was nothing flashy, but it boasted all of the latest safety features and had fared the best in a national publication's crash tests.

Leaves swirled on the street when Bryan pulled his Lexus to the curb. Morgan got out of her car and joined him on the brick-paved walk that led to the front door. He was dressed in a dark suit since he'd come straight from his office. His attire was professional, his smile personal. Upon seeing it, her pulse took off like a warning flare.

They hadn't been alone together since the

press conference. Morgan had made sure of that. They wouldn't be alone for long now. Her real estate agent was running late, but the woman would be there any time to let them inside and answer his questions during the walk-through. Even so, Morgan wondered if it had been a mistake to leave Brice in the care of Bryan's parents. At least with the baby in her arms she wouldn't be so tempted to open hers to Bryan when he reached her.

"Hello, Morgan."

"Hi." The cool temperatures turned their greetings into white mist. They eyed one another awkwardly before she asked, "So, what do you think of the neighborhood?"

Stuffing his hands into his trouser pockets, he glanced around. "It's very solid. The values here are in no danger of dropping. And there's nothing wrong with the home's curb appeal."

"The mature trees help," she said, pointing to a nearby oak. Its leaves had turned yellow and most of them had fallen, exposing a squirrel's nest high in the thick branches.

"Brice is going to have a field day around here when he gets older."

"Tell me about it. He's already impatient to

be mobile. Just this morning he pushed up onto his knees after rolling onto his belly. Any day now, he's going to be crawling and everything at his eye level will be fair game."

He glanced toward her car. "You didn't bring him?"

She shook her head. "He's with your mother."

The real estate agent arrived then. After apologizing for her lateness she unlocked the front door and waved them inside. "If it's okay with you, I'll just stay out here and make a few phone calls while you show Mr. Caliborn around."

Morgan swallowed. She had little choice but to agree. The door closed behind them with a thud that seemed to echo in the empty house.

"The parquet floors are original and for the most part in excellent shape."

"So I see."

She pointed to a room through an arched doorway to the side. "Why don't we start the tour in the dining room?"

Bryan had more on his mind than the house, but he followed her through the rooms, listening patiently and with no small amount of interest to her plans for decorating. It was clear Morgan loved the house. He liked it, too. Even though it was bare of furnishings and its walls were in need of a new coat of paint, it exuded charm and character. No doubt once she took possession of it, in short order and with little effort, she would turn it into a home.

Even now as they walked from space to space he could picture her there. In the living room sitting beside the fireplace and admonishing Brice to keep away from the flames. In the kitchen baking cookies or drinking hot cocoa at a table tucked into the nook. In the library curled up with Brice on an overstuffed couch turning the pages of a picture book.

And in the master bedroom at the top of the stairs, he pictured her in a big bed, wearing white satin and smiling as she held out her hand in invitation.

"What's wrong?"

Her question yanked Bryan from the daydream. "Sorry?"

"You're frowning. Don't you like the house?"

"That's not it. The house is perfect. I can see you here," he told her truthfully.

The problem plaguing Bryan was he could see himself there, too. With Morgan. With Brice. And with the other children he wanted to create with her to fill up the spare bedrooms. He hadn't thought it possible to want a wife and children again after what had happened. He hadn't wanted to risk his heart as either a husband or a father. He knew the reason behind his changed mind. She was standing in front of him. She was also moving on. She didn't need him.

"Then you think I should buy it?" Morgan's excitement was palpable.

"Yes. It's a good investment, although I wouldn't offer the full asking price given the current market."

"I was thinking the same thing," she replied. "Especially since the owners have already left and are motivated to sell."

He couldn't have asked for a better segue. Bryan cleared his throat. "Speaking of leaving, I'll be flying to London next week."

"The company's expansion project?" she guessed. She'd heard him and his father talk about it enough.

He nodded. "We've hit another snag. At this

point the new facility won't be operational until next summer, which puts us six months behind schedule and close to three million dollars over budget. I'm hoping that by being there I can help move things along."

"How long will you be gone?"

"A month is the best-case scenario. Three or more if we need to appeal a judge's ruling."

Her expression dimmed. "You'll miss the holidays."

He shook his head, offered a crooked smile. "They have these things called airplanes, you know. But I will miss—"

Bryan couldn't stand it any longer. He had to touch her, even if just to stroke the side of her face, which he did. His hand lingered, turned so his palm could cradle her cheek. He didn't want the contact to end or the connection he felt with her staring up at him to be lost.

"What will you miss?" she asked softly.

"Seeing Brice on a regular basis. Babies change so fast." He swallowed. "And you, Morgan. I'll miss you."

His mouth found hers. The kiss was light, soft, giving her a chance to pull away if that's what she wanted. When she didn't, he infused it with all of the feelings he couldn't yet give voice to. Dillon had been good with words and a master when it came to persuasion. His brother also had been spontaneous, never thinking beyond the moment. Bryan couldn't be like that. He always looked before leaping. But he could be persuasive in his own way.

By the time the kiss ended, a plan was forming. He needed time to put it in place, to perfect his strategy. Twenty-four hours would do it.

"I have to go, Morgan, but can I stop by the guesthouse tomorrow evening?"

"Okay," she said slowly.

"Ask my mother to sit for Brice again. There's something we need to discuss."

Morgan blew out a breath and paced the length of the living room, hoping to wear off the worst of her nerves. Brice was already at the main house with the Caliborns, and Bryan was due to arrive at the guesthouse soon. She'd changed her clothes three times before deciding on a chocolate-brown sweater and tweed pants. She blamed her indecisiveness on the way he'd looked at her after that kiss.

Bryan could be a hard man to read, but as they'd stood in the empty master suite with the late-afternoon sun filtering through the window, she'd sworn a much deeper emotion had stirred in his dark gaze than the sort that went with either sexual attraction or family obligation. It had thrilled her to see it, especially coming as it had after his admission that he would miss her and Brice during his stay in London. But a moment later he'd been his usual contained self when he'd asked to stop by the guesthouse tonight.

She was adding a little more lip gloss when she heard the knock. She glanced at her watch. Bryan was early. Morgan wasn't sure what his eagerness said about the topic he wanted to "discuss."

"Hello, Morgan."

"Hi." She managed the greeting in a casual voice and stepped back to allow him inside. "Can I take your coat?"

He handed it to her along with the bottle of wine he'd brought. Morgan was still nursing Brice, but she decided to indulge in half a glass when she poured him some of the merlot. She'd expressed some breast milk earlier for

Julia to give the baby and she'd begun supplementing his feedings with some formula and cereal so he slept through the night.

When she returned with their glasses, he was standing in front of the sofa. He took his glass of wine, but instead of sipping from it, he set it aside and then squared his shoulders as if preparing for battle. His tone was firm, his words more of an order rather than a request, when he said, "I want you and Brice to come to London with me."

"Wh-what?" Morgan's wine nearly sloshed over the rim at that. He took it from her hand and set it next to his on the side table.

"I know I won't be gone long, a matter of months at most, but I want you with me."

"You do?"

"Actually, I don't just want you with me in London, I want you to marry me, Morgan."

Her heart bucked out an extra beat as she waited for a declaration of love or at the very least a mention of his true feelings, but what Bryan said next was, "It makes sense for a number of reasons."

"Marriage makes sense?" she asked, because she wasn't sure she'd heard him right.

"Absolutely." He nodded, clasped his hands behind his back and began pacing in front of the sofa where she'd taken a seat since her legs threatened to give out. As if addressing Windy City's management team, Bryan began ticking off those reasons in a voice that conveyed plenty of conviction, but lacked the kind of passion a woman hopes to hear from a man asking her to spend the rest of her life with him.

"Brice is a Caliborn. He is an heir to one of the largest businesses in the country. It's not expected, but of course it's hoped, that when he comes of age he will take his place within the company that his great-great-grandfather started in post-fire Chicago."

"I'd never stand in the way of that."

"I love Brice. I know it took me a long time to show it, but it's true."

"You had your reasons," she said softly.

"I'd do anything for him." *Just as he would have done anything for Dillon?* "I want to look after him, Morgan." *Just as he'd always tried to look after Dillon?* "And I want to look after you." *Because Dillon was no longer there to do it?*

Responsibility, obligation, duty. Morgan

needed better reasons than those to wed. "But marriage is—"

"The perfect solution."

His use of the word *solution* implied Bryan was addressing a problem. Her heart began to ache. The pain grew worse when he said, "You and I are compatible. I enjoy spending time with you." His gaze dipped to her lips. Longing, was that what she saw? Apparently not, she decided when he said, "We share similar tastes in takeout food and home furnishings."

Her eyes narrowed. "Chinese food and room decor are a good basis for a lifelong commitment?"

"That's not what I meant." He frowned, as if sensing his argument wasn't winning her over. "It's just that a lot of couples I know got married because they were attracted to one another."

"And that's bad?"

"It's not enough. You have to have things in common to succeed long-term."

She agreed with him to an extent, but he still wasn't talking about love. Love was the only reason Morgan would marry.

"I will be faithful to you," he was saying. "Of

course, I'll expect the same from you in return. And, as my wife, I will support you in whatever you want to do." He gestured with his arms. "For example, if you want to continue teaching music weekday afternoons at the south-side community center, you may do so."

"Gee, thanks for the permission."

He coughed. "What I mean is you wouldn't be limited to only that. I have the resources that would allow you to create your own center somewhere if you'd like, or do whatever else you feel necessary to bring music into the lives of young people." He ruined that fine speech by adding, "Philanthropy is a Caliborn trait."

"Apparently   so   is   high-handedness." Morgan rose from the sofa. She'd heard enough. More than enough. Her heart couldn't take any more. Crossing her arms over her chest, she shouted, "Where do you get off telling me what I can do and expecting me to settle for compatibility in a marriage? When I marry—if I ever marry—it will be for love."

"But—"

She steamrollered over him. "As for Brice, you have no need to be concerned that I'll somehow deprive him of his heritage. As a matter of fact, I was already considering starting the necessary paperwork to legally change his last name from Stevens. As you said, he's a Caliborn. His name will reflect that soon enough."

"I didn't mean—"

"You didn't mean what? To insult me? To make me feel belittled and bullied? Well, you have. I thought—" She shook her head and shoved hurt behind anger. "It really doesn't matter what I thought now. I was wrong."

"It does matter."

She pointed a finger in the direction of the door. "Go, Bryan. Now. Because while you seem to think we have so much in common, at the moment I can't think of anything."

"Morgan—"

When he made no move to leave, she marched to the door, flung it wide for him.

"Just go. Maybe it's for the best you'll be leaving for London soon. I don't want to see you for a while. When you return, I'll be in my new home and things will be less awkward for all of us."

He stood at the threshold, looking dismayed. "You're angry with me."

The understatement grated. "And hugely disappointed." Hurt came into play, too. "But don't worry that how I feel right now is going to prevent me from allowing either you or your parents to see Brice. I came to Chicago because I wanted my child to have a relationship with his father's family. That hasn't changed. I may be a lot of things, but I can assure you that spiteful isn't one of them."

"I never thought that."

"Good." She nodded.

Frowning, he said, "I handled this wrong."

He was still *handling this wrong* as far as Morgan was concerned.

"Proposing marriage shouldn't make sense, Bryan. I know you've been hurt. I know what happened to you must have made it very hard for you to trust again. But marriage should be about love. You should want to marry the person you can't imagine living without. Not merely the person you feel an obligation to on behalf of your family."

She closed the door before he could respond. She didn't need to hear any more of his cold rationalizations.

* * *

He'd botched it. Screwed it up royally. He sat on one of the lounge chairs beside the pool and reran their conversation. He'd laid out his argument just as he'd planned. It had sounded reasonable when he'd rehearsed it in front of the bathroom mirror earlier that day.

His head dropped forward and he scrubbed a hand over his face. *Reasonable*. God, he was an idiot. He walked to the main house, pausing outside the patio doors. Inside he could see his parents doting on Brice, who was lying on a blanket on the study floor.

They were happy again. Nothing could replace Dillon, of course. But the sharpest edges of their grief had been filed down thanks to the baby. Thanks to Morgan. She'd done the same for his grief, both over his brother and the boy he'd thought was his son.

She'd given them all a chance to get to know Brice when she could have filed a paternity suit and claimed compensation. In return she'd been doubted, dismissed, investigated and libeled.

If I ever marry—it will be for love.

The one thing Bryan had kept from her, even while seeking her hand. How cold it must have sounded, he thought as he climbed into his car and revved the engine to life. Hell, it must have sounded as if he were proposing a business merger rather than marriage.

CHAPTER TWELVE

FOR the next several days, Morgan was determined not to think about Bryan and his heartbreaking suggestion that they marry because it "made sense." She was hurt and angry with him. She also was disappointed with herself, because after he'd left she'd wondered if she should have said yes. She loved him. She wanted to be his wife.

To keep her mind off his proposal and her foolish heart, she immersed herself in the upcoming move. The owners had accepted the offer she'd made, leaving only the paperwork and packing to complete. Morgan was looking forward to retrieving the rest of her belongings from storage and having the new piano she'd purchased delivered. At the penthouse, she'd had Bryan's baby grand to play. Other than at the community center, she hadn't played in weeks.

Before she could move in, however, some work had to be done, thankfully all of it cosmetic and not likely to take very long. She'd hired a painter and was in the process of picking out wall colors, had measured the windows for custom shades and draperies and had made inquires to have the hardwood floor in the living room refinished. If all went according to plan, she and Brice would be out of the guesthouse the first week in December.

Bryan would already be in London. Morgan sat down at the counter with a bundle of paint chips and tried not to think about the fact that he was leaving that day. She wasn't very successful. She could only hope that by the time he flew in for Christmas, she'd have her emotions under control.

When she glanced up and saw him outside the door that led to the patio, she almost thought she was imagining things. But he knocked then and the sound had her scrambling off the stool.

"What are you doing here?" She glanced at her watch. "Your flight leaves for London in less than three hours. Shouldn't you be on your way to the airport?"

"I should be," he agreed. "But I couldn't leave without seeing you."

Morgan's heart, bruised but apparently still foolish, knocked against her ribs. Tell him to go, her head demanded. Her feet didn't obey. Stepping back, she invited him inside. He was, after all, her son's uncle. If he could be pragmatic about their relationship, then so could she.

"So, besides seeing me, what brings you here?" She gave herself high marks for her casual tone and blasé attitude. They provided a nice cover for her clammy palms and rioting nerves.

"You and I have some unfinished business that needs settling." He shook his head then and grimaced. "Not business. Forget I used that word. What's between us is personal."

"I think we already *discussed* everything we needed to discuss when you were here the other night."

Having picked up on her emphasis on the other offending word he'd used, he told her, "No discussion this time, Morgan. I'm here to apologize."

"Okay." She crossed her arms, a reminder to herself to hold firm. "I'm listening."

He blew out a breath, looking uncharacteristically nervous. "Oh, hell, I'm no good at this."

Genuinely curious, she asked, "At what?"

"Talking." He gestured with one hand. "Oh, sure, with cue cards or memorized responses, I can come off well enough. But when I have to speak extemporaneously—" he cleared his throat "—or from the heart, I don't do so well."

Her eyebrows inched up. "I promise not to grade you."

"Right. The other night when I came here, I knew what I wanted, but my approach was all wrong. I left you with the impression that my ultimate goal was to provide for you and Brice."

"It's not?"

"No. Well, yes. Of course I want to provide for you. But that's not why—" He swore again and then reached for the fan of paint chips. "I want to marry you, Morgan, because I don't want to come home to a beige penthouse any longer. My life is beige. I want color in it. And, before you say it, I'm not talking about home decor here."

When she opened her mouth to speak, he waved a hand to stop her.

"That sounds corny. Forget it. What I meant to say is I'm lonely." He winced. "God, that makes me sound desperate and as if just anyone would do. But that's not true. I am lonely, but I don't want to be alone anymore and you're the reason."

Before she could respond, he blew out a sigh. "I'm making an ass of myself when I'm trying to sweep you off your feet. I need you. I don't want to lose you, because I love you, Morgan. I love you and Brice. And I want us to be a real family."

She put a hand over her mouth, holding in a sob and unintentionally covering up her smile. He loved her. The passion in his tone and his perfectly imperfect proposal made that clear.

"Aren't you going to say anything?" he asked.

She crossed to where he stood. For the first time since she'd known him Bryan didn't look authoritative, imposing or powerful. His expression was unguarded and sincere enough to steal her breath. Maybe that was why it took her so long to speak.

"Well?" he prodded, looking like a newly convicted man awaiting his sentence.

Morgan decided to put him out of his misery. "I have just one thing to say." Going up on tiptoe, she wound her arms around his neck. A moment before her lips touched his, she murmured, "It looks like we're going to have to call another press conference."

Rich, successful and gorgeous…

These Australian men clearly need wives!

Featuring:

THE WEALTHY AUSTRALIAN'S PROPOSAL
by Margaret Way

THE BILLIONAIRE CLAIMS HIS WIFE
by Amy Andrews

INHERITED BY THE BILLIONAIRE
by Jennie Adams

Available 21st August 2009

www.millsandboon.co.uk

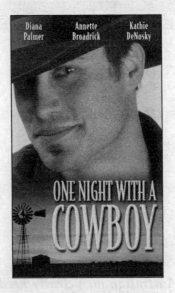

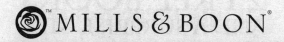

2 FREE BOOKS
AND A SURPRISE GIFT

We would like to take this opportunity to thank you for reading this Mills & Boon® book by offering you the chance to take TWO more specially selected titles from the Romance series absolutely FREE! We're also making this offer to introduce you to the benefits of the Mills & Boon® Book Club™—

- **FREE home delivery**
- **FREE gifts and competitions**
- **FREE monthly Newsletter**
- **Exclusive Mills & Boon Book Club offers**
- **Books available before they're in the shops**

Accepting these FREE books and gift places you under no obligation to buy, you may cancel at any time, even after receiving your free shipment. Simply complete your details below and return the entire page to the address below. You don't even need a stamp!

YES Please send me 2 free Romance books and a surprise gift. I understand that unless you hear from me, I will receive 5 superb new stories every month including two 2-in-1 titles priced at £4.99 each and a single title priced at £3.19, postage and packing free. I am under no obligation to purchase any books and may cancel my subscription at any time. The free books and gift will be mine to keep in any case.

Ms/Mrs/Miss/Mr_____ initials _____

Surname _____
address _____

_____
_____ postcode _____

Send this whole page to: Mills & Boon Book Club, Free Book Offer, FREEPOST NAT 10298, Richmond, TW9 1BR.